County Council

Julie Miller is an av[...] bestselling author of brea[...] with a National Readers' C[...] Maurier Award, among ot[...] an *RT Book Reviews* Care[...] complete list of her books, monthly newsletter and [...] go to juliemiller.org

USA TODAY bestselling and RITA® Award–winning author **Marie Ferrarella** has written more than 250 books for Mills & Boon, some under the name Marie Nicole. Her romances are beloved by fans worldwide. Visit her website, marieferrarella.com

014372994 X

Also by Julie Miller

Also by Marie Ferrarella

Discover more at millsandboon.co.uk

DEAD MAN DISTRICT

JULIE MILLER

COLTON 911: THE SECRET NETWORK

MARIE FERRARELLA

MILLS & BOON

All rights reserved including the right of reproduction in whole or in part in any form. This edition is published by arrangement with Harlequin Books S.A.

This is a work of fiction. Names, characters, places, locations and incidents are purely fictional and bear no relationship to any real life individuals, living or dead, or to any actual places, business establishments, locations, events or incidents. Any resemblance is entirely coincidental.

This book is sold subject to the condition that it shall not, by way of trade or otherwise, be lent, resold, hired out or otherwise circulated without the prior consent of the publisher in any form of binding or cover other than that in which it is published and without a similar condition including this condition being imposed on the subsequent purchaser.

® and ™ are trademarks owned and used by the trademark owner and/or its licensee. Trademarks marked with ® are registered with the United Kingdom Patent Office and/or the Office for Harmonisation in the Internal Market and in other countries.

First Published in Great Britain 2020
by Mills & Boon, an imprint of HarperCollins*Publishers*
1 London Bridge Street, London, SE1 9GF

Dead Man District © 2020 Julie Miller
Colton 911: The Secret Network © 2021 Harlequin Books S.A.

Special thanks and acknowledgement are given to Marie Ferrarella for her contribution to the *Colton 911: Chicago* series.

ISBN: 978-0-263-28318-1

0121

MIX
Paper from
responsible sources
FSC™ C007454

This book is produced from independently certified FSC™ paper to ensure responsible forest management.

For more information visit: www.harpercollins.co.uk/green

Printed and bound in Spain
by CPI, Barcelona

DEAD MAN DISTRICT

JULIE MILLER

This book is for your personal enjoyment only. This
paper is from sustainable forest management.

For more information, see www.harlequin.co.uk.

For the Grand Island Book Club, who so graciously took me to dinner and talked about my book! I was honored, and I had fun. Lindsey, Micki, Jessica, Jodi, Mary, Jana, Kristen—you are all fabulous, intelligent, accomplished young women and terrific moms, and I thank you.

Chapter One

Smoke.

Kansas City firefighter Matt Taylor held the handles of the resistance weights in front of him, feeling the pull along his massive arms and broad chest. He turned his nose toward the doorway of the spare bedroom, where he worked out when he wasn't on duty at the fire station, and sniffed the air.

Definitely smoke.

Slowly, deliberately, he eased the cables back through the pulley system and let the weight drop down to the stack. He grabbed the towel off the floor beside him and wiped the sweat from his face and neck, then swiped it over the top of his dark, military-short hair before rising from the machine's bench. He was a lieutenant at Firehouse 13 now, and his years of training and natural low-key demeanor kept him from panicking as he stalked through his apartment and checked the usual suspect spots. Kitchen clean and clear. Furnace running efficiently despite it being two degrees and snowing outside. Even though he emptied it out faithfully, he opened the closet where the washer and dryer were stacked and checked to make sure there was no lint in the dryer vent.

No fire here.

But his nose never lied.

And then his ears tuned in to the distinctly high-pitched, repetitive beep of a smoke detector, muted by walls and distance.

The fire wasn't here.

Pulling the towel from around the neck of his gray KCFD T-shirt, he tossed it over the back of a kitchen chair and reached beneath the sink to pull out the small fire extinguisher he stored there. Sweats and running shoes were hardly standard gear to battle a fire, but he knew it was the man, not the equipment, that was his best weapon to locate and put out a blaze. Ready to do battle, he jogged to the door of his apartment and flung it open.

A woman screamed.

Corie McGuire, the single mom who lived across the hall, pressed a hand to the neckline of her navy cardigan sweater, her small chest heaving in and out as she huddled back against the door to her apartment. "Good grief, Mr. Taylor. Don't startle me like that."

"Where's the fire?" He was sharply aware of the panic rounding her mossy-green eyes that were tilted up at him, the fact she was keeping as much distance between them as the door at her back allowed, and the charred iron skillet she clutched with an oven mitt down at her side. The sticky residue in the bottom of the skillet was still smoking. Matt quickly kicked the welcome mat from in front of his door across the wood-planked floor. "Put it down."

She hesitated a few seconds before nodding. He'd spoken in a tone that people usually obeyed, and she did, kneeling to set the hot pan on the mat. "It will leave a mark on your— Oh. Okay." He sprayed foam on the skillet, pulled the mitt from her startled hand, and lifted the pan to spray the bottom and sides as well, ensuring whatever substance had burned inside it couldn't catch fire again. "Thank you. I was going to take it downstairs and set it in the snow beside the dumpster out back. Pitch it out in the morning before school. This works, too."

With the charcoal goop in the pan extinguished to his satisfaction, Matt stood the same time she did. And swallowed hard. Somehow, he had drifted closer to his neighbor, or she had moved closer to him, and her ponytail had brushed against the *So Others May Live* firefighting emblem tattooed beneath the sleeve on his upper arm. Objectively, he'd always known Corie McGuire was a pretty woman, probably about his same age, late twenties, early thirties. But he'd never been this close to her before.

He'd never felt this gut punch of awareness about her, either.

Beneath the scent of her shampoo, he detected something salty and sweet, like pancakes and syrup with a side of crispy bacon. Maybe not the sexiest scent to most men, but he found himself craving it. It was certainly a more enticing scent than the smoky haze seeping into the hallway from beneath her closed door.

"You have smoke in your apartment," he pointed out, switching off the man to stay in firefighter mode. "I can help."

"That's all right. I've opened some windows to air things out. Sorry if it bothered you." When she knelt to retrieve the skillet, Matt stuck out a warning hand, which she instantly straightened away from. "Leave it."

"Leave it?" She shook her head. "Mr. Stinson will hardly appreciate finding a burned mess in the middle of the floor."

Matt didn't care what the building super thought—he had a more immediate problem that needed to be dealt with. But he knew he wasn't handling tonight's encounter well. From the time he'd reached his full height of six feet five inches and started bulking up after high school, his adoptive mother and grandmother had gently warned him that people who didn't know him might find him intimidating. And though the women in his family knew he was more gentle giant than scary ogre, others, like Corie McGuire here, might misread his blunt demeanor and quiet ways and be afraid of him.

Not that he blamed her for giving him a wide berth. He was a big, scary dude. When he wasn't lifting weights, he was running, partly because the physical demands of his job meant he needed to stay in shape, and partly because he had little else to do, especially in the wintertime. Other than a Sunday dinner with his grandmother and some assortment of parents, brothers, uncles and their families once or twice a month, or an occasional trip to the bar after shift with his Lucky 13 firehouse buddies, he didn't really have a social calendar.

The top of Corie McGuire's blond head barely reached his shoulder, and the woman was built on the slender side of things. They'd exchanged little more than a nod in the elevator after she and her son had moved in across the hall. Even then, she kept her boy hugged close to her and shifted to wherever the opposite side of the elevator was from him. He'd helped carry her groceries up one time, and even then, she'd stopped at her door and had taken the bags without letting him into their apartment. Since he wasn't the most outgoing of people, he hadn't immediately noticed that she was right there with him, keeping neighbors at a polite distance and never having friends over. Now that he thought about it, the woman and her son kept to themselves pretty much. He should give her the space she seemed to want from him.

But there was a haze of smoke drifting into the hallway and a beeping alarm telling him something wasn't right.

And one thing that Matt Taylor never shied away from was his job as a firefighter.

"This is what I do for a living. Would you mind if I came in and checked to make sure there are no secondary hot spots trying to ignite?"

If possible, Corie's eyes widened further. "There could be another fire?"

"You said you opened a window?"

To his surprise, she reached behind her to twist the doorknob, inviting him in. "My son is in here. Please."

The moment the door opened, the shrill beep of the smoke detector pierced Matt's eardrums. Closing the door behind them, he followed her into the kitchen. Corie braced her hands over her ears as they walked beneath the archway where the smoke detector was blaring its warning. The smoke was thicker here, with a dirty-gray plume billowing out of the open oven. Matt wasted no time closing the oven door and moving past her to close the kitchen window. Then he reached up to pry the cover off the smoke detector and pulled out the battery. The sudden silence didn't immediately stop the ringing in his ears.

But Corie lowered her hands. "Thank you." She'd already turned the oven off, but he squatted in front of the appliance, peering through the rectangle of glass, looking for any stray sparks or glowing elements. "Is something still burning?"

"You want to keep the oven door shut and all the windows closed until you're certain the fire is out. A lot of fires reignite the moment you add fresh air to the mix." He watched for a full minute before he set the fire extinguisher he'd carried in with him on the counter. "I think we're good." She had leaned in beside him to study the oven, too. But he didn't realize how close she was, and he bumped into her when he stood. His instinct was to reach for her to keep her from falling, but she grabbed the edge of the countertop to steady herself and scuttled away to the kitchen archway to keep him from touching her. Matt let his hand drop back down to his side. "Sorry."

She growled and huffed a breath that stirred the wheat-colored bangs on her forehead, and he wondered if that was her version of a curse. "No. I'm the one who's sorry. You've never been anything but polite, and now you're trying to help us, and that was rude. I've already screamed at you once tonight."

"Self-preservation isn't rude. I startled you. You do what you need to do to feel safe."

"I…" Her lips parted to argue, but they snapped shut again. Her posture relaxed and she hugged her arms around her middle. And smiled. A real smile. The tension around her eyes relaxed, and her soft pink mouth curved into a grin. "Thank you for understanding."

He could point out that with his superior strength and longer legs, he could have reached out and grabbed her without any effort at all if that had been his intent. But why would anyone want to make that beautiful smile disappear? Especially when that smile was directed at him. It made him want to smile, too.

Um, what are you doing, Taylor? Sniffing your neighbor? Smiling at her? Stop it or you'll really scare her.

Turning away, Matt checked the oven one more time, assuring himself the fire was out and whatever had burned had been starved of the oxygen it needed. Instead of moving toward Corie and the archway, he crossed back to the kitchen window and opened it. Then he turned on the hood fan above the stove and waited to see if she would move out of his path.

"Is it safe to open windows now?" she asked, maybe

just to break the awkward silence of him waiting for her to move.

Matt nodded. But when he heard the furnace kick on, he took a step toward her and the smile vanished. He quickly halted. She didn't need a firefighter anymore. She needed a respectful neighbor who would finish his business here as quickly as possible and go back to his own apartment. "Where's your thermostat?" She hugged one edge of her sweater over the other, shivering at the cold night air filling the kitchen. "You might want to grab an extra sweater," he advised. "It'll take twenty, thirty minutes to get the smoke out of here."

She nodded. "Mother Nature hasn't exactly graced us with warm weather and sunshine. I loved having all this snow for Christmas. But it wouldn't hurt my feelings any if it warmed up and melted away and spring came early."

"Spring won't happen in January. Not in Missouri."

"You're right, of course." She grabbed her wool coat off the back of a chair and shrugged into it as she led him through the apartment. "This way."

Although the layout of her apartment was a mirror image of his own across the hall, and he could have found the thermostat on his own, his training as a KCFD firefighter had taught him that a woman alone at the scene of a fire of any size probably wouldn't appreciate a man barging through her personal space—unless the whole place was fully engulfed and him storming in meant the difference between life and death. So he politely followed her out of the kitchen, through the living room and down the hall.

Corie wore her ponytail high on the back of her head, and it bounced against her collar like a shaft of golden wheat swaying in the wind. There was a sway to her hips, too. He'd noticed how her jeans had curved with a womanly flare, but even with her heavy coat, her natural slenderness blossomed in all the right places.

Matt didn't realize his gaze was still plastered to her backside until she stopped at the hallway wall between the two bedrooms and a little boy with a longish mop of brown hair stepped out of the second bedroom. "What do you want?" He stepped in front of Corie and held up a beastly-looking blob built out of hard plastic blocks—a dragon, he'd guess, based on the plastic swirls of flame attached to the creature's snout and the triangular bits that were either short wings or Godzilla-like spines on its back. From behind the colorful creation, which he held up like a shield, the boy peeked up at Matt with green eyes that matched his mother's. "The fire will get you if you come too close."

"Evan!" Corie slipped her arm around her son's shoulders. "You remember Mr. Taylor from across the hall. He's our neighbor. Now be polite."

Matt had a little nephew who had mastered that put-upon eye roll. He also recognized the stance of a young man—even this slight little boy—protecting someone he cared about. He respected that reaction as much as he worried about being the cause of it. Evan McGuire tucked his homemade dragon beneath his arm. "Sorry, sir. Hi."

Matt was equally brief. "Hi." He adjusted the thermostat to a much lower temperature, waiting for the furnace to shut off.

If Corie McGuire barely reached his shoulder, her son, Evan, barely reached his waist. They must be built on the slim side of things in the McGuire family. Matt scarcely remembered his birth parents, but they had been tall and broad shouldered like him and his younger brother, Mark, who was also a firefighter with the Lucky 13 crew.

The boy's diminutive size didn't stop Evan from stepping forward, tipping his head back and sizing up their visitor. "You're big up close."

"I'm big far away, too." He parroted the phrase his petite grandmother had often teased him with.

Corie snickered at the joke. She snorted a laugh through her nose, then quickly slapped her hand over her mouth. She looked more embarrassed than he was by her noisy amusement. Whether it was for his sake or hers, she quickly hustled her son toward the hall tree by the front door. "Evan, get your coat on. It's going to get cold in here."

Matt recalled one elevator ride together where Evan had announced it was his eighth birthday before his mother had shushed him and ended any conversation before it got started. Like any self-respecting young man, he groaned at being told what to do, even as he tromped through the living room and pulled on an insulated jacket that had sleeves that were too short for his arms and that clung to his small frame as he zipped it up.

But his demeanor changed when he looked into the hallway and saw the ruined skillet on Matt's door mat. "I'm sorry, Mom. I didn't mean to make a mess. I tried to put the fire out."

"It's not your fault." Corie ruffled his hair and kissed the top of his head, ushering him back inside. "I should have ended my phone call with Professor Nelms and fixed you a snack myself so you didn't have to turn on that old oven."

"But I made the frozen pizza just the way you showed me."

"Then maybe there's something wrong with the oven. I'm just glad you weren't hurt."

He nodded. Then tipped his chin up to Matt. "I'm sorry we bothered you, Mr. Taylor." Evan glanced over at his mom. "Isn't that right?"

Matt glimpsed the sadness and regret that tightened her features before she forced a smile onto her lips that wasn't quite as pretty as the natural smile she'd shared in the kitchen. What made a child apologize for a simple, albeit potentially dangerous, mistake, and a mother regret that he felt he needed to apologize?

Matt had never been a parent, but he'd been raised by the two finest people he'd ever known. He remembered how his adoptive father, Gideon Taylor, had coaxed him out of his silence and fear as a traumatized orphan. He'd given Matt jobs to do, small responsibilities that he could succeed at and grow his self-confidence. Gideon Taylor had worked side by side with each of his sons, showing them what it took to be a good man, how to be part of a family, how to live in the world with a sense of purpose and not be afraid of doing the wrong thing. Again.

Emulating the lesson of his own dad, Matt unhooked the multidialed utility watch from his wrist and held it out to Evan. "Can you tell time?"

Evan scoffed a little snort through his nose, reminding Matt of the adorable sound his mother had made a few minutes earlier. "Of course I can. We learned that in first grade. I'm a second grader now."

"Good man. Take this." Evan's eyes widened as he looked at all the numbers for time, temperature and barometric pressure readings. His mouth dropped open before he took it from Matt's outstretched hand. "When thirty minutes have passed, I want you to turn this thermostat back up to seventy degrees and remind your mom to close the kitchen window. Can you do that?"

Evan danced with excitement. "Is that okay, Mom?"

"You'll have to give Mr. Taylor his watch back," she reminded him.

"Not for thirty minutes," Evan protested.

"It's not a gift."

"Please?"

Matt wasn't sure he'd be able to withstand the enthu-siastic energy pouring off the boy. Corie smiled the good smile again. "All right. Homework done?"

"Yes, ma'am."

"Good. Then you can use that same half hour to play your game before bedtime."

Corie combed her fingers through his hair and cupped his cheek. When she started to kiss him again, he glanced up at Matt and pulled away, perhaps embarrassed by the PDA, perhaps trying to be more like the man he believed being trusted with Matt's watch made him. "Did I tell you I earned a ronin to fight with my dwarf? Now I can shoot arrows at the bad guys."

"That's great." She smiled again at her son's delight over the video game Matt was familiar with. "Do you even know what a ronin is?"

But Evan was already dashing down the hallway past Matt into his room. "'Bye, Mr. Taylor. See you in thirty... twenty-nine minutes."

The furnace clicked off with a noisy jerk. Matt hadn't had this much conversation outside of work for a long time, and the urge to stay a little longer and keep talking with this tiny family felt odd. Didn't stop him, though. "Sounds like something my younger cousins have played. I've played it with my brothers, too, a few times. If I re-member correctly, a shapeshifter and sorcerer are next to join the team."

"You play *Bomba's Quest*?"

Matt wondered if his cheeks were heating with a blush or if he was succumbing to some weird kind of hypother-mia. "My uncle Brett wanted to know if it was appropriate for his kids to play. My brothers and I volunteered to test it."

"I wondered if it was appropriate for an eight-year-old, too. He likes figuring out the puzzles and solving the riddles. But the characters are all cartoons, and no one dies when they go to battle. Not like real violence where people get hurt." She stopped abruptly, as though she was surprised to hear herself say those words out loud. "I'm sorry. I'm rambling. I'll be sure to get your watch back to you. That was a nice gesture."

Matt was as curious about the shadow that crossed her features as he'd been about the things he'd said that had made her smile.

Get back to being a firefighter and get out of here.

"You make pizza in a skillet?" he asked, picking up on something her son had said.

"The cast iron heats up and works like a pizza stone. The handles should have made it easier for Evan to manage." When she headed back to the kitchen, Matt followed. "Usually, his go-to snack is popcorn in the microwave, but for some reason, my microwave isn't working tonight." She pushed a couple of buttons beside the handle, but nothing lit up. "I don't know if it's the microwave or the socket it's plugged into."

If her apartment was wired like his, there should be a circuit breaker on the microwave outlet. Possibly, it had tripped and neither Corie nor her son knew to push the button back in to reconnect the circuit. But an oven fire *and* a faulty microwave in one evening? That seemed to be an unusual amount of bad luck for anyone, especially a woman who seemed as competent and careful as Corie. Matt pushed the circuit breaker button, but nothing re-engaged.

"I tried that already."

Good. So, she knew that safety measure. Either the microwave itself was broken or there was a problem with the wiring. Matt unplugged the appliance and moved it to the opposite counter where there was another plug.

"You don't have to do that. I'll call Mr. Stinson tomorrow to look at it. I'm sure you were busy doing something important."

The moment he plugged it in to the new socket, all the lights came on. "It's not the microwave. Looks like a wiring issue." He glanced over his shoulder to see Corie frowning at the now-empty socket. "Is something wrong?"

"I'm not sure."

On a hunch, he asked her for a flashlight and then knelt in front of the oven again. After testing to make sure it wasn't hot to the touch, he rubbed his fingers along the heating elements at the top and bottom of the oven. A sticky, charred residue like what he'd seen in the skillet came off in his hands. He'd fought enough fires to know there was something unnatural about this one.

He tried not to jerk when he felt Corie's hand on his shoulder, balancing herself as she knelt beside him. "What's that?"

"I'm not sure." He could easily understand food overflowing its pan and spilling onto the heating element at the bottom of the oven. But something needed to be spraying oil or grease—and a lot of it—for it to coat the top heating element like this. And nothing about pizza sprayed when it baked. "Did you squirt anything on the fire to put it out?"

"Evan threw some flour on it."

"Flour burns."

"I know that. He knows that, too, now." She pulled her hand away and stood, opening the cupboard above the stove. "I keep a can of baking soda mixed with salt in here to put out small fires."

An old-school solution that worked as well as a chemical extinguisher. "It snuffs out the oxygen."

She nodded. "I showed Evan where I keep it and taught him how to use it. I was in my bedroom, on the phone with my professor about a project for my college class. I didn't realize there was a fire until the smoke detector went off. I ran out here, saw the flames, grabbed the can..." She opened the lid and handed him the can. There was only a dusting of powder at the bottom. "It's empty. That's why he went for the flour instead. The only time we've used the baking soda mixture was when I was teaching him how to put out a fire. I lit a match in a pan and had him put it out so he could practice. This should still be full. I don't know how..." A dimple formed between her eyebrows as she frowned. "I don't remember emptying it. I don't know why I would."

Maybe she hadn't.

Curious. And a little disturbing to think that all the safeguards she'd had in place to protect her son from a fire had failed.

Matt needed some time to ponder on that. Evan seemed to be a precocious little boy. And God knew Matt understood a child's fascination in playing with fire. But would an eight-year-old know how to sabotage an electrical outlet to make his story about using the oven plausible? Or was there something else going on here? For now, Matt simply wanted to complete his due diligence as a firefighter, and as a good neighbor. If there was anything he could do to help Corie feel safer in her own apartment—even if that meant him leaving—he would do it.

"My microwave works," he offered. "I'm at home on Tuesday nights. If he wants a snack, and you're busy with schoolwork, he could come over."

"Usually, he can safely occupy himself when I'm studying. And he knows he can interrupt me if he needs something." She placed the empty can back in its cupboard. Then she pasted a tight smile on her face and headed to the front door. Did she suspect her son of setting the fire, too? "I'll show you out."

This time, he didn't follow. "You want me to move the microwave back, or leave it here?"

"Leave it. You've done enough."

He was beginning to think he hadn't done nearly enough. "Talk to the super. He needs to replace that stove and the microwave outlet before you use either one again."

"I will." She was waiting by the front door.

"Do you have a safe place to cook your meals in the meantime?"

"Afraid we're going to start another fire?"

He didn't joke about stuff like that. And judging by the frown dimple that had reappeared on her forehead, she wasn't trying to be funny, either.

What was going on here? Just a series of unfortunate coincidences that had taken their toll on a tired, hardworking single mom? Or did she share any of the same suspicion he did that something was deliberately off in this apartment tonight?

Finally, he forced his feet to move to the door. "I'll leave the fire extinguisher here until you get your baking soda solution restocked. I have another one in my truck." When he moved past her into the hallway, he picked up the torched pan and handed her the oven mitt. "I'll take this down to the dumpster for you."

Her fingers brushed against his as she tried to take the skillet from him. "You don't have to do that."

No way could she muscle the ruined pan away from him, but another unexpected touch like that, sending ribbons of unfamiliar heat skittering beneath the skin she'd made contact with, and she could probably ask him for anything she wanted. What kind of sorry, solitary soul was he to be so attuned to a woman he hadn't said ten words to before tonight? He pointed back toward the kitchen. "When I'm done, I'll come back to reset the smoke alarm. Evan's thirty minutes should be up by then."

"Okay." She hugged the door frame, her shoulders lifting with a sigh that made him think she was either too tired to argue with him, or just agreeing to whatever he said that would make him leave. "I'll lock the door behind you. Knock when you get back."

Matt carried the pan to the first floor and braved the cold air without a coat to set it on the dumpster behind their building. He spared a few minutes to pull his pocketknife from his sweats and scrape some of the residue from the bottom and handle of the pan. Although there were definitely bits of cheese and hamburger that had turned to ash, there was also more of that same sticky substance he'd found on the oven's heating element. He cut a swath of plastic from a trash bag inside the dumpster and wrapped the sample inside before stuffing both the knife and the sample into his pocket. This hadn't been a big enough fire, nor an official KCFD investigation, to warrant sending the substance to the state fire lab, but he could ask his firehouse captain and some of the other more experienced firefighters at the station house if they'd run across anything like it before. A bracing wind whipped through the alley, chilling him from his speculation.

On the way back inside, he paused in front of Wally Stinson's door and thought about asking the super if he'd worked on any of Corie's appliances or electrical outlets recently, or if she'd filed a complaint about any of them needing repairs. He'd like to ask if there had been any other small fires in the apartment, too—anything that might indicate a boy playing with matches or other flammable materials. But there was no sound coming from within the apartment, and there was no light shining from beneath the super's door, so the man had either gone to bed or was out for the evening. He'd make a point to stop by the next morning on his way to work.

Matt walked past the elevator and took the stairs, needing time to think. One strange thing in Corie's apartment he could dismiss as an accident. Two made him curious. But three missteps, all leading to a potentially dangerous fire and no way to fight it, told him something was wrong. Now whether Corie was really good at hiding irresponsible behavior, or something more sinister was happening behind the walls across the hallway, he couldn't say. In the meantime, Matt would do whatever he could tonight to ensure that Corie and Evan McGuire had nothing more to worry about and could get a good night's sleep.

By the time he'd reached the seventh floor, Corie was waiting outside her door, holding his watch and a small plate wrapped in plastic. "I went ahead and put the battery back in the smoke alarm myself. All I had to do was pull out a chair to reach it."

"You tested it?"

She nodded. "It beeped." In other words, *stop butting in, already.* She handed him the watch. "Evan says thank-you. I appreciate the way you eased his concern and made him feel useful. Although I didn't know what half the bells and whistles on this watch are for. And trust me, he asked about every one of them." After he'd strapped the watch back onto his wrist, she handed him the plate. "And here. It's not much. But thank you."

Matt didn't need a thank-you, and he certainly hadn't expected a gift. He lifted the plate to inspect the thick slice of cherry pie. He hadn't grown to 250 pounds of muscle by turning his nose up at a free dessert. But he felt awkward taking anything from this woman who wore a coat with a frayed collar, and whose son clearly needed some bigger clothes—and possibly some counseling on the dangers of playing with fire.

Misreading his hesitancy, Corie quickly apologized. "Don't worry. I didn't bake it in that rattrap of an oven. I work at Pearl's Diner evenings after school. Except on nights like this when I have class. Sometimes I bake, but mostly I wait tables."

He knew Pearl's. Classic diner food that filled your belly and made you feel at home. He'd eaten there with his family many times over the years. He knew the original owner, Pearl Jenkins, had retired and sold the restaurant to Melissa Kincaid, the wife of one of the detectives his older brothers, Alex and Pike, worked with at KCPD. But other than adding some lighter fare to the menu, he hadn't noticed any changes in the quality of the food. And the pie from Pearl's was legendary. "My boss lets me bring home any extra since we bake it fresh every day."

"You made this?"

Corie nodded.

He finally remembered his manners. "Thank you. Cherry's my favorite."

"I'm glad." She opened her door. "Well, thank you again. Good night, Mr. Taylor."

"Good night, Mrs. McGuire. Ms.? Miss?"

There was a drawn look to her features that spoke of fatigue. "I'm divorced from Evan's father. Corie will do just fine."

"Matt will do, too. For me. I'm Matt. Not married. Never have been. Never baked a pie."

She smiled in that way that made him feel like he hadn't just stuck his foot in his mouth and made an awkward conversation downright uncomfortable. "Good to know. Good night, Matt."

He waited in the hallway, hearing the dead bolt, a chain and the doorknob engage. He liked that she was cautious about her safety. Even though the City Market district was being reclaimed by Millennials and real estate investors, the transformation hadn't taken hold everywhere. The Mc-Guires were still a lone woman and a little boy alone in the city.

And Matt was the scary dude across the hall who'd come out of his solitary refuge just long enough to save the day…and scare her back behind her tightly locked door.

Dragging his door mat back across the hall, he stepped inside his apartment and locked the door behind him. He'd return to his weights later. For now, he turned the TV on the late news, leaned back on the couch and stretched his feet out onto the table beside the takeout wrappers from tonight's dinner. He unwrapped the pie and inhaled its heady scent. Sweet and delectable, just like Corie.

Matt didn't even bother getting up to get a fork. He picked the wedge up in his hand and took a bite. His grandmother was one hell of a cook, and this pie reminded him of that perfect blend of talent and experience. The second bite made him forget the niggling thought at the back of his mind that told him something was very wrong in that small apartment across the hall.

There was also something very right about that little family.

Corie McGuire had pretty hair, a pretty butt and a pretty smile.

Matt inhaled the last of the sweet, flaky crust and tart filling.

And damn, the woman could cook.

He might just be in love.

Chapter Two

"Okay, now you're just showin' off."

Ignoring the teasing voice, Matt pushed up off the snow-dusted pavement after checking to make sure there was no fuel leak and pried open the hood of the burning car with his long-handled ax. He wedged it upward, bracing the ax between the frame and the hood to keep it open. He turned away from the billowing smoke that poured out over the fenders to frown at his younger brother, Mark, who'd brought a second ax from the engine parked several yards away in the parking lot.

"Huh?" Matt lifted the hose he'd dragged to the burning car off his shoulder and pointed it toward the flames before opening the valve and spraying the engine block. The steam of water meeting fire forced them both to take a step back. They wore their turnout gear like the rest of the Lucky 13 crew, who had responded to the call to a car fire behind an office building just north of the downtown area. But since this wasn't a structure fire they had to walk into where oxygen would be scarce, there'd been no call to wear face masks and a breathing apparatus. His cold cheeks stung with the spray of steamy moisture on and around his goggles, forcing Matt to redirect the water. "Are you complaining because I'm doing my job?"

"I'm complaining because you're doing everybody's

job." Mark moved in beside him, waving his arm through the smoke and steam, clearing it away to get a visual on the origin of the fire to ensure that it was completely out. "Hell, I could have stayed at the firehouse where it's warm and finished my lunch instead of getting in the truck and riding here to watch you do all the work."

"I let you turn on the water and pressurize the hose, didn't I?" Matt covered the engine with one more spray of water before shutting off the valve and giving a high sign to Ray Jackson, another firefighter, who was waiting beside the hydrant to turn it off.

"Big whoop. I know this is small in the grand scheme of fires, but we are trained to work together as a unit. You're making me look bad in front of our adoring audience." Mark turned his blue eyes to the group of curious bystanders huddling together for warmth on the far side of the parking lot. "Unless you're trying to impress one of those ladies over there?"

Matt glanced across the way. Although he'd been aware of the small group of people, making sure they'd remained at a safe distance while he put out the fire, he hadn't really noticed that there were three women in the group. He didn't seem to notice any women since last night's visit to Corie McGuire's apartment. Honey-blond ponytails and big green eyes must be his thing. The two brunettes and a bright, unnaturally platinum blonde were attractive enough, he supposed, but not one of them had been compelling enough to divert his attention. "No."

"Of course not. Big bad Matt Taylor's just doing his job. Like always." Mark's groan echoed Matt's as Ray Jackson turned over shutting down the hydrant to another teammate and jogged across the parking lot to chat up the three ladies. "Can't say the same for Jackson."

"Maybe he knows one of them," Matt suggested, giving his teammate the benefit of the doubt.

"Would it matter if he did or didn't?" Mark swung his ax onto his shoulder and shook his head. "How am I ever going to find you a date to Amy's and my wedding if you got to compete with that?"

Matt shrugged as Ray took off his helmet and the three women eagerly shook hands with him. Matt had never possessed the gift of gab or the movie-star looks of their buddy Ray. He'd been a natural to represent Firehouse 13 on the KCFD fund-raiser calendar last year. Matt probably should be jealous. Instead, he was glad he'd never been called on to do any PR for the KCFD. Although he'd fought more dangerous fires than today's car fire side by side with Ray Jackson and was happy to let Ray or Mark do the friendly conversations with the witnesses and victims they interacted with, he was a little embarrassed to see Ray focusing squarely on the women in the group, barely acknowledging the two men standing with them.

"If we had a sister," Matt announced, "I'd never introduce them."

"Agreed." Mark clapped him on the shoulder, pulling his focus away from Ray and the onlookers and back to cleaning up after the fire. "Come on. I'll help you drain the hose and roll it back up. Water's freezing fast. Careful of that ice. I think we just turned this place into a skating rink."

They worked in silence for a few minutes while their firehouse captain, Kyle Redding, stood farther down the sidewalk talking with a uniformed police officer and the older couple walking their dog who had called in the burning car. Apparently, there was some issue in finding the owner of the vehicle. He'd like to think that Ray was following up on the investigation by chatting with the onlookers, but it didn't seem as though anyone who worked around here recognized the car or knew where the owner worked.

Matt pulled the hose out straight and began the laborious task of clearing the line before something Mark had said in jest—he hoped—sank in. "Don't set me up on any dates. Not even for the wedding."

Mark stopped abruptly and straightened, grinning from ear to ear. "Why? You seeing somebody I don't know about?"

Matt replayed the images of Corie walking away from him and the sweet smile that had softened her pretty mouth when he'd made her laugh. He wasn't sure exactly what he thought might happen with his neighbor. Probably nothing more than just that—being neighbors. But he wanted to savor last night's encounter with the small family across the hall awhile longer before he tried to work up interest in any matchmaking his brother and future sister-in-law might have in mind for him. "No. But I'm not interested in meeting anyone new."

Mark's blue eyes narrowed suspiciously. "So, you *have* met someone," he prodded, fishing for information.

Matt's answer was to pull off his goggles and toss them at Mark. "If you're so anxious to do some work, stop talking and get to it."

But Mark never gave up that easily. "Do I know her? Has anyone in the family met her? Did you find her on one of those dating sites?"

Matt gave the hose a strong tug, pulling it right out of Mark's hands. "I outrank you, Taylor," he teased, knowing with his brother, it was a useless threat. "I said get to work."

"Yes, sir, Lieutenant, sir." Although that cheesy grin

never wavered, Mark had the good sense to let the matter drop so they could get the hose prepped for the truck.

Of Matt's three adoptive brothers, his younger brother, Mark, was the only one who was his brother by birth. Unlike their older brothers, Alex and Pike, who were cops, Mark had followed Matt into firefighting, making for a friendly family rivalry in interdepartmental softball games, blood drives and fund-raisers. Sometimes the cops won; sometimes the firefighters came out on top. But nothing could ever break the bond they shared. All four brothers had lived in the same foster home and had been adopted by Gideon and Meghan Taylor—the firefighters who had saved them in more ways than one, and who had inspired Matt to follow in their footsteps. The six of them had become the family that, as a child, Matt hadn't believed he'd ever find—or even deserved.

If Alex, the oldest, was their leader, and Pike, the second oldest, was the intellectual, then Matt was the quiet one. And that made Mark the obnoxious one. There was something about being the youngest—and something about being ridiculously in love and planning a summer wedding—that made Mark particularly ornery lately. Although he'd nearly lost his fiancée, Amy, to a serial killer who'd hidden his crimes in a series of arson fires, and had nearly lost his own life saving her, Mark was now as happy as Matt had ever seen him. Amy was good for Mark. She'd brought him out of his grief and guilt after the traumatic loss of their grandfather had hit Mark particularly hard—and she thought his goofy sense of humor was actually funny. No accounting for taste, he guessed.

Mark elbowed Matt's arm, drawing his focus back to the work at hand. "What's up with you today? I just caught you smiling. There *is* a woman."

"Nah. Not me." For now, Corie McGuire and her cherry

pie were simply a good feeling Matt wanted to keep to himself. The musical trill of a woman laughing carried across the parking lot, and both Taylors paused to see Ray Jackson leaning in and saying something that delighted his captive audience. Knowing Ray, he'd have all their phone numbers before the conversation was over.

Mark snorted a laugh. "Maybe you and I ought to kick back and let Ray finish cleanup duty."

Matt shook his head, preferring to stay busy and keep moving in the cold weather. He hefted his section of hose and carried it several feet closer to the fire engine. "What would you do if Ray flirted with your Amy like that?"

Mark followed with the next length of hose. "I love the guy. But I'd lay him out flat." Mark chuckled as he dropped the hose alongside the lines two other members of their team were winding onto the truck. "Unless Amy laid him out first."

Matt laughed with him, suspecting Mark's fiancée wouldn't put up with anyone or anything she didn't want to. Matt liked that directness about Amy Hall. Not only did it make it easy for him to have a conversation with his future sister-in-law, but her honesty left him with no doubt just how much she was in love with Mark. While Matt was a little envious that his three brothers had found their soul mates, and the two older ones had even started families, he was also happy that Alex, Pike and Mark had each found the right woman. One day, he hoped for the same.

He silently wondered if anything would come of this unexpected attraction to Corie, and if he could handle the ready-made family that came with her. Not for the first time since last night, Matt debated his suspicions about the oven fire in the McGuire apartment. He'd shown the residue he'd collected to Captain Redding this morning before they'd been called out, and the captain—who had almost twenty years of experience on Matt and agreed the substance was suspicious—promised to run it by some of his old cohorts in the department. Something was off about the whole story of baking a pizza gone wrong. Something more than the sooty remains of a fire had coated the heating elements in the oven. And Corie had seemed so certain that she'd had a fire-suppressant mixture stored in her cabinet for just such an emergency that he had a feeling there was something deliberate about that fire.

Somebody had wanted it to burn.

Matt had set more than one fire himself when he'd been barely more than a toddler. He'd been curious, yes, but he understood now that he'd been acting out against his birth parents' neglect, and later against being stuck in foster care and the guilt he felt at putting him and Mark there. Was there something going on in Evan McGuire's life that was making the eight-year-old experiment with fire? It would require Matt drawing on some painful memories, but maybe it was worth prodding Corie a little to see if she suspected her son might have picked up a dangerous hobby, and if he could get the boy some of the same type of counseling that had helped him as a child.

"Yo, Matt." Mark's summons pulled Matt from his thoughts. "Take a look at this." Mark was standing in front of the sedan's charred engine block. Now that the fire was out and the smoke and steam had dissipated, they could make a clearer assessment of what might have caused the fire, despite the ice frozen around the parts Matt had hosed with water. "You're the fix-it guy. Those wires don't belong there, do they?"

Matt frowned at the blackened metal wires crisscrossing above the radiator and battery. If they'd been part of the car's makeup, they should have been coated in rubberlike polymers or plastic to prevent sparks or accidental electrocution to the unwary handler. Even with the intense heat of the fire, some trace of the insulation should have remained. Reaching under his turnout coat, Matt pulled out his pocketknife and chipped away at the ice. "Looks like some kind of homemade repair job." He peered down between the frame and engine parts. "It doesn't look like they're holding anything together, though. Just a sec."

Without regard for the snow or ice, Matt dropped down to the ground and slid as much of his bulk as he could beneath the car. Between his flashlight and the pocketknife, Matt quickly found what the wires were attached to—the melted remains of a cell phone and a wad of charred, waxy cord that fed into a hole in the oil pan.

Talk about wanting something to burn.

This fire was no accident.

"Hey, if it isn't the wonder twins." At the sound of approaching footsteps and a man's familiar voice, Matt slid from beneath the car.

"Uncle Cole." Mark was already trading a handshake and friendly back-slapping hug with the dark-haired older man by the time Matt was on his feet.

"Mark. Matt." Other than the lack of silvering sideburns, Cole Taylor was a dead ringer for their father, Gideon.

"Uncle Cole." Matt reached out to shake hands with the family member, too. His gaze dropped to the KCPD badge and gun peeking out from beneath his leather jacket before sliding back up to slightly lined blue eyes. That meant he was on duty. It didn't explain why he was here at the scene of a small fire, though. "Good to see you."

He pointed to the man with the dark sideburns and stocking cap standing beside him. "This is Agent Amos Rand, my new partner. I'm showing him the ropes while my regular partner is on maternity leave. He's on temporary assignment from NCIS."

"A Navy man?" Matt extended his hand in greeting.

"Marines." Agent Rand could give Matt a run for the money in the stoicism department. But his grip was solid and friendly enough.

"Like Grandpa." Mark shook hands with Cole's new partner. "He served during the Korean conflict, and in the reserves for several years after that. He died earlier this year."

Matt reached over and squeezed his brother's shoulder. They all missed the family patriarch, who'd suffered a fatal heart attack while helping Mark rescue the victims of a car accident. But Mark seemed to take it personally that he hadn't been able to save their grandfather, as well.

Agent Rand buried his hands in the pockets of his coat and nodded. "I would have liked your grandpa."

"You would have loved Dad," Cole agreed, erasing the wistful grief that had momentarily darkened his expression. "He'd have been telling you stories for hours. A few of them might even have been true."

Amos chuckled. "Sounds like a good man."

"He was the best," Cole and Mark echoed together.

Matt nodded his agreement. "What brings you two to our parking lot on this cold day? You're not working arson now, are you?"

Cole shook his head. "We're still major cases, organized crime division."

Amos pulled out his cell phone and nodded toward the sedan. "You all catch up." Matt watched the NCIS agent type in the license plate and send it off in a text before he circled around the car, sizing up the blackened engine block and peering into the windows. "This was an arson fire?"

"Looks like it," Matt confirmed.

Cole shoved his hands deep into the pockets of his coat, his breath gusting out in a cloud of warm air. "We're supposed to meet a CI on a case we're investigating."

"CI?" Mark asked.

"Confidential informant." Cole Taylor scanned the people around the parking lot before tilting his gaze to the windows above them on either side. "Don't suppose you've seen a skinny, hyperactive guy with dark hair? Possibly wearing coveralls. He works at a garage over on South McGee."

"We cleared the immediate area." Matt pointed to the gathering across the parking lot where one of the brunettes was typing on Ray Jackson's phone. "Except for that group over there, it's too cold to have a lot of onlookers. Is one of those men your guy?"

"In a suit? I don't think so." Cole glanced back as Captain Redding dismissed the couple with their dog. "The guy talking to your captain is too old to be our man. Our CI requested we meet on neutral ground where the chances of anyone recognizing him would be next to nil. He'd stand out like a sore thumb here in the business district. Unless he was dropping off somebody's car he was working on."

Amos returned from inspecting the car. "It's Maldonado's car," he confirmed. "Plates and VIN number are in his name."

"Ah, hell." Cole looked up at Matt, his expression grim. "Please tell me you didn't find a body in it?"

"Hadn't looked beyond the front and back seats."

"Can you open the trunk?" When Matt hesitated, Cole pulled back the front of his coat to expose his badge where anyone passing by the scene could see it. "We have probable cause that our man could be in danger. I'll take full responsibility."

"Not a problem." His firefighter's training included

a vow to save people before property. Since Matt's ax was currently wedged between the hood and frame, Mark picked up his ax and followed them to the back end of the car. He wedged the blade into the locking mechanism and forced it open. Suspecting it was useless to warn the two officers to stay back, Matt raised the trunk. Although some of the smoke from the engine has made its way through the car's interior and drifted out to dissipate in the wintry air, it was easy to see that there was nothing inside but the spare tire and a toolbox. "The car looks abandoned." He reached inside to open the toolbox. "He's got the means here to rig that fire. But then, it wouldn't take any special tools to set that up. Just a cell phone and the know-how."

Cole and Agent Rand went into investigator mode, snapping pictures of the vehicle with their phones and sending the information on to a third party—a fellow investigator or someone in the crime lab, he guessed.

"This fire was no accident." Matt led his uncle to the front of the car to point out the ignition device beneath the hood. Amos took a picture of the cell phone itself and then dropped it into an evidence bag from another pocket of his coat. "I figured it was some kind of insurance scam. Abandoned car. Remote ignition. Whoever set it only had to call the number on the cell. Like striking a match in the oil pan. A spark, oxygen and fuel to burn. Ignition 101."

Agent Rand stood on the other side of Cole and tucked his phone away. "You think Meade's people are sending him a message—keep your mouth shut or you'll be in the car next time it burns?"

"Meade?" Mark frowned at the name from Kansas City's storied criminal history. "I recognize that name. You mean Jericho Meade and his mob connections? I thought he was dead."

"Alleged mob connections. And he is." Cole shook his head. "Tori and I took care of them."

Matt had heard the story of the undercover op several years earlier where Uncle Cole had met his wife, then–FBI agent Victoria Westin. They'd both infiltrated the crime family and had been forced to become allies to protect each other's cover and complete their respective missions. Pretending to be a couple had become the real thing. They'd both left undercover work once they'd gotten married and had their twin girls. And though Cole had remained a detective with KCPD, Tori had retired from the FBI to manage a small art gallery and focus on their girls.

Cole reached up with a gloved hand to smack Matt's shoulder, including both him and Mark in the point he was making. "But, just like the next generation of Taylor clan brothers are fighting to keep Kansas City safe, we believe the next generation of Meade's crime family is fighting to regain their influence. Jericho's nephew Chad Meade was released from prison after seventeen years a few months back. He's trying to take up where his uncle left off. Our CI was going to confirm that Meade has been stealing cars and sending them to a chop shop. Auto theft may be old-school, but we suspect he's using those profits to finance his efforts to bring illegal arms into the city. And using some legit businesses to launder money for suspected terrorists." He nodded toward Agent Rand. "That's the connection that brought NCIS into our investigation."

Mark frowned at what Matt suspected was a glossed-over version of Meade's criminal enterprise. "All that's going on in KC? In *this* neighborhood? There's a lot of money here. I thought this was where the Millennials and old-school yuppies worked and tore down old buildings to put up condos."

"They do." Cole pointed to the office building where the

curious crowd had come from. "This isn't gang turf, but there are a couple of import/export and agricultural distribution companies headquartered in that building that we're monitoring. With KCI Airport and the Missouri River carrying so much traffic, Kansas City is considered a port city. That's why we've got all the embassies and customs offices here."

Agent Rand nodded. "Making it a hub for supply lines and money changing hands if the right man establishes a foothold here."

Mark snorted at the enormity of what Chad Meade was trying to accomplish after his stint in prison. "You mean the wrong man." He looked around the parking lot, tall buildings and crowd of suits and dresses that was dissipating now that the excitement of the fire was over and Ray Jackson had rejoined the team stowing gear on the trucks. "Although this would be a great neighborhood to find some nice cars to steal."

"Exactly. Not where our mechanic would be hanging out. We thought it'd be a good location to meet our CI." Cole studied the burned-out car again. "Apparently, someone else didn't agree."

Organized crime in their neighborhood? Were there really terrorist connections in the Firehouse 13 district? Matt thought of Corie and Evan McGuire, slight of build, super cautious and all alone in the world. Their building was about nine blocks from here—a bit of a long walk, but certainly doable. And Pearl's Diner, where Corie worked, was just around the corner, less than two blocks away. Several of the people working in these office buildings had probably eaten their lunch there. Maybe he should be worried about how safe any of them were.

"And you think this fire could have been set as a deterrent to your informant speaking out against Meade?" Matt asked.

Cole shrugged. "No proof one way or the other yet. Your first instinct could be right, and this is an insurance scam. If Maldonado had a change of heart, he could be looking for some quick cash from an insurance payout, or he could have torched the car to throw Meade's men—and us—off his trail. He'd have the know-how to rig a car like that."

Amos Rand shifted on his feet, looking anxious to leave. "I'd sure like to get eyes on him. Find out if he's had a change of heart, or if Meade's people got to him. Make sure he's still in one piece somewhere."

Two mysterious fires in two days. Not that Corie Mc-Guire would have any connection to a police informant and organized crime. Matt suspected her son, left to his own devices for entertainment last night, had been playing with setting a fire. This burned-out car couldn't have anything to do with that.

It had to be a coincidence.

Not that he liked coincidences. But Matt was paid to put out fires and save lives, not solve cases for his uncle or anyone else in the police department.

"You okay, big guy?" Cole asked, pulling Matt from his thoughts. "You seem distracted."

Mark grinned like the annoying little brother he was. "That's what I said. I think there's a woman involved."

Matt slid him a warning glance. "Shut up."

That big grin must be a family trait. Cole matched Mark's amused expression. "Definitely a woman judging by that reaction."

Matt wasn't ready to admit to any emotion he wasn't sure he understood yet. "Can't a man get any privacy in this family?"

But Mark wouldn't let it go. "Hey, you're the only Taylor

bachelor left until our cousins graduate from high school and college. After being the baby brother for so many years, it's only fair that I get to pick on you for a change."

"Some things never change," Cole agreed. "Mitch, Brett, Mac, Gideon and Josh used to give me grief about finding a woman and settling down. Even Jess found a husband before I met your aunt Tori." He squeezed Matt's arm, offering some hard-won advice. "It'll happen when it happens. And it'll be worth the wait. But if there is somebody special, you know we'd all like to meet her. Whenever you're ready."

"Taylors!" Captain Redding shouted. He answered the dispatch summons on his radio before heading over to the first fire truck. "We got another call!"

Mark swore. "This whole neighborhood is turning into a dead man district."

"What does that mean?" Agent Rand frowned.

Matt explained the terminology. "A dead man zone is the spot where we suspect a fire will shift and spread to, given wind conditions, structural composition and so on. It's the place you *don't* want to be because the fire is coming your way."

Amos nodded with grim understanding. "You're saying this whole neighborhood is a danger zone."

"Yes."

Cole stepped back, reaching out to shake Matt's and Mark's hands again before sending them on their way. "Go do your job. We'll work the crime scene here and copy you on anything we find out. You boys be safe."

Mark traded a quick hug before he and Matt jogged on past him. "Say hi to Aunt Tori and the girls."

"Will do. Hey, are we getting an invitation to your wedding?"

Mark turned, backing toward the engines. "They should

go out next month. Amy's designing and making them herself. She's not just an artist, she's a perfectionist."

"She and Tori should have a lot to talk about at the next family get-together."

"Taylors!" Redding shouted from the captain's seat in the truck.

Matt tugged on Mark's coat. "Gotta go."

He doffed a salute to Cole and Amos before climbing up to his seat behind the steering wheel of the fire engine and starting it up. "What's up?" Matt asked.

The captain was still on his radio across the cab of the truck. "Class B fire at the recycling plant on North Front Street." Class B meant flammable liquids—several steps up in danger from an engine fire one man could put out. The recycling plant would definitely be a dead man zone if they didn't get there quickly enough.

All thoughts of Corie, Evan and mysterious fires he couldn't yet explain had to be put on hold.

"Let's go." Matt shifted the engine into gear and turned on the lights and siren. "Lucky 13 rolling."

Chapter Three

"Mom, if we had a watch like Mr. Taylor's, you could set the timer on it, and you wouldn't have to keep checking your watch every minute to see if we get home by my bedtime." Evan hopped from one foot to the next, following Corie down the aisle and off the bus. "Or we could use it to check the temperature to see if I need to wear my mittens and hat."

The bus door opened, and the damp, wintry night air slapped her in the face. Corie pulled her scarf snug around her neck and flipped up the collar of her coat before turning to her son and tugging his knit stocking cap down around his ears. "I don't need a fancy watch to know you have to wear your mittens and hat."

She looked over his head to Mr. Lee, the bus driver, who grinned from ear to ear at her son's persistent, supremely logical argument on the merits of buying a fancy watch for his next birthday, which was nearly a year away. "Good luck with that one," he said before bidding her good-night. "He'll keep you on your toes."

"That he will." She felt lucky and a little sad that the affable older gentleman who drove them home from the diner nearly every night was one of the most familiar faces she knew in Kansas City. Other than her coworkers at the diner and Evan's school, where she worked as a para-educator until she finished her teaching degree, she hadn't made any effort to form friendships since moving across the state. Not since her last new *friend* in St. Louis had turned out to have a connection to her ex-husband, and she discovered Denise had been feeding Kenny Norwell information about her work and school schedule, and she ended up getting an unwanted and unfriendly surprise visit from Kenny at the sports bar where she'd waited tables one night. It was one of the few times she'd been glad Evan was spending the night at her mother and stepfather's. That visit from Kenny and the subsequent lecture from her mother about blowing her chance at a reunion with the man whose money and connections she liked more than his treatment of her only daughter had been reason enough to transfer her college credits and move to Kansas City. "Good night, Carl."

Corie stepped off the bus, wishing she had on jeans or slacks instead of her waitress uniform. At least her sturdy support shoes allowed her to move quickly so that she didn't have to spend any longer than necessary out in the cold air. She reached for Evan's hand and, as soon as the bus pulled away from their stop, they hurried across the street and down the two blocks that would take them to their building.

Evan danced along beside her, full of energy after spending four hours obediently sitting at a corner table in the diner, completing his homework, eating dinner and playing a game on her phone. "Honestly, if it's any help, I don't mind staying up past nine o'clock."

"I appreciate the offer," she teased. "But I know how impossible it is to get you up for school in the morning if you're up too late the night before."

"Or I could get a new watch," he countered. "My birthday's coming up in November."

"How about we just hustle for now, little man." She

tightened her grip around Evan's hand and matched his eager pace.

If she could afford a Swiss Army Knife–like watch like Matt Taylor's, she'd be spending the money on a new, warmer coat that fit her son better, making a down payment on a cheap car so they wouldn't have to wait at a bus stop or walk these last two blocks in the open air, or, what the heck, maybe pay a bill or something. Making it completely on her own in the world was proving to be more rewarding than she'd imagined, even though it was sometimes a challenge to make ends meet. Even though a single phone call back to St. Louis would instantly fill her bank account, the help came with too many strings attached. Strings she had no intention of ever reconnecting.

Her life was here now, in Kansas City with her son. It might be a small life. But it was a good one. They were safe. Evan was growing stronger and more confident every day. And she believed—she hoped, at least—that one day they could have a normal life and be happy.

Corie's sigh formed a white cloud of air, and Evan slowed down to play at making clouds with his warm breath. Even though she played along to see how big they could make a cloud before it chilled and dissipated, she kept Evan moving beside her, worrying as much about his exposure to the cold air as their safety.

Fortunately, there was a bus stop on the same block as Pearl's Diner, and bus passes were cheap. But she worried about the January night air on Evan's young lungs and every alley or parking garage they had to walk past before they got safely inside the locked lobby of their building. She wasn't above scoping out the driver of every vehicle that passed, either, checking to make sure her ex-husband hadn't made tracking her down to their new apartment in a new city his top priority since his release from prison in Jefferson City eleven months earlier. He'd contacted her through her attorney in St. Louis demanding visitation rights with Evan, but a firm no and a reminder of all the custody papers and restraining orders she had in place had been her only reply. Being told no wouldn't have made Kenny happy, but Evan's panicked reaction to the possibility of seeing his father—even under the parameters of a supervised visit—had made her decision quick and easy. Corie's job was to protect her son from the man he only remembered as a monster. She hadn't even given her estranged mother her new name or address, and she hadn't listed her new phone number. Their life in St. Louis felt like a lifetime ago, but the wariness of her surroundings and the potential threat of that past catching up to them was as fresh as the diner's cheesy burritos for tomorrow morning's breakfast she carried in her backpack.

Since the lobby of the building was locked 24-7, she had her key card ready to swipe as soon as they climbed the granite steps and reached the outer glass doors. It was noticeably warmer the moment the door closed behind them, blocking the wind. Corie's stress level went down, as well, as soon as she heard the lock clicking into place. Once she and Evan got through the interior door, she inhaled a deep, calming breath, unbuttoned the top of her coat and loosened her scarf.

She considered stopping at Mr. Stinson's apartment while they were here on the first floor, but Evan had already run ahead to press the call button on the elevator. Nodding in silent agreement that her son had a better plan than knocking on the super's door, Corie followed Evan to the elevator, catching his mittens and cap as he shed them and stuffing them into the pockets of his backpack. Not that his energy level was showing any signs of ebbing, but she'd stayed late at the diner to fix their to-go breakfast and had missed their regular bus. Getting Evan to calm down and fall asleep by his nine o'clock bedtime was a challenge, even without the late start to his nightly routine. Mothering first. She'd run back down to see about the state of the oven and electrical outlet once she got her son in his pajamas.

Corie grabbed Evan by the shoulder when the elevator doors opened, checking the interior before following him inside the empty car. When the doors opened onto the seventh floor, Evan skipped down the hallway, leaving Corie to hurry after him. "Can I open it, Mom?"

Evan's fascination with gadgets, even one so simple as a key in a lock, gave her a moment to glance over her shoulder to the door across the hall. She idly wondered if Matt Taylor was home this evening. He'd said he usually had Tuesdays off, but what about Wednesdays? And just what did he do behind that door? Watch sports on TV? Work out? Maybe he was a gourmet cook or a fix-it guy with some carpentry or painting project going on. Was he into fast cars or monster trucks? Maybe he read books.

Evan pushed the door open and tossed her the keys, running inside to shed his coat and dump his backpack on the couch. Corie shook her head and followed him inside.

It didn't matter what Matt Taylor did behind closed doors. She had plenty to deal with right here inside *this* apartment. "Hey, little man." She turned the dead bolt behind her and nodded to the coatrack beside the door. "Hang up your coat and take your backpack to your room. You know we don't leave a mess in the living room."

"Yes, ma'am."

Corie was dragging with the length of her day after working two jobs, knowing she still had to get on her laptop to do more research for the paper she was writing for next week's class. But Evan happily bopped from one spot to the next, hanging up his coat and dashing down the hall to his bedroom before she even got her coat unbuttoned. "Get your pajamas on. Do you need a snack before you brush your teeth?"

"Can I have chocolate milk?" he shouted from his bedroom. From the sound of things, he'd opened a drawer in his toy chest and was riffling through his collection of tiny plastic building bricks to add to the ever-expanding fantasy fortress he was building on the table that had once been his desk. While she worried about the significance of her son building defensive fortresses and attack dragons, the school counselor insisted they were healthy outlets for the fears he'd carried with him since he'd been a toddler. "Cookies, too?"

"One or the other," she hollered back. "Pj's before playtime, okay?"

She smiled at his answering multipitched groan, picked up her own backpack and carried it to the kitchen. She flipped on the light switch and stopped in her tracks. "What the…?"

Her oven was missing. Not blackened up the front edge. Not under repairs. Gone.

"What…? Where…?"

Before she picked up the phone to call Mr. Stinson and ask how she was supposed to cook breakfast in the morning, Corie forced herself to inhale a steadying breath. What she noticed then wasn't much better.

She sniffed the air again. Something smelled off. Different. Extra.

Then she spotted the sticky note clinging to her microwave oven. She set her bag on the counter beside it and tore it off. She read it quickly, read it twice before breathing a little easier.

Mrs. McGuire—

Got the plug fixed. Don't know how, but the wires
had disconnected. The microwave works.
Your oven will take me a little longer.
We need to talk.
Wally S.

"You're darned right we need to talk."
She crumpled the note in her fist and punched a couple of buttons on the microwave, just to reassure herself
that she could heat up breakfast. Then she pushed up the
sleeves of her cardigan sweater and got busy putting away
the takeout box and cleaning up the mess of rearranged
items and a grease smudge Mr. Stinson had left behind.
She wiped down the countertops and found a space underneath the sink where she could move the pots and pans
he'd taken from the bottom drawer of the oven and strewn
across the counter. Then she pulled the sweeper from the
pantry closet and swept out the dust bunnies that had collected under and behind the stove. She knew she should
be feeling grateful for Mr. Stinson's help instead of this
nagging sense of violation. But how could she explain to
the kindly older gentleman the sense of intrusion she felt
knowing that someone had been in her apartment while
she'd been away?

He didn't know her history. No one in Kansas City did.
Not all of it. He thought he was being helpful, doing his job.
Wally Stinson *was* being helpful. She was the one whose
sense of *friendly* and *helpful* and *normal* had been skewed
by her ex-husband's violence and control, and her mother's
opinion that everything Kenny had done to her was just
part of being married. Even when he'd been arrested for
multiple counts of arson and witness intimidation and had
taken a plea deal that guaranteed his guilt in exchange for

less prison time, Corie's mother had begged her not to divorce him. Kenny had money and connections and a veneer of status her mother accused her of throwing away.

Corie had dropped the charges of domestic battery and attempted kidnapping, just to make sure Kenny went away and she got full custody of Evan.

But any sense of security was fragile and hard-won. Yes, she'd broken all ties with Kenny and her mother. She'd moved away, changed her and Evan's names and lived as invisible a life as possible. But that didn't mean she still didn't jump at shadows, worry when Evan was out of her sight, and fear the idea of someone watching her, touching her things without her knowing, trespassing on her life.

She'd called Mr. Stinson this morning, and he'd promised to stop by. The man had keys to get into every apartment in the building. She'd *known* he would be here today. A normal person wouldn't be upset by that. Oh, how she desperately wished for the day she could feel normal again. Her therapist in St. Louis had advised her to visualize what she wanted her life to look like in the future, and eventually she'd be able to let go of the past and she'd get there. During her counseling sessions, she'd also learned to think before reacting. Her feelings of fear and distrust were to be expected, given all she'd been through. But that didn't mean she had to act on them.

Take a deep breath.
Think. Observe. Assess.
Then react to what was really here.

Corie did just that, taking the time to put away the sweeper and calm her fears. The building had been locked. Their apartment was locked. She and Evan were safe.

Mr. Stinson's presence accounted for the whisper of an unfamiliar scent that lingered in the air. She squeezed her eyes shut and tried to pinpoint the fading smell of something woodsy combined with citrus. She opened her eyes and ran the water in the sink to rinse her dish rag. When she squirted the lemony hand soap to clean her hands, she thought she'd solved the mystery. Mr. Stinson had probably washed his hands here when he was done working. Moving the oven would have required a dolly and maybe some extra help from the part-time super who lived in the apartment below hers and helped with bigger projects like replacing a damaged oven.

But to completely dismiss her suspicions, Corie needed to do a little more investigating. Did the super wear cologne? Did his assistant? She wanted to verify that the extra scent in her kitchen belonged to one of them and her paranoia was simply an overreaction. It was yet another reason to get Evan into his pajamas and hurry downstairs to speak to the building super before he turned in for the night.

As she picked up a towel to dry her hands, her gaze landed on the dessert plate sitting in the drainer beside the sink. Matt Taylor had returned it early that morning, washed and dried, before heading to his shift at Firehouse 13. Since she and Evan had been in their usual mad dash to get ready for school and up to the bus stop, she'd thanked him again, thanked him for comparing her pie to his grandmother's and then, realizing the silliness of their rushed morning conversation, had told him goodbye and set the plate in the drainer before running back to her room to throw on some mascara, blush and lip gloss, grab their coats and backpacks, and get them up to the bus stop.

But that silly conversation at her door meant that Matt had been at her apartment twice now in the past twenty-four hours. Maybe that's what felt off about the apartment tonight. Other than the movers and Mr. Stinson, who was old enough to be her father, she hadn't had any man in here.

Did Matt have a scent that lingered in the air? Somehow, she had the impression that he wasn't a cologne kind of guy. But that didn't mean he didn't put off natural phero-mones that spoke to something purely feminine inside her. Was she just projecting her thoughts, imagining something had changed in her apartment because an attractive man had been here?

Corie put the plate away and leaned against the edge of the sink, staring at her reflection in the window there. She looked a little older and a lot more tired since the last time she'd thought of any man as attractive. She hadn't thought about a man that way in years. Not since Kenny and their ugly divorce. Not since remaking her life to keep her and Evan safe.

She was human enough to objectively appreciate a good-looking man, even to be a little bit in awe of the utter masculinity of size and strength embodied by her neighbor, especially in that sharply pressed, shoulder-hugging black firefighter's uniform he'd been wearing this morning. The day she and Evan had moved in, and they'd first met Matt Taylor, she had to admit, she'd been afraid of him. Her ex-husband, Kenny Norwell, was of average height and build, and he'd been scary enough when he'd used his words and his fists and his threats against her. Sharing the close quarters of an elevator ride with Matt had made her feel practically helpless. She appreciated him respecting her need to keep her distance. She'd never heard him swear or raise his voice in anger. Over the months they'd shared the same apartment building, she'd deduced that he wasn't a seething powder keg about to blow, that he was truly a quiet, gentle-natured person, despite his size.

Still, she'd been feeling like something was off in her apartment for a couple of days now, even before Matt's suspicions about the oven fire had reinforced her own and made her anxious to get him out of her space, no matter how kind and helpful he was being. The cherry pie had been as much an apology for her sudden haste in getting rid of him last night as it had been a thank-you for allaying her fears about the fire. And for impressing Evan with the watch and timekeeping responsibility. Being estranged from her mother and stepfather meant there was no strong adult male influence in Evan's life, other than a couple of wonderful teachers. And she certainly wasn't going to get involved with another man just to give her son a father figure. She'd learned the hard way that marrying a man didn't make him a good father—or husband.

Corie reached across the sink to pull the curtains shut and cancel out both her perpetually wary expression and the cold night beyond. Maybe she could ease up a little on her isolationist rules that had become second nature to her and strike up a friendship with Matt. Just so Evan could have him as a friend, too.

Only, she had a feeling that Matt might be interested in more than friendship. And she couldn't give him that. At least, she thought she'd felt those vibes of attraction, felt the heat of a wandering gaze plastered to her backside. And her mouth.

She couldn't even remember the last time she'd been kissed. The last time she'd wanted a man to kiss her.

Then again, she was so out of practice with relationships that she could be reading Matt Taylor all wrong. Matt was a quiet man who kept mostly to himself. As far as she could tell, there was no woman in his life. He was all about his work. And clearly, he worked out. Muscles like his didn't just happen. She'd seen him coming home in his black KCFD uniform or wearing a KCFD T-shirt like the one that had stretched across his broad chest last night often enough to know he was a firefighter, even before he'd announced it in the hallway last night. He was polite, a little awkward when it came to conversation, completely unaware of, or maybe embarrassed by, his dry sense of humor. But was he shy? Or was he reclusive for other reasons like she was?

Corie hung up the towel and headed out of the kitchen toward the bedrooms to make sure Evan was getting ready for bed. Certainly, she counted a few men among her friends—coworkers, classmates at Williams University. But they were more acquaintances than anyone she'd feel comfortable hanging out with in her own home. And nothing with them had ever fluttered with interest, much less real desire. Abuse, blackmail and living in fear of her and Evan's lives had made trusting a man impossible—and being attracted to one too big a risk to take.

She barely recognized the womanly impulses inside her anymore, but last night, something had definitely fluttered. Matt had sensed she was in danger and had come to her rescue. He'd taken several practical steps to keep her and Evan safe and to prevent any further damage to her kitchen and apartment. And he'd done it all without grabbing her, threatening her or talking down to her like she was an idiot who wouldn't understand.

Although Corie doubted she'd ever feel completely safe again after surviving her marriage to Kenny, for a few minutes last night, she hadn't been afraid. She'd been worried that Evan could have seriously injured himself, and that she'd have to dig into her meager savings to come up with the money to replace the oven if the super and building owner blamed her for negligence and didn't feel like replacing it. She'd even been unsettled by her suspicions that the fire hadn't been an accident.

But she'd felt safe with Matt Taylor in her apartment, taking up a lot of space, taking care of them, smelling like a man and saying unexpectedly silly things that made her want to laugh. She'd felt safe right up until the familiar survival instincts that had kept her alive for more than eight years had taken hold, and even the temptation of touching hard muscle and the warm skin of that tattoo peeking from beneath the sleeve of Matt's T-shirt had faded beneath her need to protect Evan and herself at all costs.

She couldn't indulge these rusty sensations of sexual awareness that had awakened inside her. But those few minutes of feeling safe, of feeling like a woman, of picking up the subtle signs of a man being interested in her, had been worth at least a slice of cherry pie.

Reaching Evan's room, she knocked softly on the doorjamb and stepped inside. He was already in his pajamas and building on his fortress. Surveying the whirlwind that was her son determined to have fun without disobeying her, Corie shook her head. She picked up his backpack from where it had hit the floor and set it in the desk chair before gathering up his discarded clothes and dropping them into the clothes basket inside his closet. She folded the sweater he'd been wearing and hugged it to her chest, hating to interrupt the bad guys attacking the ramparts of the castle and the dragon lord, or whatever that winged creature was he'd created, raising the towers ever higher in the battle of Evan's desk. But she needed to settle her fears. She opened the drawer of his dresser and set the sweater inside. "Hey, sweetie. You haven't opened a new soap or sprayed some of my perfume in the apartment, have you?"

The dragon swooped down and knocked over several tiny block warriors as he answered. "Ew, no. I don't like any of that girly stuff."

"Did you spill anything in the kitchen this morning?"

Evan pushed to his feet, his saving-the-world game momentarily forgotten as his sweet face aged with a frown.

"Mom, is something wrong? I know the rules. I wouldn't break them. I know we have to stay safe now that Dad's out of prison. I haven't even told any of my friends my real name."

Oh my. Corie's heart hurt at the maturity she heard in Evan's voice.

"Evan McGuire *is* your real name now. Remember? The judge in St. Louis said so." Her mistakes and fears had forced her little boy to grow up way too soon. She crossed the room to wrap him up in a hug, cradling his head against her breasts and stroking her fingers through his shaggy brown hair. "It's okay, sweetie. I'm okay. I'm sorry if I worried you. Mr. Stinson removed the oven from the kitchen, and it's kind of throwing me off."

He let her hug him for about as long as an eight-year-old who thought he needed to be the man of the house could stand. He pushed away, tilting his wise green eyes up to hers. "I know you don't like changes in your routine. But I didn't do anything." He crossed his finger over his heart. "I swear." He glanced over at his sprawling stronghold. "I dragon swear."

Truly, the strongest vow that Evan McGuire could give. To his way of thinking, nothing could get past the dragon protecting them. If only reality could be as assuring as what this medieval fantasy world had become for her son.

"I'm not blaming you. I just wanted to check." She spared a couple of minutes to admire his dragon beast and the newest turret on his castle before catching a glimpse of the time. "You finish getting ready for bed. Remember to set the timer when you brush your teeth. I'm going to run downstairs and talk to Mr. Stinson for a minute. When I get back, we can read another chapter of that fantasy book together, okay?"

"Okay!"

With her son excited like the little boy he should be, darting off to the bathroom to do her bidding, Corie grabbed her keys from her bag. She locked Evan in and took the elevator downstairs. When her knock on the superintendent's door produced no response, she followed the sound of men's voices out the back door of the building.

A cold wind whipped through the alley, wrapping Corie's polyester dress around her thighs and cutting through to her skin. Shivering as she stepped around the corner of the row of dumpsters, she found Matt Taylor crouched in front of what had once been her oven, with the building super leaning over his shoulder, shining a flashlight inside the appliance. Corie overlapped the front of her cardigan, clutching it together at her neck. "Mr. Stinson?" Matt instantly pushed to his feet and the superintendent stepped back, momentarily blinding her with his light before he pointed it toward the snow blowing across the asphalt. Corie tried to see what they'd been in such rapt conversation about, but she mostly saw a charred black hole. "Can't it be repaired?"

If she wasn't mistaken, Matt shifted his position to block the bulk of the wind. Not that she would warm up anytime soon, but at least she wouldn't get any colder. It was a thoughtful gesture. "Did you get a hot dinner?" he asked, forgoing any sort of greeting and *not* answering her question.

Corie nodded. She was more interested in what the two men had been discussing than the temperature of the nighttime air or the condition of her stomach. "Evan and I ate at the diner. Does this mean the oven can't be fixed?" She dropped her gaze from Matt's steady dark gaze to Mr. Stinson's disconcerting frown. "Do I have to pay for a new one?"

While she was calculating how many extra shifts she'd

have to pick up to pay for a new appliance, Mr. Stinson cleared his throat. That didn't bode well. He rubbed his hand over the top of his balding head, then stepped back to gesture to the space between the dumpster and recycling bin. "Does your son like to play with matches?"

"Excuse me?" Obeying the unspoken summons, Corie scooted around Matt and peeked into the hidden nook.

In a circle of scorched asphalt where the snow had melted away sat what she assumed was her discarded iron skillet. A black stain of soot climbed the brick wall above it and surrounded the milk carton that had melted into a flat plank and sat in a pile of ash in the pan. More surviving bits of charred debris lay scattered around it, stretching out into the surrounding snow like bony fingers, as if someone had kicked snow onto the flames to put them out. She'd like to think this was a homeless person's fire that had gotten out of hand. But the fearful suspicion crawling up her spine told her that was just wishful thinking.

Corie hugged herself impossibly tighter, automatically defending her son—automatically throwing up every defensive barrier she possessed against the nightmares of her past. Another fire. Two in two days. Her voice came out brittle and sharp. "What are you implying?"

Matt adjusted his knit cap over his ears as if he was making conversation about the weather. "I found a chemical residue coating both of the heating elements in the oven. I found the same gelatinous residue inside the lip of the milk carton."

"Why are you…?" Matt still wore his KCFD uniform and insulated jacket. He must have just come from work. Or maybe he was still on the clock. Corie backed away into the deeper snow across the alley, keeping both men in view. "Are you investigating me?"

Wally raised his gloved hands in a placating gesture. "Has your son been alone in the apartment today?"

Even worse.

"You're investigating Evan?" She shook her head, all her mama bear defensiveness welling inside her and making her shout. "He was at school or with me. All day long—until we got home a few minutes ago. I saw my oven was missing and came down to ask you about it. He's upstairs right now, getting ready for bed. But you're not going to interrogate him. He's a child. An innocent child."

Matt's tone remained calm, his stance annoyingly unaffected by her losing it like this. "I'm not accusing Evan of setting these fires with any malicious intent."

Semantics. An accusation was an accusation.

She glared at the building super. "*He* is."

Chapter Four

Katie Norwell remembered the flames shooting up into the night sky as Kenny torched their first home. A wailing toddler squirmed in her arms and tears streamed from her eyes to mingle with the blood at the corner of her mouth while her monster of a husband pinned her in front of him, her upper arms almost numb with the pinch of his grip.

As he forced her to watch his handiwork, Katie felt her entire future going up in flames. Kenny, on the other hand, seemed to be getting off on the destruction of the small house she had worked so hard to decorate and turn into a family home. "Insurance will pay for a bigger, brand-new home, more befitting my new position with the Corboni family."

She didn't bother arguing that she preferred history and character over modern ostentation. She didn't bother threatening to report his crime—unless she had a death wish. She was trapped, and he knew it. He smacked his lips as he whispered against her ear. "You're lucky I let you bring the boy out."

He didn't mean he'd done her a favor by letting her save their son. Danny would always be Kenny's prized possession. He meant she was lucky that he'd let her live.

"Corie?"

She snapped out of the memory at the firm, low-pitched call of her name.

Not Katie. She was Corie now.

That flash of memory belonged to the past. The wall of Matt Taylor standing in front of her, his dark eyes creased with concern, belonged to the present.

She rapidly blinked her surroundings into focus and gathered her thoughts. The remnants of two fires. Snow. Cold. She needed her coat. Kansas City. No Kenny. Bald man. Big man.

Corie tilted her gaze up to Matt's angular, darkly stubbled face.

He thought Evan had set these two small fires.

He didn't know what a real arsonist could do.

The hardness around his eyes softened when he sensed she recognized him and could be reasoned with again. "I don't mean Evan any harm. And I won't jump to any conclusions. I promise," Matt stated, making Mr. Stinson grumble about being accused of something himself and turning away. "I want the facts first."

"The facts are my son didn't set these fires." There was something about Matt's stoic demeanor that calmed her enough to speak rationally again. "Why would you think that?"

"Several things about them make me suspicious," Matt explained. Although she was certain he was wondering why she'd blown up like that, he was too polite to mention it. Or maybe her reaction made it look like she was hiding something. The hell of it was she was hiding a lot. "I asked Mr. Stinson if I could examine them. The signatures are too similar for me to think they were set by two different perps. The residue is what dripped into the pan and set your son's pizza on fire. The whole oven was primed to burn. If the detector hadn't gone off—if I hadn't smelled the smoke…"

She'd had nothing to put it out with beyond depriving the flames of oxygen. And she'd opened a window. This could have been a disaster. But surely not… There was no way this could be anything but a horrid coincidence, right? A chemical? The unfamiliar smell in her kitchen? A different sort of panic threatened to sink its talons into her. She stepped around Matt to confront the older man. "Mr. Stinson, was anyone besides you in my apartment today?"

"Just to move the oven out," he groused, clearly feeling underappreciated and defensive now that he was no longer the one asking questions. "I fixed the outlet, and Jeff helped me move the oven out on a dolly."

"Jeff? Who's Jeff?" She tried to picture the retired gentleman who'd fixed her garbage disposal last Thanksgiving when Wally had visited his daughter in Ohio. "I thought Phil somebody helped you."

"Phil remarried and moved to Arizona with his new wife. You probably don't know that because you're not around much," he added, as though working two jobs and spending her free time with her son were crimes instead of choices. "Jeff moved in about a month ago. Gets reduced rent as my new part-timer. He lives in the apartment right under yours—612. We were in and out of your place in half an hour."

Shouldn't that make her feel better, knowing no one had been in her apartment who couldn't be accounted for? Of course, she'd feel a lot better if she actually knew who this Jeff person was and could put a face to the name. There had to be another explanation for the fires, beyond the one that scared her more than anything else. She and

Evan were safe. She had no proof that her past had caught up with them.

So, why did she feel like someone *had* violated her sanctuary?

Her shiver had nothing to do with the cold.

Matt was still calmly explaining his concerns in that deep, resonant voice. "According to my fire captain, it's a homemade fire starter usually used in vandalism. Spray or brush the flammable substance over the heating elements and crank the temperature until it ignites. Or drop a match into a milk jug filled with the incendiary compound."

She knew what he was implying. But he was wrong. Evan had been too young to know anything about his father's line of work—an arsonist for hire. All he remembered about Kenny Norwell was the yelling and the fist that had shattered her cheekbone when she picked up her toddler and drove away with nothing but the clothes on their backs. There were no tender memories—nothing but the fires and the hospital and the running and hiding until the rest of Kenny's crimes finally caught up with him. Once she'd given her testimony and the trial and sentencing were over, Katie Norwell had secured full custody of her son, cleared out her savings and sold her car, and gone to the judge to start a new life as Corie McGuire.

Logically, she knew that Matt had no idea about her past or Kenny's expertise—he wasn't making that connection. And she knew genetics didn't make Evan a firebug like his father had been. This had to be a sick joke. Yes, her son was obsessed with dragons. But that was a coping mechanism—to his child's brain, dragons were the strongest, most unbeatable creatures ever devised. A dragon would protect him against the monsters. A dragon controlled the flames—he wasn't consumed by them. Evan could not be fascinated by fire—she couldn't go through that kind of terror again. "You think Evan is responsible? He's eight years old. He doesn't know about flammable compounds, and he would never do anything risky like that to put himself in danger." She knew kids could be curious, but she also knew her son. In some ways, he was all sweet little child—but in one way, he was mature and protective beyond his years. "Evan would never do anything to put *me* in danger."

"I'm not accusing your son of anything malicious," Mr. Stinson insisted. "But part of my job is to make sure the tenants of this building stay safe. I know boys will be boys. And you can find out about anything on the internet these days."

"No." She was as emphatic as the chill in the air. "Evan did not set these fires."

Clearly both men believed they'd been deliberately set. Clearly, both men blamed her son. Both men were wrong.

Matt took a step toward her, and Corie flinched away. She glared up at him, and he retreated a step. His voice dropped to a husky timbre, probably meant to ease the import of whatever he was about to say. "Sometimes kids experiment with things that get out of hand and are more dangerous than they thought they would be. I've done some counseling with other kids who've pulled the fire alarm at school, for example. The fire department will go in and sit with the student and explain the importance of respecting their own safety and the safety of others—how answering false alarms could take us away from someone who truly needs our help."

She shoved a lock of loose hair behind her ear and held it there, creating another barrier between her and the world that wanted to attack the person she held most dear. "I'm familiar with that program. We've had firefighters come to our school and give that same talk." She glanced at the ruined oven and charred bricks. "But you're accusing my son of arson, not pulling a fire alarm on a dare or on a lark. Evan might have put a pizza in the oven, but he did not do this."

Matt glanced over at Mr. Stinson. The older man shrugged, as though he was biting his tongue on another possibility.

Corie saved him the trouble. "*I* didn't start that fire, either." She tipped her chin up to Matt, wondering if his concern was professional or personal, and wondering why the answer mattered to her. "My son doesn't need counseling. If these are arson fires, then someone else is responsible." She included the super in her warning. "You've had a break-in in this building, and you need to step up security."

Wally Stinson clutched his coat in a dramatic gesture. "You think someone broke into this building and I don't know about it?"

Someone who'd washed his hands at her kitchen sink and wore a citrusy cologne.

Someone who shouldn't even know that Corie and Evan McGuire existed.

Suddenly, the wintry chill poured into her veins, chilling her from the inside out. "I have to go." She backed toward the door to the building. She needed to see her son. Now. "I'll pay for the stupid oven and clean up that mess myself."

"Mrs. McGuire, that's not what I'm saying," Mr. Stinson started. "You'll still get a new oven. I just wanted to make sure nothing else is gonna get damaged…"

Corie swiped her key and opened the door, hearing no more.

She hurried to the elevator. The doors opened the moment she pushed the call button. She had her finger on the seventh-floor button, and the doors were closing, when a big hand grabbed the door and pushed it open again.

Corie yelped and darted to the back of the elevator as Matt Taylor filled the opening. "I'm sorry."

"Sorry." She echoed his apology, hating that she'd screamed at her neighbor, who'd been nothing but kind to her and Evan. Until tonight. And even then, he'd been cautious in explaining his suspicions about her son playing with fire.

He stepped inside, sliding to the far corner of the elevator as the doors closed. As if a few feet of distance could make him any less imposing, or the scent of the cold, fresh air wafting off his uniform and jacket were any less enticing.

"I'm sorry," he apologized again. He pulled his stocking cap from his head and worked it between his hands before flattening his back against the side wall and adding a few extra inches of space between them. His gaze dropped to the death grip she held on the railing before those coffee-brown eyes settled on her wary, wide-eyed stare. "I know I'm a big, scary guy. I just wanted you to stop for a second and talk to me. Help me understand why you're upset—why you needed to run away."

They passed the second floor before she realized he was doing his damnedest to make himself as nonthreatening as possible. Knowing he didn't deserve to be judged by Kenny Norwell's standards, Corie made a conscious effort to loosen her grip on the railing. She blinked, trying not to look so much like prey being eyed by a predator. "First, you are a big guy, yes. But you're not scary, Matt. You're gentle and kind, from what I can tell. You startled me, that's all. I'm...more skittish than the average woman. I own that."

"Why?"

His question surprised her. Most people politely kept their distance or dismissed her entirely when she went into escape mode. "There are no gray areas for you, are there? You have a question, you ask it. You see a thing that needs to be done, you do it." He waited. The elevator slowed as she hugged her arms around herself and gave him the briefest explanation possible. "My marriage to Evan's father was not a good one. I'm overly cautious around men as a result."

"He hurt you?"

"Kenny Norwell hurt a lot of people." The elevator doors opened, and Corie hurried down the hallway, aware that Matt was following her—and equally aware that he'd shortened his stride to maintain his distance. She appreciated his thoughtfulness, hated that she projected the air of a woman who needed that kind of kid-glove treatment and was rattled enough by the conversation in the alley that she unlocked her door and headed inside without looking back. "Excuse me. I need to see with my own eyes that Evan is okay."

"Why wouldn't he be—?" She closed the door on his question and quickly threw the dead bolt behind her. Her breath rushed out on a sigh full of regret as much as relief.

She didn't want to hurt Matt, but she was more used to guarding herself than being open, more used to being afraid than trusting. Corie listened for the sound of his key in his door before she fixed a smile on her face and headed back to Evan's room.

Peeking inside the doorway, she found him busy building his fortress again. "Hey, little man. Did you brush your teeth?"

Evan glanced up from his work to roll his eyes with the exhausted look of the downtrodden masses that only a small boy who'd lost precious playtime could manage. "For two whole minutes. It took forever."

Corie smiled, relieved to see he was fine, happy to hear

his dramatic personality hadn't dimmed one iota and embarrassed to admit she owed the man across the hall an apology. "Get your book and climb under the covers. I need to talk to Mr. Taylor for a couple of minutes. I'll be right back."

"Okay. Tell Matt I said hi. And ask if he needs me to use his watch again. Maybe I could borrow it for school when we talk about technology." She arched an eyebrow and gave him the mom look. "Okay. Don't ask. I don't need a watch."

Oh, the drama. "To bed, mister."

"Yes, ma'am."

Once Evan was in bed and thumbing through the pages of his book, Corie slipped across the hall and knocked softly on Matt's door.

She curled her toes inside her sensible shoes, bracing herself for the door to swing open and the big man to suddenly fill the opening again. But he must have seen her through the peephole, because the door opened slowly and Matt leaned a shoulder against the door frame, trying and failing to look less imposing, and pleasing her all the more for making the effort.

He'd taken off his jacket and cap, rolled up the sleeves of his black uniform shirt and loosened a couple of buttons that gave her a tantalizing glimpse of another one of those T-shirts that hugged his muscular body so well. "Evan okay?"

"Yeah." Corie fiddled with the buttons of her own sweater, feeling an unfamiliar stab of heat. She buried her hands in the pockets of her cardigan, hoping she hadn't looked like she was imagining undoing the rest of those buttons on his shirt. "Are you certain someone deliberately sabotaged my oven?"

Not the way she'd meant to start that apology.

But Matt didn't seem to mind. He nodded, one curt, certain nod that made her shiver again. "The fire in the alley was also deliberately set."

Just rip off the bandage and tell him.

"My ex-husband… He went to prison for arson—insurance fraud and witness intimidation. Sneaking into my apartment to destroy an appliance or tamper with a plug is the kind of thing he would have done…to harass me. To frighten me. He couldn't grasp that I wanted to end the marriage and sue for full custody of Evan." Matt's dark eyes never wavered from hers. He knew there was more to her story, but he didn't push her to spit it out. He waited patiently until she took in a deep breath and could say it. "My marriage was a lifetime ago. Kenny has spent most of the last six years in prison. He doesn't know where we live. He doesn't know his son. He doesn't know me. Not anymore."

She hugged her arms around her waist again, the momentary heat she'd felt fading as the past swept in. "I legally changed our names. Cut all ties to where we used to live. There's no way he could find me. He can't be responsible for this." She paused to take in the scope of his broad, inviting chest, wondering what he'd do if she threw herself against him. Wondering why the arms of a man—of Matt Taylor—seemed like refuge to her tonight. She hugged her sweater more tightly around herself instead, feeling it was a poor substitute for the heat and strength she could see in him. "Those two fires make me think the impossible. They make me worry." Corie pressed her fingers to her forehead, rubbing at the tension headache twisting there. "I want there to be another explanation besides Kenny tormenting us."

"If there is, I'll find it." Matt straightened to his full

height but drifted back a step into his apartment. "Do I remind you of him?"

"Of Kenny?" Honestly, the only similarity that popped into her head was that they were both men. And Kenny hadn't even been very good at that. "No." She'd just confessed to making the stellar choice of marrying an abusive loser who set fires for a living and not being the woman Matt thought she was—and he was worried about scaring her? "You're half a foot taller than he is." And though they were both well-built men with dark hair, there was a difference about their brown eyes she wasn't sure she could explain. "His eyes are like a cold, empty void, and yours are…warm. Like a steaming cup of coffee." She allowed herself a few seconds to appreciate the heat shining from his eyes before shrugging off that fanciful notion. "Most importantly, your personalities are different. Kenny would never care that I was afraid of him. He wouldn't give me a chance to explain or defend myself. And he certainly would never apologize for startling me like you did."

Matt released a slow breath and nodded. "I can be pretty quiet. It's spooky when I don't say much."

"Spooky? Who told you that?"

"My brother Alex. And a woman I once dated."

"Well, Alex and what's-her-face are wrong. I think you just wait until you have the right thing to say." Although she could easily imagine Matt being a big, brooding presence if he ever got ticked off, he'd never shown her that side of him. "I bet there's a lot of thinking and decision making going on inside that head before you ever say a word. Maybe you're a little shy. And if that's so, I think it's sweet." She quickly put up her hand in apology. "And before you argue with me, *sweet* is a good thing."

"That's what my grandma says. If a woman calls one of us sweet, not to complain."

"I like your grandmother."

"She's one of a kind." The line of his mouth softened in what she hoped was his version of a smile.

The tension inside her skull eased a little. She liked being on good terms with Matt. She should end this conversation while she was ahead. She thumbed over her shoulder across the hall. "I'd better get inside. I promised Evan a bedtime story. We both have school in the morning, so…"

"Good night."

"Good night, Matt."

"Corie." She'd unlocked her door and pushed it partway open, but somehow he managed to stop her without touching her, without startling her. Corie turned as he braced one hand on the door frame beside her head, reversing their positions from a moment ago. "If I ever do anything that reminds you of your ex, you'll tell me, right? You won't just put up with it because you're a nice lady or you're worried about hurting my feelings or you think the truth will trigger my temper. It won't. I promise. You'll tell me to back off if I scare you?"

Kenny had rarely given her the option of pointing out when he was hurting or frightening her. If anything, he enjoyed it when she'd voiced her fears. It only made him want to torment her more, it seemed. Kenny had always needed to prove his strength, his power—and when the outside world hadn't let him be everything he wanted, he exerted that dominance over her. But Matt Taylor was a different sort of man than her ex had been. He knew he was strong, but he worked hard to play down his physicality instead of shoving it in her face. He was a little awkward, a little gruff—but he seemed like such a good man. A good neighbor. Maybe even a good friend. If she'd let him be.

Corie considered the earnestness of his request, then surprised herself almost as much as it must have surprised

Matt when she reached for his hand down at his side and squeezed his fingers. "I will."

His hand was callused and warm and infinitely gentle as he folded his fingers around hers and squeezed back. "And I'll tell you the next time I investigate anything suspicious that relates to you or Evan."

She offered him an apologetic smile. "I'm super protective of my son. I overreacted."

"No. I overstepped my authority. Thought I recognized someone acting out the way I once did."

"You acted out?"

He rubbed the pad of his thumb across her knuckles in a gentle caress, but which of them he was soothing, she couldn't be sure, because the seriousness of his expression didn't change. "I started fires when I was a little boy. Younger than Evan, but still…" His grip pulsed lightly around hers. "Had some catastrophic consequences," he added without hinting at what that tragedy might have been. "I thought if Evan was dealing with something like that, I could help. Speak to him from experience."

"You played with fire?" That was an irony she understood far too well. "And yet you became a firefighter."

He nodded. "Atonement."

Atonement. That single raw word spoke volumes yet told her little. This gentle giant was a curious one. His honesty spoke to something deep inside her. His confession, whatever it might mean, lessened the embarrassment and caution she'd felt in revealing some of her own past. Her instinct was to comfort him. Her desire was to know him better. But instinct and desire hadn't served her very well in the past. Her brain told her to run far and fast from this connection she felt with Matt. But her heart was asking for something very different.

He pulled his hand from the door frame and brushed the back of his knuckles across her cheek. Her breath caught at the tender caress. But it wasn't fear of his touch that made her lips part as her skin suffused with heat. "I want you and Evan to be safe."

Corie realized they'd been holding hands this whole time. Their eyes had been locked together, and she hadn't once felt the need to bolt. But maybe she'd be smart to at least walk away. She reached up to pull his fingers from her face and grasped each of his hands between them. "Thank you for caring, Matt. But I got this."

He nodded. "Remember what I said. Be honest with me. And if anything—anyone—makes you afraid again—"

"I'll call 9-1-1 and ask for the firefighter next door."

"You could just call my number. Here." He was the one who was finally strong enough to release their hold on each other to pull his billfold from his back pocket. He handed her a KCFD business card with his name and both his cell and the firehouse numbers on it.

"Lieutenant Taylor. Impressive." She hugged the information to her chest. "Thank you. Good night, Matt."

"Good night, Corie. Tell Evan good-night, too. I'll wait 'til you lock the dead bolt behind you."

Once she'd locked her door, Corie leaned back against it. She smiled when she heard his door close and lock across the hall. Was he always this true to his word? Did Matt show this kind of caring to everyone?

They'd held hands longer than a simple thank-you called for. Corie raised her hand in front of her face and marveled at the sensations of warmth and caring still prickling in her fingers from where Matt's big, callused hand had folded so gently around hers. Then she brushed her fingers across her cheek. She hadn't cared about a man's touch in years. But tonight, she'd actually enjoyed that simple, caring contact. She drew her fingertips across her lips, wondering if his mouth would be equally gentle pressed against hers. Or would his kiss be more demanding, as befitted his size and strength? Her pulse beat with intensified interest, and her body flushed with a long-forgotten warmth. Did she even have it in her to respond to real, raw passion like that anymore? If the memory of Matt's touch still lingered on her skin, what would it feel like if her whole body was wrapped up against his?

The heat she felt deepened and spread through her body, triggering a deliciously female response to sensations she could only imagine. Her womanly responses to men had lain dormant for so long. Once, she'd shut them down to protect at least a part of herself from Kenny, and she'd never felt compelled to resurrect that sweet tingling of normal desire in her breasts and womb. She'd never been brave enough to indulge that silky heaviness that warmed her from the inside out. Matt Taylor wasn't classically handsome, and he had no smooth charm that she could detect. But there was no denying his utter masculinity, or her basic feminine response to all that maleness. He was an unexpected temptation to her rusty hormones. He was interesting. A little mysterious and seriously hot. She was tempted to get to know him better—to do much more than simply hold his hand and share a hushed conversation at her apartment door.

"Mo-om!"

Perfect timing. Evan drew out her name on two syllables, pulling her back to reality and quashing any momentary fantasy she had about Matt. She tucked his card into the pocket of her sweater and pushed away from the door. If she wasn't careful, she was going to develop a crush on the firefighter next door. Maybe she already had.

But she had a family to support, a college degree to earn, and an eight-year-old son who needed story time and some cuddling before he'd go to sleep.

Corie didn't have time to indulge in whatever her hormones or heart were trying to tell her about Matt Taylor.

Chapter Five

After the second rapid knock on his door, Matt pulled his jeans down over his work boots and hurried out of the bedroom, tucking in his insulated undershirt and shrugging on a flannel shirt as he strode through his apartment. "Coming!" he barked.

He peered through the peephole to see which of his brothers had stopped by to tell him to hustle his butt over to Grandma Martha's old condo, where they were converging tonight to continue the remodeling and repair work needed before putting it on the market in the spring or summer. But there was no annoying brother out there. His nostrils flared as he dragged in a steadying breath to tamp down the mix of concern and anticipation surging inside him before he quietly opened the door to the blonde and her young son standing in the hallway.

"What's wrong?" he asked, reading the harried expression on Corie McGuire's face.

She hugged Evan back against her stomach and retreated half a step, possibly rethinking knocking on the Big Bad Wolf's door. "Is this a bad time?"

"For what?" He buttoned his shirt and straightened the collar, waiting for an explanation.

Corie nodded, deciding the reason for being here was more important than whatever second-guessing was playing through her head right now. "I have a big favor to ask you. I don't know if I have the right…" Not an emergency. The wariness in him eased a fraction, and he rolled up his sleeves while Corie spewed out a stream of disconnected sentences. "I got called in to work this evening. One of the girls went home sick. It's a chance to pick up a few extra hours. But it means working until closing, and it's a school night for Evan." She paused for breath. Nope. He still didn't understand what she needed from him. "I know it's impossibly short notice, but I heard you come home from work a few minutes ago, and… I'm not giving you much time to relax, but would you be able to watch Evan for me this evening?"

He needed clarity. Was she in a panic caused by time constraints? Or was he missing something more serious here? He glanced down at Evan and the green, purple and yellow plastic dragon he carried. "Babysit?"

Evan's lips buzzed with a groany sigh as he pushed away from his mother. "I'm not a baby."

The boy was put out, not in distress. This didn't sound too serious. Maybe Corie was uncomfortable asking for a favor. Maybe she was uncomfortable asking *him* for a favor. Maybe she felt like she was out of options and he was the last resort. The poor choice he'd made watching his little brother, Mark, twenty-six years ago had never been repeated. He might not be the fun uncle, but in the years since, he'd been trusted with younger cousins and nieces and nephews, and they'd all survived. In his experience, you kept the kid busy, fed him and put him to bed on time, and he'd never had an issue. If she needed a sitter, he was her man. How could he make this easier for her?

Maybe she wasn't the one he needed to make friends with.

Matt leaned against the door frame and hunched his

posture a tad, turning his focus down to the green-eyed boy and trying to sound like…not the Big Bad Wolf. "Poor choice of words, Ev. My apologies. You and your dragon buddy want to hang out for a while?" He was still looking down when he raised his gaze to Corie's. "His regular sitter isn't available?"

Color blossomed in her cheeks. "Regular? Um… I don't have anyone on speed dial—"

"Usually I go with Mom to the diner," Evan volunteered, innocently unaware of his mother's embarrassment as he matter-of-factly explained their predicament. "But that's when she works the afternoon shift after school. I can only go on Fridays and Saturdays when she closes. She calls me a growly butt in the morning if I stay up too late. And staying up until the diner closes means *too late*."

Understanding dawned. Corie didn't have a regular sitter. They went to school together in the morning, and he went to campus with her when she had classes and to Pearl's Diner when she had to work. And she'd just mentioned the need to pick up extra hours, so paying for an emergency sitter might not be an option for her.

He was trained to handle emergencies—large or about the size of a small eight-year-old boy. Matt dropped his gaze to Evan again. "Can you handle a hammer?"

Evan screwed his lightly freckled face up in a suspicious frown. "I don't know."

Matt held up a finger, warning mother and son not to leave as he dashed into the spare bedroom to pull his toolbox from the closet and retrieve a hammer. He came back to the door and found both mother and son peeking into his apartment, with Corie clinging to Evan's shoulders to keep him from following Matt inside. He wouldn't have minded the boy traipsing along behind him. "Let me show you." Matt knelt in front of Evan, trading the hammer for the dragon, letting the boy feel the weight of the tool and watching how he grabbed it with both hands in the middle. Matt moved Evan's hand to the proper position and demonstrated an easy swing. "Did anybody ever teach you to hold the handle near the end, and not up by the peen?"

"Peen?" Evan giggled, no doubt thinking that was the past tense of another word. Matt had been a boy once, too. "That's not a real word."

"The peen is the heavy metal part of the hammer that you hit the nail with."

"It is? I thought you were talking about…" His mouth rounded with an O of excitement before tilting his face up to Corie. "Mom, can I try? I want to hammer a nail."

Corie frowned. "Are you working on a project? I don't want him to get in your way."

"He won't." Matt stood, firmly grasping the hammer to stop Evan from swinging it. He had a feeling it wouldn't be too hard to keep this kid entertained. "Is it all right if I take him to my grandmother's old apartment a few blocks from here? I planned to meet my brothers to work on renovations. I'll make sure Evan's buckled into the back seat of my truck. I'm a safe driver. I drive the fire engine. Never had an accident."

"You drive the fire engine?" Evan's eager response told her that was about the coolest thing he'd ever heard. Way cooler than even the chance to hammer on something. No way was Corie going to be able to say no without disappointing her son. Or Matt. Besides, there was no need for her to. Everyone else would be showing up at his grandma's apartment with a spouse or fiancée, children and probably a dog. Matt liked the idea of bringing his own sidekick to the party. "Can I drive it?"

"You're a little young for that, bud." Matt eased his no by ruffling his fingers through Evan's soft, staticky hair.

It was funny how some of the longer strands stuck straight out or up. Evan McGuire might be a curious, sheltered kid, but he was all boy. "I'll show you my Lucky 13 truck sometime. You can climb inside, sit behind the wheel. But that's another outing. And we're not going anywhere tonight unless your mom says it's okay."

"Mom, pleee-a-ssse! He drives the fire engine and I can hammer." He hoped the kid went into music, because he could draw a word out across several different notes.

Corie shook her head, looking like she'd already lost the battle. "You're sure he won't be in your way?"

"Positive."

Corie's blond ponytail bobbed across her shoulders as she shook her head, surrendering to the boy jumping up and down between them. "You'll have him home by bedtime?"

"He'll be snoring when you get home from work."

Evan finally stopped his bouncing. "Hey, I don't snore. But, can I, Mom? Please? I want to learn about peens." He beamed a gap-toothed grin, as though saying the word out loud made him want to laugh again. "And fire engines." Evan tugged on Matt's sleeve. "Will you tell me about your fire engine?"

"You bet." Matt tucked the hammer through his belt and rested a hand on Evan's shoulder before he started that bouncing thing again.

Corie tilted her soft green eyes up at Matt, and he couldn't look away. "You'll keep him away from any power tools?"

"Mo-om!"

"My brother Mark is a registered EMT, and my first aid training is current. If he gets hurt, we'll fix him."

"If he gets hurt—?"

"He won't get hurt."

Her soft green eyes rolled heavenward, and he thought he detected the hint of a laugh. "Sometimes I can't tell when you're joking. I have to get used to that dry sense of humor." Matt felt his mouth relaxing into an answering smile. *Getting used to* would require spending more time together. He liked that idea. "Okay. To all of it." She combed her fingers through Evan's hair, trying to neaten it up a tad before she cupped his face in her hands. "Homework done?"

"Yep."

She arched a suspicious eyebrow, and Evan groaned again.

"I still have multiplication tables."

"Run and get your coat and backpack. You'll finish the math before you help Matt and his brothers, okay?"

"Okay." Evan was darting across the hall and tearing through their apartment before Corie finished her question.

Unlike her son's flyaway hair, Corie's hung thick and straight. She brushed a loose strand of it off her cheek and tucked it behind her ear. Matt's fingers tingled with the urge to do the job for her. And linger. And maybe free that ponytail to see how long her hair was when it fell loose and straight. "I hope you know what you're getting into."

Matt curled his hands into his fists and tore his thoughts away from sifting her thick, shiny hair though his fingers. "I think I can handle second grade math."

"Yes, but can you handle a second grader?"

Although he suspected she was teasing him as much as giving fair warning, Matt felt compelled to reassure her. "I'll have help. My grandmother and sisters-in-law are bringing food. There'll be plenty for him to eat. My brother Pike will bring his son. Gideon Jr. is close to Evan's age. He'll be fine."

"Okay. Thank you." Corie seemed pleased with his explanation, if a little overwhelmed by the loving, crowded scene he'd described. "I'll owe you a whole pie for helping me out tonight."

"You'll owe me nothing."

She smiled—a huge, beautiful, bright curve that gave him a glimpse of straight, white teeth and softened the tension around her lips. Didn't she understand that smile was payment enough?

"I'll bring the pie, anyway." When she reached out to squeeze his hand, Matt squeezed back. He loved the feel of her hand in his. Small and soft compared to his big workingman's hands, but strong. With sensible, unadorned nails and the faded stripe of a scar between her thumb and forefinger. Her fingers tightened around his before she released him and backed across the hallway into her apartment. "I'd better get changed. And I won't forget the pie!"

Chapter Six

Three hours later, Matt raised his hands in triumph as he busted through the kitchen wall they were taking down with their fire axes a split second before his younger brother, Mark, broke through the drywall in his section. His older brothers, Alex and Pike, slapped him on the shoulder and congratulated him before razzing Mark.

"That's how you swing an ax." Pike smacked Matt on the shoulder.

Alex agreed. "Told you he'd win."

"Not fair," Mark protested, always ready to prove himself against any of his three older brothers. "Matt's arms are a good two inches longer than mine."

"Why do you think I didn't take that bet?" Alex, the oldest and shortest of the four, teased.

Pike Taylor, the only brother with blond hair, picked up a couple of pieces of Sheetrock and carried them to the trash can in the dining room that was now open to the kitchen, save for the two-by-four framework that was coming down next. "If you don't want to give Matt credit, think of it this way—Alex and I are the real winners because we didn't have to do any of the teardown work." He glanced down at Alex, who was picking up the debris Matt and Mark had created. "Right, Shrimp?"

"Really? Shrimp?" Alex tossed his load in after Pike's. "I always thought it was you and me against the wonder twins."

"Un-uh," Mark reminded him, poking Matt in the chest. "He's two years older than I am. I'm the beloved baby boy. Grandma said so. It's every man for himself in this family."

"Matt!" Evan shot around the corner and skidded to a halt when he saw the four men laughing and ribbing each other. The dragon he carried had sprouted a second set of yellow wings, telling Matt how Evan and his nephew Gideon were staying busy. The boy's wide-eyed gaze settled on the long-handled ax cradled across Matt's shoulders. "Where's your hammer? Are you okay? Did you cut yourself?"

Matt questioned the pale tinge beneath Evan's brown freckles. "I'm fine, bud."

"Do you dragon swear?"

Um, yeah?

"What are you boys arguing about now?" Meghan Taylor, the brothers' adoptive mother, showed nary a wrinkle on her youthful features, except for the amusement crinkling beside her honey-brown eyes, when she appeared behind Evan. She carried a toddler wearing pink, fuzzy pajamas in one arm, and rested her free hand on Evan's shoulder as they peeked around the corner from the bedrooms, where she and their father, Gideon Sr., were corralling Evan, Pike's son, Gideon Jr., and Pike's little girl, Dorie. "Seriously? You two used your regulation axes to take down that wall? It's a good thing that no one lives above or below Martha's apartment with the fuss you four are making."

Matt's gaze zeroed in on Evan's pale features as the boy shrank back against Matt's mother. Had the kid been startled by the pounding and crashing? Did the potential weapon he wielded make the boy think he and Mark had attacked more than the wall? "It's a noisy job, Ev," he explained, lowering the ax to cradle it securely between both hands. "We're all good here." He wasn't sure of the protocol, but he drew a cross over his heart. "I dragon swear."

Mark set his ax in a safe corner and threw up his hands. "Speak for yourself, big guy. Mom, you know these three bullied me into turning this into a race."

"Un-uh." Their mother had heard—and dismissed— that excuse many times over the years. "The axes were probably your idea."

"I told them breaking through the wall like that could be dangerous and wanted no part of it." Pike was the next to offer up an explanation, as he swooped in to pluck Dorie from their mother's arms and blow a raspberry onto his daughter's cheek, making the tiny blonde giggle with delight. Evan tilted his chin up, looking more curious than alarmed by the farting sound and resulting laughter. "Can I help it if they won't listen to reason?"

Matt was pleased to see his mother switch both hands to Evan's shoulders, perhaps sensing the boy's nervousness at being surrounded by all this noise and activity. "How hard did you try?" Meghan asked Pike with a deadpan tone of doubt.

"Not as hard as I did," Alex insisted, tossing more debris into the trash. "That's what sledgehammers are for, I said. But have these three yahoos ever listened to me?"

Their mother shook her head, then turned her soft brown eyes up to Matt. "You're my last hope for a straight answer, son. Why would you all risk someone getting hurt and making all this racket by chopping through walls?"

"The job needed to be done." Matt might have learned that deadpan delivery from his mom. "Since it's an exer-

cise we practice time and again in our firefighter training,
I knew we could do it safely."

"And we have a winner." Meghan Taylor bent down
and whispered a reassurance against Evan's ear. "I told
you they were fine. Matt just beat all his brothers in the
wall-chopping competition."

As their mother beamed him a smile, Matt was instantly
struck by the reminder of how good it felt to be the one
who could make someone he cared about light up like
that. Maybe that's why Corie's smile was such a turn-on.
It was rare and hard-won. And though he was probably a
fool for thinking it, her smile felt like it was a special gift
just for him.

While the quiet moment passed between mother and
son, there was laughter and a round of applause from their
grandmother, Pike's wife, Hope, Alex's wife, Audrey, and
Mark's fiancée, Amy, as they joined them. The younger
women were supposed to be painting the walls and trim
in the living room. But the "Yay, Matt!" from Evan was
the only voice of approval he needed to hear. Whatever
concerns the boy had had when he'd run out to the main
room disappeared with Meghan's explanation. When Matt
caught Evan's gaze across the room and winked at him,
the boy flashed his gap-toothed grin and dashed back into
the bedroom to play.

Yep. Making someone smile felt pretty damn special.

As he had many times throughout his life, Matt thanked
the fates that had landed him in this family. The competition was real, and occasionally intense, but always full of
love. And the ringleader of them all—a shrinking, widowed, eighty-four-year-old woman—quieted the room by
simply raising a plastic tub filled with cookies she'd baked
to go with the dinner they'd all eaten earlier. Martha Taylor swatted aside Pike's hand as he reached for a cookie.

She wrapped her arthritic fingers around Matt's forearm and held on to him for balance as she stepped around the debris.

"The first snickerdoodle is for our winner," she announced, handing Matt one of her delicious cookies. He promptly stuffed it whole into his mouth while she hugged him around the waist. He dropped a kiss to the top of her snow-white hair before she pulled away and handed an equally delicious cookie to Mark. "And a consolation prize for second place."

"We always try harder." Mark held his cookie up and did a misplaced victory dance before kissing Martha's weathered cheek and hugging her, too. "Thanks, Grandma."

"What about the rest of us?" Alex pouted, drawing his red-haired wife, Audrey, to his side. "I'm starving."

Audrey poked him in the flank. "You had seconds at dinner."

"Yeah, but they weren't cookies."

"Oh, all right," Martha relented, as they'd all known she would. "Time for us all to take a break. Everybody dig in." She wrapped a stack of cookies in a paper napkin and handed them to Pike's shy wife, Hope, who'd been rubbing noses with Dorie and brushing crumbs from Pike's chin. "Take some for Evan and the Gideons."

"I'd be happy to."

"I'll help," Pike offered.

Before they headed down the hallway, Hope swiped her fingers across Pike's lips, even though the crumbs on his face were long gone. When they lingered there a second and Pike's blue eyes heated at the contact, Matt felt a spike of envy. Not because he lusted after his sister-in-law or begrudged his brother his well-earned happiness, but because he wanted that, too—that connection with a

woman who had eyes only for him. He wanted that connection with Corie McGuire.

Only, he wasn't quite sure how to make that happen. Or
if Corie was even interested in him trying.

He was thirty years old and had never been in a serious
relationship. He'd dated. He'd had sex. But nothing had
ever worked out for him. Probably something to do with
being six foot five and what that one blind date his brothers had set him up with had described as *spooky quiet*.
He didn't always have a lot to say and got stuck in his
head sometimes while he thought things through before
he did speak. He lacked Mark's glib sense of humor and
Alex's outgoing personality. Even Pike had a goofy sort
of nerd charm going for him. Matt was just… Matt. Physical. Direct. He'd been a troubled kid who didn't speak for
months after his birth parents' deaths—not until Meghan
and Gideon Taylor had done their patient, loving child-
whisperer thing with him and gotten him to open up about
the tragedy he felt responsible for. And though he'd worked
through his demons, it was still hard for him not to be that
guarded, excessively observant survivor he'd once been.

Yep. A relationship with him probably wasn't for the
faint of heart.

The man who had saved Matt's life when he'd been that
silent little boy, Gideon Taylor Sr., strode into the main
room, sliding his arm around Meghan's waist, unknow-
ingly completing the image that everyone in this family
had a partner except for Matt…and his widowed grandmother. But she'd been blessed to have been married to
their grandfather Sid for more than sixty years, until his
death this past summer. "None of the cookies made it past
those two boys and Pike." His dad pointed to each of his
three remaining sons around the room. "Talk about déjà
vu." But he was grinning. "Ma, you got any more?"

Martha held out the tub for him to help himself to a snickerdoodle. "I'm so fortunate that you're all helping me with this remodeling project. I love how you've opened the kitchen up to the rest of the apartment. Makes me sorry that I had to move." She put up a hand before Gideon could remind her of her health issues and the flight of stairs leading to the front door, which was no longer safe for her to negotiate on her own. "I know it's for the best, and I admit I'm having fun finding the perfect place to put everything in my new home. But do you know how many years I was stuck back in that kitchen cooking, missing out on all the activity out here?"

"We were all in the kitchen with you, Ma." Gideon dropped an arm around her shoulders. "You never missed a thing." She leaned into the kiss he pressed to her temple. "Come on. Let's get back to my grandkids and your great-grands and stay out of harm's way while the boys finish tearing down in here." It wasn't hard for him to reach around Martha and pluck a second cookie to munch on. "And bring these with you so the big boys don't eat them all."

Martha might be in her eighties, but she was quick. She ducked from beneath her son's arm and faced the middle generation of young men who had torn up her kitchen. "But I want to hear about Matthew's young woman."

"Oh?" Gideon and Meghan stopped and turned, both looking at Matt with hope and curiosity. Great. Now his parents would be part of the inquisition, too. "You're seeing someone?" his dad asked.

Matt carried his ax to his toolbox and slipped the protective cover over the sharp blade. Then he picked up a broom and dustpan to attack the powdery drywall dust on the floor, hoping the personal question would just go away.

"Evan's mother," Martha offered when Matt didn't immediately respond.

"We're not *seeing* each other," Matt clarified for his father. "Corie and I are friends."

His brothers and sisters-in-law filled the room with teasing catcalls. His father slowly munched his cookie, his narrowed eyes assessing the full disclosure or lack thereof in Matt's response. Gideon Taylor had earned the silvered hair at his temples after raising the four of them. He knew how to wait out his sons until he got the answer he wanted.

And though Matt had gone back to work, his younger brother, Mark, ignored the shushing from his fiancée and poked the bull. "Tell us what she looks like, Matt."

Matt focused on the muscles in his arms and hands as he worked, trying to ignore his well-meaning family. Sweep. Dump. Sweep some more. But it seemed everyone was waiting for his answer now. "Prettier than you."

"Impossible." Amy swatted Mark's shoulder at that joking remark, but his baby bro wouldn't let the subject drop. Instead, Mark pulled the trash can closer, and he and Alex helped Matt with the cleanup job. "Just trying to get a sense of who's rockin' your world, big brother. Does Evan take after her?"

Although he knew everybody in the room was hanging on the details he wasn't sure he should share, Matt couldn't help but picture his pretty neighbor. "Same mossy-green eyes." He mentally compared her image to Evan—a cautious, curious boy who didn't know whether to be the man of the house or Corie's baby boy. "Corie doesn't have freckles like Evan. Her hair's the color of a ripe wheat field."

Alex paused with the remains of a shattered two-by-four in each hand. "A ripe wheat field? When did you become a poet?"

As Alex stuffed the boards into the trash, Mark continued the interrogation. "Is she the reason you were asking Captain Redding about old-school fire starters?"

Alex pulled out his phone. "That reminds me. I did a rundown on that name you asked me about—Kenneth Norwell. Career criminal with a long rap sheet." As much as he knew mentioning the word *criminal* while talking about Corie and Evan would only make his family more curious to learn about them, Matt mentally logged the information Alex was reading off his phone. "His current address is Jefferson City. Apparently, he didn't move too far from the penitentiary once he got out. He hasn't missed a check-in with his parole officer there—met with him last week. There's no indication of him living or working here in KC."

It was no surprise that their father was going to let mention of a paroled prisoner slide. "Why do you have KCPD checking the status of a paroled prisoner?" Gideon asked. "And why are you talking to Kyle Redding about incendiaries?"

Matt supposed if he had more of a social life, his interest in helping Corie and Evan wouldn't be such big news with his family tonight. "There was an oven fire at Corie's place. I made sure it was out. Another fire the next night in the alley behind the building. Something about them seemed hinky, so I was following up on my hunch."

"Arson?" his father asked. As chief arson investigator for the KCFD, Gideon Taylor Sr. certainly knew his way around a fire—probably better than any of them, except their mother, who was captain at another firehouse.

Matt nodded. "Corie insists that Evan wouldn't mess with anything like that and that he knows all about fire safety. But if it wasn't either of them, then somebody was in their apartment. Coated the heating elements with a flammable substance. Used it again in the alley fire."

Gideon's dark eyes narrowed with suspicion. "I don't like the sound of that."

Amy hugged her arms around her waist and shivered. "Arson fires are about the scariest thing I've ever had to deal with." She looked across the room to Mark, who was already crossing toward her. They'd both barely survived the work of an arsonist this past summer. "I'd still have a home, and Gran and I wouldn't be living with this guy."

Mark hugged her close. "You *like* living with this guy."

"I do." Amy nestled her forehead at the juncture of Mark's neck and shoulder. "And marrying him."

"And marrying him." She reached up to touch his face, and the unbreakable bond the two of them shared gave her the courage to smile before turning to face the rest of them. "So, big, bad Matt rescued Corie from a fire in her kitchen. Is that what all you Taylor boys do? Rescue the women you love?"

Love? Um...

Mark rubbed his hands up and down her arms, still soothing away the nightmare they'd survived. "Red, you said you don't like to be rescued."

"Well, I don't always like it because I'm a stubbornly independent woman, and I believe I can take care of myself," she teased. "But it *is* hot."

She looked to Audrey, who linked her arm with Alex's and nodded. "Super hot. It means the world to know someone's got your back and you can trust him without reservation. It allows us to be as strong as we need to be."

Alex turned and pressed a kiss to her forehead. "That little girl we're adopting will be lucky to have you for her mama."

Why couldn't his family discuss the weather or how much they missed Royals baseball like other, normal Kansas Citians?

Matt loved Amy like a sister and believed Mark had found a treasure, but the woman had no trouble speaking her mind. "Matt's hot. I bet Corie's hot, too."

Mark's cheeks turned a pale shade of pink that matched the embarrassment Matt felt at her compliment. "Could we stop saying hot? Unless you're referring to me?"

"Oh, you know how I like to refer to you, Fire Man."

Although he was grinning, Gideon shook his head as the subtext between the newly engaged couple's banter. "Hello, you two—you have an audience—and children in the next room. Save it for after the wedding."

"Did I miss something? Who's hot?" Meghan reentered the room to stand beside her husband. "Matthew's girlfriend?"

"Mom, no. I don't have a girl... Corie is a friend. I'm just watching Evan while she's at work tonight."

"And investigating some mysterious circumstances surrounding her," Gideon added, his tone laced with concern. "Sounds like you're pretty involved to me, son."

"I like to know what I'm dealing with," Matt insisted. "And if Evan has anything to do with those fires, if he's trying to emulate his father or he's crying out for attention because the creep chose a life of crime over him, then—"

"You're the best man to help him." Probably better than anyone here, his mother understood just how far he had come since he'd been the troubled little boy who'd set the fire that had killed his birth parents. "Other than being a little skittish around all of us—and who wouldn't be?—I'm not seeing any indication that he's withdrawn or hiding something."

"Evan seems like a pretty cool kid to me," Pike added as he rejoined them. "He's making sure Junior and Dorie stay safe and share their cookies, even though Mom and Dad and Hope have been in there with them most of the evening. And that castle they're building is pretty sweet. The kid's going to be an architect one day."

Or was there something so frightening in his real life that he felt he had to keep building imaginary fortresses to feel safe?

Pike crossed the room to join them in picking up the mess they'd made. "So, we're talking about Evan's mom? Is she the one who finally woke up Matt here?"

Alex helped him move the bank of old cabinets they'd taken apart to the side of the kitchen. "She has hair like a 'ripe wheat field.' Quote, unquote."

"When did you become a poet?" Pike echoed Alex's earlier question. Apparently, Matt's factual description of Corie's hair had revealed something he hadn't intended to. "This sounds serious."

Matt realized he was surrounded on all sides and commanding way too much attention. "Don't any of you have work to do?"

Martha Taylor had an answer for him. "I don't. Certainly, nothing as interesting as this conversation."

"Grandma!"

Fortunately, his mother had always been his strongest ally. "Give it a rest, boys." From the time they'd first met in the foster home where they'd all been living, Matt, Mark, Alex and Pike had been Meghan Taylor's boys. Becoming adults hadn't changed the nickname or the bond. She reached up to cup Matt's cheek and smiled. "I know you've just been waiting for the right one to come along. I'd like to meet Corie sometime. I hope she knows what a treasure you are." Then she added, in a soft whisper for his ears alone, "I hope you know, too." As she pulled away, she added, "And remember, firefighters work as a team. If there is something dangerous around Evan and his mother, you don't take it on alone." Her look encompassed the entire room. "You have allies."

"Yes, ma'am."

Despite the dramatic sigh of disappointment from Grandma Martha, the spotlight on Matt finally faded. The younger women returned to their painting as Gideon walked his wife and mother down the hall to watch the children. Matt and his brothers got to work on the last of the cleanup and prepping the expanded kitchen for the work they were going to do this weekend.

However, Mark, in all his newly engaged happiness, wouldn't let it go. He knocked loose the remaining dangling bits of drywall and tossed the biggest piece at Matt. "They say when the big ones fall, they fall hard."

Matt caught the piece squarely against his chest and shoved it into the trash. "Give it a rest, Mark."

Evan popped in again, his mouth wrinkled with concern as he eyed the dusty residue clinging to Matt's dark flannel shirt. The kid must have some kind of danger radar. Or he was more of a worrywart than anyone his age should be. "Matt, did you fall? Are you hurt?"

As worried about Evan's paranoia as he was glad for the reprieve from Let's Pick Apart Matt's Love Life Night, Matt scooped him up in his arms and rested the boy on his hip. "I'm fine, bud. You know, in many ways, you're lucky you're an only child."

"Huh?"

Matt was already striding from the room. He'd done most of the heavy lifting tonight. Let his annoying brothers handle the rest of the cleanup. "Show me this castle you and Gid are building."

Evan's arm rested lightly on Matt's shoulder, seeming to like being able to look him straight in the eye. "Can I hammer something again?"

Matt paused at the entrance to the hallway and looked back at his brothers. "Sure. I've got a trio of numbskulls you can start with…" Matt veed two fingers toward his eyes, then pointed to Mark, Pike and Alex, indicating he'd be watching them for any more teasing…and would put a stop to it when they didn't have an audience that included an impressionable child or their delicate grandmother. Alex laughed. Pike nodded, conceding that Matt was leaving with the upper hand. Mark threw his hands up in protest, as if affronted. So much love and support. So much a pain in the—

"What's a numbskull?" Evan asked.

Matt shook his head as his brothers laughed behind him. He needed to think about how he was going to explain that one to an eight-year-old.

By the end of another hour, the kitchen was prepped for new cabinets and tile. Paint cans had been sealed, dust had been swept up, his family had given the state of his love life a temporary rest, and Matt was walking Evan down the steps to the sidewalk in front of his grandmother's condo. "This way, bud." Evan kicked up puffs of snow as he shuffled along beside Matt. "I promised your mom I'd have you in bed by nine o'clock, so we'd better hustle."

"I'm not sleepy," he protested through his wide yawn.

Matt bit back his grin. "I know. If you want to close your eyes and rest for a few minutes on the drive home, that'd be okay."

"Can I come help again? Grandma Martha said she'd bake chocolate chip cookies next time. They're my favorite. She said to call her Grandma Martha because I was a nice boy, and I was helping her, even though she's not my real grandma." Since Matt's hands were full with his ax and toolbox, Evan tugged on the sleeve of his coat to stop him. "I don't have a real grandma. Is it okay if I share yours?"

This kid worried way too much about other people's feelings and safety for someone his age. Not for the first time this evening, Matt wondered what events had shaped his young life. Corie had confessed that her ex had *hurt a lot of people*. Anger burned through Matt's blood at the idea that any of that violence might have touched Evan.

"If she said it's okay, then it's fine by me." He set his tools down on the sidewalk beside his truck and lifted Evan into the bed of the pickup so the boy could help him stow his ax and toolbox in the metal cargo box behind the cab.

Matt thought he heard the scrape of footsteps on the sidewalk. But with Evan's boots raising a muffled metallic sound in the bed of his truck, he couldn't isolate the noise. He glanced behind him to see if one of his brothers had followed them out. But the circle of illumination from the streetlamp in front of the old butcher shop was empty. A glance up the block revealed no pedestrians, either. Sometimes these tall brick and limestone buildings lining either side of the street in the City Market district captured sound and reflected it back off the hard surfaces, especially on a clear, cold night like this with little wind to dampen the echoing sounds.

Of course, there were shadows at the fringes of every streetlight and in the alleyways between buildings. And with vehicles parked along the curbs, someone hunched against the cold might not be readily visible. Matt pushed up the edges of his knit cap and trained his ears to try and pinpoint the company he couldn't see. But with Evan rattling Matt's toolbox as the boy insisted on lifting it himself, as well as his ongoing commentary about all things construction and cookie related, it was pretty impossible to hear anything else.

Probably his overtaxed sense of alertness, anyway. If he had heard the last steps of someone scurrying inside a warm building, there wasn't any real need to be concerned. This might once have been a decaying working-class neighborhood, but it had enjoyed a rebirth of tourism and an influx of professionals and young families who both lived and worked closer to the heart of the city. This wasn't a particularly dangerous neighborhood. Getting Evan out of this single-degree weather was probably a more pressing concern.

"Come on, bud." Once Evan had closed the lid and locked it, Matt helped him jump down and climb up into the back seat of his crew cab. Matt buckled him in, then ruffled the bangs that stuck out from beneath Evan's stocking cap. "Did you have fun tonight?"

"I like hammering, but can I use your ax next time?"

"Probably not the ax. It's heavy and it's dangerous. But we'll see about putting a paintbrush in your hands." There was still plenty of work to do on the condo above his late grandfather's butcher shop. Once they finished the remodel, they could sell it for a nice enough price that Grandma Martha could pay off the single-story ranch home she'd moved into that summer. The question was, would Corie be willing to trust Evan with him again? Once he mentioned axes and the fact he'd asked his brother to run a check on Evan's father, she might reconsider. "It'll be up to your mom."

"Cool." The smile Evan flashed was missing two full teeth, but it hit Matt with the same intensity that Corie's smile had.

Good grief. Maybe his family was seeing something in him that Matt hadn't fully admitted yet—he was falling for the family next door—not just the pretty mom whose smile and touch could set him off-kilter, but the little boy who seemed haunted by some of the same shadows Matt remembered from his own early childhood. The McGuires needed him. Or maybe they just needed someone—and he wanted to volunteer for the job.

Matt closed the rear door and stepped out into the street to walk around to the driver's side. But a subtle alarm tickled the back of his neck, and his fingers clutched the door handle without opening it.

He hadn't imagined footsteps. They were in a hurry now, moving away from his location. Punctuated by the slam of a vehicle door, he had to wonder if someone had been watching them. But a quick 360 didn't reveal any spies. Maybe his family's conversation about arson, and Corie's suspicion that someone had been inside her apartment while she'd been at school, were feeding his wary senses.

This wasn't a place where muggings and street crime happened much anymore—and anyone with a lick of sense would think twice about coming after him. Matt could walk the walk when it came to holding his own in a physical confrontation. His firefighter training and lifting weights weren't the only skills he'd honed over the years.

Still, the tickle at his nape was never wrong when it came to fighting fires and the safety of the men and women on his Firehouse 13 team. Something wasn't right. But what he saw as intrusive might just be a curious neighbor, wondering what was going on over the old Taylor Butcher Shop, or why the loner of the Taylor clan, who'd never even brought a date to a family gathering, now had a kid in tow.

With no obvious threat in sight, Matt climbed in and locked the doors. After he started the engine, he cranked the heat and found Evan's curious green eyes watching him in the rearview mirror. "I'm going to let the truck warm up for a few minutes before we go."

Evan pushed up against his seat belt. "Can I use your watch to count how many minutes again?"

"Sure." Matt took his utility watch off his wrist and reached over the seat to show Evan the timer feature. "Now you set it for four minutes. When the alarm goes off, I'll hear it and we'll go."

"Sweet." Evan leaned back in his seat to play with the watch that fascinated him so. "We have twenty-four minutes before I have to be in bed," he announced. "After the truck warms up, we'll have twenty minutes to drive home."

Good math skills. He'd run through his multiplication problems in a matter of minutes, and gotten every answer right, before Matt gave him the okay to go in and play with Gideon Jr. "I'll get you home in eighteen."

"We'll have to run up the stairs if we only have two minutes."

"I'll race you." As soon as the watch beeped, Matt pulled out of his parking space. There was little traffic at this hour, and he quickly passed two blocks before stopping at the red light. Matt found Evan watching him in the mirror again. "Will there be someone at the diner to walk your mom to her car when she gets off work?"

"We don't have a car."

His guileless pronouncement rekindled Matt's suspicions. "Then how does she get to school and work and then come home?"

"The way we always do. We walk. Or when it's cold like this, we'll walk to the bus stop. It's not that far."

But it was late at night, she was a woman and she was alone. "Does she ever let you walk that far by yourself?"

"Un-uh."

"Then she shouldn't, either." Movement in the street behind him shifted his attention from Evan. A nondescript van pulled out of a parking space and drove up behind

Matt's truck. The van wasn't speeding. But with its headlights blinding him in every mirror, he couldn't get a look at the driver, either. "Hey, bud. Why don't you set the timer for fifteen minutes. You time me to see if we get home before it beeps."

Matt was glad to see Evan concentrating on the watch, telling him the boy wasn't alarmed by the vehicle behind them. But he was an eight-year-old boy—he shouldn't have to be worried about strange coincidences and sixth senses warning him of danger. That was Matt's job. On impulse, he turned right before the light changed. When the van turned the corner behind him, Matt pulled his phone from his coat pocket and punched in a familiar number.

His brother Mark picked up on the second ring. "Did you miss me?"

"Do you mind stopping by my place on your way home?"

"No." Every bit of humor left Mark's tone. "What's up?"

Matt took another random corner, and the van followed. The warning at the nape of his neck couldn't be ignored. "I'm not sure. But I'd feel better if I had some backup."

Chapter Seven

"Hey, blondie."

"Come on, sugar—you know you miss us."

Great. Now the two men at the back of the bus were blowing kisses at her.

After that "courtesy" message her attorney's office in St. Louis had left on her phone tonight, she sure as hell didn't need this.

"As a courtesy, we are notifying all our clients that Owenson, Marsden & Heath may have had a breach in security subsequent to an electrical fire in our offices, in which several computers and most of our files were destroyed. While we are making every effort to ensure confidentiality while we sort through the remains of both paper and digital records, we are still in the process of accounting for all our data. Rest assured, backup systems were in place, and we are able to continue working on all of your current or upcoming needs. We are happy to report that Mr. Heath is at home now, recovering from injuries sustained in the fire. Our temporary offices will be housed at…"

She hadn't listened to the rest of the voice mail. Current and upcoming needs had nothing to do with her. Her only legal concerns were in the past. But a breach in security? Missing records? Her attorney injured in a fire?

To Corie, that meant only one thing. Kenny.

Was he responsible for that fire? Had he gotten access to her new identity and other personal records Mr. Heath had arranged for her? Had he burned the place down to cover up evidence that he had been in St. Louis? If he could track down her attorney, could he also find her here in Kansas City?

"Whatcha thinkin' about, sugar? Which one of us you'd like to get to know better first?"

Corie hugged her backpack tightly to her chest and stared at her hunkered reflection in the bus window and at the city lights that seemed to float past as she made her way home after closing the diner. Normally she found the ride home relaxing, and she enjoyed seeing parts of the city still decorated for Christmas or New Year's, especially when the lights reflected off the snow. But tonight, the world outside was a blur. Her pulse thundered in her ears, drowning out any fun or peaceful thoughts. And she was shivering, despite her coat and gloves and the bus's heater blowing across her feet.

She fought to keep Kenny's verbal abuse from playing in her head. *"What the hell's a study group? You're not going anywhere. You're good for only two things. If you weren't so damn frigid, it'd be three. You make me look good and you take care of my baby. Understand?"* The words might be different, but the tone was the same. Her reaction was, too.

This is not Kenny, Corie told herself, forcing herself to take deep, calming breaths. *There is no proof that he set that fire in St. Louis and found out about your new life. Your world isn't burning down around you.* The two men hassling her tonight weren't Kenny. Even at his worst, Kenny had been all about appearances—the right look, the right woman, associating with people of money and power. *Those two losers are just a couple of drunks who hap-*

pened to get on your bus. You have value, Corie. You are strong. Think of the positives. Evan is safe. You are safe.

She repeated the mantra again and again, just like her therapist had advised her. *Evan is safe. You are safe.*

Her feet throbbed with the length of her day at school and the long night at the diner. But tips had been good, she'd timed it just right so that she didn't have to wait outside in the cold for the bus to arrive and she'd had enough time on her last break to get on her laptop and track down the last source for the paper she was writing for her English language learners class. Except for that phone call and those two yahoos in the back, nights like this were all worth it, right?

She'd made the mistake of making eye contact with Jordan and Harve when they'd first stumbled onto the bus at the stop after hers. Apparently, a brief glance had been invitation enough for the two drunks to slide into the seats next to and across the aisle from her, introduce themselves and start hitting on her. At first, she'd thought they might try to rob her when Jordan had put his hands on the backpack in her lap and leaned into her. But then Harve had grabbed his crotch and run his tongue around his chapped lips, and she realized they weren't after money or her computer.

"Mr. Lee?" She'd wasted no time calling out to the fatherly Black man driving the bus. He'd ordered the two booze-scented men—one with scraggly red peach fuzz on his jaw that blended into the tattoos on his neck, and the other sporting a chest-length beard that had a broken pretzel stuck in it—to move, or he'd call the police and drop them off at the next stop.

With much vocal protest and a stumble onto a seat with a startled young man whose earbuds had tuned them out up to that intrusion, they'd made their way to the back of the bus, where they continued to be a nuisance to anyone with a pair of boobs between the ages of eighteen and fifty. And since Corie was currently the only passenger left who fit that description tonight, she was bearing the brunt of their lewd noises and whispered innuendoes.

"Just one drink, sugar?" That would be Harve, with the snack stuck in his facial hair. "We could have a nightcap at your place."

Once upon a time, when she was young and naive and believed every man could be a hero, she would have turned to Kenny to make them stop. And no doubt, with his resources and criminal connections, he would have. But that was before she realized he'd be protecting his property— not her feelings of fear or discomfort. Kenny would have made a threat or punched one of those rummies or tracked them down and torched their car to make the point that nobody embarrassed him by putting a move on the woman— or anything else—he considered his.

Tonight, she had to deal with this kind of crap on her own.

Or find an ally she could actually trust to have her best interests at heart.

Corie met the driver's gaze in his rearview mirror and silently pleaded for his help. "Knock it off!" he ordered, quieting the pair temporarily. "Sorry about that, Ms. Corie."

"Corie? Your name's Corie?"

"Corie what, sugar?"

The driver grumbled a curse and shook his head, realizing too late that he'd just given those two losers more information about her. Although she offered him a reassuring smile, she hoped Mr. Lee didn't repeat his threat about putting them off at the next stop because the next stop was hers. At least, here on the bus, she had the relative safety of the other passengers and driver to protect her—or at least bear witness to the harassment if anything should happen to her. Corie still had a cold walk back to her apartment once she stepped off this bus. She didn't relish being alone at night for the block and a half it would take her to get safely inside the locked foyer of her building if those men decided to follow her.

As the bus turned onto Wyandotte and drove up the hill toward her stop, Corie peeled off her gloves and stuffed them into her coat pockets. Potential frostbite would take a back seat to security tonight. Then she dug into her bag and pulled out her cell phone and pepper spray, squeezing one in each hand. She might not be able to outmuscle or outrun Jordan and Harve if they should decide to follow her and prolong this torture, but she could outthink them. She could plan ahead and give herself options for escape. Then she shrugged her backpack onto her shoulders and prepared to book it as fast as she could to her building. If there was one thing she'd learned from her years with Kenny, it was to be prepared for any-and everything.

And to do whatever was necessary to keep herself and Evan safe.

Moving quickly, she slid out of her seat and hurried down the aisle to sit in the very first seat beside the stairs. She intended to be down the steps and out the door just as soon as it opened.

"Whoa. Slow down, sugar. We'll walk you home." Jordan lurched to his feet, with Harve shuffling after him.

"Sit down," Carl Lee ordered when he saw them coming down the aisle behind her. "This isn't your stop." He glanced across the aisle and whispered to Corie, "You hustle on out of here the moment I stop. I'll try to keep them inside."

Harve snickered and plopped down in the spot behind

Corie, dangling his arm over the top of her seat. "Maybe we need some fresh air, old man." She jerked away when his fingers brushed against her ponytail. "Besides, we wouldn't want our little woman walking home by herself so late now, would we?"

Corie practically threw herself against the partition in front of her seat and whirled around to tell the creep to back off. "I am *not* your little woman, and I *don't* need you to walk me home."

Mistake! She'd engaged them. Now they saw her response as a personal invitation to increase their taunts. "Ooh, she's feistier than I thought she was going to be." Jordan grinned from ear to ear.

"I like 'em feisty." Harve rose to his feet, and his long beard fell over the top of her seat. How she'd dearly love to yank it as hard as she could. Maybe he'd bite his tongue when his chin hit the seat, and that would shut him up.

Both men laughed. Mr. Lee muttered something under his breath and pulled his radio from the dash. Was he going to report these two? Call the police?

She turned her back to the men as the brakes hissed and the bus began to slow. She tapped 9-1-1 into her own phone and prepared to push the call button if she had to.

Then she peered through the glass and saw the tall man standing beneath the shell of the bus stop. Silhouetted against the fluorescent lights, his height and bulk were emphasized by the insulated winter coat he wore. Like a beacon in the midst of a stormy sea, Matt Taylor's broad shoulders and immovable presence showed her the way to the safe harbor she needed.

Relief, gratitude beyond measure and maybe even anticipation surged through her veins and she shot to her feet. Bless his big, bad self for showing up and being the friend she needed right now.

"Matt!" Corie was down the stairs and out the door the moment it opened.

Without any hesitation or warning, she launched herself at him. She shoved her phone and pepper spray into her pockets and grabbed the collar of his coat with both fists, pulling him toward her as she stretched up on tiptoe and pushed her lips against his. His startled breath didn't surprise her—she hadn't given him much of a heads-up. But she didn't expect his firm mouth to slide over hers in answer to her desperate ploy. She didn't expect the rasp of his late-night beard stubble to tease her skin with its own subtle caress. She didn't expect the frisson of heat that tingled across her lips and shocked much-needed warmth into her blood when his mouth settled over hers in a brief, potent kiss.

The kiss was longer than she intended, shorter than she wanted, and left the ground shaking beneath her feet as she dropped to her heels. Matt's lips chased after hers as gravity broke the contact between them. And Corie was far too tempted to palm the back of the black stocking cap he wore and guide his mouth right back to where she wanted it.

But the bus driver's warning to the men behind her reminded her that throwing herself at Matt was a survival tactic, not a mutual routine she had any right to pursue. She swallowed her shock and forced herself to continue the charade, although she could only manage a breathless whisper. "Hi, sweetheart."

"Sweetheart?" He rubbed his hands up and down her arms and his face hovered above hers, frowning in confusion until he heard Harve and Jordan's harassment.

"Hey, sugar, wait for us." The bearded man scrambled to the stairs behind her. "Don't you close these doors, old man."

"You said we'd have smooth sailin' with her, Harve. If I have to mess with that guy, then I want extra—"

"Shut up, Jordy."

Corie didn't need to explain her overly friendly greeting.

Matt's expression was cold, fierce and eerily silent as he lifted his gaze and looked over the top of her head to meet Jordan and Harve. He pried Corie's hands from the front of his coat and moved around her. Straightening to his towering height, he didn't have to say a word to stop the two men in their tracks.

Jordan toppled onto the curb in his haste to back away from the imposing welcome. Harve grabbed the sleeve of Jordan's coat and tugged him to his feet and up the stairs. "Get on back here, Jordy. This isn't our stop, after all." His dark eyes rounded like shiny black beetles as he nodded to Corie. "We'll be seeing you, Ms. Corie."

Jordan puckered his lips. "Bye-bye, sugar."

Just as Corie flinched back half a step at that final unwanted gesture, Matt strode forward. He boarded the bus, each step a purposeful stride. He stopped beside the driver and watched Harve and Jordan beat a hasty retreat down the aisle, all the way to their seats at the back. Then Matt lifted his coat to pull out his billfold and hand a business card to Mr. Lee. "You see those two hassling Corie again, you call me."

"Kansas City's Bravest." Carl took the card and nodded his ready agreement. "Yes, sir. You all be safe now."

"Good night, Mr. Lee," Corie called up to him as Matt rejoined her. "Thank you."

"Good night, Ms. Corie. Mr. Taylor." The Black man nodded and closed the door. With the hum of the motor grinding into gear, the bus pulled away.

A chill from the damp, wintry air seeped through the

wool of her coat and Corie hugged her arms around her waist. But the cold temperature wasn't the only thing that made her shiver. Harve and Jordan pressed their faces to the back windows, their eyes only leaving her when the two high-fived each other over the top of the seat.

She startled at Matt's touch and the sudden infusion of heat as he draped his arm around her shoulders and tucked her to his side. Playing his part of half a couple even better than she was playing hers, he was also watching the two men until the lights from the bus stop and streetlamp could no longer pierce the windows and her tormenters were swallowed up into the shadows.

Corie stood there, leaning into Matt's warmth long enough for her to realize that she hadn't put her gloves back on. Though stiff with cold, her fingers were fisted into the padded nylon of his black insulated jacket, clinging to him as though she had every right to attach herself to him for comfort or use him as a human heating pad. Shaking off those survival instincts that seemed to have her continually reaching for him, Corie released her grip and stepped away. She dug her gloves out of her pockets and slipped them back on. "I'm sorry about that kiss. I just…" She glanced down the street where the bus had merged into late-night traffic, then tilted her face to Matt's. "I needed them to stop. I suspected if they thought I was *with* you… It worked. Thank you."

He didn't seem to hear her apology. Or care that she'd taken advantage of his willingness to help her.

He didn't have anyone with him, either.

Where was Evan? Kenny had found them!

Corie tamped down the flare of panic that grabbed hold whenever she didn't know Evan's exact location. *Too soon to worry. Too soon.*

"Do you know those two?" Matt asked.

She shook her head, looking around. No, she hadn't seen them before tonight. Oh, damn. The panic was winning. They were all alone at this bus stop. There was no child here with them. Her apartment was a block and a half away. Was Evan at home all by himself again? She didn't see Matt's truck. There was a small group of patrons outside the bar down the street, huddling up to smoke their cigarettes—but no one anywhere close to Evan's age. Where was her son? She'd trusted Matt with one job. Okay, maybe two now that Jordan and Harve had inserted themselves into her life tonight—but she'd trusted Matt with the one thing more important than anything else in the world—her son.

"They seemed to know you," Matt went on matter-of-factly. "Why would they think you'd be an easy mark for them? 'Smooth sailing'?"

Corie even made the ridiculous move of peeking behind Matt's broad back, looking for her freckle-faced angel. "Where's Evan?"

Matt turned so they were facing each other again. His deep, patiently modulated voice barely changed its timbre, even though he hunched his shoulders a fraction to bring his gaze closer to hers and demand she focus on what he was saying. "Sound asleep on my sofa. My brother and his fiancée are with him. Ev is fine. Tell me about those two men."

Matt's eyes captured her attention. Unlike Harve's cold, creepy beetle eyes, their warm brown intensity moved through her like the potent drink they resembled. His coffee-colored eyes calmed her panic and chased away the chill of remembered fears. Evan was safe. Matt was a stand-up, trustworthy man who wouldn't do anything to endanger her son. *He's not Kenny.*

And as rational thought returned, the point Matt was

making registered. Was it her imagination, or had Harve sounded remarkably articulate for a drunk who'd been slurring every word a few minutes earlier? "He's asleep at your place? Evan's okay?"

"Yes. Are you?" Matt slowly straightened, his gaze never wavering from hers. His gloved hands fisted down at his sides, relaxed, then fisted again, as though he wanted to reach for her, but was holding himself back from making contact.

She wouldn't have minded. After the past six years of avoiding men—at first because she'd assumed they were all like Kenny and his thuggish cohorts, and later because work, school and being a hypervigilant single mom didn't allow time for relationships—she wouldn't have minded if Matt Taylor reached for her, at all.

Corie's lips relaxed into a wry smile and she nodded. "I'm fine. Thanks to you." Whether Matt was being exceedingly patient or endearingly shy, Corie wanted that connection he was too polite to initiate. She'd once been a confident young woman who'd gone after what her mother had told her she wanted—what she naively thought she'd wanted, too—until a kidnapping and death threats and Kenny's violent, obsessive world had scared that brave young woman into submission. It was nice to feel a little of her confidence returning with this man. She slipped her arm through Matt's and stepped toward the curb. "Could we head home now?"

"As long as you talk to me." He rested a leather-gloved hand over hers where she clung to his forearm, revealing that he liked sharing that friendly link with her, too, and didn't want her pulling away. The man was warm, and he made her feel safe. And his kiss had awakened something dormant and too-long ignored inside her. She wasn't going anywhere.

Falling into step beside him, Corie shared the bare bones of her bus ride home. "They got on at the stop just after the diner. You know—too much to drink and not enough action at whatever bar they'd come out of. I tried to keep my head down, but they spotted me, decided I was their chosen target. Mr. Lee told them to move—and they did. But that didn't shut them up. Then they became a nuisance to everyone on the bus. Only now I wonder if it was all an act. Harve seemed to sober up pretty quickly once you showed up."

"I have that effect on people."

Whether he meant to be funny or not, Corie smiled and pressed her cheek against his shoulder. The material of his jacket was cold against her skin, but she savored the supple hardness and promised warmth of the muscle she felt underneath. They crossed the street and walked a whole block like that, with Corie hugging herself around Matt's arm and his hand covering hers. Matt's bulk blocked the worst of the wind, and his ever-watchful eyes that scanned their surroundings and occasionally settled on her made her feel protected. Simply walking down the street arm in arm with Matt felt normal. Intimate. And far more romantic than any grand gesture Kenny had ever used to try to charm her. "It's just weird. Weird things are happening around me lately," she admitted. "First the fires, and I think someone's been in my apartment. That stupid phone call. Now those two idiots giving me grief."

"What phone call?"

Corie's breath clouded on a puff of frustration. Had she actually said that out loud? She tried to explain in a way that didn't make her sound like the completely paranoid woman she was. "A voice mail from my attorney's assistant in St. Louis. There was a fire in their office."

"Was anyone hurt?"

"My attorney sustained minor injuries, but he's doing fine now. I guess they lost several documents in the fire."

"Were any of the destroyed documents yours?"

She shrugged. She had immediately imagined the worst, but she truly didn't know. "It was just an FYI call."

Matt's fingers tightened briefly on hers before he slid his hands into the pockets of his coat. She might have imagined him hugging his elbows to his torso, keeping their arms linked together, encouraging her to remain at his side. But as he glanced over her head to track the line of cars and trucks coming through the intersection behind them as the lights changed, she sensed something about his posture had changed, grown wary. He wanted his hands free to…to what? "You didn't see a white van following the bus, did you?"

"No. It's hard to see much besides the lights through the windows at night." She studied the vehicles that rolled past them. Not a van of any kind in sight. The thrill she'd just admitted to herself at having Matt meet her at the bus stop to walk her home vanished. Had he seen something she had missed? "Why?"

"I saw an unfamiliar vehicle in the neighborhood earlier. It followed us from Grandma's place."

"Followed?" Corie stopped, yanking her arm from his. Futile thrills and chivalry and logical explanations be damned. There *was* something wrong. "Why didn't you say something?"

Matt turned. He cupped her elbows and ran his hands up and down her arms. "My brothers who are cops are looking into it. The van didn't come to our building or parking garage. I lost it by taking the scenic route home."

She didn't want reassurances. She wanted facts. She knew better than to dismiss the suspicion in his words and posture. "The van was following you? You're certain? Did you see the driver? Is Evan okay? Was he scared?" The last time she'd felt like the world was falling apart around her, it had been. She didn't intend to dismiss the things that struck her as odd and be caught off guard and forced into doing something she regretted again. "I need to see Evan. Right now."

This time, Matt draped his arm around her shoulders and tucked her to his side. His stride seemed to be longer now, forcing her to hurry her pace. "As far as I could tell, he spent the whole time playing with my watch on the drive home. I doubt he noticed the van."

Corie shook her head, feeling equally doubtful. "He notices everything."

"He does. I crashed through a wall tonight, made a lot of noise. He came running to make sure I was okay." She paused and glanced up at him. "I was," he answered her unspoken question, pulling her back into a quick step beside him. "Evan is, too. My brother Mark is with him. My brothers Pike and Alex are working on tracking down the van, although I only got a partial plate. Chances are the guy was scoping out my truck to see if he could steal it. I was more worried about you being out here by yourself."

"I'm fine. I'm going to be fine," she amended. "I've handled worse than a couple of drunks on the bus. Evan is my only concern."

Matt's arm tightened around her, partially lifting her to keep pace with his stride as they climbed the granite steps to their building. He swiped his key card and led her inside. Even being in the lobby, cut off from the cold, windy night, she felt chilled. Seven years ago, when the trouble began with Kenny—the worst year of her life—the terror had all started with someone following her and her son.

Matt punched the elevator call button. "You won't do him any good if something happens to you."

Corie hurried inside and pressed the button for the seventh floor. "I'm a grown-up. I can take care of myself. He just turned eight. He's trusting and curious and all I have that's worth anything." She was clearly rattled by the incident or she wouldn't still be clinging to Matt. Once she realized her fingers were clutched in the side of his coat, she tried to release him. But her grip seemed to be locked in place, and, damn it, her eyes were stinging with tears.

"Hey." As the elevator doors closed, Matt framed her jaw between his big hands, tilting her face up to his. "Next time you work late, let me know. I will pick you up. And if I'm on shift, I'll send one of my brothers or my dad."

She shook her head between his hands. "We've been riding the bus for months. We're not your responsibility. I can't ask you to—"

"You're not coming home on your own after dark again." He emphasized his resolute pronouncement by tightening his fingers against her hair and the sides of her neck, gently preventing another shake of her head. A soft huff that could be a wry laugh stirred the bangs on her forehead. "It's bad for my blood pressure."

"*Your* blood pressure?" She reached up to wind her fingers around his wrists. "*I'm* the one who's freaking out."

He stroked his thumb across her cheek. His leather glove was cool against her skin, but his firm touch and deep voice swept aside the world long enough for her to take a deep breath. "Let me do this small thing. Please."

She needed to think, not react. She needed to use her brain, not her emotions. And most importantly, she needed to get her mental stuff together so she wouldn't frighten Evan. Matt's patience and no-nonsense caring gave her enough of a break from her maternal panic to dial it back a notch. She believed him when he said Evan was safe. For that, she was grateful. But she didn't intend to become a burden to him. Besides, if these odd events did have anything to do with Kenny Norwell, anyone who got involved with her would be in danger. "We're already an imposition. It shouldn't be your problem."

He didn't try to lie and say she and the recent events surrounding her and Evan weren't an upheaval in his life. He didn't tell her not to worry. He didn't wheel and deal and promise to take care of her problems for her in exchange for her silence or a roll in the hay or custody of her son the way Kenny would have.

Instead, Matt planted himself in front of her like the unbending oak he was and held out his hand. "Give me your phone." He tugged his gloves off with his teeth and held them there while he typed his number into her phone and handed it back to her. "This is faster than pulling my card out of your bag." The boyish move and garbled sentence were as endearing as that unexpected response to her kiss had been intoxicating. She plucked his gloves from between his lips and held them for him while he pulled out his cell and typed in her number. Now that he could talk clearly, he added, "If you prefer the bus, one of us will ride with you. Offering you a lift doesn't mean you owe me anything. Just promise you'll call."

When he was done, she tucked each glove into the appropriate pocket of his jacket, just as she did with Evan almost every day when they got home from school. But instead of sending him on to his room to play, as she would a child, Corie wound her arms around Matt's waist and hugged him tightly, taking note of every hard plane and solid muscle pressed against her. Even though she was of average height, she scarcely reached his shoulders. Still, it felt like a perfect fit when his arms folded around her and he lowered his head to rest his chin against the crown of her hair. Corie nestled in, oddly sad that the elevator was slowing to a stop. "You're a better friend than I deserve, Matt. But you may not want to get involved with me."

"Maybe I do. Maybe I already am." The elevator doors opened, and he released her to walk side by side down the hallway together. "Have a little faith in me, okay?"

Corie reached for his hand and laced their fingers together. "Trusting you is the easy part."

Chapter Eight

Corie pushed open the door the moment Matt unlocked it, anxious to see Evan after hearing Matt's suspicion about the white van.

As he ushered her inside the shadowed living room, they were greeted by a slightly shorter, equally broad version of Matt. Although his eyes were blue to Matt's warm brown color, there was no mistaking that this was his brother. Mark Taylor pressed a finger against his lips, urging them to whisper as he nodded toward the couch where Evan was fast asleep with his arm thrown around his dragon and Matt's watch strapped to his wrist. A statuesque redhead in a paint-stained sweatshirt entered from the kitchen, drying her hands on a towel. She smiled a greeting to Corie and Matt without saying a word.

"My brother Mark," Matt whispered behind her. "His fiancée, Amy Hall. This is Corie, Evan's mom."

Although her eyes barely left her sleeping child, and the relief flooding through her made it difficult to speak, Corie managed to thank the couple before hurrying across the room. She peeled off her gloves and knelt beside the couch to peer into Evan's sweetly innocent face as he snored softly atop a throw pillow. She brushed a lock of shaggy brown hair off his freckled cheek and cupped the back of his head. He was perfectly fine—exhausted from what had no doubt been an exciting evening for him, but fine. Kenny hadn't found them. Kenny hadn't taken her son from her again. Exhaling a sigh of relief that echoed through the room, she pushed to her feet, adjusted the afghan covering him and kissed his cheek.

"Better?" Matt asked. He must have followed right behind her.

She looked up at him and nodded. "You were right. He's okay. It's just…a mother has to know." She turned Matt's watch on Evan's slender wrist to unbuckle it. "You'd better take this now or you may never see it again."

Matt stopped her fingers and slipped it back down Evan's slender wrist. "Let him keep it for tonight. I think it makes him feel safe, like he can cope with anything that stresses him."

She wasn't sure it was the watch so much as whom the watch represented. There were a lot of things about this man that made a person feel safe. Corie squeezed her hand around Matt's forearm, thanking him for the consideration. "I'll make sure we return it in the morning."

Corie felt a tug from the opposite side as Amy linked arms with her and pulled her toward the bright lights of the kitchen. "Come with me. Let's go where we don't have to whisper. I made some hot chocolate to warm us all up. And I want to show you the drawing Evan made." Her voice grew louder and more exuberant as they left Evan snoozing in the living room. "I'm going to turn it into one of my garden aliens, a miniature one he can keep in his room. If that's okay. He said he had a spot for it."

Amy handed Corie the colored pencil drawing sitting on the table and hurried to the stove to fill a couple of mugs with hot chocolate. "Garden aliens?"

"Unbutton your coat and sit for a few minutes." Clearly, Amy felt at home here in Matt's apartment, as she gestured to a chair at the rustic wood farm table. With Matt's penchant for working with his hands, she wondered if he had restored, or even built it himself. She didn't get time to ask as Amy pointed out the whorls of purple, red and yellow on Evan's drawing. "I see dragon overtones, which will be fun to incorporate. Evan is certainly bold with his color choices. I find that inspiring."

Should she be worried about the ever-expanding army of dragons guarding Evan's room?

Mark strolled into the kitchen, picking up a half-empty mug from the table and carrying it to his fiancée for seconds as she tore open pouches of instant cocoa and poured hot water from the kettle into each mug. "Amy's an artist. She works mostly in metals. She's set up shop in my garage."

"Only because mine burned down this past summer." She handed Corie and Matt each a steaming mug of cocoa before sitting in the chair next to Corie's. She thrust out her left hand. "Here's an example of my handiwork. My engagement ring."

Corie was left with little choice but to examine the twisted filigree work around the diamond solitaire. It was certainly one of a kind…as she suspected Amy was, too. "What a unique, beautiful ring."

Mark squeezed his hands around Amy's shoulders, and she leaned back into him, holding her hand up to admire the jewelry. "Mark gave me the diamond on a plain white-gold band when he proposed, with his blessing to turn it into whatever I wanted. I melted it down and created the two hearts knotted together around the diamond. The wedding bands I'm making will be plainer because of Mark's work."

Corie cradled the steaming mug in her hands and

shrugged. "Wow. You're making your own wedding jewelry, and I don't even have a hobby."

Matt stood at the counter next to the stove, stirring his hot chocolate. "Because you're working or studying all the time. Or doing stuff with Evan. Not everybody could handle all that on their plate as well as you do."

She smiled at him across the room, silently thanking him for the shout-out of praise. And, if she wasn't mistaken, that slight tilt at the corner of his firm mouth meant he was smiling back.

Finally feeling herself warming up, Corie shed her coat while Matt and Mark joined them at the table. She'd had every intention of walking Evan across the hall and getting out of Matt's hair so that they wouldn't be any more of an imposition on their evening. But the Taylor brothers and Amy were making her feel like a welcome guest. No, they were making her feel like a friend. Corie couldn't recall the last time she'd sat down with people her own age and talked about things not related to teaching, classes, work or legal matters. They chatted for another thirty minutes or so while they sipped their cocoa. She got the gist of the wedding Mark and Amy were planning for the summer on the grounds of her grandmother's farm. She heard a couple of stories about the Lucky 13 crew at the firehouse where the brothers both worked. Matt didn't add much more than a shrug to Mark's assertion that Matt had pulled him not once, but twice, from a fire. Even though Mark and Amy dominated the conversation, there was no mistaking the way they included both her and Matt with teasing gibes, complimentary observations about Evan and interesting questions that helped them get to know Corie while she got to know them.

She imagined the conversation would have gone on a good deal longer until the moment she failed to mask a yawn. She quickly pressed her hand over her mouth. "Sorry about that. It's not the company, I promise."

Mark pushed his chair away from the table as Amy squeezed Corie's hand and offered her a rueful smile. "My bad. I ramble whenever I start talking about marrying this guy. Matt's learned to put up with me." She glanced across the table and winked at the man beside Corie. "I think he might even like me."

"He does," Matt replied. "I said I'd be in the wedding, didn't I?"

Amy rose from the table and circled around to hug Matt from behind. "You did."

"Come on, Red." Mark tugged on Amy's hand. "Let's let these guys get some sleep. Corie put in a long day, and I've got a long one tomorrow." Matt pulled out Corie's chair in a sweetly old-fashioned gesture, and they all went into the living room, automatically dropping their voices as they got closer to Evan. After helping Amy into her coat, Mark shook hands with Matt and the two men bumped shoulders in a manly hug. "See you at work, bro."

"Thanks for helping out tonight."

"Like you haven't done the same for me."

Amy hugged Matt and then reached for Corie, her hug turning into a secretive whisper. "Matt's a good guy. The best there is. A bit of an odd duck—"

"Red?" Mark chided, pulling his fiancée away from Corie. "What did we say about matchmaking?"

Amy's conspiratorial whisper included Mark now. "That he's slow as molasses and might need a little nudge?"

"And on that note, we'll be going." Mark opened the door and ushered his fiancée into the hallway ahead of him. "Nice to meet you, Corie." But apparently, he wasn't immune to the matchmaking bug, either. He looked beyond her to Matt and winked. "Good night, Molasses."

Matt palmed his brother's face and shoved him out the door. Mark laughed, reached for Amy's hand, and the engaged couple headed for the elevator as Matt closed the door behind them. When he faced her, she thought she detected the faintest tinge of a blush peeking through his shadow of beard stubble. "Sorry about that. Those two can be…aggressively friendly."

Corie turned to hide the blush she was certain was staining her own cheeks and hurried back to the kitchen, where she carried the mugs to the sink and rinsed them out. "It's obvious they love you very much. It must be nice to have family you can depend on, even on short notice like this."

Moving with surprising stealth for a man his size, Matt appeared at the counter beside her and opened the dishwasher to place the mugs she handed him inside. "You don't have family? I suspected not here in Kansas City because you and Ev are always alone. You never have any company. But no family anywhere? You mentioned St. Louis earlier."

"That's where I grew up. Only child. I have a mother and a stepdad. He was pretty decent. But Mom and I severed ties. I miss the idea of having a mom and a grandmother for Evan, but I don't miss her." She could read the unspoken *why?* in his eyes. Corie shrugged and wet the dishcloth to wipe down the stove and countertop. It wasn't hard to talk about anymore. She'd made her peace with her choices when she'd changed her name and left St. Louis. "I told you my ex hurt a lot of people. But he also had a lot of money. Most of it made illegally, I discovered, doing jobs for other criminals. But Mom was willing to overlook that little detail as long as he showered her with gifts and kept me in a beautiful house that was way too big for the three of us."

"*Kept* you?"

Corie met a wall of Matt Taylor demanding answers and returned to the sink without meeting his probing gaze. He seemed to intuit that the irony of her word choices was more literal that most people might suspect. "He kidnapped Evan when I separated from him. The police didn't call it kidnapping since he was still a custodial parent. But if I wanted to be with my son, I had to be with Kenny."

"You could have divorced him, sued for full custody."

Corie shook her head. She'd been a young, vulnerable mess, isolated from any support system and afraid for her life. "The woman I was back then couldn't have."

"But you got stronger. Norwell's no longer in your life. You do have full custody, right?"

Corie nodded. "I legally changed our names and moved away from that nightmare. Started life over on my terms."

"Is that why the call from your attorney's office upset you? Do you think your mother or your ex was trying to locate who and where you are now?"

"My attorney does have that information. But Heath's office isn't even sure if anything is missing. They were calling all of his clients to tell us about the break-in, just to cover themselves legally, I suppose." She'd been so careful for so long, as had her attorney. As far as the world knew, Katie Norwell and her son, Danny, had disappeared from the face of the earth. "Kenny stayed in Jefferson City after he was released from prison. And my mother wouldn't know the first thing about break-ins and fires."

Matt started the dishwasher, perhaps giving her a few moments to tamp down her emotions. "It takes an unusually strong character to start over without any family or friends to help you."

His compliment warmed her. "When Kenny got arrested for arson and eventually sent to prison, I thought my mother would finally see him for the monster he was, we'd mend old wounds and become a family again." By the time she'd hung up the dishcloth and dried her hands, she'd found the composure to tilt her eyes to Matt's. "My mother encouraged me to marry Kenny in the first place— and she criticized me for divorcing him and taking his son from him, said that was a mistake I couldn't come back from. After all, arson is a victimless crime, she said."

If Matt was a more effusive man, he would have scoffed right then. "Tell that to the people who've lost everything they own. Who've lost the security of a roof over their heads—or worse, a pet or family member. Whether anyone dies or not, there are victims."

A fist of some long-buried grief over all she'd lost squeezed around her heart. Some parts of her past *were* hard to talk about, after all. Leaving the kitchen, Corie went to her sleeping son, sprawled on the couch, looking innocent and secure in a way she could never be. She reached down to feather her fingers through his hair and smooth the wispy spikes off his forehead. "You'd think a parent would do anything to protect their child. I would. I have. My mother's last words to me were, 'Go to him and beg his forgiveness.'" Corie shivered as though the air-conditioning had kicked on and pulled the front of her cardigan tightly around her polyester uniform. "He hurt people for a living. He put me in the hospital and kidnapped Evan so I'd go back to him. It took Kenny going to prison for us to get away from him—and she wanted me to beg his forgiveness?"

Without any warning, Matt pulled her into his arms and hugged her. Even with her crossed arms wedged between them, she felt his heat and unyielding strength. For several endless moments, she collapsed a little into the shielding bliss of his embrace. Just as she'd caressed Evan's hair a minute earlier, Matt tunneled his fingers into the hair beneath her ponytail, lifting its weight from her scalp and massaging the tension there. She didn't need any words— she could feel his empathy. But he offered her words, anyway. "Not everyone makes a good parent. My birth parents were drunk or high a lot. Mark and I barely had any supervision. I was literally playing with fire the night our house burned down, and they died. They were passed out in the living room. I managed to get Mark out. But I couldn't get them to wake up. If they'd been better parents…"

"Oh, Matt." She pulled her arms free to wind them around his waist and hugged him tight. "How old were you?"

"It doesn't matter."

"How old?" she insisted, tugging on a fistful of the flannel shirt he wore. "You said you were younger than Evan when you…acted out."

"Four."

"Only four?" She found the strong beat of his heart beneath her ear and nestled her cheek there. Her own heart was crying for the child he'd once been. "How frightened you must have been."

"I'm not trying to compare my pain to yours—or make any less of it. I just want you to know that I understand what it means to not have someone be there when you need them."

Corie rubbed her nose into the soft nap of Matt's flannel shirt, inhaling his honest, hardworking masculine scent. Kenny had never simply held her. He'd wanted her on his arm to show her off to his friends and employers, or in his bed for what she'd naively thought was unsatisfying sex simply because she was inexperienced. She'd eventually learned that the sex had never been about her at all, certainly not after she'd given him the baby boy he'd wanted. Holding Matt, being held by him, was a new experience, an incredibly addictive one that she didn't seem to have any willpower to move away from. Standing in Matt's arms, his body flush and warm and strong against hers, was like a soothing tonic and a sensual awakening all rolled into one.

"I only wanted them to notice me," Matt went on, his fingers hypnotically stroking the back of her neck above her collar. "Mark was the baby. He was cute. I was the… extra. Even at four, I knew we weren't a normal, *Leave It to Beaver* family." Her arms tightened as she imagined him as a lonely, neglected little boy. "I wanted them to feel something—fear, panic, maybe a little worry about Mark and me. *I* wanted to feel something."

"Like you were safe. Like someone cared enough to stop you from doing something dangerous. You probably blamed yourself for their deaths. They were the adults. They should have taken care of you."

Some of her hair caught in the stubble of his beard as he nodded. "I thank God every day that the Taylors adopted Mark and me. Alex and Pike, too. We were all in the same foster home. Not everyone is lucky enough to have a family like ours."

Matt's lips grazed her hair and Corie wanted to sink into him—hold him like this through the entire night. There was a joke in there somewhere about them both being the offspring of selfish, clueless parents. But a betrayal like that might still be too painful for him to joke about. Wanting to ease his pain—or find solace for her own—wasn't what their relationship was about.

Or was it? Had fate led her to the apartment across the hall from Matt because he was the rare man who understood what she'd been through? Was she drawn to him because she felt the pull of pain and secrets that resembled her own? Was his reserved, quiet intensity meant to resurrect the confident, outgoing woman she'd once been?

Despite these few minutes of happiness and normalcy and an unexpected desire to take this embrace to the next level, another yawn reminded her of the reality of her life. A wry chuckle shook through her, and she loosened her grip on the back of Matt's shirt. Feelings for Matt were just a foolish wish at this late hour. "Again, it's not the company." She was a little disappointed at how easily Matt let her pull away. But the man was nothing if not imminently practical. She should be glad that at least one of them could show a little sense. "It's late. I'd better get Evan into his own bed or I'll never get him up for school in the morning."

"I'll carry him."

Corie retrieved her coat and gathered up Evan's belongings while Matt picked up the sleeping boy and carried him to his bed across the hall. Something primal and utterly female stirred in Corie's womb at the strong paternal image of Matt gently placing her son in his bed. He took equal care setting Evan's protective dragon on the headboard shelf and hanging Evan's coat on the back of his chair while she tucked him in. After turning on the nightlight, she followed Matt to the front door.

The hot firefighter next door would make a wonderful father. She had a feeling Matt would be good at a lot of things, because he was patient and observant and supportive and caring. Protecting others seemed to be hardwired into his DNA, and that chest, those arms, that butt in a pair of jeans and…oh, hell. She might come with some extra responsibility and emotional baggage, but she was a healthy, needy, grown woman whose hormones had gotten a hold of her.

Matt turned in the hallway. "I'll wait until you lock the dead—"

"Thank you for everything tonight." Corie might just be making the biggest mistake of her new life when she braced one hand against his chest, slid the other behind his neck and stretched up on tiptoe to capture his mouth in a kiss. She darted her tongue out to taste the firm line of his bottom lip, then felt it soften when she tugged it between her lips.

And then she realized he wasn't touching her. Her fingers were clutching the straight line of short, ticklish hair at the back of his head and his hands were fisted at his sides. Although she'd elicited a brief response when she'd suckled his lower lip, he wasn't kissing her. And she didn't think that husky huff from his chest was a groan of ecstasy.

Corie quickly released him and retreated half a step as the heat of embarrassment crept up her neck. "I'm sorry."

His fingers pulsed against his palms. "I said you didn't have to do anything you're not comfortable with. Just because my brother and Amy can't keep their hands to themselves doesn't mean I expect you to—"

"No, you said I needed to *tell* you when I wasn't comfortable with something." Her embarrassment gave way to a burst of anger, then settled into confusion. "It's a thank-you kiss, Matt. I didn't suck up my courage and *pretend* to kiss you. I wanted to do that." Nope. Here came the embarrassment again. "Unless you aren't okay with that? I mean, I know I'm out of practice, but when I kissed you at the bus stop, you sort of kissed me back. And the way you held me in your apartment, I thought…" She raked all ten fingers through hair, pulling out most of her ponytail. "Was I taking advantage—?"

"No. You can kiss me or touch me any time, any way you like." He almost sounded angry as he dipped his head toward hers and ground the words through his teeth. He snapped up straight, as though the vehemence of his response surprised him. He glanced away for a moment, gathering his thoughts before he looked back to her. "That didn't come out right." His hand batted the air and she could see him warring with whatever words he was having trouble expressing. He batted the air again, and then he feathered his fingers into the hair she'd pulled loose and the internal debate seemed to resolve itself when she didn't pull away from his touch. He smoothed the hair behind her ear and settled his hand against the side of her neck, easing her own uncertainty. "I would like to kiss you again sometime." His tone had quieted to that sexy, deliberate timbre that told her he was saying exactly what he was thinking. "For real. Not for show. Not for any reason other than… I want to kiss you."

Well, as declarations of desire went, that was hot. And it was really good for her ego to know they were on the same wavelength, after all. She smiled and reached up to touch his handsome mouth. "I'll keep that in mind." He just wanted her to know that she could move this budding relationship along at whatever pace she needed to—but that he was interested in pursuing it. She hoped he understood that she was interested, too, and that he didn't need to be shy about voicing his feelings with her. Maybe he'd also learn that giving in to his impulses didn't mean he'd frighten her the way Kenny had. Corie drew her hand down his chest before pulling back to the door. "Good night, Matt."

He touched the corner of her mouth and traced her smile with the tip of his finger, sparking an electric current that curled through her all the way down to her toes. "Good night."

When he nodded and pulled away without a kiss, she tried not to be disappointed. As she closed the door and leaned back against it, she reminded herself that she wasn't the only one who might be cautious about putting themselves out there. Matt had held her and touched her and listened and shared and awakened her heart. She closed her eyes and smiled. Good grief, she was falling hard for that one. She was feeling hopeful that she could have a normal life one day. Maybe she could even have that loving husband and big family she'd always dreamed about.

"Mom?" She opened her eyes to the shadowy darkness to find Evan stumbling into the living room.

"Hey, little man." Corie hurried to meet him and gently turn him back toward his bedroom. "What are you doing up?"

"I wanted to make sure you were home, and you were okay."

Corie nearly stumbled over the threshold as her heart seized up with his concern for her. Maybe *normal* was never really going to be an option for them. Not as long as Kenny Norwell had this influence over their lives.

"Yes, sweetie, I'm okay. Matt said you are, too." Now that he was partially awake, she helped him pull off his jeans and slip into his pajamas. "Come on. Let's get you back to bed."

He reached up to touch his dragon before climbing into bed again. "I really like Matt, Mom."

She pulled up the covers. "I like him, too."

"His grandma bakes cookies, and I made a new friend. Gideon doesn't go to my school, but we built a castle together. Can he come over and play sometime?" The big yawns she'd had over at Matt's were contagious. Evan seemed determined to get all his words out before he drifted off to sleep again. "Mark's funny. He calls Amy Red because of her red hair, and Pike calls Alex Shrimp because he's short…" Another yawn indicated this conversation wouldn't last long. "Oh, and Matt won the ax-chopping contest."

"The what?" Alarm flared but quickly went away because Evan was out, no doubt finally relaxing and dreaming happy thoughts judging by the smile on his face. Corie leaned over to give him another kiss. "Good night, little man. I love you."

She turned out the bedside lamp and left the door slightly ajar. It sounded like he'd had a grand adventure with Matt and his family tonight. There was definitely a little idolizing going on there. But she couldn't blame him. She seemed to have a thing for the firefighter next door, too.

As she headed down the hallway to her own bedroom, she heard one of the neighborhood cats who prowled the fire escapes looking for handouts or a warm spot to curl up scratching at her window. At Evan's insistence, she'd stuffed some old towels inside a box and set it on the fire escape to give them a bit of shelter from the cold. Sometimes, she had leftovers from the diner she set out for them. It was the closest thing to a pet the landlord allowed them to have.

"No leftovers tonight, sweetie." Corie folded up her work sweater and set it on the quilt beside her while she untied her shoes and toed them off her feet. Even through the blackout drapes that covered her window, she could hear how agitated the cat was, meowing and hissing and bumping into the discarded chair she'd set out there to anchor the box and keep it from blowing away. "What in the world are you so fired up about?"

Corie padded across the room in her stockinged feet. But before she reached the window, she heard another sound from out in the living room. A soft knocking at her door. Three taps, a pause, three more.

She glanced at the late hour on her alarm clock and tensed when she heard three more knocks. Hurrying

straight to her coat on the rack where she'd hung it beside the door, she once more reached for her pepper spray.

Knock, knock, knock.

"Corie?"

Her breath rushed out in a gust of relief at Matt's deep-
pitched whisper. She slipped the spray back into the pocket
and swung open the door.

"You didn't lock your dead bolt. I was waiting—"

Corie threw her arms around Matt's neck. "Thank you.
For so many things, thank you." Her toes left the floor as
Matt wound his arms behind her waist and straightened,
completing the hug. Her toes were still dangling in the
air as she leaned back against his arms and grinned. "Ax-
chopping contest? Seriously?"

"Oh. That." Her feet hit the floor and she was no longer
cinched against him as he tried to apologize. "My brother
and I were taking down a wall. Ev wasn't in the room at
the time—"

"It sounds like a manly man thing that humans with
testosterone enjoy more than they should. But I know he
was safe. I feel safe with you, too—emotionally, physically." She shrugged, not coming up with enough words
to explain everything she was feeling. "Firewise. Otherwise." She felt giddy, partially with relief that there was
no intruder at her door, probably with fatigue, possibly because of all the new emotions swirling inside her. "I like
you, Matt. I know my timing isn't great and inexplicable
things are happening around us, but I do. Will I see you
tomorrow?" she asked, wanting these weird, wonderful
feelings she'd discovered tonight to continue.

He propped his hands at his waist and gave her the mat-
ter-of-fact answer she was getting used to. "I work the late
shift. Won't get home until eight or nine."

The giddiness fled, and she felt deflated. "I'll be at work by then. Well, thank you again for watching Evan tonight. I promise I won't bug you every time I—"

His big hands framed her jaw, and his lips covered hers, silencing her apology with a kiss. He'd cut her off midsentence, and she was surprised to realize she was okay with that. Her gasp of surprise was swallowed up by the pressure of his mouth gliding over hers. Matt's tongue slipped between her lips, but she was already opening for him, already answering him. She was already grasping fistfuls of his shirt and T-shirt and the hard muscle underneath and pulling herself into his kiss.

Matt sifted his fingers into her hair and cupped her head, tilting it back to ravish her mouth. He moved forward, backing her against the wall beside the door until she could feel the pressure of his thighs against parts of her body that hadn't felt anything remotely thrilling like this for far too long. The heat of his body trapped her there, consuming her the way his mouth was consuming hers.

Although it had been a teasing joke earlier that night, Corie thought of molasses in the very best of ways. Matt's kiss was slow and smooth, addictively sweet and very much worth the wait for him to take the initiative in expressing his desire for her. Every taste, every exploration was as deliberate as his every thought.

But with a groan of regret that matched her own, Matt lifted his head, ending the kiss. They were both breathing erratically, the proud tips of her sensitized breasts brushing against his chest with every exhale. She was vaguely aware of his arousal pushing at the front of his jeans, just as she was aware of the heavy, weepy center of her wishing this had been more than a kiss. She had been too long without a man. She had been forever without the right man. Oh, how this man made her feel—physically, emotionally—every scary, delicious way she'd long forgotten she had the right to feel.

His dark eyes replaced the intensity of his kiss as he studied her face, keeping them linked together with his gaze. He watched her hair as he brushed his fingers through it, trying to smooth it back into place until he finally pulled the band from what was left of her ponytail and let her hair fall over her shoulders.

His voice was a husky whisper as he gently pried her hands from his shirt and slipped the rubber band into her palm. "I'll see you tomorrow night." She nodded at his promise because she couldn't quite find the breath to speak. "How late is the diner open?"

"On Fridays and Saturdays, we close at midnight."

"Evan?"

"He'll be with me. There's a cot in the back room if he's not at one of the tables, drawing or playing or chatting with the regular customers."

With a nod, he released her entirely and backed away with his hands raised, making her feel like pure temptation despite her baby-blue polyester dress and messy hair. "I'll meet you guys there when my shift ends. You still owe me a pie."

She laughed out loud at that and clapped her hand over her mouth as the sound seemed to echo down the hallway. Matt smiled—just a small curve at one corner of his mouth transformed him into a handsome man. And those dark, coffee-colored eyes about swallowed her up. She reached up to rest her hand against the stubble on his jaw. "Good night, Matt."

"Good night, Corie." She drifted into her apartment and

closed the door, leaning back against it. From the hallway, she heard him exhale and whisper, "Dead bolt."

Why did that reminder sound like some kind of endearment?

Corie quickly turned and threw the bolt, alleviating his concern. She splayed her hand against the door, imagining that his hand was there on the other side, protecting her, connecting them. Corie caught her abraded, swollen lip between her teeth and savored the taste of him that lingered there.

She had never in her life been kissed like that. She'd never before understood how a man could make every part of her tingle with such a sharp need with just a kiss. She'd never understood how freeing trust could be, never understood how hope and laughter could make falling in love so exciting.

Falling in love. Was that what was happening here? Was it foolish of her to want like this? To believe she was getting a second chance to be happy? To hope that Matt was feeling this way, too?

After a moment, she heard Matt's door open and close. It had been six long years since her divorce from Kenny, and this was the first time in all those years that she was looking forward to seeing a man again. She was looking forward to seeing Matt.

She heard the cat scrabbling down the fire escape steps as she pushed away from the door and headed through the apartment to get ready for bed herself and idly wondered what was making the feline so restless. Pulling the curtain aside, she peered out into the night. It was too dark to see much beyond the glass. The box beneath the chair had been knocked askew, and the snow around it had been disturbed enough that the paw prints were indistinct. Maybe there'd been one occupant too many trying to share the box tonight. Seeing no critter outside for her to worry about, Corie made sure the window was locked and pulled the drape back into place.

Kenny hadn't found them. She'd freaked out for nothing.

Besides, she had more pleasant things to think about.

Like kissing Matt Taylor again.

Many, many times.

Chapter Nine

Matt pulled the steering wheel and hung a sharp left at just the right distance to avoid the cars parked against the curb, guiding the big fire engine onto the skinny side street beside the dubiously named KC's Best automotive repair shop off McGee Street. Talk about a dead man district. This was their third job of the day, and each fire had been bigger than the last. Counting the five medical calls to back up their EMTs, the cat that was stuck in a drainpipe and the two false alarms, Firehouse 13 was way above its daily call average.

After the engine hissed and squealed to a stop, Matt set the brakes and killed the siren. The red and blue flashing lights bounced off nearby shop windows and windshields but seemed to be absorbed by the swirling orange and yellow flames shooting out of the repair shop's garage doors. Inky smoke billowed skyward, staining the snow on the branches of the ancient oaks that lined the sidewalk and bringing an early night to the evening sky.

"Nice driving, Taylor." Captain Redding put on his white scene commander's helmet. "Mark, Jackson—priority one is to make sure we don't have gas tanks, oxyacetylene canisters or other flammables on site that haven't already gone up. Remove them if we can. Clear a perimeter if we can't."

"Yes, sir," they answered, fastening up their gear and securing their air tanks in the back seat.

Redding glanced across the cab to Matt. "You coordinate with the utility crew to make sure we've got all the gas lines cut off. I'll track down the owner and talk to whoever reported it." He studied the fully engulfed building. "This was burning awhile before anyone called it in. As far as I know, Friday's still a workday. Why didn't anyone call sooner?"

"You think we've got casualties?" Matt asked.

"I'm thinking I don't want to send any more men in there than I have to. Something's off with this one." Redding made a quick scan of the police cars blocking traffic and the local residents hanging out at a relatively safe distance from the fire scene. "Where are all the mechanics?" There was one nondescript guy with muscles and an aversion to holding his head up huddled inside his grimy insulated coveralls, talking with an older man in a suit and tie and long dress coat. "He's the only one in this crowd wearing a uniform of any kind."

Twenty-plus years of service gave Kyle Redding almost a sixth sense about fires. Hell. Matt hadn't been with KCFD for half that long, and he had a feeling there was nothing accidental about this blaze. Matt nodded toward the line of tow trucks and trailers on the far side of the building holding expensive cars and souped-up trucks in various states of repair. "Looks like they got most of their vehicles out."

"The ones worth some real money." Redding nodded. "Which is what I would do if I was going to torch my own place."

Matt followed up on Kyle's suspicion. "I'll give my dad a call and alert the arson team."

"Do that."

While the captain led Mark, Ray and the rest of the team off the truck to meet with the men and women on the second and third trucks and move them into position, Matt turned off the engine and called in their twenty to dispatch. "Lucky 13 on scene, 819 McGee Street. Captain Redding has the command. Taylor 13 Alpha out."

Then he swapped out his ball cap for his own helmet and tuned in to the chatter coming over his body radio as he climbed down to assess the scene more closely. The heat from the blaze was intense enough for him to feel it as he approached. Although hoses were out and the team was laying down a defensive perimeter to keep the fire from spreading, there was probably little they could do.

Matt adjusted his mask over his face, radioed his position to the crew and moved inside, clinging to the walls to keep his bearings as he tried to pinpoint the source of the blaze. Steam from the water gushing through the garage bay doors was as thick as the smoke, making visibility almost nil. After signaling Mark and Ray that he understood their all-clear on the ground floor, he made his way past the charred shell of a pickup up on lifts in one of the bays. A quick exploration confirmed that no one was trapped inside or beneath the vehicle. He made it to a set of metal stairs leading up to the second floor. But he was forced to reverse course as flames curled in a sinuous dance across the ceiling above him and cut off access to the top of the stairs. One by one, ceiling tiles melted and fell away, and the wood support beams holding up the second floor began to sag and crack as fire, water and heat weakened them. The thick stone walls and iron window frames would probably survive anything short of a massive explosion, but the interior of the two-story 1920s-era shop was fully involved and about to collapse.

"Taylor 13 Alpha," he called over his radio. "Everybody clear out. The top floor's about to rain down on us. Immediate source of ignition not evident. Cannot access second floor from interior. I repeat, everybody clear out."

Mark and Ray were already outside, waiting for the ladder truck to move into position to access the roof when Matt emerged. His mask fogged up as he met the wintry air and he pulled it down beneath his chin.

"Incendiaries down here are contained," Mark shouted. "The ignition point has to be upstairs."

He gave them a thumbs-up, showing his understanding. "Did you see the way the interior supports were burning? It's like somebody doused the top floor with an accelerant. This baby is going to end up a total gut. All we can do now is put it out." Matt tapped his radio, indicating to the crew that this had become strictly a containment mission. "Lucky 13, let's go to work. Watch yourselves up on that roof."

Matt was heading across the driveway to report to Captain Redding when a window exploded over his head. He jerked at the sound and instinctively raised his arm as glass rained down around him. But that was what the helmet and bunker gear were for, since falling debris and collapsing buildings were a firefighter's most common threat. Unharmed, he moved his mask up to shield his face, and looked up to see if the pressure that had blown out that window was the first in a chain reaction, and he needed to move his men back to a safe distance. Flashover would certainly occur now that fresh oxygen was flooding the confined space.

"Son of a..." What Matt saw was even worse. "Stop!"

A dark-haired man in grimy coveralls was leaning over the window ledge, engulfed by the black smoke billowing out around him. Coughing racked his body, and when he drew in a breath, Matt could hear the shallow wheeze of lungs that wouldn't fill. His face was smudged with soot and red smears he'd guess were blood, making his expression unreadable. But there was no mistaking his intention as the chair he'd smashed the window with came flying toward Matt.

Matt ran forward, dodging the chair that splintered around him, shouting to be heard over the roar of the fire and thunder of the hoses. A leg came over the edge of the windowsill. "Wait up! We'll get a ladder to you. Stop! Take a deep breath and stay put. We're coming." He waved the man back inside, pointed to the fire escape at the end of the building. "Can you reach—?" Matt turned to his radio. "Ladder! Northeast side, second floor. I've got a jumper—"

The man teetered over the edge into the smoke, leaping, falling, hurling himself away from the flames. Matt dived in one Hail Mary effort to break his fall. But he was too late. The victim hit the pavement before him with a sickening thud.

On his hands and knees, Matt scrambled forward. "Medic! I need a board now!"

Matt tugged off his mask and placed it over the man's face, giving him the oxygen he must have been starving for. He peeled off his gloves to check for a pulse. But as the EMTs swarmed in and pushed him aside, he already knew the diagnosis. Whether it was a broken neck or a broken skull, the man was dead.

Matt rocked back on his heels as Redding rushed over. Although the paramedics rolled the mechanic onto a back board to stabilize him and intubated him to push oxygen directly into his lungs, it was too late. After giving Matt's shoulder a supportive squeeze, the captain knelt beside the paramedics. "I think I understand now why someone started this fire."

Matt scrambled over to join him, needing to know why this man had died, needing to understand why he hadn't been able to save him. Faulty fire suppression system? Not passing any fire inspection period? What the hell kind of business left a man behind without making any effort to rescue him, or alerting the KCFD to attempt a rescue? "Did you find out anything from the owner?"

"That he's an entitled ass full of hot air. But take a look at this." After a sad shake of his head from one of the EMTs working on the victim, Redding picked up the man's wrist and pushed back the cuff of his coveralls. The man's fingers and knuckles were bruised and bloodied, like he'd been in a fight. Matt might have thought the fight had been with the heavy iron and leaded glass of that window upstairs, but that didn't account for the shred of duct tape clinging to his wrist.

Before the medics covered him up, Matt glimpsed the dark-haired man's bruised and swollen face. He'd clearly been in a fight. "Those wounds are hours old. They didn't happen when he impacted the concrete." Matt picked up the other wrist and discovered the skin was raw from where he'd pulled or gnawed his way free. "He didn't bind himself up like this."

"Crime scene cover-up." Redding placed the victim's hand back under the blanket and nodded for the EMTs to lift him onto the gurney and move him to the ambulance, keeping him out of sight from curious onlookers and the press photographers who were showing up to take pictures or capture some footage for the evening news. "Somebody left this man for dead in there."

"Hold up a sec." Matt asked the medics to wait while he took another look at the man's damaged wrist.

The captain leaned in beside him. "What is that? A homemade tattoo?"

Matt studied the markings that looked like they'd been scratched into the skin by the same instrument the man had used to free himself. Suspicion prickled the back of Matt's neck, and he wiped the soot away from the patch sewn above the man's chest pocket to read his name. "Maldonado." The man whose car had been remotely set on fire a few days ago. The confidential informant who was allegedly ratting out the next generation of the Meade crime family. "My uncle Cole needs to see this."

Redding ordered the medics to stay with the body and protect it. "I'll call KCPD."

Two hours later, night had fallen, and with the fire out, the temperature had dropped to a chilly twenty-three degrees. And while the Lucky 13 crew was combing the building to check for remaining hot spots and overhaul the debris, KCPD had arrived on the scene in the form of Matt's uncle Cole, along with his NCIS partner, Amos Rand.

Matt was running on fumes, taking a break and sitting on the running board of his fire truck while he downed a bottle of water. Other than removing his helmet and breathing apparatus, he still wore his bunker gear for the warmth the layers provided. He stood when his uncle and his partner walked up, extending his hand to greet them. "Uncle Cole. Agent Rand."

"Matt." Cole held on to his nephew's hand for an extra moment, his eyes narrowed in familial concern. "You look like you've been rode hard and put up wet. You okay?"

"Long day."

Cole nodded his understanding. Sometimes, first responders saw some wicked things that stuck with you— like a man desperate enough to choose one kind of death over another. "I'll need your statement when you're ready."

"Let's get it done." Matt crushed the empty water bottle

and tossed it inside the truck. He told them what he'd witnessed with Enrique Maldonado's death and his suspicion about the cause of the fire. There was only one worker on site besides the dead man, and he hadn't seen that first mechanic since he'd had time to walk away from the fire and scan the crowd again. Finally, someone had managed to save all the expensive vehicles they had on site—but not their last employee?

"Sounds like potential insurance fraud to me," Cole suggested.

Amos agreed. "Maybe Meade needed an influx of cash and decided to torch his own place."

"Or he was destroying evidence." Matt nodded toward the forensics team from the crime lab who'd been talking to Cole and Amos. "Has your crime scene team found anything?"

Amos pulled his wool cap more securely over his buzz cut of hair and hunched against the damp chill in the air. "They can't get into what's left of the offices upstairs yet, but they found a sticky substance on the arm of the chair Maldonado used to break out the window. They'll have to match it in the lab, but it looks like remnants of duct tape. He was secured to the chair and worked over before the fire started. Trapped and unable to evacuate. Maybe he was unconscious—maybe they thought he was dead. Nobody tried to save that guy."

Somebody had. But it had been too little, too late. Matt heard the sound of the victim hitting the pavement again and again in his head. "If I could have just gotten to him sooner. If I had known he was up there—"

"This isn't on you, Matt," Cole insisted. Captain Redding had said the same thing, ordered him to take tomorrow off and to check in with one of the KCFD counselors, if necessary. "Whether as a result of another crime like arson or assault, or deliberately planned to play out like this, we've got ourselves a homicide. One we should be able to tie to the owner of this place, Chad Meade."

Amos turned his back to the graying, slightly heavyset man in the suit and tie being escorted by a uniformed officer across the driveway to join them. "Speak of the devil."

Although Matt had spotted him in the crowd with the missing mechanic when the Lucky 13 crew had first arrived on the scene, he hadn't realized this well-to-do man who wore polished patent-leather oxfords instead of sensible snow boots was the business owner. He didn't strike Matt as an auto repair sort of guy. But then, he didn't look like Matt's image of a man who'd spent several years in prison, either. But this was Chad Meade, wannabe crime boss and the object of Cole and Amos's investigation.

"If it isn't Mr. Taylor and his enigmatic partner," Meade said in a friendly enough tone, although Matt got the distinct impression there was nothing friendly between him and the police. "We meet again. I was told you wanted to speak to me and, of course, I was eager to help find out who is responsible for this monstrous tragedy. Thought I could spare you a few minutes between phone calls and press interviews." He held up the cell phone he carried. "I've been talking back and forth with my insurance gal. I'm guessing this will be a total write-off." He glanced up at Matt and gave a practiced laugh. "These old buildings from the '20s are built like bomb shelters on the outside. But KCFD couldn't save much on the inside, could they?"

Cole made no pretensions of this being a civil conversation. "How much of a profit is this *write-off* worth to you, Chad? Aren't you on parole?"

He turned the collar of his coat up against the cold. "That's why I'm running a legitimate business here, Officer."

"It's Detective."

Amos removed the toothpick that he'd been chewing from the side of his mouth and tapped his chest. "And Special Agent. *You* need to try harder if you want us to believe you've gone legit."

Meade pointed to the smoking wreckage of the garage. "Can I help it if the competition doesn't want me to succeed?"

"You're claiming this was a setup?" Cole challenged.

"I have enemies, Detective. My uncle Jericho was an influential man—not everyone agreed with the way he ran his business. I've learned from the mistakes he made and I'm doing well for myself. But some people can hold a grudge for a long time." He pulled back the edge of his leather glove to check the time, as if he was calculating how much longer he'd allow this conversation to last. "You, perhaps. How is your lovely wife, by the way?"

"I'm here to do my job, Meade." Cole clearly had no intention of letting Chad Meade bait him into an argument about the last time Cole and his wife, Tori, had investigated the Meade crime family. "You've got a casualty here. One of your employees, Enrique Maldonado. He was trapped in the fire. He didn't make it."

"I heard. That's too bad."

Matt's hand balled into a fist at the lack of sympathy, or even empathy, for the life that had been lost.

Cole nodded. "Yeah, it's too bad he had his hands taped together and was probably unconscious when the fire started and had no chance of surviving."

Chad Meade met Cole's hard, unblinking blue eyes and finally smiled before looking away. Since members of Chad's family had once tried to kill Cole's wife, there was certainly no love lost between them. "I know nothing about that, Detective Taylor. But I assure you, the company takes care of its employees and their families. Now, if you'll excuse me, I need to talk to my insurance people and do a little PR spin with the press." He gestured to the burned-out shell of the garage. "Historic landmark destroyed. It breaks the locals' hearts."

Cole shoved his hands into his leather jacket, probably hiding the fists he'd made, too. "We'll be investigating this fire for arson. Maybe you think we can't get you for murder, but even a case of insurance fraud will put you back in prison."

"I'm just the investor who owns the property. An entrepreneur. What would I know about setting a fire like this?" He wiggled his gloved fingers in the air. "I don't even smoke anymore." He turned and waved to a brunette reporter who waved back and invited him to speak on camera. "Gentlemen. If you'll excuse me, I have to go."

Amos followed a few steps behind him. "We have more questions for you, Meade."

"I'm certain you do." Despite his perfect, capped-tooth smile, Meade's tone was laced with a threat now. "I'm not in the business anymore, gentlemen. And your investigation borders on harassment."

Cole was one cool customer, throwing Meade's excuse right back at him. "If you're not in the business, then you've got nothing to hide."

Chad Meade smoothed his tie inside his suit jacket before reaching into the chest pocket of his coat. "But I *do* have work to do, calls to make. A family to express my condolences to." He held out a business card. "If you want to speak to me again, contact my lawyer."

Amos snagged the card and stuffed it into the back pocket of his jeans as Meade strolled away. "That man is one smug SOB. He does know we've built a paper trail on him, doesn't he? That we can track his import and export shipment schedules to match up with trafficking in and out of KCI and the river port? What we need is witness corroboration. Several witnesses would be better."

Cole shook his head. "Now that Maldonado's gone, we'll be starting from scratch again, trying to convince someone to turn on Meade." His expression was grim as he looked to the blackened shell of the Art Deco building. "But if this is the result of turning on him…"

Matt listened to their case against Chad Meade, and a few inexplicable observations about this fire began to make sense. "Can I show you something?" The three men went to the body lying in the back of the ME's van. Cole and Amos flashed the badges hanging around their necks and vouched for Matt as a witness. With permission from the medical examiner, Niall Watson, who remained to observe their interactions with the body, the three men climbed in beside the gurney. Dr. Watson issued them all sterile gloves and proceeded to unzip the body bag.

"Can you identify the victim?" Dr. Watson asked, adjusting his glasses on the bridge of his nose. "I found no ID on him. No wallet, no phone."

"It's Enrique Maldonado," Amos confirmed. "May I?" Amos pulled a knife from the sheath on his belt and slid it beneath the top of the victim's boot. Once he'd pried it far enough from the victim's leg, he reached inside and pulled out a set of dog tags on a thin chain. He dropped the tags into a bag the ME held open before sealing and labeling it. "Perps don't usually check the boot for anything but hidden weapons. Those will confirm his ID. Maldonado was working undercover for me out of NCIS. We believe Meade has his hand in moving illegal arms in and out of the country by hiding them in those expensive cars he imports and exports. Enrique was our inside man who followed the trail here to Kansas City." Amos's light-colored eyes narrowed as he looked down at the body. "He was a good man. He wasn't even a field agent, but we gave him the job because he's so good with engines and cars. No one would question his expertise."

Cole rested a hand on Amos's shoulder. "Sorry about your man, Amos."

"He was a good Marine." The dark-haired agent closed his eyes completely for a moment, inhaled a deep breath, then opened his eyes, ready to work again. "He's been feeding us intel for months now. We still don't know if Meade is running this operation, or if he's a middleman and we still have to identify who he's reporting to."

Cole studied the victim's battered face for a moment before looking away. "Burning his car wasn't persuasion enough to keep Maldonado from meeting with us. Was his cover blown and Meade found out he was a cop? Or is this the going payback for anyone talking to the police now?"

Matt had an idea about that. "If Maldonado was working for you, that could explain what I found." He lifted the stiff left arm from the gurney and pulled back the stained, torn sleeve. "I thought you might want to see this." Dr. Watson snapped a photograph of Maldonado's forearm, and the letters and number that had literally been scratched into his skin.

N4 Jeff C FB

Cole pulled out his phone and took a picture of the code. "You think he did this? Or was it done to him?"

Matt laid the arm down and picked up the victim's right hand to show them the bloody nails. "With everything on fire around him, and nothing to write with, he carved this himself." Cole and the ME both snapped pictures of the hand, as well. "I think he jumped because he wanted to make sure you got his message. I can't be certain what it means, but it looks like he was trying to preserve the writing in case his clothes caught on fire and the body burned."

"N4. Enforcer," Amos translated. "Jeff C? Jefferson City? Meade's hired himself a new enforcer from Jefferson City. Probably an ex-con who just got out of prison there."

Ex-con? Like Corie's ex?

"Is that why the call from your attorney's office upset you?"

"My ex hurt a lot of people."

The back of Matt's neck prickled with awareness. He glanced outside the ME's van at his crewmates finishing their cleanup and joking with each other now that the danger at this scene had passed. He stepped to the edge of the van to look at the gathering of reporters and cameras closing in around Chad Meade. But he wasn't sure what his instincts were trying to tell him.

"What's the FB?" Cole asked.

Matt glanced back to see Amos scraping some goo off the bottom of the dead man's boot. "Looks like petroleum jelly." He showed it to the ME, who opened a jar for him to scrape the substance into.

What details was Matt missing here? "May I?"

He brought the jar to his nose to sniff the contents. Oh no. Hell no.

"You ever seen anything like that?" Cole asked.

Matt had. His blood sped through his veins like a freight train.

Corie said her ex started fires.

"Kenny stayed in Jefferson City after he was released from prison."

That's why the hairs on the back of his neck were standing out straight. He handed the jar back to the ME, who capped it as evidence. "Get another sample of that to my dad, chief arson investigator at KCFD." Matt jumped from the back of the van to the ground. "You need me for any-thing else, Cole? There's a phone call I need to make." The sooner the crew cleared the scene and he wrote up his preliminary report, the sooner he could get to Pearl's Diner and to Corie and Evan. But all that would wait if he couldn't hear her voice and know that she was okay.

"Go." His uncle shooed him on his way. "I'll contact Gideon about the potential arson. Thanks for your help tonight. I'll keep you in the loop if we find out anything about the fire itself."

Matt was backing away, even as he was unbuckling his turnout coat and reaching inside his BDUs to pull out his cell phone. He nodded toward the victim Niall Wat-son was zipping back inside the body bag. "FB. Firebug. Check out the name Kenny Norwell. Find out if he's got any connection to Chad Meade. And send me Norwell's picture if you can get it."

"Done." Cole called after him, "Who's Norwell?"

"Someone I hope is still in Jefferson City."

Chapter Ten

"Answer your phone!" Matt growled the order at the cell phone he'd anchored to his dashboard.

When Corie's voice mail started up again with its pleasant but impersonal greeting, he punched the disconnect button. He'd already left three messages, apologizing for running late, asking her to call him, telling her he had some information he wanted to share in person, trying not to sound completely desperate to know that she was okay.

He'd had to settle for a single text.

Hey, Matt. We're slammed tonight. Call you back when things lighten up.

At least if she was super busy, she wasn't alone. And he couldn't imagine any universe where she didn't make sure Evan was safe, as well. They were probably fine, and he was too exhausted by the day and his anticipation at seeing her beautiful smile again to be able to filter out the negative thoughts.

He forced himself to take a deep breath and slow to a stop for the red light at the next intersection.

He had no proof that her ex-husband was in Kansas City, breaking into her apartment, setting small fires around their building and killing undercover agents. Uncle Cole had texted him a copy of Kenneth Norwell's mugshot. A man could change his looks a lot in six years—grow a beard, shave his head or dye his hair or let it grow long. Still, Matt had memorized the image and had wearied his brain trying to recall if he'd seen anyone like that around Corie and Evan. If he'd seen anyone like that in the crowds of lookie-loos at any of the area's recent suspicious fires. But he'd been focused on doing his job—putting out the flames, not spotting the man who may have started them.

Cole had also shared that Norwell's residence was in Jefferson City. His parole officer confirmed that Norwell had been at every check-in since his release. Still, Jeff City was only a two-and-a-half-hour drive from KC. Close enough to get to Kansas City to set a fire and get back in time for his required daily meetings. But did that put him in the city long enough to play games with Corie's sense of security? Did that give him time to drive to St. Louis to torch an attorney's office to find her new name and address in the first place?

Someone was conducting a harassment campaign against Corie and her son. Someone wanted her to be unsettled and afraid, possibly to distract her enough to drop her guard so she wouldn't see the big threat coming—and maybe just because some sicko got off on gaslighting her and seeing her afraid. And there was no denying that someone had started those fires at their building with a flammable goo that bore a remarkable resemblance to the accelerant used to burn down Chad Meade's pricey automotive repair place.

It could all be a tragic coincidence. Or it could be that Corie's violent past had come back to haunt her in the worst of ways.

Matt drummed his fingers against the steering wheel, counting down the seconds until the light turned green and the car ahead of him pulled out. He had a portable siren and flashing lights in his truck he could turn on to cut through traffic faster, but the only justifiable emergency was the worst-case scenario playing through his head and twisting at his heart. And as far as he knew, that hadn't happened yet.

Plus, Corie and Evan weren't the only citizens he was responsible for here. An arsonist in Kansas City? An uptick in the number of fire calls KCFD had answered in the past month—everything from the woman this morning who had accidentally ignited a pile of laundry when she tried to light her water heater to the gut job at Meade's automotive shop this evening—were cause for concern that no one should be ignoring. Not every fire was arson, but every fire was dangerous—and a potential killer, even if you hadn't been bound up and left for dead in the middle of one.

Unfortunately, it was a single-digit Friday night during the long haul of January, and the bars and eateries around the City Market were open and doing a booming business. There were dozens of patrons hurrying along the sidewalks, getting in and out of cars and buses and cabs, and hundreds more were already inside, staying warm while they flirted and partied and filled their bellies with food and drink. Every one of them could be at risk if Kenny Norwell was in town, setting fires for whoever paid him the right price.

Matt tapped on the accelerator as the light changed. "Don't project the worst."

But the tension cording the back of his neck warned him that the worst was yet to happen.

He turned the corner and spotted the familiar neon sign and bright light from the interior spilling through the big glass windows of Pearl's Diner at the far end of the block.

But he was too far away to see inside, to spot Corie's bouncing ponytail or Evan's shaggy brown hair. Parking was going to be a bear around here, and he vowed then and there to pull into the first available parking space he came across that would fit his big truck, and then he'd run the rest of the way to the diner. He'd told Corie he'd get off by eight or nine, and it was half past ten. In the past, he hadn't minded the responsibilities he enjoyed as a lieutenant at Firehouse 13. But tonight, every frozen hose, every incident report that needed at least a preliminary summary, every offer of support and camaraderie from his crewmates over that last rough call had taken precious time away from getting to Corie and Evan. Even the twenty minutes he'd stopped to shower the smells of soot and death off him and change into jeans and a sweater had taken too long.

Now he was circling the block for a second time, seriously rethinking turning on his flashing lights and double parking outside the diner's front door, all because he wasn't good at putting his thoughts into words. He wasn't sure he could express his fears about Norwell finding a way to track down Corie and Evan's new names and showing up on their doorstep again without Matt sounding like he was barking out orders and scaring her.

Especially if this turned out to be nothing. Maybe the fires were accidents. Maybe Chad Meade had killed Agent Rand's man himself. And maybe this gut-deep edginess had less to do with arson fires and more to do with the feelings he had for Corie that were bottled up inside him.

His phone rang on the dash. When he saw the name on the screen, it didn't ring a second time.

Matt pushed the button to answer the call. "Corie."

Not Corie. He heard noises in the background, some garbled talking, the clink of dishes and silverware, a couple of raised voices, but nothing he could make out.

"Matt?" Evan's voice sounded small and nasally. Was he crying? "Is it okay if I call you?"

"Sure, bud." Matt's heart lurched in his chest. Was something wrong? Was that why Corie hadn't called him back? He ratcheted down the tension that threatened to leak into his voice. "Are you okay? What are you doing on your mom's phone?"

"Mom needs help."

"What's wrong?"

He heard a big sniffle, and then Evan's voice grew stronger. "The customers are being mean to her." Customers. Plural. So probably not Norwell. Surely Evan would recognize his own father. But then, he would only have been one or two when Norwell went to prison. Corie would know him, though. Would she let on to Evan that it was his father? Maybe her ex wasn't even in town, and the fires at their building were just a coincidence that overlapped Uncle Cole's investigation into Chad Meade's resurgence in organized crime and arms smuggling, and whatever was going on at the diner had nothing to do with the information he'd learned this evening.

Maybe someone had been rude about their service or had stiffed Corie on her tip. Maybe the kid took umbrage with that. Matt knew he would. But he kept his tone even and reassuring. "Not everybody is nice, Ev."

"They broke my dragon."

The night turned red behind Matt's eyes, and he bit down on the urge to curse where Evan could hear him. That plastic dragon was just a toy. But that toy clearly had emotional value to Evan. Heck, the kid literally swore by that dragon. Breaking it would damage more than the toy. It was a security blanket for Corie's son who'd grown up without a father. And damn it, it was Evan's.

"Some bullies aren't nice at all."

"The man with the beard said he was going to eat some of my bricks, but I think he hid them in his gross beard or his mashed potatoes. You can't eat plastic bricks. Mom's trying to make him give them back."

Hence the raised voices. "Is he hurting your mom?"

"I don't think so. But they're loud."

Finally. Another pickup was pulling out of a parking space across the street about half a block up from the diner. About damn time. "How many mean customers are there?"

"Two."

Gross beard? "There's the guy with the beard. What does the other man look like?"

"He has red hair and more freckles than I do."

Those jackasses from the bus. He remembered their names—Harve and Jordy. It took a lot to trigger Matt's temper. But with Maldonado's death, one too many arson fires, the possibility of Corie's ex working with Chad Meade and some stupid, drunk hicks hitting on Corie and breaking Evan's dragon, there just wasn't enough calm left in him to control his rage. "Did either of those men touch her?"

"Um…" Hell. They had. They'd put their hands on her.

Matt slammed on his brakes and angled his truck across the lane of traffic, staking claim to the parking space the moment the young couple climbing in left. "Is she okay? Are you?"

"Uh-huh."

"Do you dragon swear?"

He could almost hear the energy flowing into Evan's tone, and the confidence puffing up his chest. "Yes. I'm okay. Mom said to call you to see when you were coming before she called the police. When are you coming?"

"I'm parking my truck now."

"The red-haired guy asked Mom if her boyfriend was

going to save her this time." The sound of fear in Evan's voice eased a little as curiosity kicked in. "What does that mean? Are you her boyfriend?"

"Damn straight I am." Matt whipped into the parking space. "Hang up the phone and tell your mom I'm coming."

"Mo-om!"

Then there was no more call. Matt grabbed his cell off the dash, pocketed his keys, put a hand up to stop the car bearing down on him and jogged across the street. Thanks to the diner's booth-to-ceiling windows, Matt had a clear view of what was happening before he ever reached the front door at the corner.

Harve and Jordy were easy to spot at their table in the middle of the restaurant with their mountain-man hygiene and penchant for making a scene. Neither one could be mistaken for the man in the mugshot of Kenny Norwell.

That didn't make the scene any easier to dismiss. Matt saw a wingless plastic dragon and brightly colored blocks scattered across the table and plate in front of Harve. Despite Evan's red-rimmed eyes, he sassed something to the bearded man and grabbed his dragon. When Harve shoved Evan away from the table, Corie dropped her empty tray and scooted Evan behind her, lambasting the bearded man. Matt lengthened his stride when he hit the sidewalk in front of Pearl's, running the last few yards.

A pregnant woman in a business suit stood at the front register, on her cell, reporting everything she was seeing, hopefully on the phone to 9-1-1. One older gentleman stood up at his table in the booth opposite Harve and Jordy and the McGuires, pointing a finger at the two men and rebuking them. That earned him Jordy jumping up and shouting "Boo" or some other startling word that sent him tumbling back into his seat beside a white-haired woman. The rest of the customers watched the scene with wide-eyed shock or buried their gazes in their menus and plates, trying desperately not to get involved.

Involved was the call of every Taylor. Step up when someone needs help. Matt might not be a Taylor by blood. But he was a Taylor down to his very bones.

He swung the door open.

"It's one thing to get handsy with the waitstaff or harass a nice gentleman like Mr. Wallace," he heard Corie chide. "But you touch my son…"

The tinkling bell that jingled overhead sounded inordinately loud and somehow menacing in the sudden silence from every table. Matt made no effort to hunch his shoulders or tone down his anger. He knew how to make his presence known. Big dude at the front door. Black stocking cap, black jeans, black coat. Spooky quiet. Barely breathing hard despite a run through the cold night air. Dark eyes lasered in on the freckled hand clamped around Corie's forearm. Long, purposeful strides took him right up to the table where Harve Gross Beard and Jordy Freckle Face were harassing Corie and Evan.

"Well, if it ain't the boyfriend." Jordy announced Matt's arrival like a rehearsed line. "The boy said you'd show up tonight." But he glanced nervously across the table at Harve, unsure how to proceed.

Matt could help with that. "Let her go."

Although the younger man's grip instantly popped open, Harve chuckled, urging his friend not to panic. "This is all a misunderstanding. The waitress just brought us our pie. We're gonna sit and enjoy dessert."

"No." Simple. Succinct.

Harve fisted his hands against his thighs and Jordy shifted to the edge of his seat. Both were dead giveaways to the two men's intentions.

Matt Taylor had a brother who was a highly trained

SWAT cop. Another was a street patrolman who handled a K-9 partner. Hell, he'd grown up with three brothers. He knew what to do in a fight.

Not that this would be much of one.

When Harve shoved his chair back from the table, Matt toed the edge of the hard plastic tray on the floor, tipped it up into his hand and whacked the bearded man across the face, knocking him back onto his seat. Without wasting any movement, he jerked Harve's coat down his arms, twisting the sleeves and cinching them together behind the back of his chair. Jordy jumped to his feet and cocked his arm back to take a swing at Matt.

He heard Corie's shriek of a warning, raised his arm to deflect the blow and twisted to plant his fist in the middle of the red-haired man's solar plexus, stunning him. Before Jordy could catch his breath or yell uncle, Matt had pinned his arm behind his back and shoved his face down into his roast beef sandwich. When Harve tried to wriggle his chair back to kick out at him, Matt stomped his big boot down on his foot. The man yelped in pain and shouted for someone to call the cops, that he and his buddy were being assaulted by some bigfoot wild man. Matt was peripherally aware of a few customers snapping pictures of the altercation with their phones, but no one was calling anybody to help these two.

While Harve moaned in pain, Matt leaned over the man he had pinned to the table. "You two need to pick on somebody your own size. Not a little boy."

"We were just havin' some fun," Jordy argued. "He knows we were playin'." He turned toward Evan. "Right, kid?"

Corie hugged Evan closer to her side as the brave little man answered. "You're a bully! Bullies get sent to the office."

Matt twisted Jordy's arm a little harder, his eyes telling Harve he would do the same to him if he tried anything else. "Return everything you took from this boy. Now." With a nod to Corie, she loosened Harve's coat sleeves so he could free his hands before she backed away to hug Evan to her side again. Harve emptied his shirt pocket and dumped the plastic bricks on the tabletop. "All of them," Matt ordered.

Muttering a curse under his breath, Mr. Gross Beard dipped his fingers into the mashed potatoes on his plate and dug out three more pieces. When Matt raised an eyebrow, he dropped the pieces into his glass of water and swished them around to get most of the food off them. Then he fished them out with his spoon and put all of them in a napkin he handed to Corie. "Sorry, ma'am."

Corie took the napkin and guided Evan back to the last booth where the body of his dragon now sat. She settled her son into his seat and urged him to start rebuilding his toy.

"Mister," Jordy whined. "You gotta let me up. You're killin' me here."

No. He'd seen killing today. This was just a friendly conversation among three men who were about to reach an understanding. "Are you going to touch this woman again?"

"C'mon. She's pretty. I just wanted her attention. She smiled at everybody but us—" Matt applied the slightest of pressure to his wrist. "No. No, sir."

"Are you going to harass her or anyone else in this restaurant?"

There were no excuses this time. "No, sir."

Matt released his grip and stepped back, making sure Corie and Evan were behind him, and there was a clear aisle to the front door. "Get out."

Jordy eagerly grabbed his coat and booked it to the

front door. Harve was slower to rise to his feet and adjust his jacket onto his shoulders with a firm snap of the material. His eye contact seemed to say that this *conversation* wasn't over. "You don't know who you're messin' with, *Boyfriend*."

Matt didn't take kindly to a threat like that. "Neither do you."

Eventually, Harve, too, backed away from Matt and headed for the door.

The entire diner seemed to be holding its collective breath as the bearded man stopped at the hostess stand and pulled out a wad of cash in his money clip.

"I don't want your money." The dark-haired woman cradled one hand protectively over her swollen belly and held her cell phone up and snapped a picture. "You two aren't welcome here anymore. If you come in again, I'll call one of my close connections at KCPD—like my husband." She put the phone back to her ear. "I'm texting you the second man's picture now, hon. Uh-huh." She held out the phone again. "Detective Kincaid would like to speak to you."

"Harve, come on." Jordy waited in the open door, letting the cold air rush in and chill the air. "One of them dates Bigfoot? And the other's married to a cop? I don't care how good the money is, we're out of our league—"

"Shut up."

"I know you said we owe—"

"Move!" Harve shoved Jordy outside. The bell above the door dinged as the door finally closed behind them.

How good the money is? Was somebody paying those two to harass Corie?

He had a sick idea of who that might be.

Before they reached the curb, Harve was on his phone texting someone. Matt stood at the window and watched, waiting for them to leave, not just the diner, but the whole neighborhood. After Harve put away his phone, he glanced back at Matt and offered him a mocking salute. Then the light changed, and Jordy pulled his seething partner along with the group of people crossing the street. A dark muscle car with tinted windows screeched to a stop at the far curb and the two men climbed inside. Harve must have texted for the ride to pick them up. But that was no car service to arrive this fast. That had to be a buddy of theirs, waiting close by. Maybe close enough to have watched the confrontation through the diner windows.

Matt glanced down at the license plate and committed it to memory. But he made no effort to call it in until he was certain that the yahoo twins and their unseen chauffeur had driven away. Then he quickly texted the plate number to Cole and asked him to ID the vehicle owner and possibly find out Harve and Jordan's last names.

Finally exhaling a sigh of relief that the incident was over, Matt exchanged a nod with the woman at the hostess stand, now fully engaged in a conversation with her husband, who was no doubt feeling just as worried and far away from where he needed to be as Matt had felt a few minutes earlier. Only then did he turn to Corie. "Are you two...?" Corie launched herself at Matt, throwing her arms around him while Evan latched onto his waist in between them. Funny how much better he felt now, too. "Okay."

The elderly gentleman who'd tried to help led the applause. Matt wound one arm around Corie and kissed the crown of her hair, inhaling the homey, enticing scent of baked goods, hard work and fruity shampoo that was hers alone. He palmed the back of Evan's head and held them both close, strengthened by the needy, welcoming grasp of their hands, loving the sense of completeness he felt at holding mother and son in his arms.

After introducing himself and making sure the older

gentleman was okay, Matt thanked him for attempting to intervene. Mr. Wallace sat down, and he and the other patrons returned to their meals and conversations. Corie fisted a hand in Matt's coat and stretched up on tiptoe to press a kiss to the edge of Matt's jaw. "Thank you. I know I keep saying that but, thank you."

Every nerve ending in Matt's body zinged to the imprint where her soft lips had grazed his skin. The adrenaline that had spurred him into the diner was pulsing erratically through his system now, his hyperalertness to all things McGuire now warring with the bone-deep weariness from the day. He needed to keep it together for a while longer, trade some information, ensure they were safe—or there'd be no rest sufficient to help him recover from losing them. "Did they hurt you or Evan?"

"No."

He tipped Evan's head up to his and winked. "You dragon swear you're okay?" Evan grinned at Matt's understanding of the boy's highest code of honor. Evan crossed his finger over his heart and nodded before running back to his booth like the happy child he should be to start building again.

With Evan gone, Corie moved her arms to Matt's waist and snuggled closer. "I dragon swear, too," she teased. "But I'm not too proud to admit that I've never been happier to see anyone in my whole life. I knew when those two walked in and asked to be seated in my section that there was going to be trouble." With an angry huff, she pulled away, but only to move to his side and hug herself around his arm, turning toward the last booth by the windows where Evan was playing. "What kind of man gets rough with a child like that? Steals from him like it's some kind of joke?"

"No kind of *man*." Matt leaned over and kissed the

crown of her hair. "I figured Evan would be safe with you here. But I was scared at how far you might go to protect him."

She shook her head. "I got another waitress to cover the table for me, thinking if I wasn't there to entertain them, they'd eat fast and leave. But when they approached Evan, I had to step in." She rubbed her cheek against Matt's coat sleeve. "Of course, I know they only did it to get me to react. But it was nice to know I had backup before I charged in to do battle."

He covered both her hands with his. "I will always be here if you need me. I'm glad you called."

The pregnant boss lady had circled around the middle tables and met them near the back booth. She extended her hand to Matt. "I'm Melissa Kincaid. I run Pearl's Diner. Your meal is on the house."

"Matt Taylor. I appreciate you calling the police." Although he shook her hand, he shrugged off her offer. "I just want coffee and a slice of pie."

"Still on the house." She held up her phone before tucking into the pocket of her jacket. "And don't worry about Corie's safety when she's here. After the story I just told my husband, Sawyer, I imagine half of KCPD will be eating their meals here the rest of the weekend. Those two won't be bothering any of us again."

Corie released Matt's arm to exchange a hug with the dark-haired woman. "Thanks, Melissa."

"Thank your boyfriend here. By the way, my husband wants to meet you." Melissa smiled at Matt before nodding toward the booth beside her where Evan had spread out his toys, drawings and plastic building bricks. "Corie, take ten. I'll get your orders out for you."

Corie slid into the vinyl seat beside Evan while Matt pulled off his stocking cap and unzipped his coat. Although Corie spared a few moments to ruffle Evan's hair and inquire about the state of repairs on his dragon, when Matt settled onto the seat across from them, he felt her feet sliding between his under the table. He might have thought it was an accident until a few seconds later when her fingertips brushed against his knee. Although some surprisingly naughty thoughts leaped to mind at what they could be doing under the table, Matt chilled his brain and captured her hand in his, linking them together away from prying eyes.

"Sorry about the *boyfriend* thing," she apologized, capturing her bottom lip between her teeth in a frown. "Evan shouted it out to the restaurant as a warning to Harve and Jordy. I'm afraid the appellation stuck."

Man, how he wanted to kiss that bottom lip, ease her discomfort, ease his own. "I'm okay with that."

That sweet mouth blossomed into a smile. "I am, too."

Not for the first time, Matt noted how much he enjoyed holding this woman. How much he loved watching the nuances of her expression. How much he looked forward to hushed, intimate conversations like this one.

Sure, he'd spent part of the last few nights fantasizing about what it would be like to have Corie in his bed. As much as she seemed to like touching him, it wasn't a stretch to imagine undressing those decadent curves and tasting those soft lips and lying with her skin to skin, burying himself inside her, bringing them as close as two people could physically be. Although he knew her to be cautious, he also knew the woman who tugged him down for an impulsive kiss, who reached for him when he was being too careful for her, who stroked his lips and caressed his face and hugged herself around him in a way that was slightly possessive and made her smile that sexy, heart-robbing smile.

Yeah, even now, his body was aching to be closer to hers. But there was something just as soothing, just as satisfying about sharing a connection as simple as holding hands with Corie. With Evan babbling on with a play-by-play of how every brick fit together to rebuild his dragon, another waitress taking their order for coffees and cherry pie, his own thoughts racing as he tried to make sense of everything he was learning about the potential threat surrounding this family, holding hands with Corie under the table felt like a lot more. It was a secret bond for just the two of them to share.

It felt like something deeper, something stronger. Something permanent.

Matt was losing himself in the gentle green of Corie's eyes when his phone dinged with a text. Not wanting to release her hand, he set his phone on the tabletop and pulled up the message as soon as he saw it was from Cole.

Car registered to a Jeff Caldwell.
No record. Get this. His address is the same building as yours. You don't know him?

Matt frowned. He knew several of the people in his building. But he worked long hours. Kept to himself unless he had a family event. Or he was worried about Corie and Evan. The only Jeff he could think of was Wally Stinson's part-time super. And that was just a name to him. He'd never actually met the guy.

But he hated the idea that this guy had a link to Corie. What were the odds of another one of their neighbors showing up at the place where she worked? Of that same guy knowing Harve and Jordan? Of that man living in the apartment directly below hers?

"Ow."

For one fuzzy moment, Matt wondered at the change he saw in Corie's eyes. They were darker. Her pale brows were arched with a question.

Too late, he realized how much his grip had tightened and quickly released her hand. "Sorry."

"You didn't hurt me," she assured him. "But you went away somewhere. I'd say 'penny for your thoughts,' although I'm worried they're not good ones. Is this the spooky quiet side of you that you mentioned?"

His phone dinged with another text from Cole.

Without last names, it will take longer to ID Harve and Jordan. A buddy of mine, Sawyer Kincaid, just walked over from his desk and asked if I knew you. Said you got rid of the riffraff at his wife's restaurant. You're not thinking of switching sides and becoming a cop, are you? :)
I've attached Caldwell's license photo.
If you need anything else, let me know.
Stay safe.

He thanked his uncle and pulled up the photo. Although the man looked vaguely familiar, Matt couldn't place Jeff Caldwell as anyone he'd seen at their apartment building.

And though brown hair and brown eyes like his own were a fairly unremarkable look, he knew he'd seen this guy. But where? Matt splayed his thumb and forefinger across the screen, enlarging the picture to look for anything uniquely discernible, like a scar or crooked teeth. Beyond a spatter of brown freckles across his cheeks, he saw nothing to make this guy stand out in a crowd.

"Matt?" Now Corie's hands were both on top of the table, scooting aside their coffee mugs and reaching across to grasp his. "What's wrong? You're scaring me a little."

Right. This was the part where he usually lost the

woman he was interested in—when he got locked up inside his head and failed to communicate.

But as he struggled to find the right words to say what was necessary without alarming her, Corie picked up his phone and flipped it over, hiding the screen. Her skin blanched as she sneaked a panicked glance at Evan. As soon as she saw her son was distracted, she leaned across the table, dropping her voice to a whisper. "Why do you have a picture of Kenny?" she whispered.

"Your ex?"

And just like that, all the niggling bits of information swimming through his brain made sense. It took every ounce of strength Matt possessed not to leap across the table and pull Corie and Evan into his arms.

He picked up his phone, turning the image away from Evan and texting the information to his uncle. "His driver's license says Jeff Caldwell. This man is Kenny Norwell?"

"Yes. He's gained some weight and his hairline's receding a little, but that's him. Now answer *my* question. Why do you have that picture?" He followed the muscles contracting down her long, pale throat as she swallowed hard. "Spooky quiet isn't going to cut it tonight, Matt Taylor. I've worked hard to erase that man from my life. You need to talk to me."

Matt's gaze swiveled around the restaurant and landed on the reflections of the three of them in the window. He silently cursed that he couldn't see much beyond the glass besides traffic lights and streetlamps. How was he supposed to protect this family from a threat he couldn't see? "Have you seen him around any of the places you frequent? Here? Home? School?"

"No. Have you?"

He glanced across the table at Evan. "Maybe we shouldn't discuss this here."

She pulled her hands up inside the cuffs of her sweater and hugged her arms around her waist. Painfully aware of not wanting to alarm her son, Corie turned slightly in her seat. Although little more than a whisper, her tone was precise. "Ten words or less, Taylor. Tell me something before I get scared completely out of my mind."

He heard the sound of breaking glass in the distance and wondered if that was his hopes for a relationship with Corie crashing and burning.

"He owns the car Harve and Jordy drove off in."

For a moment, he thought she was going to pass out, there was so little color on her face. Matt reached clear across the table to cup her alarmingly cool cheek.

"Breathe, sweetheart. I'm not sure what's going on yet. But I will not let him hurt you."

Corie started to shake her head, her disbelief in his vow or his ability to make good on it evident in her hopeless expression. But then Evan suddenly rocketed to his feet, standing on the seat beside her, and her indomitable maternal instinct kicked in. "Whoa, sweetie. What are you doing?"

Ignoring her hands at his waist, Evan pressed his face to the glass, peering into the night. "Matt? Is that your truck?"

And then Matt realized he'd heard it, too. The breaking glass hadn't been in the restaurant or his imagination.

He spotted the flames shooting up from the windshield of his truck. Someone nearby was screaming. Others ran, both toward and away from the fire. He heard the squeal of tires spinning on the icy pavement, speeding in place until they found traction.

"Call 9-1-1." Matt grabbed his coat and rushed out the front door and into the street to deal with the blaze. "KCFD!" he shouted more than once, ordering pedestrians and vehicles out of harm's way as they slowed or stopped completely to watch the glowing liquid and the flames it carried with it spread across the hood and plop onto the pavement like a lava flow. He caught a glimpse of a white van racing away in the opposite direction as he vaulted into the back of his truck and pulled the fire extinguisher from the steel storage box there.

From his higher vantage point, he quickly assessed the potential hazards of the situation. The broken whiskey bottle and charred rag on the ground indicated someone had tossed an old-fashioned Molotov cocktail at his truck. Possibly the driver of the white van. Or Jeff Caldwell/ Kenny Norwell or whatever he wanted to call himself. But he didn't see any dark muscle car racing away from the scene. Maybe Harve and Jordan had come back to exact revenge for the public humiliation of being bested in a one-sided fight.

And maybe he needed to be the firefighter he was and think about preventing personal injury or property damage. The vehicles were parked tightly together here. And traffic was becoming a slow bumper-to-bumper parade as concerts at bars or games on TV ended, and the patrons who'd been enjoying them left for home or their next entertainment destination. A lot of gas tanks in a confined space was a chain reaction fire waiting to happen. And if that flammable, tar-like substance got on anyone's clothes or skin, the slow-burning gelatin would be difficult to wash away, leaving horrible, painful wounds.

"Feel free to call 9-1-1," Matt yelled to the group of young twentysomethings circling closer, filming the fire. "Stay back!"

Traffic was backing up into the next intersection now, as drivers were too curious or frightened to pay attention to where they were going. If he didn't get control of this situation fast, he'd have a traffic accident to deal with, too.

Matt jumped down from the bed of his truck, shielded his face from the worst of the slowly expanding flames and laid down a layer of foam over his windshield and hood. While the driver parked in front of him thankfully arrived and moved his car out of harm's way, Matt continued to spray the extinguisher. But he was running out of juice fast because the viscous goop that was clearly the arsonist's weapon of choice was spreading faster than he could contain it.

Then he felt a hand at the small of his back. "Where should I spray this?"

What the hell? Matt whirled around on Corie. "Get back inside!" Instinctively, he circled an arm around her waist and walked her back toward the diner. Then he snatched her off her feet and spun her out of harm's way as a car swerved around them. She hadn't even stopped to put on a coat or gloves. "What are you doing here?"

She twisted out of his grasp and held up the small fire extinguisher she'd brought from the diner. "Enough atonement. You need help."

"You think this is about me needing to be a hero?" Her cheeks were chapped with the cold, and the only thing she had on over her polyester uniform was that navy-blue cardigan. "You'll freeze out here."

She completely ignored his arguments. "I called 9-1-1. They said they'd be here in a matter of minutes."

Shouts and honking from vehicles down the road who couldn't see what was happening this far up the road forced them to raise their voices. "What about Evan?"

"Melissa is with him. At least let me divert traffic."

"It's dangerous out here. And I'm not just talking about the fire."

"You can't face Kenny alone," she warned him, her gaze boldly searching his for understanding.

So, she thought her ex was responsible for this fire, too. She wasn't running or hiding. She was here to fight.

He shouldn't be turned on by that.

Matt tunneled his fingers into the silky hair at the base of her ponytail and dipped his head to capture her mouth in a quick kiss. Gratitude and understanding and something far more primal burned between them in the short seconds of that kiss. Then he peeled off his coat and draped it around her shoulders, taking the second extinguisher from her while she slid her arms into the sleeves.

"I'll handle traffic." He was tall enough to be seen over several vehicles down the road. He pointed to the flames dripping beside his front tire and pooling against the curb. "Lay down some foam along the edge of the sidewalk. We can't let this spread beyond my truck. Stay where I can see you. The guy who started this fire could still be part of this crowd somewhere. Evan needs you."

"And I need you." With a nod, Corie went to work. "Be careful."

She was soon joined by two men who'd brought fire extinguishers from one of the local businesses. Matt heard her repeating his orders, directing the other volunteers as he stepped into traffic and warned the next vehicle to slow down and give the burning truck a wide berth. He directed the oncoming cars into a single lane and urged the eastbound vehicles to cross the yellow line and keep moving.

As soon as he saw the B shift crew from Firehouse 13 turn the corner, Matt exhaled a sigh of relief. Once the police arrived and took over traffic duty, he jogged forward to meet the team and give them a sit-rep. One of them threw a bunker coat around his shoulders, identifying him as the firefighter he was. He shooed away the medic who wanted to check him for injuries and directed her to the civilian volunteers who'd helped them fight the fire. The threat to his truck had been neutralized, but he was more concerned about the puddles of incendiary goo still burning inside the perimeter Corie and the two volunteers had laid down before running out of suppressant foam. They'd need a hazmat unit to clean up whatever chemical had been inside the bottle. And they'd need to secure a sample to send to the crime lab to compare to the samples from the other fires.

As a police officer approached him to take his statement, Matt turned to watch Corie huddling inside his coat, watching his crewmates go to work. There was little more than that wheat-colored ponytail showing above the collar. Every cell in his body wanted to go to her, but he needed to make a full report before the perp or perps went to ground and couldn't be located until the next fire or something worse.

It was that *something worse* that was turning him inside out with a sense of impending doom. This fire had been personal. A message to him—the clock was ticking, Corie belonged to another man, he'd never be able to protect her. Or something as crudely prophetic as the fire that had destroyed Enrique Maldonado's car—stop talking to the cops...or die.

The problem with an arsonist working as an enforcer and sending graphic messages like this one was that there was a huge risk for collateral damage. Jobs stolen. People injured. Lives lost.

Matt wanted an APB out on Kenny Norwell, Harve and Jordy, and that muscle car, along with the white van.

He wanted Corie and Evan in his arms now. Brave, beautiful Corie who wasn't afraid of hard work or of him, and her brave, smart son who missed no detail and cared so much about others. Matt needed to know they were safe. He needed to see Corie's smile again. Every day of his life.

He needed to admit that he was long past falling in love with the family who lived across the hall. The family who needed him.

The family who made him need things that no bullying wiseacres, ex-hubby arsonist or killer was going to take from him.

Chapter Eleven

"I want to stop on the sixth floor." Corie had her keys out as she and Matt waited for the elevator. "Knock on that bastard's door and look him right in the eye."

Matt cradled Evan's sleeping weight against his chest. "It's after one in the morning, Corie. What if it isn't him?"

"Then I will apologize profusely and come upstairs to live the rest of my life in shame and paranoia."

He didn't even try to hide that hint of a grin that creased the chocolatey-cinnamon stubble of his late-night beard. But the grin vanished as suddenly as it had appeared by the time they stepped onto the elevator. "What if it is your ex-husband? Do you have a plan for what you'll say or do when you see him? Do you really want him to see Evan?"

"I'm sure he already has!" she snapped, then immediately dropped her voice back to a whisper. "Evan is the only thing he ever wanted from me. If he's stalking me and you, then he's seen Evan with one or both of us. If Jeff and Kenny really are the same person, I want to know it. He was in my apartment, Matt. He sabotaged my kitchen to start a fire. He could challenge me for custody of Evan if a judge heard about that."

"He's a felon with a criminal record. No one is going to take your son from you legally. You're too good a mother for that. And I won't let them do it any other way." He loosed one arm from around Evan to hug her to his side and dropped a quick kiss to her lips. "All right. I'll go knock on his door. You get Evan to bed."

"No. I'm coming with you. Either I'd be alone with Evan upstairs or I'd be alone down here. I don't want to be alone if Kenny has found us."

His shoulders lifted with a stalwart sigh. "I don't want that, either. But you'll take Evan, and I'll take point so he has to get through me first. If he's there, you take Ev and run. Call 9-1-1. Ask for Cole Taylor. Ask for any Taylor. Help will come."

"What will you be doing while we're running?"

"Having a conversation. Your ex ever have a penchant for guns or knives I should worry about?"

She shook her head. "But he knows how to set fires in a dozen different ways."

"I know how to put out fires in a dozen different ways."

No doubt. "He's strong, Matt. He knows how to fight."

Matt glanced down the straight line of his nose and over the jut of his broad shoulder at her. Right. Matt was strong and knew how to fight, too. He'd made short work of Harve and Jordy tonight. And though she knew Kenny would be more skilled and aware than either of those numb nuts had been, she had a feeling Matt could hold his own in any situation.

She leaned into him, hoping she wasn't asking too much of this good man. "I just want to live a normal life. Raise a healthy, happy son who isn't always worried about the monster coming and him losing me. I want friends and more children. I want to teach and love and live the life that Kenny and my mother cheated me out of. I don't want to be afraid anymore."

"Evan's a smart kid. Stronger than you think. You're

stronger than you think. Besides, you've got that cool plastic dragon to protect you."

She giggled, patting the backpack that held Evan's creation, but her laugh was a wry sound that revealed more despair than humor. "You're our real protection dragon, Matt. You're big and strong and can harness the fire."

"I thought dragons were the bad guys until I met you two." His big yawn seemed to startle him. But Matt shook off his fatigue and stood up straighter, reaching across the elevator to push the number six button. "All right. We'll knock on our neighbor's door. If he was near the diner when we were and threw that Molotov cocktail, he won't be asleep, anyway."

A minute later, Corie was hefting her sleeping boy into her arms, along with his backpack and hers looped over either shoulder. Although he was slenderly built, Evan was a growing boy. She knew what a treat it was to have Matt literally shoulder some of the parenting burden from her. "I've got him," she assured him, reaching around Matt to knock on the door and start this meeting that was making the nerves roil in her stomach.

No answer.

Matt knocked. "Mr. Caldwell? It's Matt Taylor from the fire department." He put his ear to the door and knocked again, each time a little louder. "I don't think he's home."

A door opened across the hallway behind them and a woman in her pajamas and robe and a hot-pink scarf wrapped around her head peered through the gap between the door and jamb. "I know it's Friday night, folks. But do you know how late it is?"

Matt tipped the brim of the KCFD ball cap to her. "Yes, ma'am, I do."

She huffed at that answer and pulled her flowery robe

more securely around her. "Well, some of us have to work on the weekend. Keep it down out here."

Corie stepped in when Matt's straight-to-the-point communication technique failed. She pointed to number 612. "Do you know Mr. Caldwell? Mr. Stinson's part-time super? I'm Corie McGuire, your neighbor from upstairs."

"Jeff keeps to himself. I like that about him." Not-so-subtle hint noted. The woman tipped her gaze up to Matt and frowned. Then she looked from Corie to her son dozing on her shoulder and frowned again. "He's up a little late, isn't he?"

Since they clearly weren't going to charm any information from this woman at this hour, Corie jumped on the first plausible lie that sprang to mind. "Yes, he is. That's why we're looking for Jeff. I've locked myself out of our apartment. He has keys."

The woman dropped her gaze to the keys dangling from Corie's fingers before arching the sternest eyebrow she'd ever seen. "I'm calling Mr. Stinson. He'll deal with you."

The door closed on Corie's thank-you.

"You're a terrible liar," Matt teased, easing Evan from her arms until the building super arrived.

"Yeah. But I'm getting us into the apartment, aren't I?"

Well, technically, Wally Stinson was getting them into Jeff Caldwell's apartment.

Mr. Stinson looked less than thrilled when he stepped off the elevator in a pair of slacks and a wool robe hastily pulled on over his pajamas. His ring of master keys jingled as he shuffled along, smoothing his comb-over into some semblance of coverage on top of his head. "This isn't your place, Mrs. McGuire. Yours either, Mr. Taylor." He glanced over at the door to 613. "Miss Alice wasn't too happy that your noise in the hallway woke her up."

Corie didn't point out that his noisy key ring jangled

more loudly than their knocking had. "It's vital that we speak to Mr. Caldwell. I think he broke into my apartment."

Wally frowned, debating whether or not her claim had any merit. "You said that before, that you think he jiggered with your oven."

"That's right."

"Any proof?"

Corie touched the door. "I think it's in here. I want to talk to him about it, but he isn't answering."

Mr. Stinson pushed his glasses up on the bridge of his nose. "That's because he works most nights at a distribution center. He only helps me during the day. Now y'all go on about your business and let the good people in this building get some sleep."

"That's even better." Corie darted in front of him to stop his retreat. "We could go in there without him knowing, see if any of my stuff is in there."

"I haven't gotten any complaints about other tenants being robbed." First this man had accused her son of setting fires, and now, like the woman in 613, he seemed to be calling her a liar. "Why would you think this man is stealing from you and messing with your things?"

She glanced over his head to Matt's steely expression. And when he nodded, Corie confessed what she suspected was true. "He's my ex-husband."

Wally's posture withered for a moment. "Ah, hell. I had no idea. We went through something like this with my daughter. Her no-account ex cleaned out every television and computer in the house when they were getting divorced. He pawned most of it." Wally gave her a pitying look and patted her shoulder as he changed direction and pulled out the key to unlock Jeff Caldwell's door. "If that's the case here, if he's taking or breaking your stuff,

I'll fire him on the spot. But like I said, he usually isn't here nights."

"Then this is the perfect time to look, right? Thank you, Mr. Stinson."

Mr. Stinson opened the door to a dark apartment. He turned on the light, and the place didn't look that much more welcoming, with a card table and chairs set up in the living room, and an old recliner facing a state-of-the-art television. There wasn't a single decoration or personal item anywhere.

Matt placed Evan back in her arms and led the way inside, his gaze constantly moving to take in every detail. "Doesn't look like he stays here much at all."

"Do you see what he took from you?" Mr. Stinson asked.

"What?" The super startled her from her inspection of a stack of porn magazines beside the recliner. He'd bought them retail. There was no subscription name or address on them. "There's hardly anything here."

"What did he take?"

Her sanity, peace of mind and well-being. But, of course, Mr. Stinson assumed a much more monetary reason for Kenny, er, Jeff, to be in her apartment. "Do you mind if we look around?"

"Your boyfriend already is."

Boyfriend. She really was getting used to having others link her and Matt together as a couple. She wondered if he minded.

She didn't. She didn't mind being linked to Matt Taylor at all.

"Corie." Matt's quiet tone filled her with more dread than a shouted warning would have. Hugging Evan tighter to her chest, she followed him to the kitchen. He put out his arm to keep her from moving any closer than the archway.

It didn't stop the sheer terror from reaching her, though. The place was a science lab and an engineering station all rolled into one. There were stained measuring cups and hot plates on the counters. Jars filled with that clear, yellowish sludge that had coated the hood of Matt's truck and bubbled the paint up and melted his windshield wipers as it had burned. The same goo they'd found in the alley fire and inside her oven. There was an open toolbox with pliers and screwdrivers and a tinier metal box that looked like it was filled with delicate dental tools. On the floor was a box of wires and technical equipment—packaged disposable cell phones, computer chips, something that looked like bundles of firecrackers. On the opposite counter, there was a stash of three whiskey bottles whose labels matched the one that had shattered against Matt's truck. There were diagrams stuck to the refrigerator with magnets. There was a picture mounted there, too.

A well-worn, often-touched, picture of Evan when he'd turned one. They'd gone to the photography studio that day after Kenny had made her redress their son in a suit and Velcro tie instead of the cute baby blue overalls she'd put him in. There was a big *D* in the picture behind the posed shot—a *D* for Danny Norwell.

Even though he was sound asleep, she cupped the back of her son's head and turned him from the disturbing sight. The tears that stung her eyes were angry, fierce. This was her old life, the one she thought she'd escaped from. "This is Kenny. He used to have a setup like this in our garage back in St. Louis."

"Who's Kenny?" Mr. Stinson asked.

"Jeff, of course," she hastily corrected herself. "I guess he goes by Jeff now."

Matt had his cell phone out, snapping pictures. "I'm calling Uncle Cole. He and Agent Rand will definitely want to see this." He turned her toward the living room. "Stay here. I want to check out the rest of the place. Mr. Stinson, you'll stay here and watch her."

Although issued as an order, not a request, the older man nodded.

"We'll be fine," Corie assured him. "Just be careful."

Once Matt headed down the hall to the other rooms, Mr. Stinson pulled out one of the folding chairs for her, but she was too keyed up to relax. Not here. Not with evidence that pointed to the arson fires Matt had been forced to deal with. "Is this a meth lab?" the older man asked, nodding toward the kitchen.

"Something like." One thing Kenny had never whipped up in the garage was drugs. He'd always said he needed a clear head to work with the compounds he did create for clients who wanted a job done a certain way. "Some of those chemicals are combustible and flammable."

"What would he need those for?" Wally asked.

"Starting fires."

"Not in my building. He… I never knew any of this was here." Mr. Stinson ran his fingers through what was left of his thinning hair. "He knew his way around electricity, carpentry, plumbing—all of it. I played poker with him and a couple of his buddies one night."

"A couple of his buddies?" Corie almost sank in the chair as her knees wobbled beneath the weight of her suspicion. But she had Evan in her arms. She needed to be strong. Smart. Smarter than Kenny. "Does one of them have a dark, almost black beard? The other is tatted up. He's a redhead with freckles."

Wally nodded. "Yeah. Harve and—"

"Jordy."

He seemed surprised that she knew the men's names. Hell, she was surprised to know such things. Corie didn't know whether to be angry or feel foolish that she'd been in the dark about the danger creeping into the corners of her life for so long. "Do you know their last names?"

Wally scratched his head again, sorting through memories. "Jeff Caldwell, of course. Jordan Cox—we made a few jokes about his name. And Harve..." He snapped his fingers as the name fell into place. "Harve Mohrman. He told me he met Jeff in—"

"Jefferson City?" Prison. Harve and Jordy were prison buddies of Kenny's. Even Kenny's alias was a nod to his stay in the pen. Jeff Caldwell? Jeff City? Jeff C?

"Yeah. How did you know?"

Matt reappeared from the hallway, a dangerous purpose to his stride. "We need to go."

"Why? What did you see?"

He scooped Evan from her arms to hurry her along. "We may be disturbing a crime scene."

Something was wrong. Something was very wrong.

"What is it? A dead body?" Something worse than that? Something about her? Evan?

"Corie..."

She evaded his outstretched hand and hurried down the hallway, peeking into the first bedroom, the bathroom, ending up in the bedroom that was located where hers would be on the floor above them. As she entered the room, a sudden shock of cold seeped through her coat and clothes and chilled her skin.

But there was no window open. In the middle of January, there was no air-conditioning running.

It was the room itself, filled with hate and vengeance and the kind of obsession found only in horror and serial killer movies.

The smell got to her first. Something burned and pungent, like incense or a hundred scented candles. There was no furniture in the room besides a table and chair and a cardboard box that looked suspiciously like the one she'd set outside on her fire escape for the neighborhood cats.

Three of the four walls were a sick shrine to her. Pictures from her wedding to Kenny. Pictures from her childhood. Pictures of her waiting at the bus stop near Pearl's Diner, sitting on a bench on campus talking to a professor, monitoring recess duty at her school. There were pictures and newspaper clippings of fires, the shells of burned-out buildings, fiery car crashes and the charred remains of bodies. The images papered the walls and were decorated with bits of yarn pinned to the walls. Burned matches and broken lighters, even a perfume-size bottle of that flammable goo, hung from different strings. Spray painted over the collage of pictures were words and phrases like *child-stealer*, *kill the witch* and worse.

The fourth wall was tainted simply by being in the room with all the angry, vile images. It held pictures of Evan. Formal ones from when he was very young to candid shots of him on the playground at school here in Kansas City and one of him standing in the bed of Matt's truck, illuminated only by a streetlamp. If the kitchen had been the workspace of an arsonist, then this was his place of worship.

Corie couldn't move. She couldn't think, couldn't feel.

She could only startle when Matt walked into the room behind her, thankfully, having left Evan resting someplace where he couldn't see this. "Looks like he's been using the fire escape to go up to your apartment. That's possibly how he got in and out of your place."

It hadn't been a noisy alley cat pacing on her balcony. Kenny had been there, right outside her bedroom window, and she'd never even suspected.

There was so much hate, so much obsession in this

room. She didn't know whether to scream or cry or simply surrender to the inevitable.

"Come on, sweetheart. Nobody needs to see this except the police." Matt turned her into his arms and walked her out of the room.

She leaned into him, grateful for his strength and support. "I never had a chance of living a normal life when I left Kenny, did I."

Chapter Twelve

Another two hours had passed by the time Detective Cole Taylor and NCIS agent Rand had finished their interviews and left Corie's apartment to go back down to apartment 612, where a team from the crime lab was processing the evidence in the elusive Jeff Caldwell's apartment and members of the KCFD were safely packaging and removing the flammable chemicals and fire-starting devices her ex-husband had kept there.

They were as certain Jeff Caldwell was Kenny Norwell as she was, although no one could find him. And they were certain he was the man a mobster named Chad Meade had hired to do some jobs for him, including torching a car and a building and covering up the scene of a murder. Cole Taylor and his NCIS partner had left discussing the possibility of Kenny turning state's evidence against Meade.

If they could capture him.

If he didn't find another way to hide himself in plain sight and never be found again.

Matt's uncle had also promised a round-the-clock watch on their building while his parents, brothers, sisters-in-law and extended family members she'd lost track of stopped by to bring food, offer a place to stay and trade hugs, handshakes and promises of support that extended to Corie and her son…because Matt said they were important to him.

Corie had never seen such an outpouring of love before. Certainly, the Taylors were nothing like life with her family or Kenny had been. She'd met so many Taylors, she couldn't remember all their names, much less put faces to which branch of the family belonged with whom. But each and every one of them had made her feel as welcome as Mark and Amy had the other night. Like she was a part of something bigger than herself. Part of that family she'd always wanted. An extended family where she could let her son visit a grandparent and know he would be safe and nurtured and loved in a way Kenny and her mother never could.

While the outpouring of love and support had gone a long way to help her bury the images from Kenny's *kill the witch* room, she had no doubt Kenny was targeting her now, tormenting her for his own pleasure or because he wanted her off her guard, giving him an opportunity to steal back the son he'd accused her of taking and punishing her for daring to want something better, safer, more loving than the world that Kenny and his crime buddies offered.

Somewhere along the way, Corie had gotten her second wind. Anything she could do to help the police helped Evan, and she'd do anything for her son. She'd brewed several pots of coffee and served up multiple snacks brought by each of her guests. With all the comings and goings, no matter how quiet they'd tried to be, Evan had awakened at two thirty. He'd eagerly talked to Pike Taylor, petted his K-9 partner, Hans, and arranged a tentative play date with Pike's son, Gideon. He'd carried his plastic dragon with him the entire time he'd joked with Mark and Amy and played host to their indulgent guests.

She would carry the fear, the sense of impending doom for them both. Seeing her son so happy tonight was worth anything she'd gone through in her life—and anything that was yet to come.

But now that all the Taylors were gone, save for one tall, overbuilt firefighter who she feared would give his life to protect her and Evan, she had a different problem on her hands.

Matt was exhausted. He'd hinted at having a rough day on the job, and she suspected that was the reason he'd been so late getting to the diner in the first place. As he hugged his mother and father and locked the door behind them, Matt leaned back against the door and exhaled a deep breath. He looked haggard and tired—always incredibly strong—but now suddenly vulnerable somehow. He'd done so much for her, so much for Evan. Maybe now he'd let her do something for him.

Corie crossed the room. She watched him breathe in deeply and open his eyes to give her one of those almost-there smiles before she reached up to gently cup his stubbled jaw. "You smell good," he murmured in a husky voice.

"And you look exhausted. Come with me." She linked her arm through his and walked him over to her sofa. "You've been this big presence hovering around the room all night, keeping watch. Now it's your turn to relax and regain some of your strength. Sit. I'm taking watch over this apartment tonight."

He folded his long legs and sat back against the cushions, although his dark, hungry gaze never left her. "Corie—"

"No." She placed a finger over his firm lips, silencing whatever protest he was about to make. "I don't remember which brother it was, but they promised that someone would be watching the building all night. I'm in charge inside these walls. You can drop your guard for a little while and rest."

"I *am* beat," he admitted, his lips brushing like a caress against her fingertip. "But I can't shake the feeling that there's something more I could be doing to stop this maniac and protect you."

"Atonement?" She nudged his knees apart and moved between them to sit on his lap. It put her in the rare position of being eye level with him, and she made the most of it by leaning forward to press a lingering kiss against his lips. His hands tightened on her thigh and hip as he sighed against her mouth and then deepened the kiss. Although his deliciously languid possession of her mouth kindled the good kind of fire deep inside her belly and made her breasts feel heavy with anticipation, she also suspected his leisurely response spoke to his fatigue. The man had a physical job. He'd had a physical night putting Harve and Jordy in their place and dealing with his truck. Then there was the emotional roller coaster of discovering Kenny's dangerous workspace and heinous obsession room. Plus, for a man who leaned to the introverted, quieter side of things, dealing with all the police and family and firefighters who'd been in the building these past two hours had probably taken a toll on him. She wondered if *exhaustion* was a strong enough word for what he was feeling right now.

And so, because this was about what Matt needed, and not the deliciously sinful and cherished way his mouth and hands made her feel, she broke off the kiss and tipped his head to gently press her lips to the shadows beneath each handsome eye. Then she hugged him close and whispered against his ear. "You don't owe me anything. You don't owe anyone another piece of your heart and soul and protection and dedication. You've repaid the price for that fire you set as a child a hundred times over. Set your crusade aside for a few minutes and let someone take care of you for a change."

His hands rubbed big circles up and down her back. "Corie, sweetheart, you don't have to do anything."

She pulled away, hating that he saw their relationship in such one-sided terms. Yes, he was incredibly strong and smart and just and wonderful, but he needed to understand that she intended to be an equal partner in this neighbors–turned–friends–turned something infinitely more precious that had grown between them. Kenny had kept her—like a trophy, like breeding stock. But he hadn't loved her, and he'd destroyed any effort to love him.

Matt Taylor was too good a man to feel like he still owed the world a debt. "I don't *have* to do anything. But I want to." She scooted off his lap and pushed him back into the cushions when he tried to stand with her. "Now. What do you need?" She didn't have a lot to offer, but she would grant him whatever he asked. "Something to eat? Drink? I've got cold milk or apple juice. Or I can make more coffee. Sorry, I don't have anything stronger. Do you need a quiet place to sleep for a while?"

He grabbed her hand, stopping her from going into the kitchen. His gaze raked over her from head to toe, stopping with particular interest on her mouth and breasts, telling her one thing he wanted. One thing she would willingly give him.

But then Evan dashed into the living room, reminding them both they weren't alone. "Are you going to bed, Matt?" Evan asked, jumping onto the sofa beside his favorite hero. "Mom said it's *way* past my bedtime. Is it past yours?"

"Yeah, bud. Your mom was just telling me that I need to get some shut-eye."

Evan looked crestfallen. "Oh. You're going back to your apartment now? You're leaving?"

Matt glanced up at Corie, and she answered the question he hadn't even asked. "He's staying with us tonight, sweetie."

"Yay!" Evan's cheer was cut off by a yawn that Matt quickly echoed.

Corie squeezed her son's shoulders. "Come on. Let's get you into bed so Matt can get the sleep he needs, too."

"Okay. 'Night, Matt." Evan fell forward across Matt's chest, winding his arms around his neck.

Matt's long arms gently completed the hug. "Good night."

Evan sat back, his eyes narrowed in an earnest frown. "Do you want my dragon to keep the bad things away for a while? I put his wings back on him and fixed his face."

Matt squeezed Evan to his chest again and brushed a kiss against his soft brown hair. "Nah. You keep him with you tonight. But thanks for havin' my back. Love you."

"Love you, too." And then Evan bounced off the couch and ran to his room, heedless of the two wide-eyed adults staring after him.

After the door to Evan's room closed, Matt glanced up to Corie. "Is that okay? He really does mean a lot to me. He…feels like family."

Corie smiled as the lingering warmth from Matt's kiss expanded to bathe her heart in sunshine. "I'm very okay with that. After all, if you're going to be in a relationship with me, you're going to be in a relationship with my son. And I can't think of a finer role model for him."

Although she sensed that he wanted to ask what she meant by *relationship*, Corie focused on the offer she'd made. "Close your eyes and rest, Matt. It'll take me ten minutes to get Evan back to sleep. Then I'll come back and slice you another piece of that pie if you want."

His dark lashes were already brushing his cheeks as she chastely kissed the top of his head and hurried after Evan. "Don't you worry about us—or anything else—for ten minutes. That's an order."

By the time Evan had dozed off and she'd changed into her pajamas and brushed her teeth, Matt was sound asleep on the couch. His long frame was spread out with his feet hanging off one end of the couch and his head angled up on the armrest at the other. His staunch expression that was more serious than handsome while he was awake had relaxed in slumber, easing the harsh line of his mouth. This rare glimpse of boyish abandon invited her to run her fingers across the crisp dark hair at his temple and press a kiss there.

She was glad she could do this little thing for him, giving him a quiet sanctuary free from worry and guilt, even if just for a few minutes. Because she was certain there was plenty to worry about in their future, judging by Kenny's vindictive behavior and the promise of his own personal retribution plastered across the bedroom walls below hers.

Even though this was a different apartment, and her door and windows here had been checked multiple times by Matt and at least three brothers and an uncle, the last place she wanted to go was her own room. Not alone, at any rate. Not by the fire escape window, where they suspected Kenny had lurked on at least one occasion. Corie feared that if she went into her bedroom and closed her eyes, all she would see were the vile, violent things on the walls right below hers.

Shaking off that unpleasant thought, she checked the front door to make sure it was secure. She needed sleep, too. Her bedroom might feel off-limits, but there was a cushy chair out here where she often fell asleep reading a book. After turning off the lamp, Corie retrieved a couple of throws from the hall closet. She came back to untie Matt's boots and tug them off as quietly as she could without waking him. Then she spread one of the throws over his sleeping body.

He'd earned his rest. He'd earned her gratitude and admiration. He'd earned her trust and compassion. She tucked a pillow beneath his head and kissed his grizzled cheek. Even though she smelled the soap from his shower, she still detected a whiff of the smoke from the fires he'd fought today and tonight. It felt so right, having him here. It was reassuring to know he was safe, too. For a little while, at least. She thought of him as the embodiment of security. But tonight, she would be the one to give him shelter. She would be what he needed tonight. Something tight and guarded unfurled in her chest as she gazed down at the man whose face was softened by the shadows.

She really had fallen for this good man.

Maybe she hadn't been as careful with the boots as she'd thought. Maybe this alert, wary man had simply sensed her presence. Or maybe she'd projected her wish into his head.

Before she turned away, Matt grabbed her hand and pulled her onto the couch with him. "I guess I needed a little more than ten minutes. Is this okay?" he asked, snaking his arm around her waist and pulling her back against his chest, spooning behind her. "I'll go back to my own apartment if you want."

"You're not going anywhere," she said as he pulled the blanket over them both. The heat of his body snugged so closely to hers quickly made her drowsy. This was bliss, to feel so important, so warm and wanted by a man. This was the dream she'd always had about finding the right man, and she drifted slowly, contentedly toward that dream.

But then Matt suddenly tensed behind her, his breath a sharp huff against the nape of her neck. "Dead bolt?"

Corie laughed and turned in his arms. "Already taken care of."

There wasn't much room to maneuver on the couch, but she ended up flat on her back, smiling up at his confused expression. "What did I say?"

"*Dead bolt.* I think it's becoming my code word that means you care. You say it to me every night when you leave."

He feathered his fingers through her loose hair, smiling down at her. "So, I don't have to come up with flowery words or recite any poetry to impress you?"

She grinned at the joke. "I don't think that's your style. It's not mine, either. I like honest and straightforward."

His eyes were dark, pools of midnight in the shadows above her. "I saw a man die in front of me tonight. Plunged to his death and there wasn't a damn thing I could do to save him." His fingers tightened briefly against her scalp and then he was rolling back against the cushions, his arm thrown over his eyes. Tears pricked her own eyes at the pain in his voice. "A little too honest and straightforward, hmm? Sorry about that."

Corie turned into him, hugging him tightly. "Oh, Matt, I'm so sorry. Why didn't you say anything?"

"I was a little preoccupied tonight."

"Taking care of my troubles when you had your own." She pressed a kiss to the warm skin above his collar, stretched against him to tickle her lips against his stubbled neck and sup on the strong beat of his pulse there. "What do you need? How can I help?"

She nibbled on the point of his chin before batting his arm away from his face and crawling right on top of him to reach his mouth and offer him the gentle absolution of

her kiss. Her legs parted and tangled with his, sliding between his muscular thighs, already discovering the respon-
sive hardness behind the zipper of his jeans. The nap of
her flannel bottoms caught against the denim and muscle
underneath, creating pockets of vivid awareness where the
material caught and pulled against her skin.

His lips chased after hers as she moved to explore the
hard line of his jaw and the surprisingly supple spot beneath his ear that seemed to be packed with a bundle of
nerves that made him gasp for breath. She rode the rise
and fall of his chest as Matt sucked in several deep breaths
to control his responses to her bold exploration. "I'm not
good at explaining what I feel. What I need."

"Then show me."

At last, his arms settled around her again. He branded
her butt with the palm of his hand and pulled her fully on
top of him, dragging her most sensitive places against the
hard friction of his body. Giving him the freedom to express himself without words seemed to unleash something
powerful and hungry inside him.

With a ragged breath that sounded like her own needy
moan, he palmed the back of her head and held her mouth
against his, feasting on her lips, demanding she open for
him before his tongue swept inside to claim hers. With her
body draped over his like a blanket, they didn't need the
throw she'd brought from the closet. They were already
generating all the heat either of them could need. The
throw quickly landed on the floor beside them, and the
knit pajama top she wore followed right behind it.

Matt's hands were firebrands against her bare skin, urging her toward a euphoric release she'd never experienced
before. She found the hem of his sweater and T-shirt and
tugged them up his torso. Her hands were equally greedy
as they slid inside to explore his strong, wide chest. She

felt a quiver of muscle here, the tickle of crisp curls of hair there. The turgid male nub poking to attention beneath the stroke of her fingers.

Her world rocked in a dizzying circle as Matt suddenly sat up, spilling Corie into his lap. She helped him peel off his shirt and sweater, and then she slipped back in his arms, the heat of skin against skin making her feverish with desire. Making love with Kenny had never lasted this long, much less driven her into this frenzy of need, the eagerness to pleasure, this pure delight in being pleasured.

He lifted her slightly and dipped his head to pull the tip of her breast into his mouth. "Matt," she gasped, unfamiliar with the fiery arrows zinging from her sensitive nipples down to the weepy heaviness between her legs. "Is this…? Are we…?"

"I want you." She clawed her fingers into his hair, holding his wicked mouth against her straining breast as he worked the pebbled nipple between his tongue and lips and teeth and squeezed the other breast in his hand. "I want you," he repeated on a husky moan against her skin.

She had no problem understanding what he needed from her. Corie hoped she was being equally clear. "I'm yours."

To hell with atonement. This brave, good man needed healing, not penance. He needed to believe that whatever he'd done as a child did not make him the man he was today. He needed to know that he was perfect and loved. In her arms, he was most assuredly loved.

"Floor okay?" he breathed against her mouth before reclaiming her lips. "Need…more space."

Corie's answer was to lean back over the edge of the couch and pull Matt with her. They toppled onto the floor together, her landing eased by the rug and blanket and the support of Matt's arm. Then there was a fumble of hands, both eager and out of practice, as they shed the remainder of their clothes and pulled a condom from Matt's wallet. But every touch was a heady arousal, every bump was a perfect caress.

Then Matt was on top of her, sliding into her. Corie closed her eyes to savor her body's pure, primal response to his weight making the pressure building inside her almost unbearable. But he was holding himself back, balancing himself on his arms when she wanted to feel all of him against her.

Her eyes fluttered open and she caught him grimacing at the struggle being so patient with her was costing him. "Matt." She framed his face between her hands, ran them over his shoulders. She linked her heels around his hips. "Let go, Matt. Don't hold back. You're safe with me." She arched her body up into his. Her head fell back as he sank deeper inside her and began to move. As he took her to the peak and they crashed over together, Corie hugged him tight with her arms and her legs. "And I'm safe with you."

Sometime later, after redressing in a layer of clothes in case Evan should awaken early and find them together, Corie and Matt were spooning again on the couch, cocooned by the warmth of the blankets and each other's bodies. The weight of Matt's arm was a possessive band around her waist, but she didn't feel trapped. The tension that had consumed him earlier had eased, leaving her feeling cherished and necessary, not used the way sex with Kenny had been.

This was how it was supposed to be between a man and a woman.

Matt's body was a furnace at her back as he brushed her hair off her neck and whispered against her ear. "Dead bolt."

And as sleep rose to claim her, she smiled and closed her eyes. "I love you, too."

SMOKE.

Matt blinked his eyes open to the darkness of early dawn, unsure if the haze in his vision was due to the hangover of sleep deprivation or if something more was going on here. When he had slept, he'd slept deeply, contentedly. But two hours wasn't nearly long enough. Corie's couch was half a foot too short for his long body, as the stiffness in his neck would attest to.

But Corie herself was a dream. The woman liked to snuggle in close as she slept in his arms, either teasing him with the pillowed mounds of her lush breasts flattened against his chest, or rubbing that sweet, round bottom against his groin. The weight of her in his arms had given him a subconscious sense of reassurance that she was safe—and an arousal that had led to a second, more leisurely, yet no less incendiary round of lovemaking following that cathartic, healing tumble onto the rug where she'd encouraged him to be his big, bad self with her and let his fears and guilt and haunting memories of a boy who had never been enough be consumed by their mutual passion.

He loved Corie McGuire. He hadn't said those exact words, but he'd felt them. He'd shown her.

Did she understand?

And then the reality of the moment slammed through him like shots from a gun and he sat up, wide-awake.

He was alone. Her apartment was filled with smoke.

His nose never lied. Where was the fire?

"Corie?" Matt tossed the blanket aside and stepped into his boots. He'd lace them up later. Right now, he needed to understand what was going on here, and he needed to find her. He grabbed his wrinkled sweater and slipped it on over his T-shirt and jeans. "Corie!"

"In here." A true mother, she'd run into Evan's room first and woken him. Rubbing the sleep from his eyes, the boy was groggy, hopefully from being unexpectedly roused from bed and not from smoke inhalation.

Matt knelt in front of him, checking for any signs of pulmonary distress. "Take a deep breath for me, bud." No coughing fit. He squeezed Evan's shoulder as he stood, telling him everything would be all right. Then he reached over to cup the side of Corie's neck and jaw, sifting his fingers into the heavy silk of her hair. "You?"

"I'm fine." She pointed toward the kitchen. "Why didn't the smoke alarm go off?"

He wanted the answer to that question, too. But whys were for later. "Shoes, jeans on both of you now. We're evacuating until I know what's going on."

Corie steered Evan back into his room. "Winter coats?" He nodded.

While they dressed, Matt called it in and made a quick tour of her apartment. In the kitchen he found that the smoke detector had no battery in it. It didn't take any stretch of the imagination to believe Kenny Norwell had entered the apartment again at some point to sabotage Corie's safety protocols. But if he was so hell-bent on getting his son back, why would he endanger Evan like this?

There was a bigger game being played here, and Matt worried he was already a step behind whatever Norwell had planned.

Protecting Corie and Evan was still job one. The police and his father's arson team could work on taking down Chad Meade and his firebug for hire—Matt's focus was much closer to home.

But he couldn't find an ignition point from any of the usual suspects—appliances, electrical outlets, improperly stored chemicals. The floor in Corie's bedroom felt spongy as he jogged across it to check the fire escape. Flames and smoke were pouring out of the window right below Corie's, blocking their descent. He didn't need a degree in fire science to understand what was happening.

He closed the door behind him and ran to the living room, gathering Corie and Evan and leading them straight to the door, where they all put on their coats. Corie looped her bag over her shoulder, and Evan had grabbed his most prized possession—his dragon.

"The apartment below yours is on fire," he said, helping Evan zip up that too-tight coat of his.

Corie pulled a stocking cap over Evan's head. "Mr. Caldwell's... Kenny set his own place on fire?"

Matt checked the door to make sure it was safe to open, then ushered them both into the hallway. The smoke wasn't as thick here, but the haze hanging in the air told him it was seeping upward through every available vent, crack or open window. The flames would follow soon enough.

"We need to evacuate this floor and everything above us."

Corie nodded and jogged to the fire alarm on the wall. But when she pulled it, nothing happened. "This isn't working, either."

Matt ran to the far end of the hall and tried that alarm. Silence. Corie's ex had been very thorough.

He pounded on each door he passed, "Fire! KCFD, you need to evacuate. Fire!" A few doors opened immediately, and Matt repeated his orders. "Make sure your neighbors get out."

He rejoined Corie and Evan and guided them toward the stairwell, doing his best to ignore the twin sets of green eyes that were so wide with fear. "You need to get out of here, too. Stay off the elevator. Take the emergency stairs."

Corie grabbed a fistful of his coat. "What about you?"

"I'm a firefighter, sweetheart. I need to do my job. And I need to know you two are safe so I can do that job right."

Her grip tightened on his coat and she pulled him down to exchange a quick, hard kiss. "Do it well. We need you."

He walked them down to the sixth-floor landing, intending to part ways. He wanted to check out Norwell's apartment and get the other residents on the floor evacuated.

But a determined eight-year-old blocked his path. "I want to stay with you." Evan hugged his dinosaur in his arms. "I'm not afraid."

Matt went down on one knee in front of Evan and hunkered lower to look him in the eye. "You're the bravest boy I know, bud. But you need to respect the fire. Get your mom outside and the two of you stay together until I can reach you. Can you do that for me?" A familiar inspiration hit him, and he unbuckled his watch and strapped it onto Evan's wrist. "Here. Set the timer for ten minutes. I'll be down to join you by then."

"Ten minutes? Dragon swear?"

Matt crossed his heart. "Now go."

Hand in protective hand, the two most cherished people in the world to him walked away. Matt hurried onto the sixth floor, relieved to hear the blare of sirens in the distance. He knocked on doors and scooted the startled residents out to the emergency exits. He stopped when he reached the bowed door of apartment 612. The crime scene tape crisscrossing the door had been sliced through. He heard the rumble of something on the other side, like the whooshing ebb and flow of the tide rising along the beach. He knew that sound—heat, pressure, flames filling the confined space. This whole area was about to blow.

The snooty lady across hall was only too happy to have him knocking on doors now. As he turned her to follow her neighbors to the exit stairs, Matt tried to reason out why Norwell would torch his own apartment. KCPD and the crime lab had already been in there to gather evidence against him. The fire endangered his son. An explosion could destabilize the building's structure, bringing it down on all of them, killing anyone who couldn't get out.

The evacuation.

Matt swore. This was all about getting Evan and Corie out in the open. It was about hiding in a crowd distracted by noise and fear.

It was about kidnapping his son. Again.

Matt pulled out his phone to call Corie to warn her.

And that's when he heard the man screaming for help. From apartment 612.

"Help me! Somebody, help!"

Matt's heart sank. He had no choice. People before property. And he wasn't going to have another Enrique Maldonado flinging himself off a balcony because he couldn't escape the flames and smoke.

Matt texted his brother Mark, told him his location and what he was about to do. Then he steeled himself with a deep breath, prepared himself for the blast of heat, and kicked in the door. Fire literally poured out into the hallway as the man's screams turned to gratitude. "Hey, it's the boyfriend. Help me. Please."

In between hacking coughs, he recognized the man's voice. Jordan Cox. For half a second, Matt thought about turning around and running downstairs to Corie instead of rescuing this worthless piece of trash. But he'd already notified his team that he was going in, and they'd risk their lives looking for *him* if he didn't show up where he said he'd be.

He hoped his boots were thick enough to protect him from this walk through hell. "Shut up and do what I tell you this time," he commanded, racing into the searing heat and toxic fumes. "You take in more smoke if you talk."

The damn fool wouldn't listen. While Matt pulled out

his pocketknife and cut Jordy free of the duct tape he'd been bound with, the redheaded bully prattled on. "He said he didn't need my help anymore, that I was a liability. He said he could kill two birds with one stone. Please don't let me die."

Despite a blow to the head, probably to subdue him long enough to bind him to the chair, Jordan seemed aware and ambulatory. Still, he'd never make it through this fiery sludge in those tennis shoes. Since time was of the essence, there was no debate. Matt put his shoulder to Jordy's midsection, secured his arms and legs and lifted him up in a fireman's carry.

With flames melting the carpet and igniting the wood subfloor in the hallway now, Matt carried the smaller man to the exit stairs. There he set him down, but clamped a hand around Jordy's arm, partly to keep the man standing and moving through every cough, and partly because he intended to hand him over to the first police officer they met once they got outside.

On the third floor, he asked, "Did Norwell hire you to harass Corie?"

"Yes, sir."

"Why?"

"'Cause he's pissed at her for taking his son. He wanted us to rough her up, scare her a little. He said he was too busy to do all the work himself." On the second floor, Jordy tried to apologize. "He doesn't like that you're in the picture. He said he had to change his plans once you got involved."

"Do you know his plans now?"

Jordy shied away, knowing Matt wouldn't like his answer. "Keep the kid. Kill your girlfriend."

"Move."

The air was cold when they made it outside, but it was

also clean. Matt sucked two deep breaths of reviving air into his lungs. Most of the cops out here were managing traffic and crowd control, but he got rid of Jordy and started his search to find the McGuires.

He found the building super first. "Stinson! You got a list of tenants we can go through to confirm that everyone has evacuated?"

The older man pulled it up on his phone and started checking people off.

Where was the woman with hair the color of a ripe wheat field and whose smile lit up his heart? And that spunky little boy who was everything Matt could want in a child of his own?

He skimmed the crowd again, his training not allowing the man in him to panic. He even glanced at the passersby pausing their morning walks and commutes to work to ogle the drama of lights and fire engines and flames and dark smoke pouring out the sixth-floor window. They should have made it down and out through the exit stairs ahead of him. The tension in his neck corded up with the very worst of warnings and he ran back to Stinson. "Where are Corie and Evan?"

"They aren't with you?"

"I sent them down ten minutes ago."

The balding man scrolled through the list on his phone. There were no checks beside the tenants of apartment 712. "I haven't seen them."

When he spotted a familiar white van parked against the curb halfway down the block, Matt ran to it. "Corie! Ev!"

Inside, he found a remote arson lab with nearly all the same ingredients and equipment Norwell had kept in his apartment. He also found Harve Mohrman unconscious and bleeding from a head wound. Was he supposed to suffer the same fate as his buddy Jordy? Had Norwell's attempt to kidnap Evan from the crowd outside their burning building failed? If so, where were Corie and Evan now? Or was leaving the van unlocked and in the open like this an impromptu attempt to frame Mr. Gross Beard for all the arson fires?

Matt stepped out of the van and made three calls, summoning a medic to treat Mohrman, a cop to arrest him, and Corie's cell.

It went straight to voice mail. Again.

And then he saw the black muscle car, already three blocks down, darting through the growing crowd of rush-hour traffic, speeding away. The damn van was one more misdirection giving Norwell more time to get away with his prize.

Not this time. Matt wasn't sure what to do next. He couldn't afford getting caught by another diversion. He'd lose all trace of Norwell before he got down to his truck in the parking garage. If Norwell had Corie, she was as good as dead. If he had Evan, the boy was as good as gone.

No. No way. He'd lost one family in a fire. He wouldn't lose another.

He spotted Kyle Redding's white scene commander helmet and ran. "Captain!" Then he saw the engine parked farthest from the scene and changed direction. When he saw the Lucky 13 logo on the side, he kissed it with his hand and climbed inside behind the wheel. He hadn't understood all of the changes that had happened in his life this past week, but he knew one thing very, very well.

He turned the key over in the ignition, and the engine's powerful motor roared to life.

But Redding had chased after him, grabbing the door before Matt could close it. "Taylor! What are you doing with my engine? You're supposed to be off the clock today."

"Take it out of my paycheck, boss." The car was still in

sight but getting farther away. If it turned a corner or crested a hill… "Ignition point is apartment 612. Flames are in the hallway encroaching on the apartment above it." Corie's apartment. "I've got a secondary emergency, sir. Let me go."

His brother Mark was there, too, opening the passenger side and climbing in. "Come on, bro. Talk to us. What's wrong?"

"He took them."

"Corie's ex? He took the kid, too?"

Matt turned on the lights and siren. He'd clear a path through traffic and get to them quicker this way. "Call Cole and Rand. Tell them I've got a bead on Norwell. Give them the GPS on my engine and follow me."

"I'll handle the tracking," Redding insisted, climbing down and calling dispatch. "You're on my orders, Taylor," Redding said, giving Matt the backup he needed to keep his job. Stealing a fire engine for a personal mission tended to get one fired. And jailed. "Go find this guy who's burning up my city and give him hell."

"Captain?"

"I had a woman I loved once, too." He tapped the door of the truck, signaling Matt he was clear to move out before striding away. "Go! I want that arsonist behind bars."

Instead of jumping down, Mark put a helmet on Matt's head and tossed a coat around his shoulders. "You don't have to do this, Mark."

His baby brother grinned. "Hell yeah, I do. We're a team, remember? We have been since the day I was born." He smacked Matt's shoulder the same way Captain Redding had tapped the truck. "Lucky 13 rolling."

Chapter Thirteen

Corie woke up to throbbing headache and the coppery taste of blood in her mouth.

A pungent chemical smell hung in the air, stinging her sinuses, and making her eyes water. But when she reached up to wipe the tears from her cheeks, a sharp pain tore at her wrists, pulling out some of the hair and bruising her skin. What the…?

Crystal clarity returned with a vengeance and she sat up straight. She was strapped to a rolling office chair, her wrists and ankles bound by duct tape. That same yellow-ish goo Matt had showed her from her oven fire had been painted in a large circle around her chair. Her clothes were damp with it, too.

Now she remembered the figure she'd seen in the smoke when she and Evan had been evacuating their apartment building. She'd assumed it was another resident following them down the stairs. But then he'd run up on her.

She'd known one frightening moment of recognition as the man's face cleared the smoke. Dark hair. Thick chest. Cold eyes. She'd instinctively pushed Evan behind her as Kenny's fist connected with her cheek, splitting it open and emptying out a bucket of ball bearings that swirled inside her skull. She fell to her knees as Evan screamed and reached out for her.

But Kenny got between them first, cupping his hand beneath the boy's chin. "Remember me, son?"

Evan backed into the corner of the stairwell landing, avoiding his father's touch. Since sentimentality hadn't worked to instantly win him over, Kenny went back to the tactics he knew best. He jerked Corie to her feet, the sudden movement doing nothing to help the concussion he'd probably given her. "Kenny, don't do this," she pleaded as the world spun in circles around her. "He doesn't know you. All you're doing is scaring him."

"Good. Then he'll understand." Kenny's grip tightened painfully on her arm, keeping her upright when she would have stumbled. "You do exactly as I say, Danny, or I will hit her again. Now come with me. And act like we're all just going for a nice little stroll."

Corie had barely made it to his fancy black car when the dizziness made her puke. She'd passed out in the back seat without knowing if her son was safe. Now, minutes? Hours? Sometime later, the very chemical that was supposed to kill her had acted like smelling salts and roused her to awareness.

She quickly took in her surroundings. Judging by the large louvered windows running the length of the walls, it looked like she was on an upper floor of a converted warehouse. She seemed to be smack-dab in the center in an open commons area. But on either side of her were cubicle walls, desks, papers. It was Saturday and these offices were closed. So, there were no employees she could call on for help.

She spotted Evan at one of the windows, kneeling on a stack of office chairs and looking out at something through the window that had been propped open. Under normal circumstances, she'd have been frightened to see him leaning so close to an open second-story window. But these circumstances were far from normal, and right now she was helpless to keep either of them safe. At least he had his dragon with him to give himself comfort. He hugged it to his chest and rocked back and forth.

Corie frowned as her vision cleared. No. He was picking the dragon apart, piece by piece, glancing over his shoulder to the cubicles on her right and then dropping the colorful plastic bricks one or two at a time out the window.

They both turned their heads to the sound of raised voices as two men argued behind one of the dividing cubicle walls.

"I said no moonlighting."

"I've done every job you've hired me to. The results have been satisfactory, yes?" She recognized Kenny's voice immediately.

"Yes. But I'm not paying you to screw with your ex-wife. You're drawing too much attention to my operation."

"You said you wanted this building burned to the ground. You don't get to say how I do it."

"I pay you good money to take care of my enemies."

"And I will. These boys will be in bankruptcy long before they think of horning in on your territory again. This job takes care of two problems—yours and mine." Corie heard footsteps and knew the men were on the move. "Now give it a rest, Meade."

Corie sat up as straight as her bindings allowed, trying to get a glimpse of whom Kenny was arguing with. Maybe she could convince that man to help her. Maybe he'd at least take Evan with him and drop him off at police station or firehouse. Maybe she had a chance to at least keep her son safe.

Her movement caught Evan's attention, and he saw that she was awake. "Mom!"

He jumped down from the stack of chairs and ran toward her.

"Evan, stop!" She eyed the puddle of goopy gel and knew Kenny had rigged this whole place to go up in flames along with her. "Stay back! Don't get any of this stuff on you. It'll burn, sweetie."

A hard arm in steel-gray coveralls caught Evan by the shoulder and pulled him several feet away from the flammable gel. "Your mom's right, Danny."

"I'm not Danny!" Her boy twisted away and kicked Kenny square in the shin. "The dragon beats the monster every time!"

"What does that even mean?" Kenny was still rubbing his injured leg and cursing. "What kind of garbage you teaching my son, Katie?" He turned his curses on Evan and Corie nearly ripped her arms from their sockets trying to break free and get to him to protect him. "You need to man up, kid. No son of mine is going to believe in all this pansy fairy-tale stuff." He snatched the dragon from Evan's hands. "What is this supposed to be, anyway?" He tossed the dragon at Corie. She ducked, but the toy hit the floor hard and broke into several pieces.

"No!" Evan shouted, lunging after his longtime version of a security blanket.

"Evan, stop!" she shouted, not wanting him any closer to this death trap. "Do as he says. Please."

"Stop calling him Evan. His name is Danny, after my dad."

Evan swung his small fists at the monster who'd sired him. "It is not! Matt's my dad now. He's Mom's boyfriend and he loves me. Matt said so."

Kenny backhanded him across the mouth. "Shut up—"

Corie came unglued, sliding forward in her chair and crashing to the floor. "Don't you touch him! Evan!"

"There ain't no other man who's your daddy but me."

The man Kenny had addressed as Meade stepped out from behind the cubicle wall. He had graying hair, and though he wore a pricey tailored wool dress coat over his suit, she could tell he wasn't a classy guy. He walked right past Evan, who sat on the floor, holding his cheek and sobbing. He didn't offer a handkerchief or a smile or ask if Ev was okay. That man was no ally to her. "I'm leaving. I was never here. I've had my fill of domestic squabbles years ago. You're fired."

"I've got what I want," Kenny shot back, clearly uncowed by the man's intended threat. "I've got plenty of money in my bank account and I've got my boy."

The older man turned and pointed a finger at Kenny. "If I hear that you've stayed in the country…"

"You'll hire another enforcer to come after me?" Kenny laughed. "Let 'em try. I have a reputation as the best in the business for a reason. Your secrets are safe with me, Meade." He waved off the man who had employed him. "Now get out of here and let me work."

Kenny picked up a bag she assumed was full of tools or money or both and started packing the items he'd used to imprison her and prep the building for the fire. But he had no pity for her son, either.

Corie managed to push herself up onto one elbow, putting her at Evan's level. "Hey, son. Look at me." Her poor baby had a mark on his face, and his eyes were puffy and red. But he was her brave little soldier. He sniffed hard and swiped away his tears. That's when the saw the black watch that was far too big for him dangling from his wrist. She wasn't giving up hope until her very last breath. She wasn't letting her son give up, either. "Look at your watch and practice telling time. Start counting how many minutes it takes for Matt to get here."

Kenny laughed at what he thought was a ridiculous challenge. "Your boyfriend isn't coming to save you, Katie. I left him with plenty to do. He'll never find you. Not until this place has burned to the ground and Danny and I are on a plane to a tropical beach in the Caribbean."

Corie didn't intimidate the way she used to. She wasn't isolated and vulnerable to the likes of Kenny Norwell or her mother anymore. She had friends. She had the makings of a new family. She had a future.

She had her very own fire-eating dragon.

"You don't know Matt Taylor."

MATT DROVE THE fire engine up and down the skinny throughways and parking areas in the warehouse district north of City Market. He'd killed the lights and siren, creating as much stealth as a diesel truck this size could manage. He'd wasted too many minutes getting stuck behind a line of vehicles merging into one lane around a construction site. If he'd been thinking, he'd have had dispatch clear a construction-free route for him.

But he hadn't been thinking. He'd only been feeling. Fear. Love. Loss. Anger. He needed Corie to get inside his head and help him make sense of it all. He needed her beautiful smile to keep the shadows of the past at bay. He needed her boy to make him laugh and get him excited about being a father. He needed her. Period.

Mark's sharp eyes had kept the black Charger in sight until it had turned off into this maze of old manufacturing plants and shipping warehouses that had been converted into office buildings, condos and modern businesses.

"Where's the car, Mark? Where did he take them?"

Ironically, Mark, the comic of the family, was the one who kept a cool head. "It's only been a couple of minutes since we lost them. He probably drove into one of these warehouses and pulled down the door to hide. He's still here. This complex is locked down for the weekend. We'd have heard him driving away."

Matt glanced across the cab of the truck, wanting to believe. But searching every warehouse, garage door, even just on this single block was a daunting task. "We need backup. Call it in. Call everybody in. Alex. Pike. Mom and Dad."

Mark pulled out his cell phone and picked up the radio off the dashboard. "I'll get on the horn with them and any personnel from the nearest station who can give us a hand."

"I can't lose them, Mark. It's the first time it's ever felt right for me. I can talk to her and…she says I'm funny and…"

Matt's gaze zeroed in on the small dots of primary colors and purple and green sprinkled across the pavement in front of the shipping door off to his left. "Hold on."

While Mark chatted with dispatch, Matt climbed down from the truck to figure out what he was looking at. His mood lightened with every step. He picked one, and then another, cradling the tiny plastic building blocks in hand. He glanced up at the second-story window that had been propped open and knew these were a deliberate clue. "Evan McGuire, if you're not careful, I'm going to adopt you."

Tucking the bricks into his pocket, Matt searched for a ladder or fire escape that would give him the access he needed to see inside the warehouse. A dumpster and the drainpipe above it did the trick, too. Although Matt couldn't see into the open window from his vantage point, he could see in.

He nearly lost his grip and plummeted to the ground at the sight of Corie strapped to a chair and lying in a puddle of Kenny Norwell's home-brewed fire-starter kit. The setup was just like the fire that killed Enrique Maldonado.

After a quick descent, he climbed back into the fire engine and shifted it into gear. "That place is rigged to burn and Corie's trapped in the middle of it. She won't be able to get herself out."

"Backup's en route. Did you get eyes on Evan?"

"No. But Norwell's there, so the kid has to be around someplace." He knew a lot of different ways to prevent fires, to put out fires, to rescue someone trapped in a fire. But a locked door stood between him and getting the job done. "We get one shot at this, Mark. Once Norwell knows we're onto him, Corie will be at his mercy."

"You know I'll follow your lead. What do we do?"

And then he knew. A moment of clarity washed over Matt like one of Corie's smiles. He shifted the engine into reverse, backed into an alley, then straightened the big machine to meet the shipping bay door at a ninety-degree angle. "Hold on to something."

"You're not gonna…?" Mark buckled himself in and grabbed the hand bars as Matt shifted gears and stomped on the gas. "Whoa, baby! Who said you were the shy one?"

MEADE AND KENNY were arguing again.

Kenny never had played well with others. "When we made the agreement to work together on the outside, I said yes because the money is good. But I am my own boss. Understand?"

On the outside? Kenny and this Meade had been in prison together?

She wasn't sure how that was helpful, other than with the two roosters going at each other, each trying to assert his superiority over the other, they weren't paying any attention to her. Kenny probably believed he'd put her in an inescapable trap, and Meade didn't care.

Since she was already covered in the accelerant, it didn't

make any difference if she got more on her. So Corie was tapping every last bit of her strength to crawl her way to one of the desks. She wasn't sure how she was going to lever herself up high enough, but one of those drawers or pencil caddies had to have a pair of scissors or a box cutter she could use to free herself.

Evan was back on his stack of chairs beneath the windows, thankfully engrossed in watching the dials on Matt's watch and, without realizing it, believing in a miracle.

Corie had her teeth hooked onto the edge of a drawer and, millimeter by millimeter was tugging it open when she heard the loud roar of an engine outside. Both men turn to look toward the window. "What the hell is that?"

The entire building shook, and Corie fell to the floor as something big and powerful crashed through the garage door below them.

Evan tumbled off his perch but quickly climbed back up to peer out the window. "It's Matt! It's his fire engine!" He swung around to share the news with Corie. "He's here!"

"Evan, run!" He hesitated for a moment, no doubt concerned for her. "Run!"

He took off, leaving her sight as he raced for the far door as fast as his little legs could take him. She heard voices shouting down below, running footsteps, someone calling her name. There were sirens outside now, too. She could barely hear herself think.

But Corie could see the look of pure hatred on Kenny's face.

"You'll never take my son from me again." He flicked a match between his thumb and finger and dropped it into the puddle of chemicals that covered the floor. The goo burst into flame like a burning pool of oil and raced across the room toward her. "Die, witch."

He took off after Evan. "No!"

The next several things happened so quickly that Corie wondered if her concussed brain was hallucinating.

The nearer door burst open and two firefighters rushed in with a hose.

"Corie!"

Matt? "I'm over here."

Two police officers rushed in behind them, guns drawn. A rangy German shepherd led another officer inside ahead of a shorter man armed with some kind of assault rifle. Matt used hand signals to send them all off in different directions. "The boy is our number one priority."

He left the other firefighter to open up the nozzle and spray a gushing waterfall that wiped Mr. Meade off his feet. Then he turned the hose, catching the edge of the fire trap with a powerful stream of water.

"That's all the length we've got, Matt!" Mark Taylor. "I can't reach her."

"I can."

Matt ran straight toward her, his thick boots and bunker gear the only deterrent he needed to race through the flames and kneel beside her. "Matt! Don't!"

He pulled a knife from deep inside his coat and flipped it open to slice away the tape that bound her right wrist. He trailed a gloved finger over her bruised, swollen cheek. "Oh God, sweetheart, you're hurt."

"Should I tell you I've had worse?"

"No." He moved to her right leg.

Even though she couldn't feel her fingers, she still reached to rest her hand against his stubbled cheek. "I love you."

"I love you." He looked up from freeing her left wrist. "Wow. That was easy to say."

"You're a strange one, Matt Taylor. But I think you're the right one for me."

"Yeah?"

"Yeah. That's why you have to go. This isn't safe. I need someone who loves Evan to be with him now."

"*You* love him. *You'll* be with him." He never glanced over his shoulder while he cut the last of her restraints. But Corie had a clear, eye-level view of the fire dancing across the pool of accelerant, following the path that led straight to her. "You have to go. I'm about to go up in flames."

"Then it's a good thing I'm a firefighter." He shrugged out of his bunker coat and wrapped her inside it. Corie felt rather than saw the heat of the flames reach for her as he carried her through the fire. Seconds later, he set her on her feet and tossed the coat aside. They were near the windows now, several yards beyond the perimeter of the fire. "Get these clothes off."

She fumbled with the buttons on her sweater and blouse while he unsnapped her jeans and peeled them down her legs. "You have to go after Evan. He went out the other way."

"He's got a lot of people I trust looking out for him."

"But—"

"You've raised a smart kid. His trail of breadcrumbs is how I found you." He tossed the last piece of tape aside. "Clothes, woman. I don't want any accidental spark to trigger a reaction. I don't intend to lose you."

"My hands are numb. The circulation's been cut off."

"Understood." He took over and stripped her down to her bra and panties and gathered her into his arms. For a split second, she looked up into warm brown eyes and knew she would be safe. She knew she could trust his word that her son would be safe, too. "Hold your breath. This is going to hurt."

Corie filled her lungs with air and buried her face against Matt's chest. He clutched her tightly against him as Mark hit them with the full blast of the fire hose. By the time Matt signaled his brother to cut off the hose, several other firefighters were streaming in with longer hoses that allowed them to reach the spread of the chemicals and douse the flames.

She felt Matt's lips at the crown of her hair. "I don't smell it on you anymore. I think it's safe to move you outside now. I want you checked out by a medic."

She felt like she'd been hit by a freight train, and she was already starting to shiver after being drenched to the skin. But there was still only one thing on her mind. "I'm not doing anything else until I see my son."

"How about you put on some dry, chemical-free clothes? Blanket!" Matt gave the order, and seconds later Corie had two blankets, one wrapped around her like a sarong, and the other draped over her shoulders. "Evan's okay, sweetheart. He's with my mom and dad in an ambulance, getting checked over by medics. Norwell and Meade have been arrested by my uncle Cole. Jordy turned himself in, and Harve is on his way to the hospital. I'm guessing he's got jail time in his future, too."

Corie stared up at Matt, dumbfounded. "How? How do you know all that? How can you be so certain?"

He pulled the earbud out of his ear and showed her that he'd been listening in to official radio chatter this entire time. "A little birdie told me."

Corie didn't know if she wanted to swat him or hug him. "Why didn't you tell me?"

He smoothed her wet hair away from the wound on her cheek and tucked it behind her ear. "You were the one in imminent danger. That's where my focus needed to be."

"Atonement?"

"No. Love." Then he gently laced his fingers together with hers. "Let's go get our boy."

* * * * *

COLTON 911: THE SECRET NETWORK

MARIE FERRARELLA

This book is dedicated to

My Other Daughters.

To Sandra Lee,

Whom I have known

Since her first day of kindergarten,

And to Tiffany Melgar,

Whom I got to know when she was just a little older,

But no less wonderful.

And to my flesh-and-blood daughter, Jessica Ferrarella,

Who has never read a single one of my books,

But whom I love dearly anyway.

You make my heart smile, girls.

I'm so glad that you are all in my life.

With love,

Mama

Prologue

January Colton hurried across the restaurant's main dining area. By her watch, she was only five minutes late, but her sisters would make a big deal out of it since she was always running late. Usually just by a little bit, but never through her own fault. She just didn't have a job that could easily be wrapped up at day's end. Being a social worker just wasn't that sort of work.

"Sorry I'm late," she said to the two women who were already seated at the cozy round table.

Simone, the oldest sister and the only one of the three who had medium brown hair worn in a chin-length bob, raised her eyes to January's face. "Second verse, same as the first," she murmured with a patient smile.

"I'll have you know I was briefing the woman who's going to be taking my place for the next couple of weeks," January informed her as she set down her bag.

Centering herself, she looked around the table. There was a plate of appetizers in the middle and three glasses of champagne, one by each of their place settings.

"Everything looks lovely, as always, Tatum," January, the tallest sister despite the fact that she was the youngest, said, complimenting the middle Colton sister. After all, the restaurant, True, was Tatum's baby. It had been for the last two years. The blonde, wavy haired Tatum had worked night and day to pull the farm-to-table restaurant together, turning it into the success it was today.

January's excuse was not lost on either of her siblings. "You actually have someone taking your place next week?" Simone asked.

"I do," January said proudly, picking up the menu and glancing at it.

"So this is really on the level?" Tatum questioned January. They were all workaholics, but of the three of them, January was the most notoriously dedicated. They had lost count of the vacations that had been planned and then hadn't materialized.

"Absolutely," January replied.

They had made plans for this joint getaway, booking a flight as well as reservations at a spa, but Simone was still skeptical about its taking place. "You're really going to do this?"

"Yes," January answered with emphasis. "I'm really going to do this."

Simone pinned their baby sister with a look. "You're not going to back out at the last minute?"

January frowned. "No."

"Or say that something 'just came up'?" Tatum pressed the issue, knowing that those were excuses that January had used to beg off before.

Exasperated, January put down her menu and looked

from one of her sisters to the other. "What is it going to take to convince you two that I am really going to go on this way overdue spa vacation with you?"

"Way, *way* overdue," Tatum pointedly emphasized.

"Give it a rest, Tatum," January requested. "Now, what is it going to take to get the two of you to drop this and just move on?"

"You could try signing a statement in blood," Simone, a psychology professor with a PhD from the University of Chicago, suggested with an innocent smile. "We all know how quickly you can change your mind."

"Very funny coming from someone who just broke up with yet another lame guy," January commented, deciding to go on the offensive for a change. "Tell me, did you minor in having notoriously bad taste in men, or is that something that just comes naturally to you?"

The dark-haired thirty-two-year-old professor drew her shoulders back. "At least I'm trying, which is more than I can say for you."

January decided to retreat. She wasn't here to fight, she was here to mark the beginning of their mutually anticipated holiday.

But she did want to make a point.

"There aren't enough hours in the day for me to be able to do my job as a social worker properly *and* date, much less build a relationship with someone who might or might not turn out to be worthwhile," January said in all seriousness.

"Ladies, ladies, this is not the way to behave on the eve of our long postponed and much needed and deserved joint spa weekend," Tatum said as she inevitably picked up the reins of peacemaker.

It was a familiar role for Tatum and one she slipped into time and again. If Simone was the brains and January was the heart and soul of their trio, then Tatum represented their common sense. In addition, it had been Tatum's foresight that had goaded her to open this restaurant in downtown Chicago two years ago. And it had been her determination that helped her turn it into such a success—thanks to her innovative recipes—all in a breathtakingly short amount of time.

All three sisters were dedicated. They all sank long hours and hard work into their chosen fields. It was a work ethic that all three had learned right at home.

"Well, I don't know about you two, but if I don't get some sunshine on this all too pale skin of mine, I'm going to start looking like I've been left out in the rain much too long and I'm starting to rust," January complained.

"Well, don't expect me to feel sorry for you," Simone told her. "Nobody told you to pick up those extra shifts and work all those long hours for the city."

Right, like Simone wouldn't cave the minute she was confronted with a frightened, abused child. "You try looking into those sad little eyes in the faces of the kids I deal with, and you pick which one to say no to. I dare you," January said. She turned toward Tatum. "It's a lot harder, I promise you, than whipping up those sinfully delicious meals for the overprivileged gentry claiming to want to get back to 'nature,'" January told her other sister.

"Ouch," Tatum cried, pretending to wince. "You're tired and overworked, Jan, so I'll cut you some slack. But I'd watch that tongue of yours if I were you."

"I'm sorry. You're right. I am tired and I am overworked." January flashed Tatum an apologetic smile. "I haven't even had time to pack yet."

"You haven't packed yet?" Simone asked, her eyes widening. "Jan, we're leaving in the morning."

"Yes, I am aware of that," January replied wearily. "Just because I don't have a PhD doesn't mean I can't tell time."

"Well, nobody asked me, but I'd say that all three of us are way beyond needing that time off in order to recharge," Tatum told her sisters.

And then she raised her champagne glass, ready to make a toast. When she had reserved this table for their dinner, Tatum had seen to it that the glasses beside the place settings were all filled with their favorite brand of champagne.

"To our much needed vacation," she toasted, her blue eyes affectionately washing over her two best friends—her sisters.

They might have their differences from time to time, but there were no two people she loved more or had greater respect for than her sisters.

Simone followed suit, raising her glass to the others. "To our vacation."

"Our *spa* vacation." January underscored the sentiment, raising her glass, as well.

The sisters clinked their glasses.

"No matter what," Tatum added.

Her sisters echoed the mantra, although both Simone and Tatum did look at January with a hint of suspicion in their eyes.

"Hey, don't look at me like that," January protested. "My boss was the one who insisted I take this vacation, remember?"

"Well, I'll believe it when all three of us are on the plane," Simone said.

"I'll believe it when we're *getting off* the plane," Tatum interjected.

January knew that was for her benefit. "Very funny."

After taking sips of the champagne and then setting down their glasses, the sisters began to eat—and talk excitedly about their plans.

Their voices were intersecting and melding, and at first, they didn't hear the cell phone ringing. When the noise finally penetrated, the sisters looked at one another, silently asking where the ringing was coming from just before they each checked their own device.

And then January held up her hand. "Oh, hold on a second. That is my phone ringing."

Simone exchanged a look with Tatum. "And then there were two," the older sister said with a note of resignation in her voice.

Tatum sighed. This was not the first eleventh-hour phone call that had ever interrupted their carefully laid plans.

And, most likely, it wouldn't be the last.

Chapter One

January saw the almost identical leery looks on her sisters' faces as she picked up her cell phone and instinctively knew what they were both thinking.

"It's probably just a last-minute question," she told them.

In general, despite the nature of the sorrow that she dealt with in social services, January was an exceedingly upbeat person. She always saw life in a glass-half-full light. Consequently, January refused to believe that this phone call from her office might possibly be a death knell for her vacation plans. She believed, as she had said, that this was just a last-minute question, either from her boss or her replacement.

Rising from the table, she answered her phone at the same time that she put some space between herself and her sisters. She thought that maybe privacy might be in order. She had learned a long time ago that it was always better to be prepared than to be caught unaware or by surprise.

"Hello, this is January Colton," she told the caller cheerfully. "How may I help you?"

"January, it's Sid Blackwell," the raspy voice on the other end of the call said.

Even if the caller hadn't bothered to identify himself, all he needed to do was say a couple of words and she would have recognized his voice anywhere. It was her boss.

She did her best to dismiss the noticeable sinking sensation in the pit of her stomach that seemed to be mushrooming and said cheerfully, "Hi, Sid, what's up?" and thought it only fair to point out, "I did just leave the office less than forty-five minutes ago."

"I know," she heard her boss say, "and believe me, if there were any other way, I wouldn't be calling you like this, but turns out that this is an unusual situation and frankly, you're the only one I can think of who can help."

He actually sounded contrite, January thought, and that had her worried. After all, Blackwell was the one who had insisted that she take this vacation in the first place.

Something definitely had to be wrong.

January stole a glance over her shoulder. For now, Simone and Tatum weren't paying attention to her. Her sisters seemed busy talking to each other. She breathed a sigh of relief as she turned her head back around.

"All right, Sid, you have my attention," she said, trying to coax Blackwell to get to the point. "Why am I the only one you can think of to handle this?" Maybe her supervisor had just gotten too used to relying on her and this really wasn't as bad as he thought.

"The police just brought in a little girl—she looks

like she might be around five-ish," Blackwell said.
"Anyway, she was found hiding behind some crates
in a warehouse. One of the people in the vicinity called
the police when they heard gunfire."

Okay, maybe this *was* as bad as he thought.

"Gunfire?" she asked uneasily. "Is the girl all right?"

"From what I've been told, she appears to be,"
Blackwell answered. "The detective at the scene thinks
the kid might have been a witness to what happened
at the warehouse."

"Exactly what happened at the warehouse?" January asked.

"There were three dead bodies—all male—found
not too far from where the kid was discovered, cowering," Blackwell told her.

January sucked in her breath. It wasn't hard to envision what that little girl had to have gone through.
Alfred Colton's youngest daughter was instantly filled
with sympathy.

"That poor thing must be scared out of her mind,"
January said to her supervisor.

"Must be," Blackwell agreed in his detached sort of
way. "The thing is, the detective can't get her to talk.
According to what I heard, the kid hasn't said a single
word since they found her." January heard her boss
pause before finally saying, "I thought that maybe,
with all your experience working with special needs
children, you might consider just making a quick stop
by the police station and monitoring the situation."

Monitoring? Was Blackwell actually saying what

she thought he was saying? "Let me get this straight, Sid. Are you *assigning* me to this case?" January asked.

"Oh no, no." She heard her supervisor quickly deny that idea. "Susan Eckhardt is the social worker assigned to this case." Then Blackwell hesitated before he added, "But, well, Susan doesn't have much experience when it comes to special needs children and..."

There was such a thing as too much tiptoeing around a subject, January thought. Blackwell needed to get to the point and call a spade a spade.

"Mr. Blackwell, you and I both know that Susan doesn't have *any* experience when it comes to special needs children."

Rather than argue with her or defend the social worker he had assigned to the case, Blackwell took the easy way out. He focused on the only part that seemed to matter to him.

"Then you'll swing by?" he asked the woman who he acknowledged was one of his best, hardest working employees.

It never occurred to January to turn her boss down, even though, technically she'd already begun her vacation. The child in question had obviously been through something horrible and, at the very least, needed comfort and support. This was what she did very well. She couldn't just get herself to turn away from a child in need.

"Yes, I'll swing by," she told her boss. Taking out her pen and an envelope she had stashed in her purse, January was ready to take notes. "Tell me everything you already know about the case, Sid."

There wasn't all that much.

January listened carefully, jotting down the few facts she felt might be pertinent.

Finished, she told Blackwell, "All right, let Susan know that I'm on my way."

"Thanks, January. I promise I just need a little of your expertise on this matter. You can still start your vacation tomorrow, right?" Blackwell asked her. There was actually a note of hope in his voice.

"Right." *Provided the case doesn't wind up getting more complicated.* Truthfully, January already had her suspicions that it might. "I'll get back to you as soon as I know something," she said just before she terminated the call.

The moment she turned back to face her sisters, she found herself being scrutinized by two sets of very blue eyes. Bracing herself, she sat down for a moment, collecting her thoughts before she said anything.

"Well?" Simone prodded.

January took in a deep breath. "There's been an emergency," she began.

Simone laughed dryly. "That certainly didn't take long." She looked down at her watch.

Tatum just continued looking at January, waiting for the rest of the story to come out. They all knew that there inevitably had to be more.

Her sisters didn't have long to wait.

"The police found a little girl hiding behind some crates in a warehouse," January told them. "It sounds like she might have been a witness to a triple homicide."

Tatum sucked in her breath in horror, immediately

envisioning the whole scene in her mind. "Oh, that poor little thing!"

"They can't get her to talk—" January continued as she tried to explain to her sisters why she couldn't turn her supervisor down.

"Well, that's no surprise. The kid's probably really traumatized," Simone told her sisters.

January nodded her head. "That's what I'm thinking," she agreed. "Blackwell said he thinks that she's a special needs child—"

The expression on Tatum's face indicated that she already knew what was coming next.

"And that's your field of expertise, special needs children. Yes, we know," Tatum said. "Go." The restaurateur waved January on her way. "Give us a call later and fill us in on what's going on once you have some kind of a handle on it."

Again, January knew what her sisters were thinking. She could see it in their eyes. They thought that she was getting sucked into something.

"I'm just going in to offer some quick advice to the social worker assigned to the case. This isn't my case," she insisted, looking from one sister to the other.

They didn't believe her. She couldn't blame them. She wasn't buying into it herself, at least not a hundred percent.

"Uh-huh," Tatum murmured.

As January was telling them about the call, Tatum had placed a piece of chicken and several rolls into one of the linen napkins on the table, then wrapped it all up. She pushed the makeshift package toward January.

"Here," she said, offering the linen-wrapped bundle to January. "If this lasts as long as we all know it will, you're going to get hungry."

January sighed, then, rather than demur, she automatically accepted the impromptu care package. "I am *not* staying," she told her sisters emphatically.

"No, of course not," Tatum replied, her expression never changing.

"You keep telling yourself that, kid," Simone said, adding in her two cents. "Don't forget to call at least one of us with an update."

"Right," January agreed. "I'll call you as soon as I leave the police station."

"Uh-huh," her sisters said in unison.

They didn't believe that, either, January thought.

But she meant it. Despite the fact that she had told them that she hadn't packed her suitcase yet, January really was determined to go on this vacation with her sisters.

She had meant what she had said. Other than an occasional lunch on the run, or a quick phone call, it felt as if too much time had elapsed since the three of them had gotten together and just *talked* for any length of time.

Even now, their time together had been interrupted.

All that did for her was reinforce the feeling that they desperately needed some time to catch up. Since the very beginning, they had always been in each other's lives, and just because they were grown women now, that was no excuse for that practice to lapse.

As a matter of fact, there was more reason than ever

to reinforce those bonds. January couldn't think of anyone else she wanted to share all the things that she had experienced and was involved in than her sisters. And she wanted to know what was important and going on in their lives, as well.

She thought about her situation and what she might be getting into. No, come hell or high water, by tomorrow morning, she was going to be on board that plane with her sisters so that they could all begin that much anticipated, much needed vacation, January promised herself.

THE POLICE STATION that turned out to be her destination was an old five-story building that had seen more than its share of heartbreak and tragedy. Just the sight of it as she turned the corner and approached it in her car fostered a sadness within her.

January tried to see the building through the eyes of a child, and she found it hard not to shiver—or cry for that matter.

That poor little girl, January couldn't help thinking. More than likely, the child hoped this was all just a bad dream.

She caught herself wondering if the little girl was related to any of the dead men who had been found at the warehouse. That could very well explain why the child had shut herself off and wasn't saying anything. That kind of shock had been known to cause amnesia in an adult. How much more powerful could that reaction turn out to be if it was a child witnessing that sort of crime instead?

January really hoped that she would be able to help this child. Never mind getting her to remember and volunteer any sort of information about what happened to those men at the warehouse—*if* it turned out that the little girl had actually witnessed anything. January was far more concerned about being able to reach the child before she submerged herself in some sort of fantasy world that was totally outside the realm of reality.

Gearing herself up mentally, January hurried up the stairs, her high heels clicking against the cement. She normally dressed a little more conservatively when she worked, but since she'd been meeting her sisters after work and this really was a special occasion, for once January had dressed a little fancier than she usually did.

Pushing the glass and metal-framed door open, she stepped inside the police station. She was immediately met by a wall of ever-present noise as well as an uncomfortable warmth, despite the fact that this was winter in Chicago.

January was aware of several pairs of eyes looking in her direction. A couple displayed moderate interest before turning away and getting back to whatever had their attention at the moment.

Not wanting to waste any unnecessary time, she quickly approached the front desk and the sergeant behind it.

Hopefully, Blackwell had called ahead the way she had asked him to do. Smiling at the tall, bald, uniformed man at the desk, January took out her wallet.

She flipped to her identification and held it up for the sergeant to see.

"Hi. I'm not sure if my supervisor called ahead to let you know I was coming, but I'm January Colton with Child Protective Services. I was told that one of your detectives brought in a little girl earlier. She was found at the scene of a triple homicide," she added, thinking that would jar the sergeant's memory.

The desk sergeant nodded his head. "Oh, you must mean Detective Stafford."

"I'm sorry, I'm afraid I don't know his name. I was just told that he was the one who found and brought in a little girl—"

"Yes, he did," the sergeant recalled. His brown eyes met hers. "The one who hasn't spoken. Detective Stafford called in a social worker to get the kid to talk, but so far, nobody's had any luck." Lowering his voice, he confided, "The social worker is stymied. She hasn't been able to get the kid to say a word."

January nodded her head. "I know. My supervisor told me. That's why he asked me to come by and see if I had any better luck at getting the girl to talk. Do you think you might be able to call this Detective Stafford out here so I could talk to him? Or better yet, tell me where I can find the little girl and I'll take it from there."

But the desk sergeant shook his head. "I'm afraid I can't do that, ma'am. There are regulations to follow."

This was not what she needed at the end of the day. Blackwell was supposed to have resolved this. "I realize that, Sergeant. But I *have* been here before," January stressed.

The sergeant squinted his eyes as he looked at her. "I'm sorry, I don't recognize you—"

"And I don't recognize you." She took out her identification again and held it up closer for his review. "But I'm willing to talk to you. Look—Sergeant Wilkerson," she said, reading the tag on his shirt, "there's a very frightened little girl somewhere in your station and I'd like to connect with her so that I can help her be less frightened. Do you think you can help me do that?"

The sergeant sighed just as someone else approached him with a question. The policeman started talking, but Wilkerson held up his hand, signaling for the police officer to back off.

"Wait your turn, Andrews," he snapped. "Can't you see that there's someone ahead of you?"

She could see this quickly escalating into a heated argument. "Look, I don't want to cause any problems or interfere, Sergeant Wilkerson. You obviously have your hands full here. If you could just point me in the right direction, I promise I'll get out of your hair."

"Good one," the policeman laughed, glancing toward his partner.

The desk sergeant might have been bald, but his eyebrows were very full and bushy. They drew together now as he scowled at the police officer. "What did you say?" Wilkerson challenged him.

She was used to refereeing squabbling children and this really wasn't all that different. January raised her voice. "We're getting off topic here, gentlemen," she told the two police officers. When both men looked at her in surprise, January decided to approach the problem from a different angle.

Locking eyes with the desk sergeant, she said, "Look, if you could either call this Detective Stafford to come down to the front desk, or point me in the direction where I can find him, I can get down to what's really important here—getting that little girl to tell someone what she saw."

Wilkerson laughed. The sound had no humor in it. "Good luck with that," he told her. "I saw him trying to get her to talk to him about *anything* when he brought her in. It's like she was in her own little world." He leaned over the desk, although his voice didn't get any lower. "You ask me, it's like she's really spooked."

"She probably just saw three men get shot and killed, maybe even right in front of her. If that happened to you when you were a little kid, my guess is that you'd be spooked, too," a tall, dark-haired and ruggedly handsome man said as he approached the front desk from the far right.

Ah, January thought as she turned toward the man who had just walked in to get a closer look. *Detective Stafford, I presume.*

Chapter Two

"And you'd be right," January told the man who was now standing almost next to her.

The detective had a larger-than-life presence, even though in her estimation he was probably only about three inches taller than she was, and she was wearing three-inch heels.

January put out her hand to the detective.

"Sid Blackwell sent me," she told Stafford by way of an introduction. "My name is January Colton and as you've probably already guessed, I'm with the Department of Social Services."

Sean blinked as he suddenly got a good look at her and became aware of the vivacious, classy blonde standing in front of the desk sergeant. In his estimation, she looked more like a model than a social worker—and young, quite young. She certainly didn't look old enough to be a social worker.

His eyes met and held hers. After a beat, the detective took the hand that she was offering.

January caught herself thinking that the sexy detective's grip felt strong, but not overpowering. There was something about him that seemed genuine. She decided that she liked him.

"Nice to meet you, Ms. Colton," Sean said. His smile was tight, but polite. "I'm assuming that Blackwell told you what the problem seems to be."

"He did, but sometimes things get lost or omitted if a third party is involved," January told the detective. "Why don't you tell me about the problem in your own words?"

What January was trying to get was the detective's perspective on the situation. She had learned that a lot of things could be revealed through the words a person used or didn't use. Besides, the detective had been at the scene and her supervisor hadn't been.

Sean was about to tell the woman that, since she already seemed to know what was going on, he wasn't about to jump through hoops just for her personal amusement. But he also knew that was just his frustration talking. So, instead, the homicide detective took the social worker aside so he could talk to her and fill her in on the details away from the desk sergeant and anyone else who might be listening.

"We got a call from someone in the area claiming that they heard shots being fired at the old, abandoned toy warehouse. The patrolmen who took the call figured it was probably just a car backfiring, but because the call was logged in, they had to go to the location and check it out." The detective's expression was grim as he told her, "When they did, they weren't prepared for what they found. Three adult males, shot dead."

January tried not to wince. Because of her job, she

was used to dealing with abuse in various forms, but so far, she had never had to deal with murder. This was something new for her.

"They were murdered, I take it?" she asked. That was what she had been told, but somehow, saying it out loud made it that much more real for her. January's breath felt as if it had just solidified and backed up in her throat.

Sean caught himself studying this woman.

Closely.

Judging from her clothes and her bearing, she looked a little too polished to be doing this sort of work for a living. Given her last name, Sean couldn't help wondering if this was all just a diverting lark for her, or if she actually took this job seriously.

Belatedly, he realized that the social worker had asked him a question and that he hadn't answered her.

Nodding, he said, "Yes, they were murdered. Execution style," he added, watching her face for a reaction.

To her credit, the woman seemed to take the news in stride. "How was the little girl found?" she asked.

"The coroner was just logging the bodies in," Sean answered, "when his assistant heard this high-pitched whimpering noise coming from not too far off."

"Whimpering?" January asked. She could almost picture the scenario and her heart ached for the frightened little girl.

Sean nodded. "One of the patrol officers said it sounded a little like a frightened puppy. Thinking it might be another victim too weak to call out, the responding officers spread out, looking for him or her."

The detective frowned as he described the scene. "They found Annie crouching behind some crates, apparently attempting to hide."

"Annie," January repeated. Blackwell had told her that no one knew who the little girl was. Had he made a mistake? "Then you found out her name?" she asked, curious.

The detective shook his head. "No. One of the patrolmen referred to her as Annie. You know, like Orphan Annie, the kid in that old comic strip," Sean explained.

"I know who Orphan Annie is," she told the detective. "So did she respond to that name when you called her Annie?"

The detective shook his head. "No, and that's part of the reason why you're here. As far as I know, Annie, or whatever her real name is, hasn't responded to *anything* that has been said to her. I tried to get her to talk, but it was like I wasn't even there. The social worker your department sent tried her hand at communicating with the kid, but she didn't get anywhere, either.

"As a matter of fact, after she made several attempts to get the little girl to say something, *anything*, your Ms. Eckhardt got this confounded look on her face like she felt she was completely out of her depth. I got the impression that she was afraid to call her supervisor about it, so I did. Seemed like the best way to go. Blackwell said he would send reinforcements. Apparently—" Sean gestured at her "—you're the reinforcements."

Okay, January thought. She needed to clear a few things up for this detective.

"First of all, she's not *my* Ms. Eckhardt. We just work in the same department and I've been there a couple of years longer than Susan has," she began to explain.

Sean held up his hand, stopping the social worker before she could continue. "No offense, but I don't need—or want—your whole backstory here," he told January impatiently. "What I *do* need to know is the kid's backstory and the sooner you can help me get that, the sooner I can start piecing together what happened in that warehouse today, as well as finding out who shot those men and *why* they were shot."

January waited until the detective paused to take a breath and then she surprised him by laughing at his agenda. "You're not asking for much now, are you?"

Sean's eyes met hers. It was almost a contest of wills. Neither one looked away. "Not if you're as good as I was told you were," the detective responded.

January eyed him a little uncertainly. Was he just trying to use flattery on her, or was he actually telling her the truth? "And just who told you this? That I was good," she clarified. She didn't think that Susan would have said something like that. The social worker was too involved in moving up to waste any compliments on her coworkers.

"Your boss. Blackwell."

That surprised her. Blackwell wasn't generous when it came to handing out compliments.

As if reading her mind, the detective said, "And if

you don't believe me, that nervous social worker I left with my half-pint witness confirmed it when I asked her about you—before I was 'summoned' to come get you."

January focused on one term: *witness*. "I thought you said that you weren't sure if the little girl witnessed the shootings or not," January said, recalling what Blackwell had passed on to her from his conversation with the detective.

For the first time, she saw the detective grin. It was like watching beams of warm sunlight stretching out and brightening the immediate world.

"Hey, what can I say? I'm an optimist," the detective said with a shrug.

"Thinking that a little girl is the key witness to multiple homicides and then viewing that as being optimistic wouldn't be the way I'd describe it," January informed him.

The detective noted the cool tone of her voice.

"I'm not heartless," he told January. He wasn't sure why it seemed so important to him that she know that, but it was. "The way I see it, this gives me a way to get the jump on whoever did this and allows me to eliminate the threat against the kid at the same time."

"Threat?" January repeated uncertainly.

"Threat," Sean said again. "Because, trust me, if the killer even *suspects* that he was caught in the act and that there is the smallest possibility that 'Annie' here can identify him, her life won't be worth the proverbial plugged nickel."

January found that promise completely unnerving. "Well, since you put it so bluntly, let's go talk to her, shall we?" she urged the detective. "In my experience, kids are like sponges. They absorb everything and anything around them and—barring a really traumatic incident—they are usually able to recreate what they saw, at least to a reasonable degree."

"We have her in one of the interview rooms," he told her. "Your Ms. Eck—" Sean stopped himself and began again, this time correcting his initial mistake. "Ms. Eckhardt is in there with the little girl."

January hardly heard him. She had been at this station a couple of times before, but each time she had only gotten as far as the front desk or somewhere in that general vicinity. She had never been asked to go into the police station proper before. Certainly not to one of the interview rooms.

As she followed the detective now, she scanned the surrounding area. January found it to be exceedingly depressing, what with its drab, faded pea soup green walls and its decidedly oppressive atmosphere. She caught herself thinking that a weak-willed person would confess to almost anything if it meant that they could get out of here.

"When was the last time this place was painted?" she asked the detective.

The question seemed to come out of the blue, catching Sean off guard. He looked at her to see if he'd heard wrong for some reason.

"Why would you ask something like that?" he asked.

"Because just look at this place," she told him, gesturing around at the walls as they continued to make their way down the hall. "It's depressing."

"Our chief objective at the station isn't to make people happy," Sean told her, still thinking her question rather odd.

"You know," she said speculatively, "you might want to think that strategy over. If the people you're questioning are in a better frame of mind, it might make them more willing to respond to what you're asking in a positive light. It might make them want to cooperate. Just a thought," she added quickly before the detective could become defensive—or worse. She didn't want to make him combative; she was trying to offer some constructive criticism.

"I'll pass your suggestion along to the police station's interior decorator," Sean said.

"You do that," she responded. "So where's the interview room?" It seemed to her that they had been walking for a while now and she didn't see anything that came close to looking like an interview room.

"It's on the next floor," he told her just as they came to an elevator. Stopping, Sean pressed the button.

January heard the elevator approaching. It was making a grinding noise that was far from soothing.

"If it's just on the next floor, we could take the stairs," she suggested.

Just as she said that, the elevator came to a halt. The door opened, albeit almost in what appeared to be slow motion.

This was a really bad omen, January couldn't help thinking.

"You don't mind?" Sean asked, responding to her suggestion to take the stairs.

The elevator looked almost ancient, January thought, glancing into it. "I'm just thinking in terms of expediency."

Sean shrugged. "Well, it's here now," he pointed out. "We might as well take it."

If it had been up to her, she would have taken the stairs. But January didn't feel like arguing about it. She was sure that there would be other things to argue about with this detective soon enough.

"Whatever you say," she said philosophically as she walked into the elevator ahead of him.

Was it her imagination, or did she hear the elevator creak?

"Oh, if only," Sean murmured under his breath in response to her comment as she walked into the elevator.

Having entered the small elevator car, January turned to look at him. "Excuse me?"

"Nothing," the detective answered. "Just commenting in general." With that, Sean reached around January and pressed the button for the second floor.

"It's been a long day," he explained, since she was obviously waiting for more.

January gave him the benefit of the doubt. He was probably referring to the triple homicide he had caught—and his uncommunicative possible witness.

"So I gather." She thought about why she was there. "I'll see what I can do to get your witness to open up and talk."

The detective nodded. He believed her. "I'd appreciate it," he told her with sincerity.

The elevator door seemed to close in slow motion,

just the way it had opened. Then it appeared as if it was thinking about its next move. He reached around her again and pressed the button a second time.

When still nothing happened, January asked, "Is the elevator thinking it over?"

"Sometimes it's slow to respond," Sean told her, frowning slightly.

"Maybe it wants you to pick a different floor," she cracked. When the elevator continued to remain where it was, door closed but not moving, January had another suggestion. "Maybe we should just have the elevator open its doors again. If we had taken the stairs, we'd already be there."

As far as she was concerned, they were pushing their luck.

Just then, the elevator suddenly came to life. It lurched, and then moved upward, inching its way along. "It just takes patience," Sean told her, although it was clear that he was running out of his.

"What it could probably take is getting a complete overhaul," she responded. "Maybe if it had that, then it would run more smoothly."

"Yeah, that, too," Sean agreed.

The words were no sooner out of his mouth than the elevator came to an abrupt, jarring stop.

January waited expectantly in front of the door, but it didn't open, even though the whining, grinding noise that the elevator had been making had completely ceased.

The door still didn't budge. "Are we there yet or not?" she asked Sean.

He bit back a terse response and just said, "No way of knowing."

They both looked up at the top of the elevator. The light that indicated which floor they had reached had gone out, giving no indication as to whether or not they had come to their destination or if the journey had been suddenly aborted between floors without any warning.

"My guess is 'not,'" she said, still looking up at the unlit array of numbers at the top of the elevator. The numbers that were supposed to alert them as to what floor they were coming to.

"Certainly looks that way," the detective agreed.

"Okay, now what?" January asked, turning toward the man.

Sean sighed as he opened the small, metal door that housed the phone to call for help.

"Now we call maintenance to let them know that we're stuck here and to send someone to get this tin box moving again." Sean didn't bother looking at her, but he could feel the woman's green eyes on him. "And yes, I know. You were right," he conceded, albeit unwillingly. "We should have taken the stairs."

She didn't think he would acknowledge that so quickly and she felt a certain amount of satisfaction because he did. It allowed her to be magnanimous.

"I didn't say a word," January told him innocently.

"But you were thinking it," he said with certainty, growing more impatient as he waited for someone on the other end of the line to pick up. He didn't feel like standing here like this. He wanted someone to come to their aid and get this damn elevator running. The stalled car was growing stuffy.

January didn't particularly care for the detective's attitude. "If you're that good at reading minds, why did you need me to come here and deal with your witness?"

The last thing he needed was a wisecracking social worker. "Look, lady—"

"Back it up, Detective," she said sharply. "My name is January, not *lady*," she informed him. There was something very impersonal and almost insulting to her about being addressed as "lady." She felt as if he was saying she didn't care or get down in the trenches in order to work hard on her cases so she could solve whatever problem had reared its defiant, spiky little head.

Sean backed away and nodded. "January," he said obligingly. "I called Child Services because Eckhardt wasn't up to doing her job and I thought that maybe if I made the call, it would carry more weight."

"Mystery solved," she declared glibly, smiling a little too brightly at him.

"One of them, anyway," he murmured. Sean frowned at the phone. It was still ringing. No one was picking it up on the other end. "Where is everyone?" he asked irritably as it rang again.

"Probably having dinner would be my guess." She looked up at the elevator ceiling and tossed him an idea. "Listen, if I stand on your shoulders, I could probably get that trapdoor open."

January didn't actually see the detective staring at her in speechless wonder—but she could swear that she felt him doing it.

Chapter Three

"And then what?" Sean finally asked. He couldn't begin to imagine this long-haired, blond vision in the light blue dress and high heels actually climbing up on his shoulders, much less pushing open the trapdoor right above their heads.

January barely glanced in the detective's direction. She couldn't help thinking that, for a detective, he didn't have much of an imagination. "And then I see just how far between floors the elevator actually is."

Sean continued to watch her, utterly fascinated. Just how far was this woman prepared to go with this superheroine fantasy of hers? "And then what?" he asked her again, this time supplying a guess. "You shimmy up the cables to get to that landing?"

January sighed. Obviously, this man was *not* prepared to do anything about their situation.

"Unless you have a better idea," she told him. Maybe he didn't grasp the full import of this. "Look, there's a frightened little girl one floor above us. Getting to her and comforting her is my only objective at the moment."

He came across a lot of people in his line of work. This woman sounded as if she was nothing short of a crusader. Great, just what he needed. "You really mean that."

"Of course I mean it. I'm not playing games here, Detective. Now boost me up so I can climb onto your shoulders," she told him as she looked up at the ceiling.

But instead of doing as she asked, Stafford just smiled at her.

"Why are you grinning like that?" January asked, growing more impatient by the minute.

"As intriguing and appealing as the idea of having you sitting astride my shoulders is, I think it might be simpler if I just talked to maintenance."

As she began to point out what was wrong with that idea—he had just told her that no one was picking up—Sean cut her short by pointing to the receiver and saying, "Someone finally answered the phone."

And then he turned his attention to the person on the other end of the line. "Yes, hi," Sean said. "This is Detective Stafford. Social Worker Colton and I are stuck in elevator number three. It stopped moving between the first and second floors. Uh-huh. Okay, do what you have to do to get this thing moving before we grow old in here. Thanks."

January blew out a breath. "So?" she asked. "How long did whoever answered you say it was going to take them to get this thing moving again?" As good-looking as the man was, she didn't welcome the idea of being stuck with him in this elevator for an indefinite period of time. "Because if he thinks they can't fix the problem for a number of hours, I'm still willing to give it a try my way," she told him.

The woman was obviously stubbornness personified, Sean thought. He wasn't sure if that was a good thing or not. He was about to repeat what the maintenance man he had spoken to had told him when the elevator suddenly lurched again. Without any warning, Sean found himself colliding with her. He grabbed January by the shoulders to prevent any sort of real damage or injury.

"Sorry," he apologized, releasing her as the elevator car began to move arthritically to the next floor. "Are you all right?" he asked, his eyes taking inventory very carefully as he looked January over.

"Yes, I'm fine," she answered almost haltingly, obviously trying to get her bearings.

"I'll take a rain check on those proposed acrobatics just in case this doesn't pan out," Sean told her, referring to the revived elevator car.

She frowned. "Very funny."

"No, I'm serious," he told her. "I think I'd like to see you in action."

"The elevator appears to have come back to life. But I'm taking the stairs down after I interview that girl," she informed the detective.

"Understood." They reached the next floor and the elevator door slowly opened. Sean put his hand out against it, ensuring that the door remained opened and secured in place.

January stepped out quickly. He followed right behind her. "Let me guess," he said as he led the way to the interview rooms. "You were the youngest in a family of all boys."

"You got the youngest part right," January told him. "But I had two sisters. No brothers."

His brow furrowed a little as he tried to make sense of what she was saying. Why would she be so competitive if there were no brothers egging her on? "Then I don't understand," he confessed.

"You don't need to understand, Detective Stafford. All you need to know is that I'm very agile if the situation calls for it."

She'd made the comment in complete innocence. But the way the detective smiled at her told her that he hadn't taken it in that light.

She shouldn't have said anything, she thought.

"Good to know," Sean told her. And then his smile faded as he approached the interview room where he had left the other social worker and the little girl she had been sent to help.

He found himself hoping that this woman turned out to be more helpful than the first one.

Relief washed over Susan Eckhardt's rounded face as she caught sight of the detective through the upper, glass portion of the door. By the time Sean quietly opened the door, the social worker was on her feet and at the threshold.

"I was beginning to think that maybe you weren't coming back," she told him.

If she hadn't known better, January would have

said that the other social worker was flirting with the detective.

"Hello, Susan," January said, nodding at the other woman.

Any thoughts of a continued flirtation seemed to instantly vanish as Susan drew back her shoulders. "January, I heard you were supposed to be on vacation."

"Rumors of my vacation are greatly exaggerated," January quipped, and then smiled a little wearily. "It actually starts tomorrow. Sid called and said you caught a difficult case."

Susan rolled her eyes as she glanced back at the little girl who wasn't facing them. She seemed preoccupied with something on the back wall. "You can say that again. I can't get the kid to talk to me or even acknowledge me."

January thought of what she would have done. "You've tried to talk to her about something simple?" she asked the other social worker.

Susan grew slightly irritated. "I'm not a newbie. Of course I did."

"And?" January pressed. She wanted any input that Susan could provide.

Susan raised and lowered her wide shoulders in a helpless manner. "And nothing. It's like I'm not even there." She blew out an exasperated breath. "If I wanted to be ignored, I would have stayed married to Geoff," she said, frustrated. And then she looked at the detective. She obviously didn't want him thinking that she was involved with anyone. "Geoff's my ex-husband."

"I kind of gathered that." Sean noticed that the

woman who had been so ready to do acrobatics to get them out of the stalled elevator wasn't saying anything. She seemed to be observing the little girl he had brought back with him. The little girl was wandering around the other end of the room, completely oblivious to them.

"When I found her, she was all but curled up in a ball," he told January. "Like she was trying to pull into herself. It was almost as if she was trying to become invisible."

January nodded her head. "That's kind of theme and variation on the concept some kids have that if they close their eyes and don't see you, you can't see them." She continued to thoughtfully regard the nameless little girl.

Then she turned toward the two other adults in the room. "And she's made no attempt to say anything to either of you?"

"Not a word," Susan answered. And then the woman laughed to herself. "You'd think that would be rather refreshing after some of the kids we have to deal with, you know? But the silent treatment gets old really fast, too."

January was only half listening to Susan. Her eyes on the little girl, January approached her slowly. The child still had her back to her when January started talking in a low, nonthreatening tone.

"Hi, my name's January. Like the month," she said, since so many children had commented on her name, saying it was funny or odd. "It's kind of silly, I know, but my mom was hoping for a boy and she didn't have any names ready for a girl. She just looked at the calendar and picked that one."

The entire time she was talking to the child, the little girl was making no response. She didn't even turn around to acknowledge the fact that she was being spoken to.

January thought that was a little odd—and possibly telling.

"See?" Susan said, irritated as she gestured toward the girl's back. "She's rude."

"Or scared," Sean countered.

But January was beginning to suspect that there was a third alternative to this scenario. Turning toward them, she said as much. "Or deaf."

Susan's head jerked up. It was clear by the expression on her face that that possibility had never occurred to her.

"You think she's deaf?" Sean asked, surprised. That thought hadn't occurred to him, either.

"Very possibly," January answered, cautiously approaching the little girl who still had her back to them. "If she's deaf, that would explain why she didn't look toward the door when we walked in. She was looking away at the time—and didn't hear it."

Coming up behind the girl now, January lightly tapped her on the shoulder. The little girl almost jumped out of her skin as she whirled around to look at who had come up behind her, her braided brown hair flying.

There was a look of utter surprise on her face. It was apparent that she hadn't realized that there were two more people in the room now than there had been a moment ago. It was also obvious to January that the little girl had not connected with Susan in any fashion, but she looked very happy to see Sean.

The little girl quickly crossed the floor to get to him and then shyly wrapped her arms around his waist, or what she could reach of it.

"If you ask me, I'd say that you made a real connection with your potential witness," January told him.

Sean appeared to be surprised by the social worker's conclusion. "I thought she was just responding to the fact that I carried her in here."

"There's that, yes, but in her limited little world, you also represent her only friend right now," January pointed out.

Watching Sean, she saw him smiling at the little girl. It wasn't a patronizing smile, or one that was being forced out of some sense of obligation. January liked to think that she could tell the difference and she noticed that his eyes were smiling at the child.

"Not only that," January added. "But she senses that you're a good man."

Susan turned her thousand-watt smile on Sean, as well. "Yeah, me too," she said, adding her voice to the tally.

January frowned. She didn't have time for whatever this was devolving into. Nor did she have the patience for it, not when there was a genuine, real problem before them. She made a snap decision.

"Susan, I've got this," January said, glancing at her

watch. "It's getting late. Why don't you go home? It's way past the end of your day."

The suggestion was met with instant relief. "You don't mind?" the other woman asked, barely able to contain her eagerness.

"No, of course not. I wouldn't have said it if I did." January waved the other woman toward the door. "Go home." And as the other women began to leave, she called after her. "And Susan?"

The younger woman stopped in her tracks and turned around. "Yes?"

"You might want to think about a change in careers," January suggested.

Susan frowned, briefly torn and confused. But that quickly faded. Coming to, she lost no time in leaving the room.

As Susan closed the door behind her, January saw Sean looking at her quizzically. She could almost read the question in his eyes.

"I told her to go home because she wasn't being any help and I got the sense that she was growing more and more frustrated with the whole situation. Not to mention the fact that she didn't seem to realize that this little doll was deaf. That was rather sad," she told him.

"I didn't realize it, either," the detective pointed out.

"Yes, but you thought she was traumatized, and you did have a lot of other things going on at the same time, like a triple murder. It's not your job to be in tune with a scared little girl who can't hear you speaking to her. It is, however, part of Susan's job, as it is part of all our jobs in social services."

The sight of the little girl curled up on his lap warmed her heart. It told her that despite the detective's tough-guy act, there was a warm human being beneath that exterior facade.

"So now what do we do?" Sean asked, looking at January above the little girl's head. "How do we go about communicating with her?"

She gazed down compassionately. "Well, hopefully, someone taught her how to sign."

"You mean talking with her hands?" Sean asked, admittedly out of his depth here.

January smiled at the detective, nodding in response to his question. "Exactly."

The little girl looked as if she was falling asleep on his lap. He had never given having children a second thought—until just now. "Isn't she a little young to know how to do that?"

"The younger they are, the easier a time they have learning something. The school of thought is that foreign languages should be taught to children when they're very young. Signing is just another form of a foreign language," she told him. "Hopefully, her parents or parent was smart enough to get her into some sort of program as soon as they realized that she was unable to hear anything or anyone."

"Maybe she's not deaf," he said, thinking the matter over. "Maybe she's just blocking everything out because she was so traumatized and she doesn't want to deal with anything."

Rather than answer the detective, January took several steps back. "Annie" had her face buried against

Sean's chest. It was turned away from her. Taking in a deep breath, January let loose with an ear-splitting whistle.

There was no reaction on the little girl's part.

January looked up at the detective. "She's deaf, all right," she told him.

Sean, in turn, looked down at the child he was holding. There was a sadness in his eyes. "I guess she is," he agreed, then forced himself to move on. "I take it that you know how to sign?"

January smiled at him. "Yes, I do. Luckily, I made learning that as part of my training. There are more hearing-impaired, or partially hearing-impaired children, in the social services system than you might think. Working within this system also brings one to the inevitable conclusion that there are parents out there who should have never become parents."

She shivered as she thought the matter over. "Sometimes they take out their frustrations on their children in ways that are absolutely horrifying. Thank heaven that I have a family that not only keeps me grounded, but also makes me mindful that there is a brighter, more optimistic side to life. I sometimes cling to that, especially when I'm dealing with children who have been abandoned."

He raised his eyes to January's. "So you *do* know how to communicate with her?"

She smiled at the detective. "If she knows signing, I do."

"And if she doesn't?" Sean pressed.

She was up for that, too, if she had to be. "Then I'll find an alternate way to communicate with her."

"But wait a minute." Sean suddenly remembered something. "Didn't that other social worker say you were going on vacation tomorrow?"

"No," January corrected him, "she thought I was already *on* vacation. It technically wasn't supposed to start until tomorrow."

"Okay, so it starts tomorrow," he said, going along with her explanation. "If that's the case, how can you help? You're not going to be around to work with her." Sean nodded at the sleeping girl.

January had already considered that. Being exposed to the child had convinced her that she couldn't just abandon her.

"Regarding my vacation, there's no requirement as to where I can take it," she informed him. "Which means I can choose to take it in my house if that's how things play themselves out."

He stared at her, surprised. "So is that what you're planning to do?"

January looked down at the sleeping child, a smile playing on her lips. "I think so."

Chapter Four

The little girl stirred on the detective's lap. One moment she appeared to be sleeping peacefully, the next, her eyes flew open. She looked surprised, as if she didn't know where she was and was desperately trying to figure it out.

As she scrambled up into a sitting position, her large light-brown eyes darted back and forth, moving from Sean to January and then back again. Her agitation escalated by the second.

"Can you communicate with her, let her know she's safe?" Sean asked, doing his best to try to calm the little girl down by rocking back and forth in a soothing, comforting motion.

"I can certainly try," January answered.

Okay, here goes nothing, she thought as she tapped the little girl on the shoulder to get her attention. Huge fearful eyes looked up at January.

January smiled at her, then brought her fingers and thumb together and tapped them to her lips several times. Then extended the sign to include Sean.

To her relief, the little girl seemed to understand.

She bobbed her head up and down as a small smile blossomed on her lips.

"What just happened here?" Sean asked. He didn't like being kept in the dark and this was a world he knew nothing about.

January's triumphant smile was nothing short of dazzling as she turned toward the detective. "I think we've just had a breakthrough, Detective." She smiled warmly at the little girl. "She does know how to sign."

"Are you sure?" he asked. "Did you just communicate with her?" When it had become clear that the little girl was deaf, he had thought that getting through to her would be really difficult. She represented a whole new, mysterious world to him. Now, judging by the smile on the small face, there was hope.

"Yes I did. I asked her if she wanted to eat and she said yes," January informed him happily. "Well, she nodded yes. But it's practically the same thing."

"But she can understand you?" Sean asked, wanting to be perfectly clear on this. His eyes never left January's face. If she was lying for some reason, maybe to bolster her own self-image, he would know.

The social worker's green eyes crinkled. "It would appear that she does," she answered. She was so genuinely happy about the matter, she was positively glowing.

As far as Sean was concerned, they had just dipped their toes in the water. Now the real work began. He had a whole list of things he wanted to know. "Can you find out her name?" he asked eagerly.

She wanted to tell him to take things slowly, but she

sensed that he wouldn't take well to that. He would probably think she was trying to tell him his job. So, instead, she decided to make a suggestion.

"Why don't we get her something to eat and then, once she has something in her stomach, we can try to get some information from her—like her name." January watched the detective's face to see if what she was proposing irritated him.

Sean could barely harness his impatience, but he also knew that she was right. "Okay," he agreed. "I'll get her something to eat." He began to leave but he heard January call out after him.

"Detective?"

Sean stopped just short of the doorway and turned around. "Yes?"

"Don't take the elevator. If the vending machines are on another floor, you need to be able to come back. So make sure you use the stairs," January suggested.

The detective nodded his head. "Point taken," he acknowledged.

But as he started to leave the interrogation room for a second time, the little girl at the center of this drama broke away from January. Dashing up to him, the child wrapped her arms around his leg.

"Looks like someone doesn't want you to go," January commented, her mouth curving in an amused smile. "I tell you what. Tell me where the vending machines are located and I'll go get her something to eat."

Sean slowly returned to the table, careful not to cause the little girl to tumble backward. "That wouldn't be very gallant of me, sending you," he told January before taking out his cell phone.

She thought that was rather an odd thing for him to say. She had to admit that the detective and the little girl made quite a picture together.

"I didn't realize being gallant was in play here," January told him.

"Being gallant is *always* in play," he remarked. Reaching the party he was calling, his focus shifted. "Hey, Martinez." Detective Eric Martinez was the man he occasionally partnered with since his old partner had left the Homicide Division. "I didn't think you'd still be here."

"Actually, I'm not," Eric answered. "I'm just on my way out."

"Well, this won't take long. I need you to get a sandwich and a soda from the vending machine and bring it to the second-floor interview room. No, it's not for me," Sean assured him when Eric made a comment about being his errand boy. "It's for a potential witness to those warehouse murders I caught today. And don't forget the soda," he told Martinez, thinking the little girl had to be thirsty.

She smiled at him, as if she somehow knew what he was doing. "Oh, and see if you can find some cookies, too. Any kind of cookies," Sean said in response to the question the other detective asked.

Terminating the call, Sean put his phone back in his pocket. "Okay, that's taken care of. Food's on its way." He looked down at the little girl and repeated what he had just said, moving his lips very slowly. Then he felt foolish. "She probably doesn't read lips, does she?" he asked January.

"She might," the social worker answered. "But right now, we have no way of knowing one way or another. Like I said, after she eats, maybe we can find answers to some of the rest of the questions that come up."

Just then, the little girl pulled the bottom of Sean's jacket. When he looked at her, the little girl hooked both of her pointer fingers together in an X, then switched their positions.

Sean looked at her hands in confusion, then raised his eyes to January's face. "Is she trying to tell me something?"

"I think so," she answered the detective. January couldn't help grinning broadly. "She just called you her friend."

"Is that what that means?" he asked, nodding at the little girl's hands.

January inclined her head. The child had obviously connected with the detective. This would make things easier in the long run, she hoped. "Yes."

And then, to her surprise, she watched as Sean did his best to mimic what the girl had signed to him.

"Did I get it right?" he asked January, still looking at the little girl.

January smiled at her and then at Sean. "I think that big grin on her face should answer your question."

She saw a similar expression totally encompass his face. "You're right," he replied.

Just then, there was a knock on the door. Opening it without waiting to be invited in, Detective Eric Martinez walked in, a wrapped sandwich and bag of cookies in one hand, a can of soda in the other.

"I brought you that sandwich, cookies and soda you asked for," Eric announced. "Is this your hot date, Stafford?" he asked, smiling broadly at the little girl. "Hi, honey," he said to her.

"Save your breath, Martinez. Your charm is wasted here," Sean told his partner, taking the items from him. "She can't hear you."

"Haven't you heard?" the other detective asked, making eye contact with the little girl. He smiled broadly at her and she shyly returned the smile. "Charm transcends words."

"Uh-huh. What do I owe you?" Sean asked as he placed the sandwich, cookies and soda on the table in front of the little girl.

"That's okay," Eric answered. "I think I can cover this magnificent spread."

Meanwhile, the little girl was looking at the food hungrily, but she made no attempt to pick up anything. January tapped her on the shoulder and signed for the little girl to eat.

Beaming, the little girl picked up the cookies. But before she could tear open the plastic bag, January shook her head and indicated that she needed to eat the sandwich first.

The child's eyes darted toward Sean, who nodded his agreement. The little girl bobbed her head up and down, and then picked up the food. The bright brown eyes looked from January to the detective, as if to make sure they were both in agreement. When they both nodded at her, the little girl happily sank her teeth into the sandwich.

"Looks like you both speak her language," Martinez observed.

"This part doesn't take much," January replied. "The rest of it might be harder, though."

"And you are…?" Eric asked, raising one brow as he waited to be filled in.

Sean did the honors. "This is January Colton. She's the social worker that children's services sent to work with this little girl."

"She the one you found hiding in the warehouse?" Eric asked.

Sean nodded. "One and the same."

Martinez had more questions, and he knew who to direct them to. He turned toward the social worker. "You think you can get her to tell you what we need to know?" he asked her.

"All I can do is try—provided she does know something." January watched as the little girl consumed her food. For a hungry child, she ate rather daintily, January couldn't help thinking. Someone had definitely taught her manners. "You forget, she might not have seen anything going down. You said she was found hiding behind the crates, which were some distance away from where the bodies were discovered," she recalled.

Eric nodded. "That's what I heard." He turned toward Sean. "Well, keep me posted if you do find out anything," he said. Eric paused to smile at the little girl as he told Sean, "I've got to get going. It's Alicia's third birthday and Rachel will absolutely skin me alive if I don't show up until after she's tucked in bed and sound asleep."

Sean nodded, gesturing for his partner to be on his way. "Go," he urged. "Give my best to Rachel."

Eric grinned in response. There was nothing innocent in his expression.

"Oh, I fully intend to," the detective promised with enthusiasm. "But it'll be *my* best, not yours." He gave Sean a wide grin just before he left the room.

"Have you two been partners for very long?" January asked the detective as Eric closed the door behind him.

"Under two years," he answered. Remembering what had come before was hard for him and he wasn't about to get into it. Instead, he went on the defensive. "Why would that be important to you?"

"Not important. Just trying to get a handle on the kind of person I'm dealing with," she told Sean, her eyes meeting his.

"Does it make a difference?"

"Sometimes," she allowed. She looked at the little girl who was now working her way through the cookies with gusto. January kept her tone steady. "Children are extremely intuitive about things. You want her to be able to trust you."

"I think I've already established a rapport with her," Sean pointed out, smiling fondly at "Annie." She returned the smile in kind. "It's safe to say that she trusts me."

"It looks that way, but if you don't mind, I'd like to cover all my bases," January told him. "This is all very new to her—and that includes you. In the next few hours, something might come up that could make her change her mind." She knew he couldn't argue with that.

And he didn't.

Sean nodded. "Duly noted. You have any way of finding out her name?"

She decided not to answer his question just yet. "Look, before we go any further, I need you to tell me everything that she might have experienced."

He felt like the social worker was leading him around in circles. "Why should that make any difference, one way or another?"

"So I know what I'm up against," January said simply. "What *she* might be up against," she added. By the expression on his face, she could see that the detective didn't understand what she was telling him. She put it in the simplest terms she could. "I need to be able to get her to trust me and to relate to me. Now tell me what you know."

Sean laughed under his breath. "That's usually my line," he told her.

The corners of her mouth quirked in a fleeting smile. "Welcome to the other side," she said. "Now tell me."

The detective sighed. Just his luck, they had sent a stubborn social worker. But there was no point in wasting any more time going back and forth about this. Besides, it wasn't as if he was revealing any secrets. The story had probably made the news by now.

"There's not much more to tell you than I already

have," Sean said. "There were three men found dead in that warehouse where she was hiding behind some crates. One of the dead men was an informant of mine. I was working with him to bring down a well-connected drug lord."

"What's his name?" she asked. "The guy you were trying to bring down."

Sean debated telling this social worker that she had no "need to know," as the popular phrase went, but then he decided that there was no point in withholding the information from her. "His name is Elias 'Kid' Mercer. Anyway, my informant and two other gang members were found shot dead at the scene."

"And you think this little girl you found there, she saw who killed these men?" January questioned him, looking at the child uncertainly.

Sean ran his hand over the little girl's soft brown hair. He smiled at her as they made eye contact. "I have no way of knowing. That's where you come in."

She frowned as she thought over what he had just said. "You do realize that if word gets out that she witnessed this execution, her life could very well be in danger."

Sean's face clouded over. "You think that hasn't crossed my mind? Look, I don't know the kind of people you're used to dealing with, but I'm not in the habit of endangering children."

The detective had gone from neutral to red-hot in seconds, right before her eyes. It didn't take a degree in psychology to know that she had obviously touched a nerve.

"I didn't mean to imply that that you were," January told him.

In her estimation, he didn't exactly look placated, although the color of his face did return to a normal shade. "Just so you know that I'll do whatever it takes to keep this kid safe."

"Understood," January replied. She made a mental note to ask Stafford's partner about this whole incident if she saw him again. She had a feeling that Stafford wasn't being completely honest with her about what might have happened, and it had something to do with why he was so touchy when she questioned him.

As if realizing how he must have come across, Sean apologized. "Sorry. I didn't mean to snap at you like that. It's been a really long day and I did just lose an informant." He hoped that would satisfy her.

What he didn't say was that finding the informant dead brought back some very bad memories. His former partner, Harry Cartwright, a man he had worked with since he started on the force, lost his wife and daughter while he and Sean were working on a case. The wife and daughter had been collateral damage, a completely unfeeling term for a very personal loss.

The wife and daughter he, Sean, was supposed to have been able to protect but couldn't.

To this day, Sean hadn't been able to shake the guilt that haunted him. He should have been able to save them—should have, but somehow wasn't able to.

After it was all over, Harry didn't leave the force, the way some people had expected him to, but he did leave the department. Left Homicide and transferred over to the Narcotics Division.

The move had hit Sean really hard. Harry had been like a brother to him and not a day went by that he didn't miss working with the man. Sean especially missed the camaraderie that they had shared.

Eric Martinez was a good man, Sean thought, but it just wasn't the same. Because of that, and everything that had gone into what had happened, Sean found himself unable to open up. *Afraid* to open up. Worried that if he did, the same thing might happen again. He knew he couldn't bear that.

"Apology accepted," January was saying to him.

Sean forced himself back to the present.

"Is there anything else I should know?" she asked.

"Nope."

He had answered her a little too quickly, in her opinion. January couldn't shake the feeling that something else was going on here, something she couldn't quite put her finger on.

She had no idea what it might be.

And then again, maybe she was being too suspicious, she thought.

"Okay," January said, nodding and looking back at the little girl. "Let's see if I can find out her name."

"The crime scene investigative unit said they didn't find anything that looked as if it belonged to her, so there was no personal information we could tie to her," Sean said, offering her another nonproductive piece of the puzzle.

"I love a challenge," January murmured with absolutely no enthusiasm. "Let's see what she can tell us."

Coming up to the child, January gently put her hand on the little girl's shoulder to get her attention. The girl looked up at her.

At least there was no fear there, January thought, counting that as a small victory.

With very careful, deliberate movements, January held her breath and began to sign, asking the little girl if she would tell them her name.

Chapter Five

As Sean watched, January's hands almost seemed to fly, forming a number of different positions, which he assumed was the way she asked the little girl for her name. What it did manage to accomplish was to convince the detective that he didn't even know how to *begin* to actually communicate with the little girl whom he had rescued.

When January rested her hands in her lap, he assumed that she had finished the exchange, even though he couldn't make head or tail of it.

"So," Sean asked, "is she willing to tell us her name?"

"She already did," January told him, smiling at the child. "Her name is Maya."

"Maya," he repeated. It had a nice ring to it. "What was the sign for that?" Sean asked.

"There was no isolated sign," she told him. "Maya spelled her name out." Then, for the detective's benefit, she showed him each letter slowly, saying them as she formed them. "M-A-Y-A. Maya."

Sean appeared confounded as he shook his head.

"There is no way in the world that I'm going to get the hang of that."

"Well, it's nice of you to want to try," January told him, surprised that the detective said that. "But there's no point for you to attempt to do that if we're going to find her parents."

Sean had his doubts about that. "Provided at least one of them is alive and around," he pointed out. He looked down at Maya's small, heart-shaped face. All sorts of emotions went through him, making him feel outraged and angry that Maya had wound up at the scene of the crime the way she had. "If you ask me, parents who can just lose track of their little girl like that are either dead—or don't deserve to have her in their lives in the first place."

"Hey, don't jump to conclusions yet," January warned him. "In my experience, there are as many reasons for things happening when it involves children as there are children in the system."

He wasn't clear where she was going with this, but he did know how he felt. "Yeah, well, if she were my kid, I wouldn't take my eyes off her. I certainly wouldn't let her run off and play in some abandoned warehouse," Sean said, his emotions bubbling just beneath the surface.

Maya pulled on the edge of his jacket. When Sean looked at her, Maya let go of his jacket so she could talk to him. Keeping her hand open, the little girl tapped her thumb on the side of her forehead. Then, when he didn't respond, she did it again.

Lost, Sean looked over his shoulder at January. "What's she saying?"

"She's asking for her daddy," January told him.

That was when something occurred to the detective. Something unpleasant. Sean exchanged looks with January. "You don't think he was one of the two unknown men who were found dead in the warehouse with my CI, do you?" he asked.

January had another take on the situation. "Could Maya's father have been your contact?"

He thought for a second but realized that he didn't honestly know the answer to that. "I don't think the guy had any kids, but I can't say that for sure. But even if she was his kid, would he have brought her with him, knowing how dangerous it might be?"

January shrugged. "Hey, he's your informant. You would know the answer to that better than I would." And then she pulled back her shoulders, as if she was anticipating something she didn't consider pleasant.

"What are you doing?" Sean asked. In his estimation nothing had changed from a moment ago.

"I'm bracing myself to ask Maya a very jarring, unpleasant question," she told the detective.

Then, before he could say anything one way or the other, January began to sign her question to Maya. This time, for Sean's benefit, January also slowly verbalized it as she signed for Maya.

"Was your dad there in the warehouse today?" she asked the little girl.

Rather than sign something back, looking surprised, Maya moved her head from side to side.

"He wasn't one of the dead men?" Sean asked, a little uncertainly. That was good news in his estimation, but at the same time, it seemed rather unusual to him that the little girl had just wandered into the warehouse by herself.

"Apparently not," January replied.

Maya looked from one adult to the other and then directed a question to January. Because Maya was agitated, her fingers flew even more quickly.

Sean stared, mystified. "What's she saying?"

"Just that she wants her daddy. My guess is that the man is obviously alive somewhere," January said to the detective.

As he watched, she signed something else to Maya and the little girl apparently answered.

"Now what did you ask?" he asked.

"If she saw her dad recently," January answered.

"And?" he prodded.

"She did," the social worker said. Then, as Sean watched, January took the little girl into her arms in an attempt to comfort and soothe her. "Shh, it's going to be all right," January promised her.

He looked at the social worker, puzzled. She had lost him. "I thought you said that Maya can't hear."

"As far as I know, she can't. But a hug is universal. And Maya responded to it. The words just came out automatically," she added.

"I can see that," Sean said, watching as Maya curled up against January.

Who are you, little girl? How did you get inside that warehouse? Were you lost, or did someone lose you there on purpose? Sean wondered. He really wanted to get to the bottom of this, but it wasn't going to happen tonight.

January glanced in the detective's direction and saw the considering expression on his face. "What are you thinking?"

He wasn't comfortable admitting to having any personal thoughts when it came to his job. He snapped back into work mode.

"That right now, I need to figure out what to do with her for the night." His eyes met January's. "I guess you'd better call your boss, have him send someone to pick her up." And then he smiled down at Maya. Something told him that, in a way, she did understand him even if he couldn't talk to her. "We certainly can't leave her here for the night."

He sounded like he was talking to Maya, January thought, except she knew that *he* knew he couldn't communicate with her in a straightforward manner. Still, January had to admit that she found the whole thing rather touching.

"No, we can't," January agreed. She looked at Maya thoughtfully. "The trouble is, I don't think that there's anyone in our present system who can just take her in. They wouldn't be able to communicate with her. We're shorthanded right now." Although, she thought, that really wasn't anything new.

"Okay," he said, stretching out the word. "So what does that mean, ultimately?" Sean was not quite sure what the social worker was telling him. Where was Maya going to wind up staying tonight? Whether he wanted to or not, Sean found himself being protective of the little girl.

January unconsciously chewed on the inside of her bottom lip, thinking the matter over. "Well, I've got those two weeks coming to me that I have to take."

"Yeah, so you said. The two weeks you told me you were using to go away on vacation," Sean recalled.

"Yes," she confirmed. "I am supposed to be on vacation, but there're no rules about *where* I take my vacation—or how." She could see that she had lost the detective. With effort, she tried to be clearer, even though her own thoughts were jumbled up. "I can temporarily take Maya home with me and foster her. At least until things can be straightened out and you find her parents—or her father, since that's who she's been asking for." She looked at the detective's face to see if she had cleared things up for him.

"Can you do that?" he asked doubtfully. "Just take her in and be her foster parent?" he asked. "Aren't you supposed to be qualified for that or something?"

Sean hated admitting his ignorance about these matters, but in this case, there were huge gaps in his education when it came to knowing things about the foster system. In his defense, he thought, he'd never had a case like this before. The people he dealt with were usually a lot taller—and came with criminal records.

"I do," she said, surprising Sean.

"You're licensed to be a foster parent?" he asked.

January nodded. "Thinking that this might come up as a possibility someday, I became approved to be a foster parent in case the need ever arose. This is the first time that it has," she admitted. "Right now, to complete this temporary arrangement, I just have to get my boss's approval."

"Why don't you call Blackwell, then?" Sean suggested.

They needed to resolve this. He didn't want to see Maya get passed around and possibly traumatized any further. The little girl responded to this woman, and as the social worker had already pointed out, feeling safe could go a long way in getting Maya to trust her.

That also meant that if there was any information to be obtained from her, they would be able to—at least eventually.

But, information or not, Sean had to admit that his first priority was to make sure Maya was safe and *felt* safe. In this case, apparently January was his instrument to help him do just that.

January had crossed to the far end of the room and taken out her phone. It rang five times on the other end before she heard it being picked up.

"Blackwell."

Good, she had caught him. "Hi, Sid, it's January Colton. I know it's late, but there's a problem with the case you wanted me to look into," she told her boss.

"What kind of a problem?" he asked. "And what are you still doing there? I figured that you'd just see what you could find out from the little girl and then have Susan take over."

"Well, that's part of the problem," January admitted, keeping her back to the detective and the little girl. "I sent Susan home."

She could tell by Blackwell's tone that he wasn't exactly overjoyed with her news. "Oh? And why would you do that?"

"Because she was in completely over her head in this case. There wound up being extenuating circumstances. Look, I can fill you in on those in the morning if you'd like," she offered. "Right now, I'm just calling to get your approval."

"My approval. Regarding anything in particular?" her supervisor asked, a partially amused note in his voice. January was one of the best people he had, but she didn't exactly do things by the numbers.

In general, Blackwell was a decent man. January went with that thought, hoping he wouldn't give her an argument about this. In the very short amount of time she had been here, she felt she had managed to forge a bond with Maya. She found herself caring about this child. Her tendency to become personally involved was what more than one person had predicted would wind up being her undoing someday.

But someday wasn't now.

"That little girl the police found in the warehouse, the one that you asked me to communicate with," January began to explain.

"What about her?" Blackwell asked.

January couldn't gauge his mood by his tone, but she pushed ahead anyway. "She needs to be placed with a temporary foster parent until things can get further straightened out."

"And?" Blackwell prodded impatiently when January paused.

"And I'd like to volunteer to be that foster parent," January told him, talking quickly as she added, "I have been vetted and I do have my foster parent license."

She heard Blackwell blow out an annoyed, frustrated breath. "You can't take her on vacation with you, January."

"I know that. I'm not going on vacation, at least, not to that spa and not now. I'll be staying at my town house with Maya instead of going away."

"Maya?" Blackwell asked.

"Maya's the little girl's name. I got her to tell me that," January replied.

"Very good. Progress. So what's her last name?" he asked.

"I haven't gotten that far yet," January admitted. "She's only about five and the police didn't find anything on her or in the area that would give us her last name or her address. But she trusts me, Sid."

"And this is why you want to foster her?" he questioned.

"I know we're shorthanded. The child is deaf and I want her to get special care. Look, Sid, I'm the best hope she has of being reunited with her family which is, after all, our end goal."

"Then there *is* a family?" Blackwell asked, his interest piqued.

"Detective Stafford and I think so," she said, thinking that adding Sean to her side might help tip the scale in her favor. "Maya keeps asking for her father, so I'm hoping that means that he's actually out there somewhere and that we can find him."

Blackwell sighed. "I guess you make a good point. All right, I'm going to grant you temporary custody. But I'm going to have this case monitored by another social worker."

"Of course, Sid. Whatever it takes," January said, relieved that she had won the man over. She saw that Sean was watching her even though her voice was low. She gave him a thumbs-up sign.

"All right. Come in tomorrow, January, and we'll make it official. I'll have you fill out all the paperwork and sign it," her supervisor told her.

January smiled even though she knew he couldn't see her. "I know the drill, Sid."

"Yes, I imagine that you do. One question for you, January," he said before she could terminate the call.

"Yes?" She had no idea what he could think of to ask her. They had already gone over all the important points.

"Don't you know how to relax?" he asked her.

January laughed. "You're the one who sent me here, Sid."

"I was just sending you in as a temporary measure to see what you could ascertain. I didn't realize you were going to use it as another excuse to keep on working."

She didn't want Blackwell pretending to be her conscience. "Goodbye, Sid. I'll see you tomorrow."

"Good," he told her, adding, "I'm looking forward to you telling me how your sisters reacted to this."

Oh Lord, my sisters, January suddenly thought. She had forgotten all about them. She needed to notify them as soon as possible.

This wasn't going to be easy.

"I've got to go, Sid," January said, terminating the call.

"Problem?" Sean asked. He noticed that she was still clutching her cell phone instead of putting it away.

"With my supervisor?" she asked, thinking that was what Sean was referring to. "No, everything's fine there. He signed off on my being Maya's foster mother."

There was more, he could tell. "But…?"

"But?" January asked.

"There's a definite *but* in your voice," Sean told her. "Something's bothering you about this," he guessed. "What is it?"

"Well, it doesn't have anything to do with my supervisor, or with Maya," she said, answering his question slowly.

"But there's someone who isn't going to be happy about this sudden change in your life, even though it is temporary?" the detective guessed.

His immediate thought was that there was either a husband, or at least a significant other, in the picture and that he wasn't going to be happy about this.

"Oh yes," she answered. "Actually, two someones." January thought of Simone and Tatum.

"Two someones?" Sean repeated. "Well, that seems rather ambitious."

"Ambitious?" she asked. She didn't see the connection. "That's rather an odd way to put it."

She was kidding, right? "Well, it isn't every day that I meet a woman who is openly juggling two guys—"

"Two guys?" she echoed, totally confused.

"My mistake, two women," Sean corrected his previous statement. Apparently, his mistake was even bigger than he had thought.

Damn. First time he found himself attracted to someone in longer than he could remember, and it turned out to be someone wouldn't give him a second glance.

"Yes," January acknowledged, wondering what his problem was. "Two women. My sisters, both of whom are going to give me endless grief over my bowing out of our vacation, especially since it was planned around my choice of location."

"Your sisters?" he asked. Why did that piece of information suddenly make him feel happy?

He had no explanation for it, yet there it was.

"Both older and both are going to relish saying, 'I told you so' to each other—and to me." She took a deep breath, still clutching her phone. "I'll be right back," she promised. Then she repeated the message, signing it to Maya, just before she slipped out of the room.

Chapter Six

January looked down at the cell phone in her hand, debating which sister to call. Tatum had always been the more easygoing of the two to deal with, but Simone was the one who had made all the plans and consequently had booked the spa as well as the plane tickets. She knew that telling Simone that she had to bow out because of a work commitment would be the more respectful thing to do.

On the other hand, Tatum wouldn't lecture her and Simone would.

Both sisters loved her, there was no question about that. But Simone was more sharp-tongued and did, on occasion, wind up assuming a superior air when she talked to January.

This is ridiculous, January thought. She decided to face the music and not put off the inevitable. Because even though she might call Tatum instead of Simone to tell her sister that plans have been changed, somewhere along the line, Simone would call her and let her know that she had "expected this all along."

Just before she dialed Simone, January glanced at

the little girl who was the reason she was doing this in the first place.

She was right to do this. There would be other vacation getaways with her sisters, but Maya needed her right now.

Taking a deep breath, January placed her call.

The cell phone on the other end was picked up before the second ring had completed.

"I had a feeling I'd be hearing from you, Jan," Simone said. There was that touch of smugness, January thought, pressing her lips together. "So, what excuse are you going to give us?"

"No excuse, Simone," January replied. "Just the truth."

"And that is?" Simone asked, waiting.

January didn't hesitate. She gave her sister the story straight. "There was a little five-year-old deaf girl found crouching behind some crates in an abandoned warehouse. There were three men found in that same warehouse. They had been killed execution-style. It turns out that I'm the only one here who can communicate with her. So instead of going on vacation, I'm taking Maya—that's her name—home with me so I can try to make her feel safe. Do you have a problem with that?"

For a moment, Simone didn't answer. And then, using a very different tone, her sister said, "Well, if you put it that way, no. We'll just postpone our vacation and go to that spa some other time—"

"Don't you dare," January cried. She didn't want to ruin everyone's vacation because of something she felt she had to do. "I want you and Tatum to go and have fun for all three of us, do you hear me?"

"While you're getting fitted for your angel wings?" Simone asked.

"No angel wings, Simone," January replied. "I swear, if you saw this little girl's face and thought you could help her, you'd be doing the same thing I am. Now I want you to promise me that you and Tatum are going to be on that plane tomorrow, flying to that spa getaway. Okay? I don't need to feel any more guilty about not being there for this vacation with you than I already do. Now go!"

"Are you sure?" Simone asked her.

"Yes, I'm sure," January assured her sister with feeling.

She heard Simone pretend to sigh. "Okay, we'll do our best. But you're not off the hook by a long shot, little sister," Simone told her. "You owe us a sister getaway, and Tatum and I intend to collect."

"You got it," January promised. "Now I've got to go. But tell Tatum I'm sorry."

"Will do." Simone began to talk quickly before January hung up. "To tell you the truth, I half expected you to call her and not me. Why did you call me?"

So Simone was aware of the way she could sound sometimes, January thought. Apparently, there was hope. "Because it was the right thing to do, Simone," January told her.

"You know, someday those merit badges of yours are really going to start weighing you down, Jan. Take care of yourself—and try to let someone else save the world once in a while," she told her baby sister.

If she argued over Simone's assumption, January knew she wouldn't be able to get off the phone, so she just promised, "Will do."

"Uh-huh," Simone murmured. But before she could say that she knew January was just humoring her, January terminated the call.

January sighed as she shook her head.

"So, did you wind up managing to placate everyone?" Sean asked when she reentered the interview room, putting her cell phone away.

Her head jerked up. January had almost forgotten that he was there. "Yes. For the time being," she told the detective.

Sean had another point he wanted to raise with her. He decided that now was as good a time as any. "Listen, I heard you tell your supervisor, that Blackwell guy," he added for good measure, "that you were planning on taking Maya home with you."

Dealing with Simone had taught her to recognize the signs that she was about to be ambushed. "I am," she answered guardedly.

"Well, to be honest with you," he began, sensing that if he just flat out told her he didn't want her doing something, she was the type who would just roll right over him. "I'm not really very thrilled with that idea."

"I didn't realize that was a requirement, having you thrilled over my taking her into my home," January told the detective.

Okay, maybe he would have better luck being direct,

Sean thought. "Look, everything points to this being a dangerous situation."

January stopped him right there. "No kidding, Sherlock," she said. "Isn't that why it was decided that she needed someone to take her in the first place? Because she could be in danger?"

"Yes, but—" Sean began to answer, but got no further than he had the first time.

"Tell me, were you planning on keeping Maya at the police station indefinitely? Because if not," she said, answering her own question before he had a chance to, "then I'm going to take her with me to my town house so I can look after her."

Sean found himself struggling to keep his temper. "Damn but you are one stubborn woman," the detective told January, annoyed.

She met his glare, and for some reason, the expression on his face made her laugh. "You're just finding that out?"

After a moment, Sean's mouth curved. He knew he had one of two choices. He either had to see the humor in this or strangle the woman. Sean decided to see the humor in it, as well as give her credit for having a bigger heart than he had expected.

"No, I kind of figured that out earlier," he admitted. Well, if she was taking Maya home with her, he was going to have to know just where home was. "Look, I'm going to need your address," he began.

January placed her hand over her heart like a Southern belle in an old-fashioned melodrama. "Why, Detective Stafford, this is all just so sudden."

Sean never skipped a beat as he ignored her sarcasm. "So I can have a police car patrol the area every half hour," he told her. He was not about to get sucked into a discussion he had no place taking part in, especially since he found himself reacting more strongly to this woman than he felt was wise on his part. "Unless you have some kind of objections to that," he added.

She surprised him by smiling up into his face. "As a matter of fact, I don't. I appreciate the fact that you are going to be looking out for Maya—and for me," January added after a beat.

He wasn't sure how to respond to that and said the first thing that came to mind. "Yeah, well some things can't be helped."

January suppressed the laugh that rose to her lips, then fluttered her lashes at him. "You mean, like your winning personality?"

He didn't rise to the bait. Instead, he reminded the social worker, "Just remember that you were the one who wanted in on this, Ms. Colton."

January's deportment changed right before his eyes and she became serious as she admitted, "Yes, I know, and I'd do it again in a heartbeat. Let's not lose sight of the fact that Maya is the important person in all of this."

"Not losing sight of that even for a moment," Sean assured her. "Okay, give me your address and I'll see to it that a patrol car will be out in your area, keeping an eye on things. In the meantime, I'm going to escort you home."

"You don't have to do that," January began to tell

him. She was perfectly capable of taking herself and Maya home.

Oh no, he wasn't about to get tangled up in that discussion. He was accompanying them to her home and that was the end of it.

"Read my lips," Sean told her, leaning into the social worker to get his point across as he slowly enunciated, "I am going to escort you home."

She nodded. "Okay, then," she replied breezily, reversing direction. "You're escorting me home." January prided herself on knowing when to charge ahead and when to back off.

Taking a notepad from her purse, she quickly wrote down her address for the detective, then handed him the piece of paper.

JANUARY PULLED UP in front of her town house and stopped her vehicle, turning off the ignition. She glanced up into her rearview mirror.

Yup, the detective was still there. True to his word, he had followed her all the way home, staying right behind her.

She got out of her car just as he pulled to a stop.

January glanced toward the back seat. Stafford had managed to procure a child seat for Maya from the lost-and-found department at the police station. She was going to return the seat as soon as she bought one for her car. Right now, she had no idea how long the little girl was going to actually be staying with her.

January considered herself to be a very good driver and she knew that, once upon a time, children just sat anywhere they wanted to in the car. However, accidents did happen no matter how safe a driver might be. She was not about to take any chances, even if there weren't laws on the books about this. It was much better to be safe than sorry. Maya needed to be in a child seat that had seat belts holding it in place.

Glancing at her, she saw that Maya looked as if she had fallen asleep in her seat. So, for now, January left her where she was and turned toward the detective as Sean approached her vehicle.

"Well, this is it," she told Sean, gesturing toward her town house. "I can take it from here."

Sean leaned over and glanced into the car. "She looks asleep."

"I think she is," January confirmed. If Maya was, it might make things easier, at least for now, January reasoned.

He put his hand on the passenger-side door. "I'll carry her in for you."

She didn't want him thinking of her as helpless. "I'm perfectly capable of carrying her in myself, Stafford," she told him.

"I'm sure you are," Sean replied, not about to get into an argument with the woman over this. "Okay, you can carry her in if it makes you feel better—but you bring her into the house *after* I check everything out there and clear all the rooms."

January looked at him, surprised. What he was proposing sounded like something that was on one of those detective programs that were so popular on TV these days. "You're kidding, right?" she asked, waiting for him to say "yes."

"Do I look like I'm kidding?" Sean asked her pointedly.

"To be honest, I really don't know you well enough to be able to confirm that one way or another," January told him.

"Well, I'm not," Sean answered. "If someone followed you to the police station, they might have wound up putting two and two together and whoever killed those three men could very well be waiting inside your town house."

She had a feeling that there was something he wasn't telling her, but it was obvious that she wasn't going to be able to force it out of him right now.

"Are you determined to get me nervous?" January asked.

"Not determined, no, but when dealing with something like this, it's never a bad idea to be on your guard," Sean told her.

Her first instinct was to tell the detective that he was wasting his time and that he should just go home. But she had to admit after listening to Sean that there was a very small part of her that did entertain the possibility that maybe he was right. That maybe someone had broken into her town house and was waiting for her, for Maya, actually, to walk in so that any witness to the murders was eliminated.

So it was for Maya's sake that she agreed to have Sean go inside and clear each room, one by one.

"Go ahead," she told him, gesturing toward the town

house. "Have at it." With that, she handed him her house keys.

Meanwhile, Maya had woken up. She instantly began to try to get out of her car seat. Seeing her struggle, January quickly unbuckled the little girl and, taking her into her arms, drew Maya out of the seat. Maya wiggled, as if she was trying to get down. January set her on the ground, thinking that the child would feel more in control of her situation if she could walk into the house under her own power.

Sean waited, the house keys in his hand. Once January reached him, holding Maya by the hand, the detective unlocked the front door. After giving the keys back to January, he slowly drew his gun out, carefully keeping the muzzle pointed away in order not to frighten the little girl.

"All right," he told January. "I want you both to wait right inside the front door until I come back down for you."

"You're actually going to go from one room to another?" January asked him. Part of her thought this was overkill, another part of her thought that perhaps this wasn't enough of a precaution.

"That's what I intend to do," Sean confirmed.

"Be careful," she warned. When he raised his brow in a silent question, January said, "I might have unintentionally left some things scattered around on the floor when I left this morning. I was going to come back and pack for the trip."

"I think I can avoid tripping over scattered luggage and shoes," he told her with an amused smile. "You don't have a dog that's suddenly going to come charging out at me, do you?"

"No, no dog," she answered. "I would have loved to have one," she confided, "but given my lifestyle, it wouldn't have been fair to the dog. I wouldn't be home all that much and I would never have the kind of time for it that the animal would deserve."

"You're that dedicated, huh?" Sean asked as he began to head for the kitchen.

"I don't clock in nine-to-five if that's what you mean," she told him.

"Yeah, I get that," he told her, already putting distance between them as he began to search from one room to another. "We have that in common."

And then he was gone.

Maya stared after him, then looked at January. Making sure she had January's attention, Maya moved her pointer finger from side to side beneath her chin.

"You want to know where he's going?" January asked aloud, knowing Maya was reading her lips. She was a smart little girl, January thought. "He's making sure the house is safe," she told the child as she signed the same message to her.

January felt she should try to make sure that the child had reinforcement and could more easily associate hand signs with spoken words.

She was already thinking beyond tonight, focusing on the days that were to follow. Whether or not they found the girl's parents, she felt that Maya was going to need to be introduced to the world—and she intended to help with that as much as she could.

She hated the idea of Maya being helpless.

Chapter Seven

January saw Maya looking around, her eyes opened extra wide as she appeared to try to take in the entire town house from her vantage point by the front door. January was afraid that the little girl might want to just run off and start to explore the place on her own, but instead, Maya remained at her side, her small fingers wrapped tightly around January's hand.

The little girl might not be impatient, but she definitely couldn't say the same thing for herself, January thought.

What she wanted to do was shout up the stairs to Stafford and get him to tell her how the process was going. But even she knew that shouting was definitely not part of the deal. If she shouted, and there *was* someone on the premises, that would alert the intruder and even, possibly, put Stafford in danger.

Still, there was no denying that she ached to ask the detective if he was done up there, and, if not, how much longer it was going to take until he was.

Instead, January pressed her lips together to keep the words from escaping and sighed.

Because she was learning to become more in tune with Maya, January was aware that the child had turned toward her.

Maya drew her hand from hers and signed, "Where did he go?"

By "he" January assumed the little girl was asking about Stafford. She signed, "He is upstairs, making sure everything is safe."

Maya's furrowed brow vanished after a moment. The answer she'd been given seemed to satisfy the little girl. She took hold of January's hand again, as if that was the position she felt she had to maintain until the detective returned.

They didn't have long to wait.

"All clear," Sean announced, coming back down the stairs. "Doesn't look like anyone's been here," he told January. "And you are probably the neatest 'messy' person I have ever met," he said, referring to the suitcase she had warned him not to trip over.

Sean had found the suitcase standing on the bedroom floor, off to one side and waiting to be opened so that she could begin packing.

"Thank you—I think," January told him a little uncertainly.

His job was officially done, but he could stay in the town house a little longer if it made her feel more secure. He offered as much to her.

Turning around to face January, he said, "I can stick around for a while if you'd like."

She turned him down, just as he'd suspected she would. "Thanks, but we'll be fine, Stafford. It's late and I'd like to get her to bed. You know, try to approximate some semblance of a routine for Maya." January glanced in Maya's direction. "Kids appreciate routines."

"I'll take your word for it. I never had any. Kids, I mean," he added, in case she thought he was referring to having a routine. Those he'd had, one way or another, all of his life.

Even now.

Her eyes crinkled. "Neither have I, but I deal with kids all the time. You get to pick up things," she confided, "even if you don't really realize it."

"I'll keep that in mind."

Time to wrap this up, January thought. "I'll walk you to the door," she volunteered.

"What's your hurry? There's the door." Sean laughed, amused at the less-than-subtle attempt to get him to leave. "I know where the door is, January, but you should lock it after I leave."

She looked at the detective, pretending to widen her eyes. "Thank you. I would have *never* thought of doing that."

"Very funny," he replied drolly, going and then stopping in the doorway. "I'll be back in the morning, Ms. Colton."

The man just didn't let up. "You don't have to check on us," January insisted.

"I'm not checking on you," he informed her. "I'm coming by to take a DNA sample from Maya. I'm going to see if it matches any family member in the database so that we can ultimately get a handle on who she is.

Don't forget, there's going to be a police car patrolling the area. During the night, if you hear or see anything that makes you uneasy—anything at all—I want you to call 911. Better yet, here's my card." He took a card out of his pocket and pressed it into her hand. "Call me anytime. I'll be here in a flash."

"Are you planning on sleeping at my doorstep in your car?" She meant it as a joke because of his "flash" comment, but he didn't seem to take it that way.

"Just call my number," Sean instructed again. And then he glanced down at Maya who was still standing beside January, appearing a little lost and more than a little sleepy. "Tell her I'll see her tomorrow morning," he requested.

January signed the message for Maya's benefit. The little girl's fingers immediately flew, responding to the promise from the man who had rescued her.

"What did she say?" Sean asked, looking at January.

"She said she would be right here, waiting for you," January told him.

Sean's smile was warm in response. Somehow, Maya had managed to burrow her way into his heart in an incredibly short amount of time, he thought.

The detective ran his hand fondly over her soft brown braids, his gesture telling her what he was still unable to on his own.

"Okay, then," he said, turning toward January. "I'll be going," he told her, although he felt a reluctance to do so. His eyes met January's. "I'll see you in the morning," he said, then repeated pointedly, "Lock the door."

"Go, before I give in to my impulse and kick you in the shins," January said, shutting the door behind him.

The second she did, she heard his voice coming from behind the door. "I didn't hear the lock click into place."

"Then you need to have your ears checked," she informed him, raising her voice so he could hear her as she turned the lock.

"Better," Sean acknowledged as he left January's doorstep.

She gave it to the count of five, then turned toward Maya. She found the little girl watching her. There was a question in Maya's expressive brown eyes. It didn't take much for January to guess what was on Maya's mind.

"He's gone home," January signed to the little girl, then added, "He will be back in the morning."

Maya met the assurance with a wide smile followed by a sleepy yawn.

"Okay, time to get you to bed, little one," January said.

When Maya raised and lowered her slender shoulders, January repeated what she had said, this time signing it to Maya. Maya's hands made no response, but January could see that the little girl wasn't about to fight it.

Linking her fingers with Maya's, January took her upstairs. Once she was on the landing, January signed, "I don't have anything for a little girl to wear to bed, but I think that the top half of my two-piece sleepwear might work for you." She offered Maya an encouraging smile. "We'll give that a try."

Maya tilted her head, looking at her. It wasn't hard to figure out what she wanted to know.

January signed the last part of her statement to the girl, then took her by the hand again and led her into the bedroom.

January rummaged through one of her dresser drawers, then another, looking for a particular set of nightclothes. Finally finding what she was looking for, January took the top portion of the outfit out and held it up in front of Maya.

She was rewarded for her efforts with a beatific smile.

You would have thought that that I was holding up Cinderella's ball gown instead of a simple nightshirt top, January thought.

Even so, the little girl looked at her with total, unabashed excitement bubbling wildly just beneath the surface.

"I'd thought you might like it," January told her, then signed the same thing.

She was about to start helping Maya out of her clothes, which were really in pretty bad shape, especially considering the day she had been through.

But she stopped herself in order to sign to the little girl.

"May I help you put on this nightgown?" January asked her.

January felt it was safer that way, since she had no way of knowing if the trauma that Maya had gone through in the warehouse had extended to a physical aspect, as well. The last thing January wanted to do was take a chance of further traumatizing her or bringing up any bad memories for her.

To her relief, the little girl bobbed her head up and down, her eyes appearing to all but shine as she stared at what was, for January, just an ordinary, light pink nightshirt.

With very careful movements, January took off the little girl's dirty jeans and even dirtier T-shirt. She folded each and placed them on the floor beside the bed, leaving them visible as she went on to help Maya slip on the pink nightshirt.

Maya seemed very pleased as she held out the garment from her body, looking down at it. She was even more pleased when she caught sight of herself in it in the wardrobe mirror. She approached the mirror with cautious steps, inspecting herself from all angles.

Her eyes were smiling as she looked up at January. The next moment, she hugged the social worker's arm, beaming at her from ear to ear.

"Glad you like it," January signed to her, then added, "You can keep that if you like. It's yours."

Instead of hugging her arm again, Maya threw her arms around January's waist, gleefully hugging as much of her as she could reach.

January hugged her back. Any second now, she was going to cry, January thought, and she knew that would only confuse Maya. Struggling to regain control over herself, she released the little girl and took hold of her hand instead.

In response to the obvious question in her eyes, January signed to Maya, "Let me take you to your room now."

"My room?" Maya signed back, her small face the picture of wonder and disbelief.

January smiled as she nodded, then signed. "Yes, it's the extra bedroom, but for now, you can think of it as your room."

With that, she led Maya to one of the two guest rooms in the town house. She chose the smaller of the two because that one was located next to her own bedroom instead of down the hall. She didn't want to take a chance on being too far away from the child in case something came up, or Maya became frightened during the night for some reason.

By the look on the little girl's face as they entered the bedroom, in January's estimation, Maya felt as if she had entered paradise.

Pulling back the comforter, January helped the child into the double bed. Like her own bed, this one was made up with 1500 thread count Egyptian cotton sheets and a super-soft comforter. To January there was nothing more important than soft sheets when it came to getting a good night's sleep, and that went for her guests as well as for herself.

She thought, because of everything that had happened today, not to mention that this was all so new and strange to Maya, that it would take the little girl a long time to fall asleep.

January was prepared to sit up with Maya for as long

as it took. In her estimation, it would probably be at least an hour, if not more, before the little girl was out.

As she tried to figure out just what to do with herself during this time, January happen to glance at Maya.

She was already fast asleep.

It had taken her all of seven minutes.

January decided to linger for another fifteen, just in case Maya woke up.

But she didn't.

Releasing the breath she had been unconsciously holding off and on for that duration, January carefully slid off the bed.

Even though she logically knew it wasn't necessary, she made her way silently to the bedroom door. Instead of closing it, she made the decision to leave the door open so that if there was any noise during the night, or Maya tried to leave, January would be able to hear that.

This was the same reason January didn't close her own door when she went into her bedroom. Above all, she didn't want Maya feeling as if she was being closed off from anything.

When she got to her room, January decided that she wasn't going to change out of her own outer clothing and into pajamas. She left her clothes on so she would be able to spring up out of bed, ready to handle whatever needed addressing at a moment's notice.

Stafford had done that to her, January thought. Stafford and his story about those dead men in the warehouse. Men who had been executed by other men who could very well be searching to eliminate any witnesses to what they had done.

Men who might suddenly make an appearance in her home. She was a very logical, calm person, but that was in the light of day. There was something about the darkness that coaxed out uneasy, frightening thoughts and they were what she found herself battling right now.

This was ridiculous. She was a grown woman. She wasn't afraid of things that went bump in the night.

Get a grip, January, she ordered herself.

Lying on top of her covers instead of under them, January took a deep breath. She reminded herself that she had just put in a long day and that by all rights, she should have been exhausted, not coming up with scary, outlandish scenarios.

"Close your eyes, January. You need your rest," she insisted. "And you're going to need your rest so you can face tomorrow without sleepwalking. You can do this. Close your eyes and take a deep breath. In, out. In, out," she repeated as she forced herself to close her eyes.

After a while, she could feel herself relaxing, one tight muscle at a time. It took a few more minutes, but she had almost convinced herself that she was actually drifting off to sleep.

Curling up on her side, January buried her face against her pillow. Her self-hypnosis began working. She slipped into a dreamlike state.

Before long, she was one step removed from actual sleep.

The strange screeching noise penetrated the wall of sleep she had begun to construct around herself.

At first, she thought it was all part of her waking-dream state.

But when the screech-like moan came again, January realized that it wasn't a dream, or even some trapped animal, which had been her next thought.

Maya!

Bolting upright, January's feet hit the floor before she even realized what she was doing.

The next second, she was racing to the room next to hers.

She found Maya cringing in the bed, her eyes shut as she went on whimpering, making those awful noises that had woken January up.

January lost no time scooping Maya up into her arms.

Still asleep, her eyes squeezed shut, Maya began to beat her fists against January, crying and desperate to break away.

But January went on holding her, rocking her body and doing her best to soothe the little girl until Maya finally stopped making those strange, frightened noises. Her eyes suddenly flew open.

They were filled with terror.

When she finally became conscious—and realized where she actually was—Maya stopped hitting January. Instead of making that unearthly sound, the little girl began to sob, her body shaking. Her small arms tightened around January, as if she was trying to draw strength from her.

"It's okay," January said in a soothing voice, even though she knew the little girl couldn't hear her. She could only hope that on some level, Maya could "feel" the words she was saying to her and that by their very utterance, they would wind up comforting her.

Or at least they would wind up negating the effects of Maya's nightmare or whatever it was that had wound up terrifying her.

"I bet that there are a lot of things you've seen and gone through that have scared you," January whispered against Maya's hair. "But I'm right here and I'm going to protect you, I promise."

Chapter Eight

It took January a while before she could get the girl to calm down. Once Maya finally did, January tried to get her to talk about her nightmare.

But instead of signing an answer, or attempting to elaborate, Maya just vigorously shook her head.

January knew better than to push.

"You'll tell me in your own time," she signed to Maya, offering a smile.

The little girl continued to seem pensive. And then, a few minutes later, Maya wanted to know when her daddy was coming to get her. Signing, she repeated the question to January not once, but several times. Each time she did, she appeared to grow more agitated when January told her she didn't know.

January tried another approach. "Maybe I can call him for you. What's your daddy's last name?" she signed. As intelligent as Maya seemed to be, the little girl had no answer for her. All she did was to once again make the sign for daddy.

"Okay," January murmured, resigned, "No last name. Do you know his first name?" she signed, trying again and hoping that this might be the start of solving this particular puzzle.

Maya looked up at her and signed, "Daddy," in response.

As a last-ditch approach, January asked the little girl if she knew her address. Just as she had expected, Maya had no answer for that, either.

This was getting her nowhere. Maybe she could make a little headway with Maya in the morning. At least she could hope, she thought, mentally crossing her fingers. Right now she was fresh out of ideas and too tired to try to come up with any new approaches.

Rather than leave the little girl alone in the guest room again, this time January lay down next to her, thinking that having her close by would somehow comfort Maya.

She was pleased to have guessed right. The little girl began to relax.

Maya was asleep within a few minutes.

This time, January wasn't all that far behind her. Falling asleep with her arm loosely tucked around Maya's waist, January remained that way for what was left of the night.

However, when she woke up, January hardly felt as if she had slept at all. For half a second, she thought she was late. She still needed to pack for her flight to the spa getaway with her sisters.

She had no sooner thought that than she remembered. She'd had Simone cancel those reservations for her so that she could spend her vacation with Maya until the little girl's parents, or at least someone in her family, could be located.

January felt no regret over her canceled plans, only a sense of anxiety that maybe they wouldn't be able to locate *any* family members. That would mean there wouldn't be anyone to take Maya in.

January sighed, trying to blink the sleep out of her eyes. "Well, aren't you just the ray of sunshine?" she asked herself in a mocking tone.

She stretched, feeling less than fresh. Her body protested. But this wasn't the first time she had deliberately gone to sleep in her clothes or in an awkward position. She had stayed up all night in a hospital chair recently, keeping vigil. It had been at the bedside of a little boy who had been badly abused by his stepfather while his mother had done nothing to step in or try to save him. The boy, Daniel, had been rescued by a neighbor who had heard his screams. Because of internal bleeding, Daniel wound up needing surgery, and because she had been assigned to his case at the last minute, she had stayed with the boy while he recovered.

That was how she had wound up sleeping in a chair next to his bedside. She hadn't wanted the nine-year-old waking up to feel as if he had been abandoned and was all alone.

The only difference between the cases, she thought, other than the gender of the children, was that Daniel could hear her when she spoke. Getting Maya to understand her took a little extra effort. She had also known more about the boy and his background than she did about Maya.

Patience, she told herself. *Patience.*

Quietly slipping off the bed, January went into the bathroom. She threw some cold water in her face in an effort to try to feel human again.

When she came out, January found Maya sitting up in bed, obviously watching for her to reenter the bedroom.

"Hi, sleepyhead," January signed, then asked, "Are you hungry?"

Maya's face lit up in response and she nodded her head.

"Good, let's get some breakfast," January signed, then took Maya's hand, getting her to stand up. "After that," she continued, "we'll find you something clean to wear."

Maya looked over toward where her dirty jeans and T-shirt were lying folded on the floor. She pointed to the clothing.

"Something cleaner," January emphasized.

With that, she put her hand out to Maya again, waiting for her to take it. Maya immediately grasped it, reaffirming that the little girl trusted her. January gave her a quick hug, then they went downstairs.

Once in the kitchen, January put on the coffee. In all the excitement the previous night she had completely forgotten to do that. Her morning didn't start until she had the dark liquid coursing through her veins.

As the coffee maker began to make noise, going

through its paces, January opened the refrigerator door to see what she could offer Maya for breakfast. Because, until last night, she had been scheduled to leave on vacation today, she purposely hadn't restocked certain items. If things had gone according to plan, she would have been away for almost two weeks. She hadn't wanted her refrigerator filled with things going bad in that time.

Consequently, although her supply of coffee was as healthy as it always had been, the rest of the food was limited: eggs—two—bread—two slices—and as for meat, she had one hamburger patty on the shelf in case she'd been feeling particularly hungry before she left for the airport.

Beyond that, there was nothing.

"Looks like the cupboard is practically bare," January murmured as she rummaged through the crisper drawers at the bottom of the refrigerator.

As she concluded the inventory, she felt Maya tugging on her sleeve. When she glanced at the girl, Maya raised her hands, indicating that she didn't understand what January had just said.

"Sorry," January signed, then went on to repeat it, this time signing it to Maya.

As if to disprove what January had just said about the cupboard being bare, the little girl opened the refrigerator door farther and proceeded to point to the two eggs, the all but depleted bag of bread, and the lone hamburger patty on a plate.

"You're right," January signed back with a laugh. "It's not really bare. Where are my eyes?"

In response to that, Maya tugged January down to her level, then with a surprisingly gentle touch, she pointed first to one of January's eyes and then the other.

January tried not to laugh as she said, "My mistake again."

Straightening up, January went on to make Maya two scrambled eggs along with two slices of toast. When she put the meal on a plate in front of Maya, the little girl lost no time starting to eat. But then Maya abruptly stopped and looked up. Putting down her fork, she signed, "What about you?"

The very act tugged at January's heart. Not everyone, child or adult, was that thoughtful.

"I'll eat later," January said as she signed the answer.

Maya shook her head, as if she didn't believe her. Taking a bread plate that was on the side of the table, she divided what was left of her breakfast so that January could have something to eat, too.

"You've got a good heart," January told her quietly. "If your parents *are* alive, I know they've got to be looking for you. I hope Stafford can find them."

Rather than asking for her to sign what she had just said, Maya looked at her with a wide smile. January felt that she seemed to understand.

AFTER BREAKFAST WAS over and the dishes cleared, January took Maya upstairs again to find her something to wear. Rummaging through her closet, January found a pretty peasant blouse that, with the proper tie acting as a cinch around her waist, became a slightly large pink peasant dress on the little girl.

"There, you look lovely," January signed, pleased with her handiwork. "And just in time, too." Her cell phone was ringing.

January was rarely without her phone and it was a good thing, too, she thought as she looked at the name on the screen.

Sean Stafford.

"Looks like your admirer is going to be here." January signed as much to Maya, ready to explain what she meant by that term. But she didn't have to. The little girl seemed to know who January meant, and she immediately grew excited. "Ah, so much for playing hard to get." January laughed.

When Maya asked her what she had just said, January signed, "Never mind," and gestured for the little girl to follow her downstairs.

Reaching the bottom of the steps, January answered her phone and asked, "So, when are you getting here?"

"Try now," Sean told her. "I'm standing on your front step."

Well, that certainly wasn't much warning. "And what if I wasn't dressed?" she asked.

She heard a warm chuckle rumbling against her ear. January pressed her lips together. She had obviously said something that struck him as funny.

"I don't mind," he told her cavalierly.

"Very big of you," January commented as she

walked over to the front door. She hung up, opened the two locks and turned the doorknob.

"I try to be easygoing," Sean said just as she opened the door. His eyes met hers a second before he walked into the house. "I take it you didn't get much sleep last night."

"What makes you say that?" she asked. She closed the door behind the detective and then proceeded to flip the locks as he looked at her. She wasn't about to give him the satisfaction of reminding her to lock the door—again.

"Oh, I don't know. Maybe because you don't exactly look all that rested," he answered. "Since you didn't call me last night or this morning, I'm assuming that nothing out of the ordinary happened here."

"Other than Maya having nightmares," she said, sensing he would want to know about that. "No."

By now Maya had thrown her arms around Sean, greeting him affectionately.

"Hi, little one." He smiled at her as he ran one hand over her curls. Looking in January's direction, he asked, "She had nightmares?"

She could see that he was concerned. "Given the way you found her, could you expect anything less?"

"Taking what happened into consideration, I don't think I would have been able to fall asleep if I were her," Sean said.

"Well, luckily, she did for a while—until the nightmares woke her up."

"And you, did you get any sleep?" he asked.

She shrugged. "Me, not so much. At least it didn't feel like I did." Then, uncomfortable talking about herself, she changed the subject. "If you're hungry," she continued, leading him into the kitchen, "I can offer you a hamburger patty or coffee."

"Ah, a regular feast," he commented, his lips quirking to form an amused smile.

"My refrigerator was expecting me to go on vacation," January told him. "I didn't think it was smart to leave a full refrigerator if I wasn't going to be home."

Opening the refrigerator door, Sean looked around the shelves. Except for a barren plate and a couple of empty wrappers that had fallen off and been overlooked, the shelves were all but empty.

"I'd say mission accomplished," he concluded. Closing the door again, the detective turned to her. "I thought you were kidding."

"Well, let that be a lesson to you. I never kid about food," January said, deadpan.

Sean nodded his head. "So I see. After I take that DNA sample I came for and drop it off at the lab, I can go shopping for you and this lovely little lady dressed in pink," he said, volunteering his services as he smiled at Maya.

January signed what the detective said, and Maya responded by covering her mouth and giggling.

"You flattered her," January explained, then added, "and we can do our own shopping, thank you. As a matter of fact, I intend to make going grocery shopping our little project for the day. I get the feeling that she doesn't get to do a lot of normal, everyday things.

"By the way, you should know that she asked for her father again. Several times, actually. Most adamantly right after she woke up from that nightmare she had," she told Sean.

He looked at the DNA kit he had brought with him, which, in essence, was a large cotton swab. "Well, let's see if we can narrow the playing field and find her daddy for her—and her mommy, too, if the woman is anywhere in the picture."

"I get the feeling that Maya would be asking for Mommy if that were the case. I'm guessing that Mommy either left or is dead," January speculated.

"You're probably right," Sean agreed, "but until we have confirmation one way or another, let's just assume that she is somewhere out there."

"Fine by me," January agreed. She wanted to move this along. "For now, why don't you focus on getting that DNA sample from Maya so the lab can run the test on it? You'll tell them to put a rush on it, right?"

He surprised her by laughing. "You obviously haven't had all that much contact with police labs, have you? I'll make it easy for you," Sean told her. "The lab techs all plead overwork."

"You can't flex your muscles or bat your lashes or whatever it takes to get the tech to respond and put you at the head of the list?" she asked.

Her inexperience in this matter really amused Sean.

"Well, it's obvious that someone's been watching way too many TV crime procedurals."

"I don't have time to watch procedurals," she informed him with a touch of indignation. "I'm way too busy dealing with the real world and kids who have been abandoned or abused by people who were supposed to love and care for them. And, if you must know, I also think that you have a way about you that gets people to do whatever you want them to. I'm just telling you to use your 'special power' so that if Maya's father or mother is alive, we get to unite them as quickly as possible."

Intrigued and more than a little fascinated, Sean cocked his head and asked whimsically, "Anything else you'd like me to do while you're making requests?"

An answer rose to her lips, but she wasn't about to make the mistake of actually giving voice to it. Although, admittedly, there was a part of her that would have loved to find out what Sean's mouth would feel like pressed against hers.

Given that there was a child in the room, not to mention that giving in to the impulse would create a host of other complications, she couldn't actually *say* that to the detective—or even have him suspect it.

So, instead, January merely said, "No, that'll do for now."

"Okay, then, why don't we go somewhere comfortable so I can get that sample we need from this little princess?" he asked, smiling at Maya.

"Or we could just do it in the kitchen," January suggested.

"Sounds good. Tell Maya for me," he requested, turning his attention back to the little girl.

January did as he asked, signing to the little girl exactly what the detective was going to do.

After looking uncertain at first, Maya finally sat back down at the table and opened her small mouth.

Chapter Nine

When Sean took the long cheek swab out of its plastic wrapper, Maya's eyes grew huge and she scooted back on her chair, clutching at the seat, as if that was enough to get her out of the detective's reach. She also closed her mouth—tight.

January immediately signed, telling the little girl that it was all right.

Maya shook her head. "No, it's not," Maya signed back. "I will choke on the stick if he pushes it into my throat."

Before January could explain that all the detective was going to do was rub the swab against the inside of her cheek, Sean had taken out a second swab. He had brought the swab with him just in case something happened to the first one.

Getting Maya's attention, Sean elaborately unwrapped the swab, then went on to use it on himself to demonstrate to the little girl just how quick, painless and harmless the whole process was. He rubbed the swab on the inside of his cheek, took the stick out and proceeded to hold it up for her inspection.

Glancing at January, he asked, "How do you sign *done*?"

Raising both hands, January moved them from the area at the top of her shoulders down midway to her waist as if she was trying to brush off sparkles.

Flashing him a smile, she declared, "Done."

"Okay." Mimicking the movement, he looked at Maya as he did it, then said, "Done."

Very slowly, a small, shy smile bloomed on Maya's heart-shaped face. The next moment, she tilted her head back and opened her mouth. Everything about her body language told the detective she was ready for this to happen.

"Very brave," he told Maya, his eyes shining with approval.

Out of the corner of his eye, he saw January sign his spoken sentiment to the little girl.

Sean swabbed the inside of her right cheek quickly, then held up the long stick he had used for her inspection. When she nodded her head, satisfied, he felt it was safe to proceed.

With the same sort of elaborate movements he had used with his own swab, Sean took the swab he had just used on Maya and placed in the plastic bag, pressed the edges on either side together, locking the bag, and then put that in a paper bag.

January had watched the whole thing without saying a word. She was very impressed, not just with his patience, but with the amount and degree of empathy that the detective had displayed.

"They teach you that at the police station?" she asked him when he had finished taking the sample.

"Some things can't be taught," he told her with a simple smile.

"You mean like putting pressure on tab techs?" she asked him.

He snorted, shaking his head. "You just don't stop, do you?"

She held up her hands. "I have no idea what you're talking about," she answered, giving him an innocent look. And then she gave credit where it was due. "But you're very good with her. You put her at ease."

His eyes met January's, and just for the briefest second, he caught himself entertaining thoughts that had no business being in his head.

"Too bad I can't seem to do that with her handler," Sean responded, just as he banished the thought from his head.

"There's no need to put me at ease," she told her. "I work best when I'm on the edge." She cleared her throat before he could draw her in any further with those magnetic bright-green eyes of his. "Now, if you've finished that coffee I poured for you, my suggestion is that you get yourself to that lab posthaste," she told him, pointing at the bag with the swab in it.

"What about my offer?" Sean asked. When January looked at him quizzically, he elaborated. "You know, the offer to go grocery shopping for you and fill your refrigerator."

Hadn't he paid attention to what she had said to him? "How long have you had this problem retaining things?" she asked. Before he could ask her what she was talking about, January told him. "I said that Maya and I were going to make a day of it, going food shopping and just doing something normal. I thought it would be good for her."

He wasn't keen on her being out there with Maya, even in broad daylight. He would definitely feel better if he—or at least a patrol officer—was with her.

"And if I asked you to wait until I got back and could go with you?" he asked.

She didn't like being viewed as helpless. "Sorry, Stafford. No can do."

Two could play this stubborn game, he thought. "All right, then I'm attaching a plainclothes officer to follow you."

She frowned, but she supposed she could see his reasoning. "All right, as long as he puts enough distance between him and us not to spook Maya. She's been through enough," January stressed.

"No argument, but I don't want her possibly having to go through even more," Sean pointed out, "which means keeping her safe."

January rolled what he said over in her head. The way January saw it, her choices were between bad and worse. She pressed her lips together, looking at the detective. Sean represented the lesser of two evils and, happily, he didn't scare Maya. She actually responded to him.

"All right," January said with a sigh, surrendering. "You win."

The corners of his mouth curved. "And what is it that I win?" he asked, taking the DNA sample with him to the door.

He was really going to make her say it, she thought, surprised.

Looking at his expression, she realized that he was. With another sigh, she said through clenched teeth, "Maya and I will wait until you get back before going grocery shopping."

Sean nodded his head. "I take it back," he told her.

January stared at him, confused. She didn't understand. "Take what back?"

Sean's smile widened. "What I was thinking about you."

Which meant, she thought, that initially it had been something less than flattering. "Careful, Detective. I'm not as harmless as I look," January warned, making a fist at her side for emphasis.

They were back, those thoughts about her that he had absolutely no business entertaining in the present atmosphere.

With effort, Sean managed to shut them down.

Again.

He looked at her intently. "Oh, I know you're not," he quietly agreed.

January had no idea what he meant by that, but his tone was way too sexy to be construed as being harmless. It took her a moment to find her tongue. Her mouth felt far too dry.

"You'd better get going," she told Sean. Belatedly, she began to walk him to the door.

Maya was directly behind them, shadowing their every move.

"If you're going to be any use to us, you need to hurry back as soon as possible," January told him.

"You got it. Be back as soon as I can," Sean said, opening the door. But he paused just before he pulled it shut behind him. "You are going to stay put, right?"

"Absolutely." She gave him a quick salute. "Scout's honor."

Sean turned to look at her dubiously. "You were a Girl Scout?" he asked.

The way her eyes sparkled when she smiled at him, Sean didn't know if she was being serious or pulling his leg.

"I've got the merit badges to prove it," she responded cheerfully.

He decided that, for the sake of expediency, he had no choice but to believe her. "All right, I'll take you at your word." He paused to wave goodbye to Maya and then he was gone.

The little girl looked up at January, then signed a question.

"Yes," January assured her, signing. "He's coming back."

Her statement drew a huge smile in response. It didn't take much to figure out what was going on in Maya's head. "You, little girl, have a serious case of hero worship going on," January murmured under her breath.

January happened to glance down at her clothes and realized that she still hadn't changed them, not since yesterday morning. Well, if nothing else, she could use this down time to put on a fresh outfit, she consoled herself.

"Come with me," she signed to Maya.

"To where?" the little girl signed back, cocking her head.

"Definitely not a trusting soul," the social worker in her decided. Maybe that was a good thing.

"To my room," she signed, then smiled as she added, "So I can put on something that doesn't look as if I slept in it."

"But you did," Maya signed.

January laughed, then pointed to the stairs, raising her hand from the bottom step to the top of the landing.

Maya lost no time in running up the stairs, as if she thought it was a race of some sort.

With that in mind, January took her time going up, sensing that winning something as insignificant as getting to the top of the stairs first was somehow important to Maya. She had a feeling that gratification was not something that happened often for the little girl.

So, when January did reach the top of the stairs, she inclined her head toward Maya, as if she was conceding the race.

"You win," she signed. "I'll win next time."

Maya signed back, "Maybe," and smiled from ear to ear.

There was a touch of humbleness about Maya, January thought, warmed.

She put her arm around the girl's shoulders and guided Maya into her bedroom so January could pick out something to wear for this proposed grocery shopping field trip.

A couple of minutes passed before she realized that she was looking over the outfits hanging in her closet with a critical eye. The clothes were all very serviceable, of course. She had worn all of them to work at one time or another. But even so, for some reason, January caught herself dismissing each and every one.

What was she doing? *This isn't a date*, January silently insisted, annoyed with herself and where her thoughts were. She was just picking out something to wear while she was grocery shopping, for heaven's sake. Any one of the outfits she had looked at would do as long as it covered all the essential parts. And they all did.

With that in mind, she took out a pair of gray slacks and a turquoise, long-sleeved V-neck pullover. Because Maya was there on the bed, watching her intently, January held up her choice for the little girl to view, wanting Maya to feel as if she was an active part of this whole process.

Maya beamed and nodded her approval.

"Okay, I'll just go and put this on," January signed, stepping into the bathroom.

But before she could close the door so she could change out of what she was wearing and put on the slacks and top, Maya had squeezed herself into the room right behind her. The little girl proceeded to sit down, cross-legged, on the tile floor.

And then she looked up, waiting.

January's natural inclination was to tell the girl to wait for her in the bedroom until she had finished changing. But again she sensed that Maya felt better if she stayed close to her.

For better or worse, it seemed that the girl had formed an attachment to her as well as to the detective—or maybe she was being substituted for Detective Stafford until he could return. Either way, January wasn't about to make Maya feel as if she was being abandoned or rejected. Not even if the gesture was perpetuated by something as small and insignificant as closing the bathroom door to separate them.

So, with Maya sitting right there on the floor, January hurried out of the outfit she had been wearing since the previous morning and put on the slacks and top that she had picked out today. The available space in the bathroom made the change of clothing tricky for her, but January managed.

After pulling a hairbrush through her long blond hair so it didn't look like something the wind had just blown in, January put on some lipstick and turned toward Maya.

"All ready. Let's go," she signed to Maya as she put a hand out to her.

There was a look of utter gratitude on the small, angelic face that January couldn't begin to describe.

Maya curled her small hand around hers. The warmth pulsating in January's chest spread out soft, tender fingers that reached throughout every part of her.

It was becoming a very familiar feeling for her.

"Okay," January said to herself once they reached the bottom of the stairs again. "Now all we have to do is wait for Detective Stafford to show up here. But he better hurry," she murmured, "or you and I are going to fly the coop."

Maya looked at her and shook her head, indicating that she didn't understand. She had been trying very hard to read lips, January realized, but her efforts weren't proving all that fruitful.

"Sorry," January signed, then went on to sign to Maya roughly what she had murmured to herself.

With a nod of her head to indicate that she understood, Maya surprised January by walking up to the front door. She positioned herself by one of the windows that framed the upper portion of the door. For all intents and purposes, she looked as if she was standing guard there.

"Looks like you have got yourself a groupie, Stafford," January said under her breath to the absent homicide detective.

Maya's sweet, unassuming behavior made January think about the girl's parents again, or at least about the daddy she kept asking after.

Why weren't those people combing the streets, looking for her? Or more to the point, why hadn't there been a missing person report filed on Maya, offering a reward and searching for her whereabouts the moment they realized she was gone?

"If you were my little girl, Maya," she said to the child's back, "I would be out there, searching and leaving no stone unturned until I found you."

She saw Maya's back suddenly grow rigid and the little girl all but stood at attention.

"What do you see?" January asked as she made a beeline for the door. And then she remembered that Maya had been watching through the glass that framed either side of the door. That way, she would have been able to see Stafford coming up the front walk.

The next moment, as she heard the doorbell, January knew her conjecture had to be right.

"Speak of the devil," she said as she opened the front door.

"Oh, were you speaking of the devil?" Sean asked, walking in.

"No, but you're the next best thing," January said, even as Maya threw her arms around him.

Sean laughed as he scooped the little girl up and gave her a quick, warm hug. "Hi, princess, did you miss me?"

Maya seemed to get the general gist of what he was asking without having January sign what Sean had said.

Setting the girl back down on the ground, the detective looked at January. "Ready to go?"

"We've been ready since you left," she told him.

He didn't know if she was being sarcastic or critical, but he let it go. Glancing at January's new attire as he held the door open for her and Maya, he said, "Nice outfit," then closed the door behind them.

Chapter Ten

"Was that sarcasm?" January asked as she walked out holding Maya's hand.

"No. Why?" he asked. "Haven't you ever been on the receiving end of a compliment before?"

"Yes, of course. But when it comes to you, I'm not exactly sure if you're being on the level or putting me on."

"I promise, you'll know when I'm not being on the level," he told her as he watched January go directly to her vehicle. He didn't understand. "And why are you opening up your car? We're going to go to the store in mine."

January stood her ground, making no move to comply. "That car seat we got from the police station is already installed in my car. Why go through all the trouble of uncoupling it, putting it into your vehicle and making sure it is all secured there?" she asked. "Seems like an awful lot of trouble to go through for the same results. Besides, I already know the way to my market. I might as well drive there instead of giving you the directions."

He wasn't entirely sure what she was telling him. "I wasn't planning on driving blindly around," he told January. "I was going to ask you how to get there. I'm sure you're very good at telling people where to go."

She congratulated herself on not responding to his comment. "Well, now you don't have to ask," she said, smiling brightly at him. Perhaps a little *too* brightly, she conceded, but it was better than snapping at him. "Just buckle up and enjoy the ride there."

He frowned as he waited for her to secure Maya in the car seat in the back. "Tell me, is everything always a debate with you?" he asked, addressing the back of her head as she worked.

January smiled as she glanced at the detective over her shoulder. "Not if you go along with whatever I tell you. You know, it takes two for a debate."

"Yeah, it does," Sean agreed, looking at her pointedly.

She had a feeling that they were standing on the edge of a possible blowout, or at least what could turn into a very nasty argument. Taking a breath, she decided to retreat. There was nothing to be gained by locking horns anyway.

"Did they by any chance tell you how long you'll have to wait before they can give you Maya's DNA results?"

That hadn't taken her long to get to, he thought. Sean gave her the outside estimate that he'd been given, even though he knew it could be done faster. "Forty-eight hours," he said.

"That long?" she asked, turning around to look

at him. "And you couldn't get them to try to speed things up?"

"Sorry," he deadpanned, winking at Maya just before he got into the front passenger seat. The little girl looked very pleased even though she had no idea what was going on. "The lab tech I talked to told me that the department's magic wand was out getting repaired."

January frowned as she got into the front seat behind the steering wheel. She resented the detective's flippant response.

And she wasn't about to back off, at least, not yet. "It's just that I remember hearing that a top lab can get results to a test in about twenty-four hours—or less," she told the detective.

"Yeah," he agreed, seeing no reason to contest that. "If they don't have anything else waiting to be processed. Unfortunately, this is Chicago," he said with emphasis.

It wasn't as if this was the heart of the city, she thought. "A *suburb* of Chicago," January stressed, buckling up.

"Still not exactly a sleepy little town," Sean answered. "Look, I'm as anxious as you are to get an answer and find Maya's parents—*if* they're still alive and *if* they're in the DNA database."

"And you're sure that her father wasn't one of the dead men in the warehouse?" she asked. They had already gone over this once, but, January thought, it wasn't exactly inconceivable to think that a mistake might have been made in the identification.

"He wasn't," Sean confirmed. "The crime scene investigators identified all three of them. They were all drug dealers, including my source. They were all trying to get out of the life and start new somewhere else by giving me the information I needed. Coincidentally, neither of the other two men who were killed at the scene was the guy I was looking to bring down, either."

He hadn't mentioned this before. "And who is that—or is that one of those 'need to know' things that I have always found to be so damn infuriating?" January asked him with feeling.

He noticed that her hands were gripping the steering wheel a little more tightly than he would have expected. This being kept out of the loop really bothered her, he thought.

"Considering that you've gotten pulled into this, I suppose I can tell you," Sean said. He kept his expression neutral so as not to somehow convey to Maya that something was amiss. "I'm trying to bring down a well-connected criminal in this drug cartel."

"What's his name?" she asked again.

"Elias Mercer. He goes by 'Kid' Mercer because the guy has this baby face. It throws people off because, trust me, there's nothing kid-like about the man," Sean told her grimly. "I think either he or one of his people killed those three men at the warehouse to keep them from talking to the authorities about what they knew about Mercer's operation."

He glanced over his shoulder at Maya. Now there was total innocence, he couldn't help thinking. "That's also why I'm worried about the princess here. Most likely she didn't see anything. And I know she certainly didn't hear anything, but if Mercer suspects that she might have—even if it wasn't possible—a man like that wouldn't think twice about having Maya eliminated. For a man like that, there is no age restriction," he told January.

He saw the social worker turn pale. "Look, I'm not trying to scare you," the detective began.

"Too late," she informed him. But she knew she couldn't afford to just stick her head in the sand. These were dangerous people who had killed those men in the warehouse. "But better forewarned than blindsided," she said philosophically. January stole a glance at Sean. "You're sure that patrol car you told me about is going to be passing by my house on a regular basis?" It wasn't herself she was worried about. She was thinking of Maya.

Sean didn't hesitate. "Absolutely."

She blew out a breath, then forced a smile to her lips. "Well, that's good enough for me."

The next minute, she turned a corner and drove into a large parking lot, looking for a space near the front of one of Oak Lawn's larger grocery stores.

"Okay," January announced. "We're here."

Then, pulling up the handbrake and turning off the ignition, she turned toward Maya and signed what she had just said to Sean. That they had arrived at their destination.

Maya peered out her window, seeming a little uncertain at the sight of the store. Sean saw her expression and wondered if she was afraid or if this was just new to her. In any case, he wanted to set her mind at ease.

"Why don't I get her out of her seat?" he suggested to January.

He really was turning out to be a very thoughtful person, January thought. "I think that might be a good idea," she responded, adding, "It's obvious that Maya feels safe with you."

Sean grinned at the little girl. "Well, she has to be the smallest damsel in distress I've ever worked with to feel that way," he told January. There was a touch of humor in his voice.

Just before they entered the store, January grabbed a cart, then brought it over to Sean. She assumed he would deposit Maya in the seat so that they could get around the store faster, thereby making shopping easier all around. She was certain that he wanted to get this over with as quickly as possible.

But Sean surprised her with another idea. "Maybe Maya would like to push the cart instead of sitting in it?" he told January.

"I just thought it would be easier for her—and us," January said.

"Yeah, but maybe easier is not the way to go," Sean said. "I've got a feeling that Maya would be happier if she was being challenged."

"She's a little girl," January pointed out.

"Little girls need challenges if they're going to grow up to be competent, smart big girls, and more importantly, competent, smart young women," Sean concluded.

For a second, January was speechless. The detective's answers and insight really intrigued her. There was apparently a lot more to this man than was obvious at first.

January laughed softly. "I thought I was the social worker," she said.

"Oh, you are," Sean readily agreed. "I'm just here to offer advice and to provide protection."

"I thought you were here to show off your shopping prowess," she teased.

"That's just a bonus," Sean cracked. Standing behind Maya to help her with the cart if it turned out to be too unwieldy, he asked January, "Okay, where to first?"

"Why don't we start at the meat department and then work our way out to the other aisles?" she suggested, signing her words to Maya as she said them out loud for the detective's benefit.

Maya looked as if she was getting all excited and was more than ready to begin this adventure with the people she apparently viewed as her two new best friends. The little girl wrapped her hands around the cart's handle, looking very intense. She made January think of a racehorse at the starting gate, pawing at the ground and poised to react the moment she heard the sound of the starter's pistol.

January observed Maya as the little girl made her way down the aisle, with January walking on one side of the cart and the police detective walking on the other. What impressed her most was that Maya didn't act as if she was Alice in Wonderland. She behaved as if being in a grocery store of this caliber was extremely familiar to her.

"You know, I think Maya might know this neighborhood," January speculated as she looked at Sean over Maya's head. "At least, that's my working theory."

"Given that theory, it broadens my search base," Sean told her, and then he nodded toward Maya. "Why don't you ask her what she would like to eat tonight?" he suggested.

She didn't quite follow him. "Why? You think what she wants to eat will tell us something about her?"

Where had that come from? "I think that'll tell you what she likes to eat so you can make it for her and wind up with a contented little girl on your hands. A contented kid tends to be more cooperative."

Sean had managed to impress her again. "You know, if you ever feel like leaving the police force, there might be a spot for you in social services," January told him.

"Sorry, but dealing with all those kids without families, or with families that they're better off without, I'm afraid that's just too depressing for me," he told her, keeping his voice deliberately low. He knew Maya couldn't hear him, but there was a part of him that thought somehow the vibrations from his tone would register with her.

January smiled. "Not like the happy-go-lucky life of a homicide detective, is that it?"

He nodded, knowing that what he'd said might come across a little hypocritical, but he did view what he did as a service to those whose lives had been affected by deadly crimes. "We each dance to the music we like," he told her.

Coming to a stop in the dairy aisle, January stared at

the detective. "What does that even *mean*?" she asked him, stunned.

He gave her a mysterious smile. "You think on it and tell me when you've made up your mind," he said. "Meanwhile—" he put one hand lightly on Maya's shoulder to help guide her down another aisle "—let's see if we can finish up this shopping trip before nightfall." He looked down at Maya and gave her a wink.

The smile she returned said she understood him even if she didn't hear the words he'd said.

IN THE END, they loaded up on all the essentials, picking up bread and eggs, several packs of chicken breasts and legs, one package of hamburgers along with buns, and the required carton of milk for Maya, as well as a box of cereal with some sort of nutritional value.

For herself, January picked up an extra container of dark-roast coffee and a large container of creamer guaranteed to sweeten her coffee as well as rendering it a very pale color.

Sean looked down at the creamer. "I take it you don't like black coffee."

"Only as a last resort if there's nothing else," she confessed. "Otherwise, life's just too short to drink sludge."

"Is that what you think of black coffee?" Sean guessed.

"No," she answered with a straight face. "I also think it's good for fixing potholes and cracked tar."

"You know," he said, reevaluating the coffee he had had at her place when he dropped by that morning, "I thought the coffee tasted kind of funny when I had it this morning."

"And yet you drank it like a trouper." January pretended to marvel.

"Hey, I'm a Chicago police detective," he told her with a smile. "I've learned how to put up with a lot of things." And then Sean glanced at Maya, who looked as if she was trying to follow what was going on even though January wasn't signing anything at the moment. "Why don't you ask her if she wants any cookies or ice cream?"

That, she realized, had been an oversight on her part, not because she wanted the little girl to eat only healthy foods but because she herself rarely indulged in anything that, for the most part, came under the heading of junk food. While that was a healthier way to go, she knew the worth of sweets when it came to a child and she didn't want to impose her own standards on someone as young as Maya.

She signed Sean's question to the little girl and was immediately on the receiving end of an enthusiastic response.

"You certainly called that one right," January congratulated the detective.

"Well, that really wasn't much of a challenge," Sean responded. "I never met a kid who didn't like cookies or ice cream. All things sweet, actually."

"Since we've already picked up all the basics— and then some," January said, looking into the cart, "let's see if we can find something to appeal to Maya's sweet tooth."

With that she guided the little girl and the cart to the cookie aisle.

After Maya debated for several minutes and finally made her choice—several kinds of cookies, including mint chocolate chip—the next stop was the ice cream aisle.

That choice turned out to be even more difficult. There were so many flavors to choose from. Maya finally narrowed it down to three.

Watching her try to decide between the different flavors, Sean finally turned toward January. "Why don't we just get all three? This way she has a variety to choose from—my treat," he added, in case the extra cost might be why the social worker would hesitate.

"I wasn't thinking about the price," she told Sean. "I was thinking about the temptation of having so many flavors so readily available," January admitted.

"Well, the princess doesn't strike me as the type to break into your refrigerator in the middle of the night and gorge herself on ice cream," Sean told her, smiling down at Maya.

"You're right," January confessed with a sigh. "I'm overthinking the situation—as usual." When he looked at her, curious at her admission, she explained, "In my line of work, I always try to be at least three jumps ahead."

"I can understand that, but why don't you just try being in the moment and enjoying that for a change?" he suggested.

Damn it but the man was good, she thought. It bothered her a little, because she was the one who was supposed to be that way, not him. Still, it didn't detract from the fact that he came across as a man who didn't just do things by the numbers.

She peered at him as they moved away from the ice cream aisle. "Are you sure you don't have any kids, Stafford?"

"No, but I've got cop instincts," he answered. "Let's go get this paid for." As he smiled at Maya, Sean took control of the cart.

January had the impression that the little girl would have gladly followed him to the ends of the earth and back if that was what she thought he wanted.

She caught herself thinking that she really didn't blame Maya one bit.

Chapter Eleven

Sean wound up staying for dinner.

After going out of his way as he had, January felt she at least owed him a meal. She had intentionally bought extra chicken cutlets so she could make Chicken Parmesan, a meal that came across fancier than it actually was.

She knew having Sean at the dinner table would make Maya happy, and if she were being totally honest, it didn't exactly make her feel as if she was enduring a hardship, having Sean at her town house.

Despite the fact that he didn't know how to sign, Sean got along well with Maya, managing to entertain her as January prepared dinner.

After the meal had been consumed, Maya, looking as if she couldn't contain herself any longer, signed a question to January.

Watching the little girl, Sean sensed that whatever she was asking might have something to do with his being there—especially since she pointed toward him.

"What's she saying?" he finally asked January.

The social worker chose to answer Maya before addressing Sean's query. Signing, she shook her head in response to Maya's question, then turned toward the detective.

"She wants to know if you're staying the night with us," she told him.

"No," Sean answered, looking at Maya. *Not that it isn't tempting,* he caught himself thinking. "That reminds me," he said to January. "I'd better get going. I've still got some paperwork to catch up on."

"Ah, yes, the glamorous part of police work," January commented, remembering the way one of the people she associated with said her husband referred to the dreaded paperwork that cases generated.

Rising from the living room sofa they had all adjourned to after dinner, January offered, "I'll walk you to the door, Detective. *We'll* walk you to the door," she amended when she realized that Maya was right behind her, ready to shadow her every move.

"An escort comprised of two lovely women. Who wouldn't welcome that?" Sean mused.

January signed what he had just said to Maya, who beamed at Sean, her eyes shining.

"You know," Sean said to January as he paused by the front door, fighting the urge to linger. "I could stay a little longer…"

As appealing as Sean seemed right at this very minute, she wasn't going to allow herself to get roped into saying yes. "A little longer" had a way of transforming into something greater and she couldn't allow herself to get distracted. Maya was her main, and *only*, focus.

"No," she told him. "Like you said, you have work

to do and we've kept you here long enough. Besides, it's close to Maya's bedtime."

The news surprised the detective. "You've managed to establish when her bedtime is?" he asked.

"Not exactly," January was forced to admit. "I gave her the same bedtime I was made to observe when I was her age."

That brought him to another question. "You know her age?" he asked, glancing at Maya.

She was glad to give Sean at least one positive answer. "That I did establish," January confirmed. "I asked her if she knew how old she was this morning and she nodded vigorously, holding up five fingers." She smiled at the detective. "Maya's five."

"Well, that's good," he replied. "But nothing so far on her last name or her address, right?"

"Right," January signed. "I'm still coming up empty on that—for now."

Sean grinned. "So, now you're an optimist," he concluded.

She leaned into him, unaware that it caused him to catch a whiff of her light, floral perfume. "I'll let you in on a little secret. In this line of work, I have to be, or I'd wind up crying myself to sleep every night," she confided.

Straightening, she told herself it was time to have him leave before she thought of an excuse to get him to stay permanently. "All right," she said, signaling an end to the evening. "You'll give me a call as soon as you know anything about her DNA?"

He thought of reminding her about the time he had

already told her it was going to take, then decided it wouldn't do any good.

"You'll be my first call," Sean promised. "By the way, you make a really great Chicken Parmesan," he said by way of parting.

The compliment warmed her more than she would have expected. "Thanks. I'll look for your endorsement if I ever decide to open a restaurant." A whimsical smile played along her lips.

Her smile sorely tempted him, drawing him in and making Sean *really* want to kiss her. But he exercised restraint, knowing that to give in would be going way over any line he was allowed to cross. He was a police detective working a case that involved the little girl January had temporarily taken into her home, and that was where their connection began and ended. He couldn't afford to let himself lose sight of that.

No matter how much he wanted to.

"Don't forget to lock up," he reminded her as he started to go.

"Yes, Detective," she responded in a sing-song voice. "I also have an alarm system I plan to engage the minute I shut—and lock—the front door. Now go."

"Yes, ma'am." Sean saluted. And then he turned toward Maya, and to the surprise of both January and the little girl, Sean signed, "Goodbye."

Overjoyed, Maya signed the same thing back to him, her eyes dancing.

"I'm very impressed," January told the homicide detective.

"Don't be. I used the search engine on my computer," Sean told her.

"But you did think to use it, so I'm still impressed, Detective." She smiled her approval at him.

"Call me Sean," Sean prompted.

She inclined her head, humoring his request. "Good night, Sean."

"Good night, January," he said just before he walked to his vehicle, still parked in front of her house. He couldn't resist saying one last time, "Don't forget to lock up."

January sighed, murmuring something under her breath she was glad that Maya couldn't hear as she closed the front door. She shook her head. The man had to ruin it, she thought.

"C'mon," she signed to Maya. "It's time to get you ready for bed."

Maya seemed disappointed. "So soon?" she signed, crestfallen.

"It is not soon," January informed her firmly. "It's late."

Maya looked as if she actually wanted to put up a fight, but the next moment she nodded, giving in.

January smiled and kissed the top of the little girl's head.

"Atta girl," she signed, or something close to it.

AFTER SHE HAD gotten Maya ready for bed, January went downstairs to finish cleaning up in the kitchen. Maya followed her down, but January hadn't really expected anything else.

"You lie down on the sofa," she signed to Maya. "I'll be finished what I'm doing here soon."

January turned away, then heard an unfamiliar noise. She was about to sign that she wanted the little girl to settle down when she realized that the noise wasn't coming from anything Maya had done. It was coming from outside the front of the house.

Her attention piqued, January went to the window next to the front door and looked out. Scanning the street, she saw a black sedan parked in front of the town house next door.

The same one that she had seen pass by her own home several times yesterday evening. What was it doing parked in front of the Walkers' place?

Weren't they still on vacation?

She couldn't remember if the couple had returned recently or not.

You're doing it again, Jan, she upbraided herself. *You're overthinking things. The Walkers probably came back from their vacation this week and they have company now. People with normal lives do that kind of thing. They have people over. They have fun.*

She needed to stop borrowing trouble. With that, she looked around her kitchen. She had cleaned up everything and put things away. Now it was time for her to do the same thing with herself and Maya.

"Okay, sleepyhead," she said, addressing the dozing child stretched out on her sofa. "Time to get you to bed." Saying that, January scooped up the little girl and slowly carried her upstairs.

"At least someone is going to sleep well tonight," she said, placing Maya in the bed next door to her own bedroom.

January stood there for a moment, just looking at the little girl before she finally draped the blanket over Maya. She pressed her lips together ruefully. Instead of looking after other people's children, she could have had one of these of her own, she thought with a trace of longing.

"Right. Just what the world needs, another Immaculate Conception." She mocked herself because that would be the only way she would be able to have one of her own. She had no social life to speak of, other than the fund-raisers she attended from time to time with friends of her parents who were old enough to—well, be her parents. No chance for romance, much less a child there.

"You're doing just fine, Jan," she said aloud. "Stop feeling sorry for yourself. You live a great, fulfilling life. Now drop the pity party."

With that, she went into her bedroom. This time, unlike the previous night, she changed into an old set of pajamas she favored and then crawled into her bed.

The second she did, she realized that she could barely keep her eyes open. January was just about to drift off to sleep when a sudden noise penetrated her consciousness.

Her eyes flew open.

She knew that noise. It was the one made by her back-door alarm.

Someone was trying to come in.

January immediately thought of the black sedan she had seen earlier. The same one she had seen driving around yesterday.

Bolting out of bed, she paused only long enough to grab her cell phone—not even her shoes. Moving as fast as she could, she flew into Maya's bedroom.

"C'mon, baby, we've got to go," she signed as quickly as she could.

Maya had barely opened her eyes. January wasn't sure she had even gotten her message across to the girl, but there was no time to stop and sign it again.

They needed to hide.

Now.

There was a deep closet at the back of the second floor that had initially been put in as a panic room. The first owner had had it installed when he bought the town house. It was generally known that the senior citizen was a rich recluse who everyone had said was basically paranoid.

When she bought the town house, January had used the panic room as a storage area for things she meant to eventually go through and get rid of. The only problem was, she had never managed to find the time.

Her heart pounding as she held on to Maya, January hurried down the hall and made her way into the panic room now. She was praying that the lights inside still worked. She couldn't remember the last time she had tested them.

Completely awake now, Maya looked at her with sheer panic in her eyes.

It killed January to scare the little girl this way, but she had no choice. Someone was in her house and she couldn't think of any reason for them to be there other than that whoever had killed those three men in the warehouse had realized that there might have been a witness to what they had done. They had obviously tracked her down and were here to eliminate Maya before she could point them out.

This time, January didn't feel as if she was over-thinking the situation. If she was, for some reason, then this was all Stafford's fault and he had to get himself over here to make sure that everything was all right.

Signing for Maya to sit down on the floor and give her a few minutes, January quickly tapped out Sean's number on her cell phone. She had programmed the number into her phone earlier that day.

Sean answered on the third ring.

Convinced that January wouldn't be calling him at this hour for some inane pillow talk, he picked up his cell and immediately asked, "January, what's wrong?"

"Someone's trying to break into the house," she answered in a breathless whisper. "I think he or they might already be here. Where's the damn police patrol you said was supposed to be out here, driving by my house?"

Her voice had gone up. If January was hiding, she sounded much too loud, Sean thought. That prompted him to ask, "Where are you right now?"

January took in a deep breath to try to steady her nerves.

"There's a panic room on the second floor of this house. Maya and I are in there right now, but I have no idea how secure it is. It came with the town house." Before he could ask, January told him, "I use it for storage."

She hadn't said anything about a panic room before,

but that was a conversation for another time. "I'm leaving right now," he told her, dropping everything he'd been working on. "Hang tight," he instructed.

As he ran to get his vehicle, Sean put a call in to the detail he had assigned to maintain a patrol around January's town house.

"Hemmings," the patrolman answered.

"Hemmings, this is Detective Stafford. I'm on my way to the Colton town house. January Colton just called to tell me that someone is breaking in. You're supposed to be patrolling that area," he reminded the officer.

"Sorry, Detective. We're not there because Jonah and I got called away on another case," the police officer apologized.

"Another case?" Sean repeated in disbelief as he got into his vehicle. Securing his seat belt, he started up the car. "I had you doing *surveillance* on Ms. Colton's house," he told the officer sharply.

"Sorry, sir," Hemmings apologized again. "Lieutenant Walters said he needed us for something a lot more pressing than a babysitting detail. His words, sir, not mine. Again, I'm really sorry, Detective," the officer repeated.

Sean could feel his blood pressure going up. "Yeah, right."

Furious at being overridden without even the courtesy of being told, Sean terminated the call to the patrolman. The next moment, he was putting in a call to the dispatch desk.

"Nine-one-one, what is your emergency?" a calm female voice on the other end asked.

Sean identified himself, giving the dispatch desk his name and badge number. "There's a break-in taking place right now," he told the woman, then recited January's address. "The owner is home with a little girl. I think the people breaking in are involved in a drug gang and they believe the child was a witness to a triple homicide." He stressed every gory detail he could think of to get the police there as fast as possible.

For good measure, he ordered, "Get there now. I'm on my way and about ten minutes out. I had a patrol car cruising the area, but I'm told they got pulled for another assignment."

"I can check on that for you sir," the woman volunteered.

"Don't bother. Just get someone out there right now," he instructed, then repeated, "The little girl could have been a witness to a triple homicide and whoever is responsible could very well be trying to eliminate her, as well."

"I've got two patrol cars in the area," she informed him.

Sean never hesitated. "Send them both!" he ordered, stepping on the gas as he turned on his siren.

Chapter Twelve

The one thing that Sean had never managed to do, either as a policeman or as a homicide detective, was to effectively divorce himself from an ongoing situation. More specifically, he couldn't manage to separate himself from the details of any case he was investigating.

He envied those in the police department who could compartmentalize their minds or put up barricades within themselves so that what they saw or were dealing with did not weigh heavily on their minds.

Although Sean was able to maintain a calm outward facade, he just couldn't seem to do that inwardly, no matter how much he wanted to. Once he was on a case, he lived and breathed it until it was finally resolved, one way or another.

And then there were those cases that he couldn't seem to put to rest because, even now, they hadn't been properly resolved.

Right now, he was vividly imagining someone—or several someones, for that matter—breaking into January's town house. Sean summarily cursed the patrol car that was supposed to have been in her vicinity—but wasn't.

If anything happens to January or Maya—

Sean abruptly blocked the thought from his mind, staunchly refusing to entertain it. He just couldn't allow himself to go there because to carry the thought out to its possible conclusion seemed much too horrible to contemplate.

Sean pushed down on the accelerator. The speedometer went to eighty—then past that.

With an eye out for traffic—and his throbbing heart lodged in his throat—he went faster. He just wanted to get there.

He'd estimated getting to her town house in ten minutes.

He got there in just under eight.

To his relief, the two patrol cars that dispatch had told him they were sending had already arrived.

Coming to a screeching halt in front of January's town house, Sean's vehicle had barely stopped running when he leaped out and went racing up the walk.

The front door was standing wide open. He couldn't make up his mind if that was a good sign or not, he only knew that his heart was pounding so hard against his chest, it felt as if it would crack through his rib cage at any moment.

One hand on the butt of his service revolver, the other holding up his identification for the benefit of the two officers he saw just within the foyer, Sean announced, "I'm Detective Stafford. Where are they?"

Before either could answer, he shot a second, even more urgent question at them. "Were they hurt?"

Before either officer could speak, Sean had his answer. January was standing barefoot in her pajamas, holding a huddled Maya in her arms. January had apparently, just this moment, come down the stairs.

His first inclination was to throw his arms around both of them and hold them to him, but he managed to refrain. He had a feeling that January wouldn't appreciate this show of emotion right now.

"We're all right, Sean," January told him in a voice that indicated she was clearly shaken.

"We found them in what looked like a panic room, sir," the first officer, Jim Crawford, told Sean. "She had just opened the door. Although the lock on it looked kind of flimsy. I'd have it replaced, ma'am, if you want it to be of any real use."

Sean had a more important question for the officers. "What about the intruders?" he asked. "Did you get them?"

The other officer, Jacobs, an older man with thinning gray hair, spoke up. "We saw two men, dark clothes, medium build, running from the house. My guess is that the sirens must have scared them away."

Sean could only imagine what January must have gone through. He didn't want to think what could have happened if the intruders hadn't taken off but had managed to break into the panic room.

"Yeah, thankfully. Are you two all right?" he asked

the social worker, stroking Maya's head in an effort to convey a sense of calm to the little girl.

January nodded. "Getting there," she answered honestly.

Sean had never been one to shirk a responsibility or to try to cover something up he thought might be his fault. And this, he felt, could very well have been his fault.

"I'm really sorry you had to go through this," he told January.

She was doing her best not to get angry, but that anger wasn't directed at him. She felt that there had to be some miscommunication at fault here.

"Where were the police officers you said were patrolling around here?" January asked.

Sean was having trouble controlling his outrage. "They were apparently called away on another case. No one told me."

"Well, if you didn't know, you didn't know," January said, resigned. She told herself that getting upset over what had happened wouldn't lead anywhere.

"That's no excuse," Sean bit out, furious about the oversight. "Luckily, Jacobs and his partner and a second squad car were in the area," he told her, but there was no abating the red-hot outrage he felt. "I'm sorry you had to go through that."

January didn't want the detective blaming himself. "Well, it's not your fault."

"Oh, but it is," Sean said, contradicting her assumption.

Her eyebrows drew together. "Maybe it's because

of the hour," she told the detective. "But I don't understand." She looked up at him. "Why would it be your fault?"

"Because I'm thinking that whoever broke into your house had to be after Maya. That means that they followed me from the police station parking lot to your house. I am sincerely sorry, January, if I was responsible in any way for bringing those thugs to your doorstep."

She looked at him and saw the genuine regret in his eyes. He was sincerely sorry and there was absolutely nothing to be gained by making him feel even worse about it.

"Well, you didn't do it intentionally," she said, absolving him of the guilt. "But now what?" She glanced at Maya.

Maya had to be protected at all costs and they both knew that.

"I'm not leaving you unprotected again," Sean promised her.

That sounded good, but she wanted specifics. "What does that mean exactly?" she asked Sean, then made a guess. "Are you planning on camping out in the middle of my living room?"

"No, I'm taking you and Maya to my place," Sean informed her seriously, explaining, "You're moving in with me."

January hadn't expected that. "With you?" she repeated a little uncertainly. "Do you have enough room?"

"I have enough room," the detective assured her. "Besides," he added with a smile, "Maya's little. She doesn't take up much space." There was a fond look in his eyes as he looked down at the little girl. And then he raised his eyes to January again. "Why don't you go and pack a few things for you and Maya? And then we'll get going. The sooner I have you out of here, the better."

This was really happening, January thought, stunned. It almost felt surreal. She needed to focus, to center her thoughts on things she could control. "How much should I pack?" she asked.

"Why don't you pack enough clothes for about five days," Sean told her, doing a quick estimate. "If you wind up staying at my place for longer than that, we can always come back here and get some more of your things."

January blew out a breath, frustrated. It was hard wrapping her head around this turn of events. "I feel like a nomad," she confessed as she began to go up the stairs again.

"Better a live nomad than the alternative," Sean quietly pointed out.

He was right, January thought, pressing her lips together.

She was doing her best not to lose it.

She was a Colton, damn it. And Coltons could handle anything that was thrown at them.

January started up the stairs again.

Maya looked torn between following January and staying with her protector.

Seeing her dilemma, Sean made a decision. "Wait up, January. You're going to have company." And with that, the detective took Maya's hand and went upstairs behind the woman.

Coming to the landing, January looked at the little girl. "Are you going to help me pack?" She smiled as she signed the question to Maya.

For the first time since this whole terrifying thing had started tonight, Maya smiled at January and nodded her head.

"Good," January signed back to her, saying the words aloud for Sean's benefit. "I could use your help."

"You know, I really appreciate that," Sean told January as he followed her and the little girl.

"Appreciate what?" January asked, not sure what the detective was referring to. Right now, the inside of her head felt like a giant jumble. It was hard thinking clearly and keeping everything straight.

"That when you sign to Maya, you say all the words out loud," Sean said.

"Oh, that. Actually, I do that as a form of reinforcement," she confessed. "I say something out loud because it seems to help my fingers make the right moves to convey the words."

"Well, whatever the reason," Sean said, "I fully appreciate not being kept in the dark about your communication. It's hard enough on me not to know what's going on."

"Think how Maya feels," January reminded the detective.

He flushed, embarrassed that he had made it seem that he was emphasizing himself. Maya was the important one in this.

"Yeah," he agreed. "You're absolutely right."

Packing, January caught herself smiling at the detective. In her experience, there weren't many men who would be willing to give a woman they hardly knew her due the way he did.

Detective Sean Stafford, she thought as she got another pair of jeans out of the closet, was a rare man indeed.

The next moment, she ordered herself not to get carried away. She knew that she had a bad tendency to do that when she dropped her guard—and this was definitely *not* the time for that.

Forcing herself to focus, January raised her guard again.

Moving quickly, she managed to pack one suitcase for herself in short order.

"What about Maya?" Sean asked. Watching January pack, he noticed that the only clothes that had gone into the suitcase were the ones that fit the social worker.

"Well, we had plans to go clothes shopping tomorrow," January told Sean. "But after what happened tonight, I suppose that's out now."

Sean looked at her. "Why?"

Was he playing games, or just testing her? "Well, because you just said we were going into hiding," she reminded him.

"No, what I said was I was transferring the two of you to my place. I didn't say anything about actually physically going into hiding," he told her.

Okay, this *was* a test, she decided. She wasn't about to have him trip her up. "I just assumed that going to what amounts to a 'safe house' wasn't going to include any shopping sprees on the agenda. Was I wrong?"

"No, not a shopping spree," he agreed. "But there isn't anything against going to buy some much needed clothing for a pint-sized princess," he told her, smiling at Maya.

Every time he found himself looking at Maya, Sean couldn't help smiling. By the same token, he couldn't help feeling furious and incensed that someone out there was willing to heartlessly do away with the child because she had had the misfortune of being in the wrong place at the wrong time.

Sean was beginning to think that she had nothing to do with the dead men who had been part of the drug organization.

For all he knew, Maya had just gotten lost while she was out with someone from her family. Without any identification on her and a limited ability to communicate, the little girl had been at the mercy of whoever's path she had wound up crossing.

Luckily, he thought, the path she had crossed had been his. Otherwise, who knew where she might have wound up? He abandoned the thought because to go on with it made him sick to his stomach.

"So, how about it?" he asked January. She had closed her suitcase so he picked it up and carried it down the stairs for her. Maya was right behind him. "You think you might be up for a small shopping excursion tomorrow, once you two get some beauty sleep?"

To be honest, she was having trouble thinking past the moment.

"Right now," January admitted, "sleep seems like a million miles away."

"Oh, it's a lot closer than that," Sean assured her. "And I've got a very comfortable mattress in my guest room."

"Guest room," she repeated, stressing the singular. "Not rooms?"

He shook his head. "Sorry, just the one," he told her. "After all, I'm just a poor public servant. What that means is that I can afford a two-bedroom apartment, not a fancy town house. It is on the second floor, though." In case January didn't follow him, what he was telling her was a good thing. "That means we can hear the bad guys coming."

She knew he was trying to make light of the situation in order to put her at ease and she did appreciate that. But the whole ordeal was still far too fresh in her mind for her to make peace with it yet.

January highly doubted that she would be able to sleep at all for the remainder of the night, much less get enough sleep to feel refreshed enough in the morning to be able to go on this excursion he was proposing.

Still, January reminded herself, she had been able to function on essentially an eyedropper's worth of sleep several times before. She could certainly do it one more time.

Standing on the first floor, she looked around for a moment. The first set of police officers had left, but the ones who had arrived in the second squad car were still there.

"Are you looking for something?" Sean asked January. "Maybe I can help."

"No, I'm just trying to see if I've forgotten anything essential I might need for my sleepover at your place," January answered.

Well, at least she was keeping a sense of humor about it, he thought. In his book, that made her a pretty remarkable woman.

Careful, Stafford. Keep it low-key. You don't want to get carried away, he warned himself.

"You know, if you think of anything you need later, like I said, we—or I—can always come back and get it for you," Sean told her.

"In other words, let's hit the road?" she asked, amused.

"Well, if you put it that way," he allowed. "Yes, in *any* words, let's hit the road." And then he turned toward the two police officers. "I want the two of you to follow me in your car. I am not taking any more chances with these two."

"Understood, Detective," said Officer Webber, the senior partner of the duo.

The officers were more than happy to be Stafford's escorts. They left the town house and January, glancing in Sean's direction, locked the front door and set the alarm system.

The officers traveled behind Sean's sedan, acting as his safeguard, until he reached his apartment with his precious cargo.

Chapter Thirteen

"I know what you're thinking," Sean said as he let January and Maya into his apartment. He set down her suitcase in order to be able to reset his security system. "You're thinking that the apartment looks small."

January cut him short. He had come to their rescue and was now taking them in. There was absolutely nothing negative about that.

"Actually," she told the detective, "I prefer the word *cozy*." January smiled at him. "It seems to fit better."

Sean made eye contact with her. She was attempting to flatter him. There was no need for that. "Well I prefer the word *honesty*," he responded.

"Okay." She could go along with that. And, since he put such a premium on honesty, she had a question for him. An obvious one, in her opinion. "When was the last time you had this place cleaned?" she asked. While the dust wasn't exactly an inch thick, Sean's clothes were scattered around, looking as if they remained on the floor where he had dropped them—possibly in a hurry.

There was also the very real possibility that tidiness was not a really big deal on his list of priorities.

"Not sure," he deadpanned, then quipped, "My maid has the month off."

"Was that after she ran screaming from this place, or before?" she asked, humor playing on her lips.

He scanned the area through her eyes. "I guess I could stand to be a bit neater," he admitted.

January could only laugh in response. "You think?" she asked, amused, then added for emphasis, "You could stand to be a *hell* of a lot neater."

She glanced around the room again, imagining what the rest of the apartment looked like. "I take it that you don't do much entertaining," she commented.

He saw no point in denying it and attempting to maintain some sort of an image of a life. "My job doesn't exactly leave much time for that," he told her.

January would have definitely thought that a man as extremely attractive and sexy as the detective would have found some time to bring women into his life.

Actually, she mentally amended, she would have thought Sean would have had to beat those women off with a stick.

"I guess we have the same job." When he raised a quizzical eyebrow in response to her comment, she explained. "I don't have any free time, either. Being a social worker requires putting in a twenty-hour day—plus overtime," she added whimsically. Maya was yawning, drawing her attention back to the little girl. "Okay, show me to your guest room so I can put this munchkin to bed."

Sean looked at Maya. She was swaying where she stood.

"She looks like she's about to fall asleep standing up," he commented.

January laughed under her breath. "I'm counting on that," she admitted. Sympathy filled her eyes. "She really needs to get some rest."

"No argument here," Sean agreed. "This way." He paused only long enough to gather Maya up into his arms. She curled against him, resting her head on his shoulder.

January picked up her suitcase, following the detective.

"This layout is deceptive—actually larger than I'd expect," she observed, looking around as he led her to the second bedroom.

"Glad you approve. Tomorrow, after we buy some clothes for Maya, I'll see about getting the two of you set up in a hotel."

She didn't understand. January thought they had agreed about having Maya and her stay here. "Why would you do that?" she asked.

Sean set Maya down on the double bed.

Her lids fluttered. The little girl smiled up at him. It was obvious that she could hardly keep her eyes open. The next moment, they were closed again. Sean hadn't even had time to tuck her in.

Thinking that January was undoubtedly better at it, Sean stepped back and left that up to the social worker to do.

"I thought you'd prefer that," he explained, referring to her question about the hotel room, lowering his voice before it hit him that he didn't need to. "You know," he continued in a normal voice, "a bigger bedroom with two double beds. I'd take the sofa," he added quickly in case January was worried that he was going to take one of the beds. Or that he wasn't going to be there.

"No," January said, vetoing the idea. "This arrangement is fine. Besides, this is your home territory. I think you'd be more comfortable defending it. It would certainly be more familiar to you."

"True," he said, thinking her comment over. It actually did make more sense to remain here. "Okay, if you have no objections, then, consider this your home until further notice. Can I get you anything?"

"Peace of mind would be nice," January answered wistfully.

His smile was sympathetic. "I'm working on it."

Not nearly fast enough for me, she thought. Out loud she said, "I know. Thanks. And no, I don't need you to get me anything."

"Good night, then," he said, reluctantly closing the door behind him, even though he would have really liked to have stayed with January in the room, at least a while longer.

January took in a deep breath and held it for a moment, then slowly released it. She spread her hand and pressed it against the door frame, imagining touching Sean's face.

"Good night," January whispered to the door.

AFTER TWENTY MINUTES had passed, she knew she was far too tense and restless to fall asleep any time in the near future. Right now, she definitely needed something to make her relax.

But January had never been the type who believed in taking sleeping pills. Having any sort of alcoholic beverage to help her unwind wouldn't have been her choice, either. This was *not* the time to start doing either one.

That left hot tea, she thought. Hot tea used to do the trick when she was in college.

She thought the odds of Stafford having any tea in his cupboard were probably slim to none, but she supposed she'd never know unless she ventured out and looked around.

So, still in bare feet, January quietly padded into the kitchen. It was past two o'clock in the morning and the stillness that was both outside and in seemed to undulate around her, slipping under her skin.

She could actually hear herself breathing.

The apartment complex was silent. The residents in the area had long since gone to sleep.

For all intents and purposes, January thought, at this moment in time, she was alone in the world.

"Can I help you find something?"

The voice, coming behind her, made January jump and gasp in surprise as she swung her fist at him.

Standing behind her, Sean caught her arm before she could make a connection.

"Hey, Champ, I'm one of the good guys, remember?" the detective asked.

It took her more than a minute to still her pounding heart. Sean had definitely surprised her. She had thought that he was one of the home invaders, trying to break in again.

Realizing her mistake, it occurred to her that Sean was standing much too close to her. She could *feel* herself responding, growing warm. January struggled to regain control.

Finding her voice, she said, "I thought you were asleep." Damn, why wouldn't her heart stop pounding like this?

A faint smile curved his lips. "A good detective sleeps with one eye open."

"Is it always the same eye, or do you alternate?" She knew she was making inane conversation, but right now, she was stalling for time until she felt her brain was back in gear.

"That all depends on how long—or short—the night is," Sean said wryly. "What are you doing up?"

Belatedly, he released her arm before he gave in to the temptation to draw her closer and kiss that full mouth of hers. A mouth that, for some reason, seemed even more tempting here in his kitchen than it had been earlier.

Maybe the moonlight, pushing its way in through the blinds, had something to do with it.

But he sincerely doubted it.

"I couldn't sleep," she confessed to Sean.

"So I see," he replied. "I could offer you a drink."

But January shook her head, turning him down. "That would only make me more tense," she told him.

Sean nodded, understanding. "And if I gave you enough to make you relax, that would probably wipe you out for the next day," he guessed. He thought for a minute. "How about some tea?"

Even though she had come to search for some, she looked at him now in surprise. "You have tea?" she asked, adding, "You don't seem like the type, Detective."

"I'm not," he admitted. "Personally, I detest the stuff."

Okay, this was making no sense, she thought. "Then why—"

"Every once in a blue moon, my stomach acts up, and I found that drinking that swill helps settle it," he told her. "It tastes disgusting, but it does the job and that's all that really counts, right? Now, do you want me to make you some tea or not?"

January smiled and could feel her eyes crinkling. The man really was full of surprises.

"Yes, please," she told him. And then it occurred to her that she should be the one who was making the tea. There was no need for him to stay up. She didn't want to keep him from getting his rest. "Or you could tell me where you keep your pot and I can just boil some water. You don't have to stay up."

Sean pretended to study her face. "Are you telling me that you don't want my company?" he asked.

"No, it's not that," she assured him with feeling. "I'm just—"

He found it hard not to laugh, but he managed. "Then just sit down and shut up, Ms. Colton. I am not impressed—or intimidated—by who you are."

Sean was still kidding, but he also suspected that

there were people who bowed and scraped before her because of her last name and who her family was. Personally, he found that to be dishonest. To his way of thinking, people should be treated for who they were, not who they were related to or associated with.

"I didn't say that you should be," she protested. She had no use for people like that. In her opinion, they were dishonest.

"Good, now sit," he told her again.

"I'm beginning to understand why those women I felt would be flocking to your door aren't flocking," she told him.

"You thought women would be flocking?" Sean asked, amused—and just a little mystified as to why she would even think that.

"Never mind, I'm delirious," she said, waving the remark away. "I don't know what I'm saying."

Sean looked at her, a wicked grin rising to his lips. But when he spoke, there was no trace of amusement in his voice.

"Understood."

Opening the cupboard, Sean looked on first one shelf, then the next, the contents of his cupboard pretty much of a mystery to him. He finally found a half-filled box of individually wrapped tea bags pushed to the back of a third shelf.

"I'm really not sure how old these are," he admitted. "If the tea winds up tasting ancient, feel free to toss it. I won't be insulted."

"If the tea bags are individually wrapped, they should be good indefinitely. Don't worry. I'm not picky," she assured him. "If it tastes reasonably like tea, that's good enough for me."

"We'll see." Sean poured the boiled water over a tea bag in a mug, then waited several minutes for it to turn into something acceptable. "I believe it's tea now," he told her, moving the mug in front of her. He left the tea bag in for good measure. "I've got a little bit of what passes for cream if you want to try adding that to the tea," he suggested.

She smiled. "No, I'll quit while I'm ahead. But thanks," she told him. "I do appreciate the effort."

He heard something in her voice and looked at her, all thoughts of continuing their banter gone. "Are you sure you're all right?" he asked, concerned.

"I am. Now. It's just that I can't get myself to stop thinking about *what if*," January confessed.

Sean shook his head. "You can't go there," he told her firmly. "Thinking that way will totally paralyze you and then you won't be any good to yourself—or that little girl you've taken under your wing."

January blew out a very shaky breath and took a long, slow sip of her tea. The warmth curled all through her, swirling in her chest then moving its way down through the rest of her.

"You're right," she told him.

Sean sat down opposite her at the table. "I usually am."

His unshakable confidence made her smile. "There's that ego again."

The detective didn't think of having an ego as a

bad thing. "Hey, that ego is what keeps me alive," he told her.

January's green eyes met his. And then she slowly smiled. "Thank goodness for small favors," she said seriously.

"Or big ones," he corrected. "Now promise me that, other than being on your guard for Maya's sake, you are not going to spend any time dwelling on what *might* have happened. Just focus on the fact that the two of you managed to survive. By the way, answer a question for me."

"If I can," she equivocated, taking another sip of her tea.

"Just how did you happen to buy a place with a panic room in it?" he asked. "Did you actually want one?"

"That's just it," she told him. "I initially had no idea it was there. I honestly don't think that the Realtor who sold the town house to me even knew. In her defense, when you open the door, the first thing you think of is that it looks like a regular closet. It's not until you're actually *standing* in the closet and push against the back wall—which swings open—that you discover it's really intended to be a panic room."

Sean shook his head. "That must have been some surprise."

"Oh, it was," she agreed. "I accidentally found it about a month after I moved in. When I did, I thought that someday, when I got married and had little people in my life, the so-called panic room would make a really neat place for them to play in and have creative adventures in." January looked into her mug. The contents were almost gone. "I never imagined that I would wind up using it for the very reason the guy who first installed it had in mind."

Sean heard the catch in her voice.

"You're thinking again," he admonished.

"Sorry." January flashed the police detective a quick smile. "Nasty habit I keep falling into. So," she said, clearing her mind and focusing on a new, lighter topic, "were you serious about that shopping trip you promised earlier?"

"Absolutely," he told her with all sincerity.

"But aren't you supposed to be working tomorrow?" she asked him. "How would you explain shopping for clothes for a five-year-old?"

"That's easy enough," he told her. "Guarding you and Maya is my new assignment. The warehouse where she was found was the site of a triple homicide. Maya was either an eyewitness, or the killer thinks she was. Sooner or later, he—or they—are going to come looking for her and try to find her. That's reason enough for me to be hanging around, guarding both of you." And then their eyes met. "Okay?"

January nodded, then drank the rest of her tea. Setting the mug down again, she told him, "You make a great cup of tea. Don't let anyone ever tell you otherwise."

Rising, she was about to take the mug over to the sink.

"I'll take care of that," Sean told her. "You just get to bed."

Starting to protest, January suddenly felt too tired to argue. "Okay," she agreed.

She was asleep within five minutes of entering the guest room and lying down.

Chapter Fourteen

Sean's eyes flew open.

When he told January that he slept with one eye open, he hadn't been exaggerating. An unfamiliar noise had him instantly awake. It was coming from somewhere inside his apartment and he couldn't place it. It had to be too early for January to be up, especially considering how tired she had been.

Throwing off his blanket, Sean's feet hit the floor at the same time that he reached for his sidearm in the nightstand next to his bed.

He took the safety off as he silently made his way toward the front of the apartment and the source of the noise. His alarms hadn't been tripped, but the detective was well aware that a savvy intruder could figure out how to bypass any security system no matter what might have been used to arm it.

Moving as quietly as he could, Sean came into the living room, then froze in his tracks at the same time that he exhaled a long sigh of relief.

No intruder had broken in.

As near as he could ascertain, January was cleaning his apartment. Didn't the woman ever do what was expected of her? he wondered, irritated.

"What do you think you're doing?" he asked, putting the safety back on his sidearm.

January dropped the makeshift dust cloth in her hand, which, until an hour ago, had doubled as a kitchen hand towel. She pressed her palm against her pounding chest, trying to regulate her heart rate.

She turned around to face the detective. "You have *got* to stop sneaking up on me like that, Stafford, or I swear that you're going to wind up giving me a heart attack."

"That goes both ways, you know," Sean told her pointedly. He tucked his weapon into the back of his waistband. "Now, I repeat. What do you think you're doing and why aren't you in bed?"

"I got enough sleep," she replied simply. "As for your first question, I know you're not familiar with the idea, so you might not recognize it when you see it, but what I'm doing is cleaning."

His eyebrows drew together to form a dark, foreboding scowl.

"I know what you're doing," he informed her, annoyed. "But *why* are you doing it?"

"If you have to ask, you really don't understand the concept of doing it. Cleaning happens when a place *needs* it. And trust me," she said, her tone lightening, "your place really needed it."

Looking around now, she felt satisfied. She had made a dent in cleaning up the apartment, at least when it came to the kitchen and the living room. She told herself that she would tackle the rest later.

"You do *not* have to do this," Sean insisted. He assumed that the social worker felt she needed to pay him back for taking her and Maya in.

"Oh, but I do," she answered simply. Her reply surprised him. She wasn't doing it to pay him back, it was for an entirely different reason. "If the dust bunnies had gotten any worse than they were," she told him, "I would have risked losing Maya in them."

She said it with such a straight face, she almost sounded serious, Sean thought.

Just what he needed. A social worker who doubled as a comedian.

"Very funny," he commented.

"Sadly, not really," she told him. January looked around at her handiwork. "I'm going to stop now and look in on Maya. If she's up, I'm going to get started on making breakfast. This—" she gestured around the general area "—will be continued later."

"About breakfast," he interrupted. "I thought we'd just go to a drive-through place."

"No need," January told him cheerfully. "I looked in your refrigerator. You have eggs, you have bread, you have me. Everything you need for a balanced meal."

Maybe she was the type who needed to hear the words out loud, he thought. "Look, I did not bring you here to cook and clean."

"I know," she answered. "That's one of the perks of having me here. Had you *asked* me to clean, I might have dragged my feet a little. But you didn't ask, so I'm more than happy to do it."

Sean shook his head. That really didn't make any sense to him, but he had a feeling she wasn't trying for sense.

"You women are a very befuddling species," he told her in all seriousness.

January didn't bother correcting him. Instead, she just smiled as she headed out of the room. Her eyes looked like they were laughing at him. "Keeps you on your toes, doesn't it?"

That wasn't the only thing it did, he thought, watching January as she left the room, her hips swaying in an enticing rhythm that was beginning to reel him in.

The next moment, Sean sternly upbraided himself. Thoughts like that were bound to get him into trouble. It didn't take a crystal ball for him to know that.

Fully awake now, he went to the kitchen to get the coffee started. He found to his diminishing surprise that January had beaten him to it. There was a freshly brewed pot standing at the ready on his coffee maker.

In a pot that had been recently cleaned, he noted as he poured his first cup of the day. Just when did this woman get up? More important than that, how had she managed to do all this without waking him up until now?

Did she get *any* kind of sleep?

He doubted it as he looked around at what January had already managed to get done.

Somehow, she had cleaned the entire kitchen and had gotten most of the living room straightened up.

Hell, he felt he was doing well if he managed to wash the dishes every couple of days or so—and that was without ever putting them away. His philosophy was that he planned to use the dishes at some point or other, so there was no real reason to empty the rack.

That rule of thumb had served him well so far.

"Guess who's awake," January said as she came back into the living room with Maya. The little girl was dressed, wearing the same converted blouse-into-dress that she had had on yesterday.

Sean noticed that her hair had been neatly brushed and rebraided. He also noted that not only did she seem less frightened than she had yesterday, but she actually looked happy.

"I don't need to guess," he said, lowering his voice before he remembered that Maya couldn't make out anything he said. But even so, he did add, "You're talking about my favorite princess." He enunciated the words right in front of her in hopes that, eventually, the little girl would be able to read his lips.

If for some reason Maya's stay here wound up being for a longer time, he would try to learn a few basics when it came to signing. Just a few frequently used words and phrases, because there was only so much that could be conveyed by a smile, he thought, trying not to get frustrated.

As she walked into the room, Maya surprised Sean by coming up to him and tugging on the edge of his shirt. It got him to bend down.

"Okay, I'm down to your level," he said, waiting to see what was next. "Now what?"

He sincerely doubted that the little girl could read his lips, but when he asked the question, Maya threw her arms around his neck and hugged him.

"I believe you have your answer," January told him. "And it looks like you won yourself a pint-sized heart," she added with a smile, smoothing down Maya's bangs. "Okay, now on to breakfast."

"I found the coffee," he told her, toasting her with his mug.

Her eyes crinkled as January smiled at him. "It wasn't hiding," she pointed out.

"I know that," he replied. "I'm trying to say thank you."

"Then say it. Nobody's stopping you. No preamble necessary." Her smile widened. "Was it to your liking?" she asked as she took out what she needed to make the simple breakfast. "The coffee," she prompted when he didn't respond.

"It wasn't as dark as I usually make it," Sean acknowledged. "But it was good."

"I wasn't sure how sludgy you liked it," she confessed. "So I took my best guess. Next time, I'll go a little heavier with the coffee—or lighter with the water." Then she decided that maybe it would be prudent to add, "If there *is* a next time."

"Are you resigning from the breakfast detail so soon?" Sean asked, surprised she would give up so easily.

"No, I'm not planning on it," January told him.

She had lost him—again. "Then why the *if*?" Sean asked.

"I was making reference to the fact that you might

get the bad guys," she told him. "Then there no longer will be a reason for Maya and me to play house at your place. The flip side of that is that you might find a member of her family and she will go with them."

"I'll say one thing for you. You certainly have more faith in the police department than most people do. Especially the people I've run into lately," he said, thinking of recent events that hadn't gone as well as he would have hoped.

"Sounds like someone might be badly in need of a vacation," she commented as she started preparing breakfast.

He laughed under his breath. The sound definitely lacked any humor. "No argument there, but that doesn't change my opinion about the way that a lot of private citizens in Chicago regard their local law enforcement agents."

She turned away from the stove for a second. "I'd say that, at the very least, you need to mingle with a different crowd of people—and soon." The moment the words were out of her mouth, an idea flashed through her mind. "And I have got the perfect solution for that," she declared happily.

He had to confess that the woman fascinated him. She seemed very pleased with herself—and the look became her, not to mention that it drew him in.

"I'm almost afraid to ask," he told her. Despite the smile on her face, he found himself feeling more than a little leery about what she was going to propose.

"Don't be afraid to ask," she said playfully. "You're

a police detective. Asking questions is a way of life for you."

January waited a beat as she cracked four eggs into a bowl.

When he didn't pick up the opening she had left for him, she felt she had no choice but to prod a little.

Turning to look at him over her shoulder, she urged, "So ask."

"Okay," he said gamely. "What is this perfect solution you have for me?"

"You, Detective Stafford, are going to come with me—with us," she corrected, looking at Maya, "to attend a family gathering."

"Any particular family you have in mind?" he asked, bracing himself as he watched her face and waited for her response. He had a feeling that he knew what she going to say.

"Yes, wise guy, a very specific family in mind," she told him, then said, "Mine."

"Since it's your family—and since I'm *not* family," he stressed, "wouldn't I be, you know, *crashing* this gathering?"

"Technically, you're my—*our*—bodyguard," she amended, glancing toward Maya. "That makes you as much a part of all this as my clothing. In case you're not following me, I wouldn't leave my clothing home, either."

Sean couldn't help but laugh. "That is a very novel way to describe it—but by the same token, very effective," he added, doing his best *not* to envision her without her clothing.

"As long as you get the message," January told him with a wide smile.

She put the eggs on low as she deposited the four slices of bread into the toaster. When they popped up, she buttered them all quickly, then placed two slices each on two plates and went on to distribute the eggs among the slices.

"So?" she asked as she set the plates down in front of Maya and Sean.

Sean flashed her a smile. He wasn't accustomed to being served in his own home. "Breakfast looks great," he told her.

"I know," she said, accepting the compliment as if there was nothing else he could have logically said. "But what about the invitation?"

"Shouldn't I wait to get it before I answer?" Sean pointed out.

It was clearly a stall tactic on his part and January knew that, but right now she really wasn't in the mood to play.

"You just did get it," she informed him. "From me."

"Well, if you put it that way," Sean allowed, "I guess the answer is yes."

"Finally," she declared as if she had just won a tournament that had taken way too long to win. "You certainly believe in making a person work for everything, don't you?"

"You mean that there's another way?" Sean asked innocently.

She didn't bother suppressing the smile that rose to her lips. "Yes, I believe they call it being straightforward."

"Oh, but this way, it just feels so much more rewarding when it finally comes through," Sean told the social worker.

She studied him for a long moment. "You know," January said, "with your rather unconventional sense of logic, you might be a Colton without knowing it."

Sean raised a puzzled eyebrow. "Is that your idea of a compliment?"

"No," she replied with an innocent expression, "just a simple fact."

Sean had been watching her. January had been moving around this entire time, preparing their breakfast and then serving it to them. There were only two plates, he noted.

"Aren't you going to eat?" he asked.

"Oh, I nibbled while I was preparing your breakfasts. And I did have toast earlier—two slices," she volunteered, knowing he would probably ask for a number.

"Nibbling?" he questioned. "Shouldn't you have more than just a nibble?"

She grinned at the detective, her eyes once again warming him.

Try as he might, he couldn't seem to get used to that. It was a pleasant surprise each time it happened. And he caught himself thinking about how it might feel, nibbling on her very tempting neck.

"A bodyguard *and* a nutritionist," she marveled, her eyes teasing him. "Anything else?"

"Yes," Sean answered seriously, doing his best to shut down these feelings threatening to run riot through him. "I also have a pretty short fuse when it comes to comments from wise guys."

"Duly noted," she said, nodding her head as she gave him the point.

"Just trying to look out for your best interests." Sean felt he needed to add that.

"And I appreciate it," she told him in all sincerity. "Now, I'll take care of the dishes, and then Maya and I will get ready for this shopping trip you're taking us on."

He took the plate out of her hand. "*I'll* do the dishes," he informed her. "You and the princess go get ready."

"Are you sure?" January asked, nodding at the dish. Most men weren't fans of washing dishes and he had already proven that he only did so when there was no way out. "It won't take me long."

"I'm sure," he said, still holding the dish in his hand. "Just because I don't wash dishes very often doesn't mean I don't know how. It just means I don't like to, which, the last time I checked, makes me a normal male. You find me a man who claims to like doing dishes and I'll show you a man who belongs in a museum under glass—or a notorious liar who's trying to impress the woman he's dating."

January grinned at him, amused. "As a matter of fact, you're probably right," she agreed.

Sean blinked several times and then pretended to cover his heart with both hands. Taking a "shaky" breath, he declared, "Be still my beating heart."

"You are also most definitely a wise guy," January told him.

"Guilty as charged." Then he ordered, "Now get going."

January took Maya's hand, turning toward the doorway. He didn't have to tell her twice.

Chapter Fifteen

Sean had never been a fan of shopping for clothing.
Ever since he became an adult, he had never entered
a mall of his own volition unless it was an absolutely
unavoidable necessity. The last time he remembered
actually walking into a mall was more than two years
ago. It had been to help Harry Cartwright, his former
partner, go shopping for his wife's birthday. Harry had
wanted to buy her something special, and true to form,
he hadn't had a clue what to get.

Sean had gone with him during lunch for moral
support. Three weeks later, Sean grimly remembered,
Harry's wife and child were dead.

January saw the faraway, distracted expression on
Sean's face as she brought Maya out to model one of
her choices.

"Where are you?" January asked the detective.

Sean shook off the unwanted memory. "Nowhere
where you would want to be."

January knew when not to pick at a scab and this
had all the signs of being a bad one, so she tactfully
backed off. But for Maya's sake, who was looking at

him as if the sun rose and set around the man, she knew she had to get the detective to respond to the little girl.

"I think Maya's trying to impress you, Detective," January told him pointedly. "You need to smile your approval."

"Sorry," Sean said, his eyes washing over Maya as he warmly smiled at her.

Sean's smile, January noted, did wonders for both the detective and the little girl who was on the receiving end of that smile. Maya lit up right before Sean's eyes, causing the detective to respond even more.

January nodded her head. "Good," she declared with approval.

Sean wasn't sure if that was meant for him, but he saw no harm in taking it that way.

Taking his hand, Maya fairly skipped along beside Sean as they made their way through the store. He smiled at her, determined to make her feel safe and carefree despite the fact that he couldn't shake the feeling that they were being observed. It might have been his natural paranoia acting up, but he didn't think so. He remained vigilante and alert.

BY THE TIME the shopping trip was officially over—and they had managed to hit three different department stores during that time frame—Maya was completely outfitted with a supply of fresh new clothes. Sean had offered to pay for them, but January told him not to worry about it. Social Services would take care of it.

Sean knew for a fact that, the way that particular department operated, it would be a long time before

January would be reimbursed. He had a feeling that she was actually footing the bill, but he wasn't about to press her on it. He trusted that if she was inclined to pay for Maya's wardrobe, January's family would probably take care of it in part.

"I think that Cinderella's going to be all decked out when it comes time to go to the ball," January told him once they finally returned to his vehicle.

Sean had carried almost all the items to the car while January and Maya each brought along a few items. And everything was summarily deposited into the trunk.

Putting away the last of it, Sean turned to see January sign something to the little girl. He assumed the message had something to do with what she had just said to him. He was sure of it when he saw the way that Maya laughed in response.

"My guess is that there's enough here for several balls," he told the social worker. "By the way, when is it?" he asked, because with everything that was going on, the date had slipped his mind.

It. Sean's question seemed to come out of the blue. She wanted to be sure they were on the same page before she answered him.

"Are you asking about my family's gathering?" she asked him.

"That's the only 'ball' that I know of," he told her, waiting for January to secure Maya in the car seat that had, in his mind, become hers.

"Saturday," she told him.

"This Saturday?" he asked uncertainly. It really

didn't seem possible, since the event had almost come out of nowhere.

January was convinced that the detective was attempting to stall again, but why? Supposedly, in attending this event, he was just going to be her escort, the way he had for grocery shopping and now at the mall. Granted, attending the gathering wasn't going to be as impersonal as escorting them to the supermarket and the department stores at the mall had been. But it wasn't exactly as if she was bringing him as her date for the afternoon and definitely not as her "significant other," although the idea wasn't as off-putting as she might have once thought.

Sean was just going to be a warm body watching over Maya and over her, she reminded herself.

Why was he behaving as if he was suddenly spooked by the idea?

"Uh-huh," January confirmed with an attempt at nonchalance. "This Saturday." She glanced at him. "I didn't think you'd have a conflict since you said you were going to be our bodyguard until you or your department are able to find Maya's family as well as who killed those three victims in the warehouse. The same people," she pointed out, "who probably broke into my town house."

"No, I don't have a conflict," he replied, then decided he might as well own up to the problem. "I just don't do well at family gatherings."

She looked at him. There was no *do well* about it, January thought. There was just being there, and he could certainly do that.

"Don't worry. Nobody's going to ask you to perform or do any magic tricks. You'll be fine. Tell you what," she said as she got into the front passenger seat and buckled up. "Why don't you pretend that you're undercover? That way, you can assume another personality during the time that we're over my parents' house. Would that make it easier for you?"

But he was stuck on another point. "Your parents' house," Sean echoed.

"Uh-huh. They're very nice people," she assured him. "Mom made Dad take down the photograph of the body of the last police detective he shot. It's no longer hanging over the fireplace," she told Sean with an incredibly straight face.

"Okay, point taken," Sean conceded.

"My parents are very nice people. My entire family is comprised of nice people. Don't get me wrong," she said, in case he thought she was just trying to whitewash her family. "There are times when they can make me crazy, but those times don't last and at bottom my whole family all mean well. Personally, without going out on a limb, I think that you'll find you like them.

"And, if you find any time during the course of the day that you just can't take it, all you have to do is say the code word and we'll leave," she promised.

"Code word?" Sean repeated. She hadn't said anything about a code word, he thought.

January looked over her shoulder to smile at Maya as they drove away from the mall.

"Uh-huh." He could swear that her eyes were laughing at him. "Everyone's gotta have a code word," she said solemnly.

"Okay," Sean replied gamely. "What's my code word?"

"Stratosphere," January answered. She smiled brightly.

He shot her a look. "Stratosphere?" he repeated incredulously. "How the hell am I supposed to work *that* into the conversation?"

January's smile just grew wider. Sean could have sworn that she lit up the interior of his vehicle.

"You're intelligent," she told him in all innocence. "I have great faith in you."

Sean snorted. *Yeah, right*, he thought. Out loud he said darkly, "Very funny."

"Not half as funny as the expression on your face," January said. "Relax, detective. I promise you'll have fun. Everyone in my family is easy to talk to—with the possible exception of my cousin Jones, but his only difficulty is with my uncle, not anyone else in the family. Personally, I think you and Jones will probably get along famously." She added, "He owns Lone Wolf Brewery, you know," to cinch the argument.

That managed to surprise Sean. "You're kidding," he cried, looking at her. "Your cousin actually owns that brewery?"

"I wouldn't kid you about that," she answered. "It's certainly an easy enough fact to look up."

Sean rolled that surprising piece of information around in his head, trying to absorb it. "Son of a gun," he murmured.

Satisfied that Maya was all right in her seat, January turned back around and returned her attention to the detective.

"Is there a reason behind that remark?" she asked, curious about his reaction to the information.

"Lone Wolf happens to be my favorite local brewery," Sean admitted.

That pleased her. It would certainly help matters when it came to the gathering. "See? You've already got something in common with a member of my family. This will be fun," she assured him again. "Really."

"Yeah, maybe it won't be so bad after all," Sean allowed, driving back to his apartment.

"Wow, you really know how to dish out high praise," January said with a laugh. The man would probably announce the advent of the second coming by saying, *Looks like He's back.*

Sean shrugged. "It's the best I can do at the moment," he told her. He tended to try to be low-key whenever possible. "Look, I said that I'm going with you. Why don't you just take the win and be done with it?"

"Okay. You're right. I'll take it," January said, then quietly added under her breath, "For now."

"You're bringing someone?" her mother asked later that evening when January called to tell her about Maya and Sean. She could hear Farrah Colton struggling not to sound as excited as she actually felt. "What's his name? Where did you meet him? Why haven't you—"

"Calm down, Mom," January said, raising her voice

to be heard above her mother's. "Believe me, it's not what you think—"

"Not what I think?" her mother echoed. "Why? Is he a robot? A rubber doll? What? Talk to me, January."

January didn't know where to start. She didn't want to scare her mother, but she wasn't about to let her think that this was a boyfriend she was bringing. That would definitely kill any future between them.

"He's a police detective, Mom."

"So?" Her mother obviously didn't see a problem. "You know that I've always had the greatest respect for the law enforcement community. You're not handcuffed to him, are you?"

"No, I'm not handcuffed to him, Mom, but he is coming to this gathering in his police detective capacity," January told her.

She could tell that she had managed to lose her mother. The next thing Farrah Colton said confirmed her suspicions. "Okay, you're going to have to explain that to me, Jan."

Maybe if she went back to the beginning. "You know I didn't go on vacation with Simone and Tatum."

"I am aware of that," her mother told her. "Are you aware of the fact that they didn't go on vacation, either?" she asked, assuming that might have not registered with her youngest, even though she and her husband were throwing this party and wouldn't be having it if two of their daughters were unable to attend. Sometimes, her children got too involved in what they were doing and just became oblivious to key points.

"What?" January cried. Both of her sisters had told

her that they were still going on that vacation. She felt a stab of guilt. Had they done this because of her?

"They decided to postpone until you were able to come with them. They didn't think it would be enough fun without you, which I think is a really nice compliment. They also said something about you taking in a little deaf girl because your department was short-handed and there was no one else available who could communicate with her."

Her mother paused, waiting for confirmation. When January didn't respond, she asked, "Did I get that right, January? Is that why you didn't go on that vacation?"

"Yes, Mom, you got it right," January told her. "Maya's been staying with me and it was necessary to get a protective detail for her. That's why Detective Stafford is coming with me. With us," she amended. "He's the protective detail." January was doing her best to word it so that she didn't wind up alarming her mother about how dangerous the situation potentially was.

She should have known that her mother wouldn't just leave the matter alone.

"Why does she need a protective detail?" her mother asked. "Is she in danger?" And then another question, far closer to home, occurred to January's mother. "Does that mean that *you* are in danger, too?"

"Mom, don't get ahead of yourself. I'm just taking care of her until Sean…um… Detective Stafford locates her parents." She attempted to divert her mother by appealing to the woman's incredibly kind heart. "You can imagine how scared that little girl had to be, surrounded by a bunch of strangers in a world where she's unable to hear anything that's going on."

"That's why you were assigned to her."

January gave her mother a slightly more rounded explanation of the circumstances. "That's why I volunteered to take Maya in and be with her until she can be reunited with her family."

"How did she get separated from them?" her mother asked. "Can't you get her to tell you how that happened?"

"I'm working on it, Mom. First, I need to get her to really trust me," she told the woman. "That's why this gathering you're having will be so helpful. I'm thinking that maybe just having her around everyone, absorbing all those good vibrations, getting to feel secure—" January stopped abruptly, realizing that she wasn't being clear. "Oh, you know what I'm trying to say, Mom, right?"

She heard the smile in her mother's voice. "I know, darling, I know. You come with… Maya, is it?"

"Yes, Mom, it's Maya," January replied.

"Well, you know you're welcome to come with Maya and your police detective—"

January needed to nip this in the bud before her mother got carried away. This was all Sean needed to hear. "He's not *my* police detective, Mom."

"All right," Farrah said, changing her direction. "You come with whoever's detective he is and we'll all show the three of you a very good time."

January wasn't completely convinced that there

wouldn't be a problem. "You won't embarrass him—or me—will you?"

"Sweetheart, we wouldn't dream of it," her mother assured her. "Your happiness and well-being is our only concern and if, by extension, that includes Maya and Detective…?"

"Stafford, Mother. Detective Stafford," January told her. She knew she had already told her mother his name once and really doubted that the woman had forgotten it so quickly. Her mother was just enjoying this far too much.

"Detective Stafford," her mother repeated. "If that includes both of them, as well, well I say all the better. Now stop talking and start getting ready, dear."

"The gathering is tomorrow, remember, Mom?" January pointed out.

"Tomorrow will be here before you know it, darling," her mother said.

January sighed. "That's what you always used to tell me when I tried to put off doing my homework or studying until 'tomorrow.'"

"And I was right, wasn't I?" her mother asked, amused. "I also succeeded in getting you into the habit of studying before the very last minute. I'm very proud of that."

"Yes, I know," January answered with a laugh. "You're a great mother, Mom. Simone, Tatum and I are in complete agreement on that. Now, if you'll excuse me, I have to go. There're some things I need to do before we come over tomorrow."

"Just bring yourself, Maya and your *protective de-*

tail, dear," Farrah added with emphasis. "That's all any of us want—or need—to see."

"And you will all be on your best behavior?" January asked one last time.

"When have we not been?" her mother asked innocently.

"You really want me to answer that?" January responded with a dry laugh.

Farrah chuckled, her tone vetoing that idea. "On second thought, you're probably tired. Get some rest, dear, and we'll talk tomorrow when you and your entourage get here."

She was about to tell her mother not to refer to Maya or Sean as being part of an entourage, then decided to drop the matter. Her mother, she knew, would be on her best behavior once she finally got to meet Maya and Sean. At this point January knew that it was a toss-up as to which one of them would hold the most appeal for her mother, although, in truth, she had to admit that she did have her suspicions about the matter.

Despite her concerns, January couldn't wait for the next day to come.

Chapter Sixteen

"Hey, Sean, could you come here for a minute?" January called to him.

It was the day of the party and she was dressed and ready to leave for her parents' gathering. She had gone into the living room to make sure that Maya was still ready, as well, even though she had gotten the girl dressed earlier. January was taking no chances since she was accustomed to children who could get dirty and disheveled at the drop of a hat.

To her relief and delight, not only was Maya still neat and clean, she was actually entertaining herself. Sitting on the floor in front of the coffee table, the little girl was drawing on the sheet of paper January had given her.

Expecting to see wide, unrecognizable circles and squiggles, January was surprised at how well Maya was able to actually draw. The end result was a picture of animals gathered together. It was definitely better than most five-years-olds were capable of doing.

The girl had real talent, January thought.

Reacting to her summons and expecting the worst—

because that was the nature of his work—Sean came hurrying into the living room. He hadn't tucked his shirt in yet, but his service weapon was in his hand and ready to use if necessary.

Seeing his gun, January realized how she must have sounded to him and she immediately apologized. "I'm sorry, I didn't mean to make you think that something was wrong." She gestured toward the coffee table at the drawing Maya was working on. "Look at what Maya drew while waiting for us."

Sean looked at the drawing more closely. To his surprise, he was able to make the figures out. "Is that supposed to be us?" he asked.

"Well, two tall figures and one short one with long brown braids. Judging from the clothing the taller figures are wearing, they're definitely supposed to be a man and a woman. So, taking that into consideration," January told him with a smile, "my guess would be yes, Maya made a drawing of us."

She slanted a glance at the detective. He wasn't picking up on the important part. "Look at it. She drew us as a family." She indicated the figures. "Look, we're all holding hands."

"Son of a gun, you're right," he said, smiling at the drawing. Maya looked up at him and he signed "Good," pleasing the little girl while surprising January.

"You just told her *good*," January said, amazed. He hadn't said anything about continuing to learn how to sign.

"I know," Sean replied as if being able to do so was nothing out of the ordinary.

January smiled at him. The man just kept surprising her. "You've been studying."

Sean merely shrugged. "I thought it might be a good idea to try to keep up a little," he said, as if learning to do so was no big deal on his part, even though January knew it had to be. The detective was incredibly busy. Learning how to sign, even in a very minor way, would have taken a lot of concentrated effort on his part.

The man really cared.

He looked back at the drawing. It was impressive for what it was. "She's pretty talented for a half-pint," he told January.

"And, on that note, I think we should be leaving," she said. "We don't want to be late."

"Why? Do the doors slam shut at the mansion if you don't arrive on time?" the detective asked. But it wasn't a hostile remark. His mouth curved as he asked the question.

"No, it's just not polite to be late, that's all," she informed him matter-of-factly. She had been raised to always be punctual. "And it's not a mansion. It's a regular house—just a little larger than most," she added, then felt she needed to tell him one more fact—or maybe two. "My parents' house and my uncle and aunt's house were built on the same property next to one another. The houses are exquisitely furnished. That's because both my mother and my aunt Fallon are interior designers. They have their own company."

"And your father and uncle are into developing medical technology," Sean recalled as he held the front door opened for January and Maya.

"You *have* done your homework," January said, impressed. "By the way, anywhere in that homework you did, did it happen to mention that my dad and my uncle Ernest are twins?"

"I might have read that somewhere," he replied vaguely, resetting the alarm system before he walked out to join Maya and January.

"Uh-huh. Did you also happen to read that my mom and my aunt Fallon were twins, too?" January asked.

That caused Sean to stop short for a moment before he finally got to his car and unlocked the doors. He held the rear door open so that January was able to secure Maya in her car seat.

The part about her mother and aunt had eluded him. "Twins marrying twins?" he asked, saying the words out loud as if to make sure that was what January was telling him.

She couldn't help laughing at the expression on Sean's face. He appeared stunned. She could relate to that.

"When you're a little kid," she told him, remembering various incidents from that time, "you think you're always seeing double. And then you start to think that everyone's parents have look-alikes. Wrapping your head around the fact that your parents are actually unique turns out to be a little harder."

"I'll bet. Well, if nothing else," he said as January got into the car on the passenger side, "today should really prove to be interesting."

"And fun," she reminded him, buckling up. "Don't forget fun."

"So you said," he told her as he started the car. At

the time, he'd just thought she was trying to talk him into going, but now, he was beginning to think that maybe she was actually right.

As he started up the ignition, January realized that she hadn't given him her parents' address. "Oh, let me give you the directions," she offered.

But before she could say anything further, Sean told her, "Not necessary. I've already got them."

January could only shake her head in total wonder. "You really are prepared, aren't you?" she marveled.

He didn't see why that should surprise her. "In my line of work, my life could depend on that," he reminded her.

"Well, for today your life is secure. All you need to be prepared for is to enjoy yourself," she informed him. "If you ask me, I think you both could use it."

"I can see Maya needing it," Sean admitted. "But not me."

He could feel January looking at him. "Oh, I think you need it a lot more than you think, Sean," she told him. "If you ask me, you're in a dark place, Detective. You need to find a way to get out of there before it winds up swallowing you whole." Her eyes met his. He was blocking her, she thought. "I know what I'm talking about."

"Is that the social worker talking now?" Sean asked.

His tone told her that he was humoring her, but it also told her that she was right.

Sean was harboring something, something he didn't want to talk about. Maybe he had suffered some sort of breakup, January guessed. Or maybe it was something else, but whatever it was, it had definitely left its mark on the man and wounded him.

He looked as if he was visibly shutting himself off from her.

"I also volunteer for several charities and deal with a lot of emotionally wounded people," she told him, trying to explain why she felt he was being secretive about something.

"I see. Well, you save all that insightfulness for them," he told her. "With me, what you see is what you get. No trapdoors, no secret hiding places."

Smiling at him, January said, "If you say so, Sean."

"I do," he told her emphatically, his tone a little more serious than he had intended. Gripping the wheel, he stared straight ahead as he pressed down on the gas pedal.

"Um, Sean?" January tried to get his attention as he continued driving.

"Yeah?" he bit off, then instantly regretted it, trying to get hold of the temper that had gotten away from him.

"We're here," she told him. "Or, we were, except that you just passed it." She nodded toward the house that was growing smaller in the rearview mirror.

Sean bit off a sharp curse, aimed at himself. He was relieved that the little girl sitting behind him wasn't able to pick up on what he had just said. He needed to get a better grip on things, especially when it came to himself, Sean thought.

Frowning, he shot January a look. "You distracted me."

She caught herself grinning. "I think that's the nicest thing you've said to me so far," January told him. She tried to hide the grin.

Sean spared January a glance, seeing the fight she was waging. Several things popped into his head as a response, but what ultimately wound up coming out was, "The day's still young."

Why what was, for all intents and purposes, a throw-away comment would wind up warming her heart was anyone's guess, January thought. This was not the time to analyze it.

"Ah, something to look forward to," January said flippantly. "But let's just table that for now, shall we? Looks like we're here."

Turning in her seat, she signed as much to Maya, then got out of the vehicle.

Sean was already out on his side. "You think it's all right if I park here?" he asked. There was a lot of open space in front of the palatial house, but he wasn't sure just what protocol dictated and he didn't want to accidentally cross anyone.

"I'm sure that my mother would tell you that you can park anywhere you want to, short of in the bird-bath," she told the detective with a laugh.

Then, because she was afraid that might somehow wind up intimidating him, she explained. "Because you rescued Maya and me from those intruders, you pretty much walk on water as far as she's concerned," she told him.

He nodded. "Yeah, well, since that's pretty much my job, I have no idea why that puts your family in my debt."

She flashed a smile at him. "We're a very close family and we're partial to keeping all the members alive," she quipped. Then, looking at the somewhat imposing house, a house she had thought of as home all of her life, she asked, "Ready?"

"Maybe you should give me another minute or so," Sean said. He knew that this should be like any other encounter, but for some reason, he felt as if he actually needed to create a good impression.

January had a feeling that in another minute, the detective would find a reason to either bolt or, most likely, remain outside, acting more like a protective detail and less like a guest.

She didn't want to drag him inside, but she also didn't want to have to explain to her mother why the man she was obviously looking forward to meeting had suddenly decided to disappear.

So, instead of giving Sean that minute he had asked for, January got out of the vehicle, took Maya by the hand and walked up to the front door. She heard Sean closing the car door behind her. She hoped that was a positive sign.

January rang the doorbell.

The next instant, the massive front door flew open, and as she had prophesied, Sean found himself seeing double. Both her mother and her aunt Fallon were standing in the doorway.

"Welcome!" her mother cried, delighted as she extended the greeting.

Equally pleased, Fallon's eyes swept over the police

detective who had escorted her niece. She proclaimed, "You're here!"

Both women welcomed Sean with open arms at the very same time that they embraced the little girl they had been told about.

For her part, Maya seemed both overwhelmed and slightly enchanted at the same moment. Her head moved back and forth as she looked from one woman to the other, and finally to January, an obvious question in her eyes.

January quickly signed to Maya, introducing her to her mother, Farrah, and then to her aunt Fallon. Belatedly, she realized that she had neglected to do the same for Sean.

"Wow, where are my manners?" January admonished herself. "I'm sorry." The apology was meant for all three adults. "Mother, Aunt Fallon, this is Detective Sean Stafford. Our bodyguard."

"And here I was, feeling sorry for you for having to give up your vacation," said a tall, very pretty blonde, walking up to them. She momentarily gave Sean her undivided attention. "Hi, I'm January's cousin, Carly Colton." She put out her hand.

Sean shook it. It was obvious that he was trying to place her—and failing.

"I'm sorry, I don't mean to stare. It's just that you look very familiar," he explained.

"There might be a reason for that," Carly told him. "I'm a pediatric nurse at Chicago University Hospital. If you've ever had any reason to come by the hospital on police business or for any other reason, our paths might have crossed."

Her words unexpectedly brought back an image that he had struggled for two years to bury. It was never that far from his mind, but the mention of the hospital managed to quickly unearth it.

His expression grew grim. Carly didn't notice, but January did.

Unable to ignore it, January leaned into Sean and whispered, "Is everything all right?"

"Yes. Sure." Sean was quick to rally. "Just a little overwhelmed by how much your mother and aunt look alike."

He was lying, January thought, but for now she knew she had to let it go. Sean clearly needed space, and maybe even some time to cope with whatever was going on in his head.

So she said, "Well, if you think that's something, then you had better brace yourself."

He didn't understand. "For what?"

There was no need for her to answer because at that moment, a deep, baritone asked, "Was that the lilting voice of my youngest daughter, or am I just imagining things?" Alfred Colton, a tall, imposing man with very thick, dark-blond hair, walked into the front room.

January turned around, beaming at the larger-than-life man.

"You're not imagining things, Dad. It's me," January answered, affectionately kissing her father's cheek.

"So, you're not a figment of our joint imaginations,"

Uncle Ernest said, coming up to her other side and pressing a kiss to her cheek in turn.

"Wow." The word escaped Sean's lips without his meaning it to. He heard it belatedly and flushed as both men and January turned in his direction.

January was the first to say anything. "I told you they looked eerily alike."

That they certainly did, Sean thought, stunned despite having been warned ahead of time.

"January, that's no way to talk about your father," her uncle said.

Ernest's comment was echoed by his brother. "Or your uncle," Alfred Colton told his youngest daughter.

"In my defense, I don't think that Sean was prepared for just how very alike the four of you look," January said.

"Well, your mother and I don't look alike," her father teased.

"You know what I mean, Dad," January told him, looking at the foursome who had been the reason for so much confusion in her younger days.

"Uh-huh." Disregarding his daughter's words, Alfred Colton took Sean's hand and shook it. "Nice to meet you," he told the detective. "You're the first breathing male January ever brought home who wasn't in foster care."

January's face turned bright red as she cried in protest, "Dad!"

"Alfred." Her mother chided her husband at the same time.

Alfred Colton appeared the soul of innocence as he asked, "What did I say? It is true."

"Women," Ernest Colton said with a shake of his head. "Who can understand them? Am I right?" he asked Sean with a conspiratorial smile.

Sean glanced over at January. "Absolutely," he agreed.

The funny thing was, he found himself falling—not only for January, but for her family, as well.

At least, the members he had met so far.

Chapter Seventeen

No one was as surprised as Sean at how much he really liked and got along with January's family. Not just one or two of the members, or because he felt he had to be polite to the Coltons who were, after all, a very big, important family in the area. Sean had never kowtowed to someone because of who they were or how much money they had.

But in this case, he quickly discovered that these people—every single one of them—were all genuinely nice and down to earth. He felt he could see through an act and these people really did seem like they took an interest in him as a person.

Sean found himself caught up in the various family dynamics playing out before him. Moreover, at no time did he feel as if any of January's relatives felt themselves to be above him in any manner, shape or form.

The detective was also surprised to find that he wasn't the only nonfamily member attending the gathering. Shortly after he, January and Maya arrived, he saw Cruz Medina in the group. Medina was Tatum Colton's newest employee at her restaurant. Since Sean had assumed that this was a family-only gathering, and that he and Maya were the exceptions, seeing another nonfamily member there was a surprise.

When he questioned January about it, she told him that her restaurateur sister had just hired Cruz as a sous chef for True and had brought the man to meet her family. It was her way of getting him entrenched. Sean found all of this to be unusual, given that he recognized Cruz from the Narcotics Division. As far as he was aware of, Cruz knew his way around a coffee maker, and that was the sum total of his culinary abilities.

Sean made no comment when they were introduced, but as soon as he found an opportunity to do so, he made his way over to Cruz.

Pouring a glass of wine for himself and one for the Narcotics detective, Sean handed the other man a glass and asked, "Hey, what's the deal, man?"

When Cruz raised his dark, expressive eyes to Sean's face, indicating his ignorance about the comment he had just made, Sean asked plainly, "Are you moonlighting these days?"

Since news traveled fast at the police station and rumors even faster, Cruz saw no reason to pretend. Sean, he reasoned, knew enough to keep this quiet.

"Something like that," Cruz replied evasively. Then he said, "Way too complicated to get into right now."

Just in case this was something other than he thought, Sean felt a warning of sorts was in order. "These are good people," he said to the man he knew as Harry Cartwright's new partner. "I wouldn't want to see any of them get hurt." The smile on Sean's lips never wavered, but there was no mistaking his warning. He was telling Cruz to be on his best behavior.

"Don't worry," Cruz said as he raised his glass to his lips. "I have no intentions of hurting anyone here. I have a completely different target in my sights, but that's all I can say on the subject right now."

Sean nodded his head, dropping the topic for the moment. "Understood."

"Hey, what are you two talking about?" January asked as she came up to join the two men.

"Just sharing some common interests," Sean replied vaguely. "Speaking of common interests—" he quickly scanned the room "—where's ours?"

He had really expected to find Maya hermetically sealed to January's side since the little girl wasn't with him at the moment. That she was with neither one of them worried him more than he let on.

"She's with Carly," January explained, pointing her out to the detective. She had kept one eye on the little girl at all times, even when she wasn't with Maya. "Everyone's doting on Maya," she told him with a touch of affectionate pride. "But, as it turns out, Carly also knows how to sign, and she and Maya have been talking up a storm, so to speak."

January looked again toward where she had left the little girl. Observing Maya with Carly and her mother now, she thought Maya was positively glowing. With a sigh, January said, "I think we're going to have a tough time getting her to come home with us."

The moment the words were out of her mouth, she

immediately looked at Sean to see if he had caught her slip.

The look on his face told her that he had.

I'm going to have to be careful, January told herself. She hadn't meant to make it sound as if the three of them were a unit.

To her surprise, as well as relief, her inadvertent comment didn't seem to bother Sean.

It was getting harder and harder for her to maintain that barrier she had put up between them. Harder for her to remember that Sean was just here with her—and Maya—in a professional capacity. She found that his constant presence was generating some very *un*professional thoughts in her head.

And those thoughts were really beginning to get in her way.

"I agree," Sean was saying, watching the little girl. "Good thing that Maya seems to have such a soft spot in her heart for you."

"For both of us," January corrected emphatically. She wanted to give credit where it was due and to make Sean realize that, without even meaning to, he had formed a bond with Maya. But this situation couldn't go on indefinitely and she knew it. "Has any progress been made with that DNA match?"

"No, not yet," he told her. When he caught the sharp look that crossed her face, he quickly added, "but it turns out that the lab is really swamped, so it's going to take longer than the promised forty-eight hours to get back to us."

"It's getting really hard to be patient," she told Sean.

He caught the edge in her voice. His eyes met hers.

"Yes, I know," he replied, even though he wasn't thinking about getting the DNA results or anything even remotely close to that. Instead, he was thinking about the impatience that longing had created within him.

Apparently feeling as if he was intruding, Tatum's pseudo-chef took this opportunity to break away. "I'll see you around, Stafford," Cruz said.

Nodding at January, he made his way back to where he had left her sister.

"You two know each other?" January asked, mildly interested.

Sean had no desire to be caught in a lie, but at the same time, he didn't feel he should volunteer too much at this point.

"Yeah," he answered, leaving it at that.

January drew in a breath. At times Detective Sean Stafford could be the most uncommunicative man, she thought in frustration.

"From where?" she asked.

"Long story," he answered flatly.

She supposed that was meant as her cue to back off. "Maybe some other time," January replied.

She wondered if the man realized just how much slack she kept cutting him.

"Maybe," he agreed, leaving it at that. "Let's get back to Maya before someone in your family decides to permanently whisk her away." Sean began to make his way back to the circle of people around the little girl.

Despite the fact that a perpetual wall of silence surrounded her, effectively separating her from everyone else there, Maya seemed to be very happy, even thriving, in the ongoing atmosphere.

January began to appreciate the fact that, in every way except for one, Maya was a normal, happy little girl. It made the social worker in her more determined than ever to attempt to find the little girl's family and unite her with them.

January made a solemn promise to herself that, with or without Sean's help, she was going to make this happen for Maya.

THEY WOUND UP staying at her parents' house a lot longer than January had intended. Initially, she'd thought that they would leave the gathering a great deal sooner than they did. She didn't want to abuse Sean's good nature.

But as it turned out, he was the one who demurred when she suggested leaving.

He seemed to be really enjoying himself, January thought. She had the distinct impression that the detective was not accustomed to this sort of celebration. Her guess was that, being exposed to it now, Sean was trying to absorb as much of it as possible.

January had watched in fascination as her father and her uncle took Sean aside at different points in the afternoon and evening, undoubtedly sharing some sort of guy thing that ultimately pleased and/or amused the detective. She saw him smiling, *really* smiling.

For her part, she would have loved to be able to hear what was being said, but she instinctively knew it had to be something to do with "man talk," a term both her father and her uncle favored. Quite simply, it referred to imparting "wisdom" along the lines of older man passing down acquired knowledge to younger man.

She'd been afraid that Sean would initially brush it off, but she discovered that she was worrying needlessly. Going by Sean's expression, he seemed to take it all well, and each time she saw that his demeanor remained easygoing. Possibly, in part, thanks to his police training.

By the time they finally did leave the family gathering, Maya appeared to be all but spent. She did attempt, for a while, to get across how excited she felt. For a little bit, her small hands seemed to fly, talking almost nonstop, sharing as much as she could with January and Carly.

But then, perforce, Maya's hands grew still, and her eyelids kept drooping, signaling she was about to lose the battle against encroaching sleep.

By the time they finally reached Sean's apartment, Maya had fallen sound asleep. She didn't even wake up when January unbuckled her from her car seat.

Nor did she wake as Sean slowly picked her up from that seat and drew her into his arms.

Careful not to jostle his precious cargo, the police detective moved almost in slow motion. He didn't want to wake Maya up.

"I think she's completely worn out," Sean whispered, holding the small body to him as he began to go up to his door on the second floor.

"Sean, you don't have to whisper," January reminded the detective, once again pointing out, "Maya can't hear you."

"Logically, I know that," Sean replied. "But on some level, I think maybe she can. I know it's dumb."

"No, it's not dumb," January argued. "It's sweet. I know that's not something I'm supposed to say to a homicide detective, but it doesn't change the fact that I think it is. So sue me." She raised her chin as if she was issuing a challenge.

His mouth curved. "Suing is just about the *last* thing on the list of things I want to do with you," Sean confided as he came to the landing. Crossing to his door, he realized that he would have to shift Maya in order to get his house key out.

Which probably meant waking her up.

He looked over toward January. Positioning his hip in such a way that she would be able to get into his side pocket, Sean said, "Would you mind?"

January wasn't following him. "Mind what?"

He supposed he hadn't exactly been clear. "I can't get my key out to open the door without shifting and jostling Maya. But you can."

That didn't jibe with what he had told her earlier. "I thought you set the alarm before we left for my parents' house."

"I did. But I need to put the key into the lock to disarm the alarm so I can input the right combination in order to open up the door." He looked at her to see if she was following what he'd just said.

January rolled her eyes. "Oh, for the days when you

could just kick down a door," she said with a wistful note in her voice.

"Yeah, right." He laughed, trying to envision her actually kicking down a door. "You and what army?" Shifting, he waited for January to slip her hand into his pocket in order to secure his house key.

January took in a deep breath and then slipped her hand into his pocket to retrieve the key. "I'll have you know I can kick down doors," she informed him. When he gave her a skeptical look, she qualified her remark. "Little doors in dollhouses, but still doors."

Sean nodded. "If I'm ever trapped in a dollhouse, you'll be the first one I send for," he told her with an aura of solemnity in his voice.

"Deal," January agreed.

Her hand seemed to tingle where she had slipped it into the pocket of his jeans. It had taken her longer to locate the key only because she was trying her best not to turn the hunt for the key into something a great deal more tantalizing and physical.

She failed.

It was exactly that.

But that was because she was trying so very hard to divorce herself from the process.

Finally securing the elusive key, she held it up in front of his face. "I got it," she declared. "Now what?"

"Use it?" he suggested. "Before the night gets too old?"

"Right," she murmured, utterly embarrassed that, just for a moment, she had managed to get *really* distracted by her hunting errand.

Slipping the key into the lock, she input the combination, then turned the doorknob and opened the door to his apartment. She quickly looked around the immediate area. "Nothing looks as if it's been touched."

"That's good to hear," he said, looking around himself. "But I am the detective, so I'd better act like one. I'll check everything out. You take Maya."

Very carefully, Sean passed the little girl to her.

"This must be what the changing of the guard feels like," January quipped, taking Maya into her arms. The little girl didn't even stir, she noticed with pride. "I'd better get her to bed," she told Sean.

"Not until I clear the apartment," he said emphatically.

She thought he was being needlessly overcautious, but she didn't want to spoil the night by arguing with him. *Better safe than sorry*, she reminded herself for the umpteenth time.

"You're right," she agreed. "I'll wait here with Maya."

She stood there, holding Maya against her, thinking that this had to be what having a child was like.

A warm, protective feeling flooded through her as she waited for Sean to return.

Someday, she promised herself. *Someday*.

She felt as if she had been standing there, waiting forever, when Sean finally returned to the front of the apartment.

"It's all clear," he told her. "Nobody is in here except for us." He gently took Maya back into his arms. "I'll take her to her room and put her to bed. You look as if you're about to fall over if you try to do that."

"I'll have you know that I'm fresh as a daisy," she informed him.

"Right, a daisy that's been growing in the desert for the last two months—without any water." He laughed.

"Flattery is definitely not your strong suit," she said as she followed Sean to the guest bedroom.

"Maybe not, but observation is," he pointed out. "It's what I do for a living, remember?"

"I keep forgetting," she said, deadpan. "I guess that's why I have you to remind me." She watched as he laid Maya down.

"You want to get her ready for bed?" he asked, although if it were up to him, he would opt to leave the little girl dressed.

"I don't want to risk waking her up," she said, agreeing with him without realizing it. "This will do fine for tonight." And with that, she stepped back and accidentally bumped up against Sean.

Chapter Eighteen

Without meaning to, Sean brushed his chest against her back. It was just the most innocent of contacts, and yet the moment it happened, January was on the receiving end of an electrical shock that went shooting right through her.

Sean reacted instantly without even thinking about it. He put his hands on her shoulders and slowly turned January around. There was nothing more to his action than wanting to steady her.

At least, that was what Sean told himself.

But when he turned January around so that she was facing him, he was suddenly aware of all sorts of emotions vibrating through him. Without meaning to, Sean found himself acutely conscious of every single part of the woman. At the same time, every shred of his own desire was making itself known to him.

It was as if he was attempting to put a lid on a pot that was threatening to explode at any second.

In that one moment in time, their eyes met, and suddenly, there were no more secrets between them, no more hiding places where those same unvoiced secrets could be tucked away.

The very intense desire that seemed to have been there right from the start took over, ready to govern her every move, her every thought.

January had never felt like this before, whether because she hadn't had any time, or because she had never been attracted to another man to this extent, she didn't know. All she did know was that whatever this was was threatening to explode within her, drenching every part of her, promising to be exquisite when it finally emerged.

She couldn't put any of this into words, and when she did try, Sean gently placed his finger against her lips, letting her know that right now, words really weren't necessary.

"We don't want to disturb her," he told her softly, nodding toward the sleeping Maya.

January still wasn't sure if they were on the same page, even though something—some deep inner instinct—told her that they were.

For now, January just took the hand that Sean offered her and followed him out of the room.

Without saying a word, as if talking at this moment would somehow break the spell, Sean took January into his bedroom.

Looking around the room, January couldn't help smiling.

"You made your bed," she noted, although the rest of the room still looked like a hurricane had recently touched down, then left.

His eyes smiled at her as he said, "You're rubbing off on me." Then, because he was aware of what the rest of the room still looked like, he added with an appealing smile, "A little."

"Hey, Rome wasn't built in a day—or cleaned up in one, either," she told the man who had managed to totally hijack her heart without any effort whatsoever.

Every part of her smiled at him even as he began undoing her by slow, languid increments.

"No," Sean agreed, his voice low, husky, as he pressed a kiss to her throat. "It wasn't. But it's always good to have something to aspire to," he said, touching soft, tantalizing kisses along first one side of her neck and then the other.

Her pulse quickened and she could feel her knees being reduced to the consistency of well-cooked spaghetti, all but dissolving beneath her.

January found herself all but gasping for air. She dug her fingertips into his shoulders in an effort to remain upright.

He could feel her swaying against him, trying to regain her balance. "Am I going too fast?" Sean asked.

It took her a moment to actually comprehend the words. What she was really aware of was the feel of his warm breath along her skin as he formed them.

Pulling herself together in order to focus on what he was actually asking, she finally answered, "No, not fast enough."

Her response pleased him, but at the same time, he wanted to be absolutely sure that she was a willing participant. That he hadn't somehow managed to overwhelm her so she couldn't think clearly. He needed this to be real.

With what seemed like lightning speed, this woman had become incredibly important to him and he didn't want to risk losing her because he had given in to the moment and, in so doing, had robbed her of her free will. He wanted her more than he could possibly say, but not that way.

"You're sure?" he asked.

January drew back just a little so that she could look at him. The detective made her feel almost dizzy, she realized—and she reveled in the sensation.

"Detective, I can sign a sworn statement to that effect if that would make you feel better, but could it wait until later?" Standing up on her toes, she brought her mouth up to less than an inch away from his. "Because right now, my hands have got better things to do than write," January assured Sean just before she pressed her lips against his.

Hard.

At the same time, she managed to undo Sean's belt, slipping it out of the loop that was holding it in place.

She felt his grin forming beneath her lips. "Multitasking?" Sean asked her.

There was nothing short of a wicked expression in her eyes as she answered, "Always."

She wasn't sure if, in the end, it was he or she who slid his trousers down his very taut, appealing hips. January was only aware that the garment was no longer an obstacle.

And neither was her dress.

Sean had sent hot shivers down her back as he slowly lowered the zipper. But the way her dress managed to all but sigh as it fell to the floor, no longer creating any sort of barrier between them, remained a mystery.

January wasn't interested in the why, only in the end result. And the end result was that very, very quickly they went from being dressed to being naked. They were cloaked only in red-hot desire. It was coupled with a network of pulse-scrambling kisses mutually pressed to every conceivable place on their throbbing bodies with superb results.

January had never even entertained an inkling of the fact that she could actually feel this beautiful, this overwhelmed. This incredibly exquisite. Accustomed to giving, she desperately wanted to share this wondrous feeling, to make Sean feel exactly what she was experiencing at this very moment. She could honestly say that every single part of her body was smiling and cheering at the same time.

While she had no idea exactly what was happening to her, she did know that she didn't want this to end— even though it had to.

Still, January tried to hang on to the mind-blowing sensation that had suddenly taken hold of her.

Sean felt his breath growing shorter and shorter. Like a man who had fallen overboard and was only marginally able to swim, he found himself close to being overwhelmed.

He never would have guessed, not in a million years, that this sweet, kind, thoughtful person he had impulsively kissed harbored a powerful storm within her. A storm that stirred his blood and made him unbelievably happy to be here with her tonight. This unexpected surprise completely took his breath away and made him want to pleasure her within an inch of both their lives.

Maybe it was foolish, but Sean couldn't shake the feeling that what was happening right at this moment was something that two people had never experienced before. Not to this extent.

It wasn't conceit or vanity that made him feel this way, just a secret insight that had taken over and was now, inexplicably, holding the reins.

Every kiss between them gave birth to one more. Every eager caress cloned itself into yet another, more stirring touch.

Heaven help him, but he couldn't seem to get enough even as he tried his very best not to overwhelm her.

Or scare her off.

When he heard her labored breathing, he drew his head back, concerned. Had he gotten too carried away?

"Are you all right?" he asked, his eyes sweeping over her face.

"If I were any more all right," January told him, her eyes shining, "I'd probably be in heaven right about now."

Sean laughed then, relieved as well as delighted at the way she had assessed the situation.

"How do you know that this isn't heaven?" he asked. "Because it is, for me."

Then he filled his hands with her, bringing her body closer to his and exulting in every warm, giving inch of it as he caressed her.

He slowly kissed her over and over again, feasting

on her lips before moving down to the swell of her breasts, thriving on the sounds of ecstasy that escaped her as she reacted to him.

When he found that he couldn't hold himself in check any longer, Sean laced his fingers through hers and drew himself up along her body.

January shivered in anticipation.

And then, his eyes on hers, Sean slowly entered her. The rhythm between them seemed to come on its own, filling his soul as well as hers.

Sean began to move.

At first it was just ever so slowly, but then the tempo increased. January matched it, moving with him beat for beat. She managed to delight him and tantalize him without even knowing it.

Sean kissed her harder as he continued to up the tempo until it was all but a frenzy throbbing between them.

Bound together in this inner paradise, they went faster and faster until they raced together as one to the very highest pinnacle on the summit.

The explosion that seized them echoed through their bodies simultaneously. They clung to each other, savoring the experience and wishing that it would never end, even though they knew that it would.

The euphoria melted away in layers, eventually leaving them in each other's arms, in awe of the moment and savoring the memory.

January felt her heart pounding so hard she thought it would stop. She waited for it to regain its normal rhythm.

It took a little longer for her to steady her breathing.

"Detective," January finally managed to say to him in a voice that was barely above a whisper. "You definitely have some hidden talents."

"That would probably be thanks to my earlier undercover work," he said wryly, kissing the top of her head as he held her close against him. "And you. Let's not forget you." He returned the compliment. "You are a total revelation."

"You mean I'm not the boring dud you thought I might be?" January asked, amused, as she continued to try to catch her breath.

Sean's grin grew wider. "The words *dud* or *boring* never crossed my mind. Give me a few minutes to regroup and I'll be ready for round two."

Not that she wasn't sorely tempted, but she knew she couldn't give in to that. And she told him as much. "Oh, as enticing as that really is, I think that might be pushing it."

Sean raised himself up on his elbow to look at her. "Don't tell me I drained you," he said incredulously. The way she moved, Sean was convinced that the woman had enough energy to go on like that indefinitely.

"No, it's not that," she told him with more than a tinge of regret in her voice. "But I feel like I should be getting back to the guest room before Maya wakes up and wonders where I am. She's much too young to understand what happened here, and on top of that, I never learned the proper signs to explain to her what we just did—even if I wanted to, which I really don't," January added with feeling.

Getting off his bed, she looked around for her discarded clothes while Sean caught himself looking at her—and aching for her all over again.

"Yeah, maybe you'd better go," he reluctantly agreed. "Before I totally disregard all the sense you're making and give in to this overwhelming desire to seduce you."

"Seduce me?" January echoed, amused, as she pulled on her dress. Since she was going back to bed once she reached the guest room, she didn't put on any of her undergarments. "Is that what you call it?" she asked him. "Because from where I was, it looked pretty much like we were seducing each other."

Sitting up on the bed, Sean reached over and hooked his arm around her waist, pulling her to him. He was unable to resist one last, deep kiss.

Releasing her after several beats, Sean took in a long breath. "Yeah," he agreed with a grin. "I guess you're right." Nodding his head, he allowed his eyes to wash over her one last time. "We're going to need to talk about that."

She looked at him, uncertainty undulating through her. Why did he want to talk about it? Was he already beginning to regret what had happened tonight? She had next to no experience with men, but she knew a lot of women who had poured out their hearts to her, telling her about being tossed aside after having what they thought was the perfect romantic interlude. They had thought they were building something when it turned out they had experienced the vibrations of a death knell.

"Why would you want to talk about it?" she asked, even as she warned herself to drop the subject.

"Well, I don't know about you, but after what just happened between us, I really don't want that to be the last time," Sean told her.

As he talked, Sean quickly got dressed again. All he could think of was that Maya might accidentally come looking for them. He didn't want her education to take a turn for the adult at this point in her life.

January blinked, staring at him. Did he just say what she thought he had, or was that purely wishful thinking on her part?

"You don't?" she asked him.

"No, I don't," he answered with emphasis, then asked her pointedly, "Do you?"

She stared at him. "Would I be too pushy if I said no, I don't?"

"I'm sorry, my head's a little scrambled," he admitted. "Is that no, you don't want it to be the last time, or no, you—"

She leaned over and stopped his mouth with her own. It was the best way she knew to end this line of conversation that seemed likely to go around in circles and not lead to the desired destination.

When she stopped kissing him this time, January told him, "No, at the risk of sounding like a complete pushover, I do *not* want this to be the last time you and I build our own stairway to heaven."

He grinned. "That is a very interesting way to put it."

"Well, right now, that is the only way I am going

to be able to put it. I've really got to get back to Maya before she wakes up, gets scared and comes looking for me."

"She might *not* wake up," he told her.

"Maybe not," January agreed, "but I really don't want to risk it."

"Yeah." Sean nodded, even though it cost him. "You really shouldn't."

Her mouth dropped open at the same time that her heart swelled. The words escaped her mouth before she could react to stop them.

"And that's why I love you."

The next moment, she was stunned as shock—not to mention instant regret—filled her. January had no idea what had come over her. She had allowed words that should never have seen the light of day emerge, unencumbered, on their own.

Chapter Nineteen

She realized that attempting to backtrack at this point wasn't going to do her any good.

"I mean—" January had no idea how to take back what she had just said.

Sean could only look at her, speechless, because of what he had just heard her say. "You what?"

"Nothing," January cried, unable to take it back and at the same time very aware that she was attempting to close the barn door a second after the horse had managed to gallop off, escaping. "I'm delirious," she quipped. "I don't know what I'm saying."

"Well, from here it sounded like you said you loved me," Sean told her. The expression on his face was totally serious.

Tossing her head, January tried her best to brazen it out. "If I were you, I'd get my hearing checked," she informed him, avoiding his eyes as she headed for the bedroom door.

"It's good to know," Sean continued, ignoring her disclaimer and commenting on what January had just said.

"And why's that?" she asked without turning around.

"Because," he replied very matter-of-factly, "I think I love you, too."

That statement, uttered without any fanfare, stopped her dead in her tracks. It took her a minute to recapture her breath. Very slowly, she turned to look at Sean, then she immediately turned back toward the hallway.

This was just too much for her to deal with, January thought.

"I've got to get back to Maya," she said, her voice all but stilted.

Sean nodded as if they were having a regular conversation. He wasn't about to stop her from leaving. Instead, he casually told her, "I'll put this on the list of things we need to talk about."

January made no comment. She just continued down the hallway.

Still, she couldn't get herself to stop smiling.

HE NEEDED TO get his mind off January and back on the reason he was here in the first place, Sean upbraided himself. His priority was protecting Maya. But he was also focused on finding a way to bring down Mercer. He needed to find out if the drug lord was the one who had executed those three men in the warehouse, or if he'd paid someone to do it for him.

Sean's search for answers hadn't led him anywhere, but he wasn't about to give up. His gut told him that there had to be something that he was missing.

It had to be somewhere in his records, he thought.

He just needed to find what it was that he had managed to somehow overlook.

His thoughts kept him up for most of the remainder of the night.

HE FINALLY MANAGED to drift off. And when he did wake up, it was to the warm, tempting smell of fried eggs and bacon.

January was making breakfast, he realized.

A man could really get used to this.

Throwing off the covers, the detective took a five-minute shower then quickly got dressed. He was making his way to the kitchen within ten minutes after opening his eyes.

Because of the aroma, Sean had expected to find January in the kitchen, preparing breakfast. But he was surprised that she had a pint-sized assistant helping her. The chord that this utterly domestic scene struck made him smile.

"Is she really helping?" he asked, nodding at Maya. "Or does she get underfoot?"

January hadn't heard Sean entering and, remembering last night in all its glorious detail, she smiled warmly at him.

"Let's just say that she's *learning* how to help," January answered. "But she's not really getting underfoot. She is helping." Changing the topic slightly, she asked him, "How do you want your eggs this morning?"

He suddenly realized that he was so hungry, preparation didn't matter. "Cooked," he answered simply.

January could feel her eyes crinkling at the corners.

She was trying very hard to divorce herself from this euphoria that had seized her soul, but it was extremely hard to achieve that impartial distance.

"You really are very easy," January told the detective.

Sean nodded, doing his best to look serious. "I try to be," he replied, looking at Maya. He smiled at the little girl before he signed a greeting to her.

January brought over Sean's plate and placed it in front of him. Since he hadn't asked for anything special, she gave him the sunny-side-up eggs she had already prepared.

"You just said good morning to her," January observed, stunned and impressed.

Sean nodded. "I know what I said," he replied, smiling at Maya.

January wasn't ready to let the subject go. "You're really getting good with that," she said, commenting on the way he had taken to signing.

"The internet is a great source of information on just about everything," he told her. "I just decided to look up a few terms after you went to bed last night." His eyes met hers. "I couldn't sleep."

January's delighted smile seemed to encompass her entire face. "I could," she told him. "As a matter of fact, I slept like a baby."

He considered that for a moment, then shrugged. "Not sure just what that says about me," Sean admitted.

A wicked twinkle entered her eyes. "I guess we'll just have to figure it out as we go along," she told him.

"But for now, eat your breakfast." January pointed at his plate. "You need to keep up your strength."

Though he was trying to separate himself from last night's events, he wasn't quite as successful as he would have liked to be. "I certainly will if I plan to share another go-round with you any time in the near future."

Anticipation undulated through her and her grin grew that much more wicked.

"We'll see," January told him. Finishing her breakfast, she moved back her plate. "So, what do you have on tap for today?"

His answer would sound deadly dull to her, he thought. "I've got to get some work done on my ongoing investigation," Sean told her, then anticipated her next question. "And yes, I'll check with the lab to see if they've managed to make any progress with finding a match on Maya's DNA test."

January remained seated for another minute or so. "Nice to know you're on top of things," she told him.

Maya had scooted into her seat earlier, sitting down opposite Sean. She was watching him with adoring eyes and for all the world appeared to be absorbing each of his words, even though January knew that was really impossible.

Listening to January, it was Sean's turn to smile wickedly at her. "I guess I have my moments," the detective admitted.

"THAT WAS A really great breakfast," he told January less than fifteen minutes later. His plate was completely denuded of every last morsel of food. "Want help with the dishes?" he offered.

Smiling, January shook her head. "You'll just get in the way. Maya and I will handle what's here. Go, do your thing," she told him, waving the detective off. "Make the world safe."

Sean rose to his feet. "Never let it be said that I ignored a lady." He gave her a formal salute and winked at Maya. "I'll be in my office if you need me—and even if you don't," he added whimsically, then left.

TRY AS HE MIGHT, he kept coming to the same dead end time after time, Sean thought. He was staring at the same array of photographs depicting Kid Mercer at different stages of his notorious career.

"What the hell am I missing, Mercer?" he demanded of the subject of all these photographs. "And just where did you disappear to? Was that why you killed those three men? Because one of them could tell me where to find you?"

Sean flipped through the various images, feeling frustrated and utterly stymied. "Too many questions, not enough answers," he complained to the cartel leader who wasn't there.

Sean was so immersed in looking through the drug lord's file, he didn't hear Maya come in at first. He had deliberately left his study door open to get a little air circulating through the tiny room. Otherwise, with his computer running, the small bedroom/study became much too warm all too quickly, even though it was still winter.

Seeing the shadow cast over his computer, Sean looked up. And smiled.

"Hi, princess," he said, greeting her even though he knew Maya couldn't hear him. He reasoned that talking to her somehow comforted him. "I'm a little busy right now. Maybe I can play with you later," he suggested.

Maya cocked her head, making him think of a bird that was trying to understand what a human was saying. It was frustrating for him. Sean wanted to be able to communicate with her, to get the basic gist of what he wanted to say across to her.

"Bear with me, princess. I'm not very good at this yet," Sean said as he did his best to sign at least a little of what he had just said.

Maya stood by his desk, watching him with wide, patient eyes. He had the feeling that at least a part of her felt sorry for him.

That was okay, he thought. Sympathy acted in his favor.

But as he awkwardly tried to tell her that he would play with her as soon as he had done a little more of his work, Sean watched as Maya's eyes suddenly grew very large.

"I sure hope that I didn't just say something I shouldn't have," he told her, knowing his words were only a comfort to him, not her.

It took him a second to realize that Maya wasn't focused on him anymore. She was looking at one of the photographs he had pulled up on his computer screen. Guilt shot through Sean.

She shouldn't be looking at those, he thought. The man on the screen was a killer. He was—

Maya had suddenly grown very excited, shifting from foot to foot and signing the same word over and over again.

The third time she did it, Sean realized that he recognized what she was signing—or thought he did.

Stunned, he heard himself asking Maya, "Did you just sign *daddy*?"

That was the first word he had seen her signing. It couldn't be a coincidence.

"January," he called out, raising his voice. "Can you come in here, please?"

A minute later, January came into the room, drying her hands on the dish towel she had slung over her shoulder.

"Sorry," she apologized. "I didn't realize that Maya had come in here, looking for her idol. I'll just take her to—"

Sean waved away her apology. "I think Maya just signed *daddy*." Raising his eyes to January, he said, "I think that Kid Mercer might be Maya's father." He grew more excited as he entertained the possibility. "You know what that means, don't you?"

Not waiting for January to answer, he told her his theory. "Those men we thought were after Maya weren't after her to *kill* her because she was a witness. They were trying to kidnap her in order to bring her back to Mercer. She's his daughter. Look at how excited Maya got recognizing him." He pointed to the little girl's face. "She's too innocent to be devious. Mercer has to be her father." The moment he'd said that, Sean took out his cell phone.

"Are you calling the lab?" January asked Sean.

He nodded, repeating the words and confirming her suspicions. "Calling the lab."

The moment Sean got through, he told the CSI tech who picked up to compare the DNA sample he had brought in to Mercer's DNA that was on file. He asked the tech to get back to him as quickly as possible.

Hanging up, he looked at Maya, still somewhat surprised. "Who would have ever thought Kid Mercer was your daddy?" he marveled.

January, meanwhile, had arrived at her own decision about this situation. "She can't go back to him," she told Sean flatly. When he looked at her quizzically, she said, "I don't care if he is her father." She was not about to be argued out of the stand she had taken. "Maya obviously loves him, but it's not safe for her to be with him. I am not about to allow her to go back to live with a killer."

The man had to understand why she was taking this position. "Think of what could happen to her," she said emphatically, shaking her head. "No, there has to be another way."

While they were talking, Maya had gone up to the computer, spreading her fingers out over Mercer's image as if she could actually *feel* his skin beneath her fingers.

Observing her, January could only shake her head. "Breaks your heart. Some people just don't deserve the love that they get. That DNA test," she asked, turning toward Sean, "can it help us to locate her mother?"

"Yes, if the woman is in the system for any reason," he told January, then added an all-important qualification. "And if she's still alive."

"We need to get Maya into protective custody," January argued. Especially if they couldn't identify her mother.

But Sean shook his head. "Mercer will find her," he predicted. "Mercer's good. He's got feelers out everywhere. It'll just be a matter of time before he finds her."

"All right, so how do you propose we keep her safe?" January asked belligerently.

"Well, I've got an idea," he told her.

She could have sworn a chill shot up and down her spine. Her eyes met his. "I'm not about to risk Maya's life by using her as bait," January informed him.

"Dabbling in mind reading?" he asked her.

Her eyes narrowed. She had her answer. "Then you *are* planning on using her as bait." What was he thinking? "You can't do that," she told the detective. "I won't let you."

"Relax, tiger, I'm not going to use her as bait, not really," he clarified. "I am using the *thought* of her as bait."

She stared at him, shaking her head. "You're going to have to make that a little clearer for me."

"I will," Sean promised, adding, "All in due time. But first, to set this plan in motion, I'm going to need to get in contact with that so-called new 'chef' your sister Tatum hired."

Her eyes narrowed as she tried to make sense out of what Sean was saying. Where was he going with this? Unfortunately, he had managed to completely lose her.

"I said clearer, not muddier," January reminded him.

He told her as much as he was free to share. "I need to call Cruz," he told her. "And then call in a few favors. In order to assure ourselves that Maya remains safe, we are going to need to set a trap for Mercer. If he takes the bait, we can get him permanently off the streets."

"And you can do this without putting Maya's life in any sort of jeopardy?" January asked, never taking her eyes off his face. She hated this plateau they had suddenly reached, but the little girl's life depended on her being careful.

That meant not blindly following Sean just because she had fallen in love with him.

"Trust me. When I'm finished setting this trap, she's never going to be in danger again," he told the worried woman beside him. Seeing the doubt in her eyes, Sean said, "You're going to have to trust me, January."

January sighed. She knew he was right. Even so, she knew she had to ask, "Do I have a choice?"

Sean's eyes met hers. "Ideally, no."

"Well, then I guess I trust you," January said, resigned. "Let me get hold of Cruz for you," she offered.

"I'd appreciate that," Sean responded, already taking out his cell phone to make another call to someone at the police station.

Chapter Twenty

"You wanted to see me?" Cruz Medina asked, closing the door behind him as he slipped into Tatum Colton's office at the rear of True Restaurant.

He was on his break, which he judged was the perfect time to meet with the man he knew was a Homicide detective. The same man he had just run into at the Coltons' house during the family gathering.

"Yes," Sean replied, gesturing toward a chair facing Tatum's desk. Cruz chose to stand. Sean took it as a sign. The undercover detective was leery.

"Look, why don't we just spare ourselves the needless dancing around the facts," Sean suggested.

Cruz looked at him blankly. "I'm not sure what you're talking about."

Sean could appreciate the man being careful, but right now, he didn't have time for this. "Then let me explain it to you," he said flatly. "Your current partner used to be my old partner when he worked in Homicide. Before he switched over to the Narcotics Division. You can call and ask him." He knew that was taking a chance, after how he and Harry had parted, but he trusted his former partner to vouch for him.

"All right," Cruz replied vaguely, neither confirming nor denying Sean's assumption. Taking quiet measure of the man before him, Cruz sat down. "So where is this thing going?"

"I need to have someone plant some information for Elias 'Kid' Mercer to 'uncover,'" Sean told Cruz without any preamble.

"What kind of information?" Cruz asked, eyeing Sean suspiciously.

In an ideal world, he would have been able to work his way up to this, feeling Cruz out as he went. But the world he found himself in was far from ideal.

Okay, here goes everything. "I want it known that his daughter, Maya, is being moved to a safe house. Once we have her there, it's only a matter of time before she's going to be put into witness protection. He'll never see her again."

"Maya," Cruz repeated. An image immediately clicked in his head. "You mean that kid you brought with you to the party—"

"—is Mercer's daughter, yeah," Sean confirmed. "I thought that because she might have witnessed a triple murder, Mercer had sent out his people to eliminate her. Turns out I think he wants his people to bring her home to him." The more he thought about it, the more he believed that January had been right about Mercer. Daughter or no daughter, he couldn't be allowed to get his hands on Maya.

For his part, Cruz looked stunned. "How about

that?" he cried. "I knew Mercer had a kid, but I thought she was older." He thought about the other fact he had learned, watching some of Tatum's family interact with the little girl. "And I definitely didn't know that she couldn't hear."

"Yeah." Sean nodded solemnly. "Changes the playing field, doesn't it?"

Cruz made no comment one way or the other. Something far more important had struck him. The social worker had seemed very protective toward the child in her care, more so than he would have thought was usual. "Is January okay with this?" he asked Sean, elaborating in case the detective didn't catch his meaning. "Using the kid as bait to catch the kid's father?"

"The story we're putting out is the bait," Sean corrected him. "The little girl definitely isn't."

That sounded like a pretty gray area to Cruz. "Someday, you're gonna have to explain that, but right now—" he glanced at his watch "—I've got to be getting back.

"And don't worry, I'll see to it that this 'information' winds up on the streets." He had one question for Sean. "Your end game is to lock up that SOB, right?"

"Right," Sean confirmed. "I want to lock Mercer up and not only throw away the key, but weld the door permanently shut."

"Okay, then count me in," Cruz said, surrendering the last of the pretense he had cloaked himself in. For the first time since he had entered the office, he grinned. "Damn, that means I can finally ditch this undercover gig and start living a normal life again."

Sean couldn't help but laugh. "You call what we do for a living *normal*?"

To Cruz there was no question about that. "You mean in comparison to this dual life?" he asked, gesturing around Tatum's office. He had come to Tatum's restaurant for a specific reason. He was here pretending to be a drug dealer who in turn was pretending to be a chef. There were times when he felt himself dangerously close to losing track of all the pretenses that were involved. "Hell, yes," Cruz said with enthusiasm.

Sean had done his homework, looking into the reason that would have brought an undercover agent to Tatum's door in the first place. The answer was more than a little surprising.

"You really think that Tatum's restaurant is laundering drug cartel money?" Sean asked the dark-haired pseudo-chef bluntly.

Cruz shrugged noncommitally. "I can only go with the evidence," he answered.

"But you don't believe it," Sean guessed, reading between the lines.

"What I believe doesn't matter," Cruz told Sean.

Sean knew better. Every good law enforcement agent he had ever met relied heavily on their own gut feelings. And he had a feeling that Cruz's gut exonerated Tatum.

Wanting to get away from this line of conversation, Cruz repeated, "I'll make sure the word about Maya's safe house gets spread around. We'll see if that gets the big fish to bite."

Sean rose to his feet. He had another appointment

to get to. "I'm counting on it—for everyone's sake," he said as he left Tatum's office.

SEAN'S NEXT—AND LAST—STOP before he went back to January and Maya was the police station. If everything went according to plan—meaning that he would wind up taking down Mercer—Sean knew he would need backup.

Since, technically, taking down Mercer and his associates was the province of the Narcotics Division, that division would be the one that he needed to approach for backup if his plan were to be pulled off. Under perfect conditions, he could go in, make the necessary arrangements and then get back out again in a matter of minutes.

But conditions, Sean had learned almost from the start of his law enforcement career, were never ideal. In this case that meant that, preoccupied the way he was with the myriad details involved in catching Mercer, he was not in the best frame of mind to run into Harry Cartwright.

Which was exactly what happened. Murphy's Law was alive and well.

His path and Harry's crossed almost immediately. Had he *wanted* this, Sean thought, he definitely couldn't have pulled it off any better.

Standing by the elevator on the first floor, Sean had just pressed the up button when an old, familiar voice coming from behind him said, "Hi, stranger. How's everything going?"

Recognition was immediate. He didn't even have to think about it.

He knew in his heart that this wasn't the time or the place to have this conversation, but since he didn't know when the next time might come up—if ever—this, by default, *was* the right time and place.

Turning around to face his former partner, Sean pasted a smile on his lips. "Hi, Harry. It's been a long time."

"Two years," Harry acknowledged. The six-foot detective had lost some weight and had gained a beard, Sean noted.

"I know," Sean replied. Since he *had* run into his former partner, there was no way for him to remain aloof. "And I've been aware of every single hour of every single one of those days." It was now or never, he thought. He really needed to get this off his conscience. "Harry, I just want to tell you one more time how very sorry I am for what happened to your wife and daughter."

Having started this, he just kept going. "The amount of guilt I've been carrying around because I wasn't able to get there in time to save them almost crushed me," Sean solemnly admitted. "And I *never* meant for what happened to them to wind up chasing you away." Sean felt as if he had suffered a double loss, losing what he had considered to be his secondary family, and because of that, he had lost his best friend.

"Chasing me away?" Harry repeated, bewildered. "Is that why you think I left?"

"Well, didn't you? Because you blamed me for not

being able to get there in time to protect them? Trust me, I've lived with that guilt every day for the last two years."

"Then stop blaming yourself," Harry ordered. "Because I don't."

I don't believe that, Sean thought. "If that were true, then why did you get a transfer?" He didn't believe Harry's protestations.

"I didn't get a transfer because of you," Harry told him. "I got a transfer because I needed a fresh start. I wanted to be around people who didn't have pity in their eyes every time they looked at me. There's just so much silence a man can endure when he enters a room. Hell, it was bad enough that I was pitying myself. I didn't need to have that reinforced a dozen times a day because of the people I encountered."

Sean could see his point. And it was a total relief to know that his old friend didn't hold him responsible for what had happened.

"So how are you doing?" Sean asked. They hadn't talked in those two years. There was a lot to catch up on once this whole episode was in his rearview mirror.

Harry shrugged, not certain where to begin. "Well, it's been over two years and I've started to move on—I think," he added a little hesitantly.

Sean thought of the women he had met at January's parents' house. "If you're interested in testing the waters, just say the word. My girl has a couple of single sisters and a female cousin who are nothing short of knockouts. I'm sure I can get you fixed up with any one of them."

Harry looked stunned, but not for the reason that Sean would have assumed. "Hey, hold it a second. Back up."

"You don't want to get fixed up?" Sean guessed, thinking that maybe he had gotten his signals confused.

"No, it's not that." Harry quickly denied that idea. "*My girl*?" he repeated quizzically. "You have a girl? Since when?"

"Well, I haven't exactly been living under a rock," Sean protested. He didn't have time to go into that now, but he definitely would, he promised himself.

Harry laughed. The elevator arrived and they both got on. For now, they had the car to themselves. "The Sean Stafford I knew had a permanent residence under a rock. As I recall, you were always saying you were too busy to socialize." Harry grinned at him. "Congratulations for coming out from under that rock and finally joining the living."

"Does that mean you want me to fix you up?" Sean asked.

"That means that when this is finally over," Harry said, referring to what Cruz had told him was going on, "and we have that rat-bastard Mercer behind bars, we can give it a try. But for now, tell me what you're involved in and just how much backup you think you're going to need."

"Does the word *army* bring an image to mind?" Sean asked.

The elevator stopped and opened its doors. Harry put his hand on Sean's back, ushering him out. "Why don't we go see my lieutenant and you can tell him what you need?" Harry urged.

"Sounds like a good idea," Sean agreed, following his old partner.

"I DON'T LIKE IT," Sean declared.

After his meeting with the lieutenant at Narcotics Division, he had come home to tell January that all the pieces looked to be in place and his proposed plan was a go.

That was when January had informed him that she was going to be at the safe house, as well.

She was not about to be talked out of it and dug in. "Sean, if I'm not there, this guy is immediately going to be suspicious. If he gets word of it, he might not even show up." She saw the expression on his face. Sean was definitely resisting the idea. "In order to sell this, I *need* to be there. Mercer is not stupid. He's not going to believe that I let his daughter out of my sight, not after everything that's gone down."

"I don't like you taking chances like this," Sean said with feeling.

"I appreciate your concern, Sean," she replied patiently, touched at where he was coming from. After all, he was worried about her. "But it's not up to you. It's up to me. I'm the only one who gets to vote on this and I vote yes. Like you said, this is the only way that we will ever be rid of Mercer. Rid of the threat he represents to her—and to me. I want to be able to sleep again, Sean."

Sean shook his head. He only had himself to blame.

He had inadvertently pulled her into this. "You know, I should have never told you anything."

"Too late," January said. "You did," she told him, adding, "Now let's move on from there. By the way, where is this safe house?"

"Not all that far from here," Sean said, reluctant to disclose the exact address until the time came. He still looked rather dubious about having her take up residence in the safe house. "Are you sure I can't talk you out of staying there?" He had no idea when Mercer was going to show up at the house. Most likely when they least expected it. "You know you would make my job a whole lot easier if you just go where I tell you to."

"What fun is that?" she asked innocently. And then January became serious. "You know I'm right, Sean. And besides, what safer place for me to be than in the heart of a police operation?"

"Any one of a dozen places," he answered. "Maybe two dozen."

"Why Detective Stafford," she cried, blinking her eyelashes at him in double time. "I never knew you to exaggerate."

"Desperate times call for desperate measures," he told her.

"So now you're desperate?" January asked, amused.

His eyes met hers. "Now I'm a lot of things I never was before."

But even as he said it, he knew there was no talking her out of this and he would be lying if a part of him, albeit a very small part, didn't admit that her feisty spirit was one of the things that he loved about her. The only thing he worried about was that that same feisty spirit would wind up getting her into trouble that neither one of them was prepared for.

"Don't worry," she told him, brushing her lips against his in a quick, affectionate kiss. "I'm not going to take any unnecessary chances."

"That doesn't exactly comfort me," he told her, "because the way you think, you probably see a lot of chances as being necessary."

January laughed, tickled. "You, Detective Stafford, have just got to stop peeking into my diary. A woman needs to have some secrets."

He was not amused right now. He was worried. "A woman needs to remain alive in order to have those secrets."

They were getting nowhere, and she didn't want to keep going around in circles. "We are going to argue this into the ground, Sean. Let's just agree to disagree—and let me go ahead with your plan," she told him.

He had an alternate idea. "I could just tie you up and leave you in the closet," Sean suggested.

But January was not about to budge. Mentally, she was already living in a world where all this was behind her, and she wasn't about to give that up.

"You could try," she told him. "But I promise you, it's not going to be easy—and there'll be bite marks and bruising," she added with a confident smile.

Sean shook his head as he slipped an arm around her shoulders and drew her closer to him. "You are one hell of a handful," he told her.

January saw no reason to argue. "I am," she agreed, then said with a smile, "And I'm all yours."

"Lucky me," he commented.

The corners of her mouth curved just as her eyes joined in on the smile. "And don't you forget it," she told him.

"Me? Forget the best thing that ever happened to me?" he asked innocently. "I wouldn't dare. All right, if you're determined to go through with this, are you ready?" he asked, even as he told himself he shouldn't be doing this.

"Detective, I was *born* ready," she said, just as her heart began to pound.

"That," he responded grimly, "is exactly what I'm afraid of." He looked at the screen on his phone and read the text that had just come in. His backup team was in place. "Okay, get 'Maya' and let's do this," he said.

Chapter Twenty-One

Sean was beginning to think that this whole safe-house setup had been a bad idea.

It had been two days now since "Maya" and January moved into the safe house. At some point, the real Maya would be permanently transferring to another state and another identity.

Two days and there had been no unwanted visitors.

No visitors at all, Sean thought, feeling restless. The only one who had come by in all that time was a delivery boy from a local supermarket. That had been on the first full day that residency had been set up.

Sean was really becoming antsy, not to mention that his body was cramping up. Except for a few hours when one of the Narcotics detectives had taken over the watch—Sean had slept in the back seat of the car then—Sean had remained on duty and on his guard the entire time.

If something didn't happen soon, like by tomorrow, he would be sorely tempted to just pack it all in. Admittedly, this plan had been a shot in the dark, and like so many of those, Sean thought ruefully, it had hit nothing.

It looked as if, he decided, they would have to find some other way to bring down the drug cartel chieftain.

But what?

Sean had been banking on Mercer's attachment to his flesh and blood to reel him in. What else could be used to motivate—

Sean sat up straighter. He was positive that he had heard a noise. When all of this had been set up, a sophisticated version of a baby monitor had been put in the living room and another one was placed in the bedroom where January was staying with Maya. He had quickly become attuned to all the normal noises in the house and this particular noise definitely wasn't normal, he thought.

Every single bone in his body told him that someone who shouldn't be was in the house.

Scanning the area, Sean tried to zero in on something that didn't belong. A car parked where it shouldn't have been, someone walking their dog who normally wasn't out at this time. Two people taking an evening stroll.

But nothing was out of place.

That didn't mean that there wasn't something amiss, Sean thought.

"Hey Donavan, are you hearing this?" he asked Donavan, talking into a walkie-talkie to one of the officers who was staked out in a vehicle a block away.

There was no answer.

That wasn't good, Sean thought.

Feeling uneasy, he decided not to bother checking

in with January. He would go to the house and scope things out for himself.

But even as he got out of the car and began to head for the safe house, he heard January's voice. There was an edge to it.

She was talking to someone, challenging them and enunciating clearly.

Sean knew that was for his benefit. He stepped up his pace.

"Who are you?" he heard January demanding angrily. "How did you get in? What are you doing here?"

"You ask too many questions, lady," a deep voice answered. "That's a quick way to wind up dead. Too bad no one ever taught you not to be so nosy."

Sean heard her ask, "What do you want?"

Damn it, January, stop trying to goad him, he thought, afraid for her.

"I'm here to claim what is mine," the man answered.

Mercer!

Sean was running now, but he still wasn't close enough to the safe house. He would have preferred using his car, but the sound of the approaching vehicle would have definitely tipped off the drug lord.

Sean had his phone in his hand.

He hit the conference call button, connecting with all the other police officers staked out in the immediate area.

"Mercer's in the house. I repeat, Mercer's in the house. I need every available backup closing in *now!*" he said emphatically.

"I'd leave now if I were you," Sean heard January saying to her unwanted visitor.

Just stall, January, Sean thought. There was such a thing as being foolhardy and he was terrified that she had crossed that line.

"Not without my daughter!" he heard Mercer growl. It wasn't hard to envision the rest of the scenario.

As January held her breath and watched, Mercer made his way over to his daughter's bed. The drug lord pulled down Maya's covers so he could grab the little girl and make off with her.

For one frozen moment, Mercer stared at the uncovered figure in the bed, stunned.

"A doll?" he cried. "You put a *damn doll* in her bed?" Pure rage contorted the man's deeply tanned face. "Where is she?" he demanded. "You've got one chance to live. Tell me where she is! Maya!" he called out in frustration, searching for the little girl.

"Don't you know your daughter can't hear you?" January asked him in disbelief.

Mercer's face had darkened to the point that January found it frightening.

"I know that!" he screamed in her face. "Don't tell me about my daughter! She belongs with me!" The cartel leader raised his weapon, aiming his gun at January. "Now where is she?" he demanded. "Tell me and I'll make this quick, otherwise—"

He didn't finish.

He didn't have to.

January was stalling, attempting to give Sean as much time as she could to get here. She knew he had to be listening—unless this monster had already done something to him, she suddenly thought.

Oh Lord, please let me be wrong, she prayed, afraid of where her thoughts were leading her. Sean had to be all right. He *had* to be.

Her eyes met the drug lord's. "If you really cared about your daughter, you'd give her up and let her live with someone who could give her a decent, normal life and help her live it."

Mercer sneered. "Same garbage that her mother tried to pull." He waved away the suggestion. "That didn't end well for her. Now this is *your last chance.* Tell me where my daughter is or you're going to suffer a very painful, slow death!" he threatened nastily.

"She's where you can't get her," January answered defiantly.

"Too bad for you." The cartel lord raised his weapon, ominously cocking it.

"Drop the gun, Mercer!" Sean declared. Weapon drawn and aimed, he made his way into the room.

January was so relieved, her knees almost buckled out from under her. She came as close as she ever had to collapsing. Only strength of will managed to keep her on her feet.

"Where *were* you?" she asked, quickly hurrying over to Sean's side of the room.

"I would have been here faster if you didn't lock the damn windows," he told her, trying not to give in to the frustration that had created for him. He caught the drug lord's movement out of the corner of his eye. "I said drop it!" he ordered. Sean cocked his weapon to bring his point home. "You're under arrest, Mercer. It's all over."

"The hell it is!" Mercer declared, discharging his weapon.

Anticipating what Mercer was about to do—he had a reputation for acting irrationally, another reason for the nickname Kid—Sean pushed January down to the floor and covered her body with his own as he exchanged gunfire with the cartel leader.

A wave of nausea seized January. She came very close to throwing up, but somehow, she managed to keep it all down.

She could feel her heart pounding in every part of her body.

It was all over in less than a minute, over even before backup had a chance to break in. Mercer was on the floor, a growing pool of blood forming around what appeared to be his lifeless body.

January scrambled to her feet. "Are you all right?" she cried, looking at Sean as she quickly took inventory of all the visible places on his body.

"Yeah," Sean started to answer her. "I think that I'm—"

"Sean!" January screamed as she saw the supposedly dead drug lord raising his gun. He was aiming it directly at Sean's back.

Alerted, Sean spun around and fired his weapon at Mercer again. Mercer's gun dropped out of his limp hand as the drug lord fell over again, this time totally immobile.

Not leaving anything to chance, Sean placed two

fingers against the killer's neck and checked for himself. There was no pulse.

"He's finally dead," Sean told January. And then he smiled grimly at her. "You saved my life, January."

It was as if all the air had suddenly been drained out of her. She slumped against Sean, quietly sobbing. "You're welcome," she said, unable to still the quiver in her voice.

Sean spun around when he heard the door being opened, his weapon raised and ready.

"Hey." Donavan raised his hands. He looked relieved to find them both alive. "We come in peace," he quipped. Looking at the bloody scene, the detective said, "Looks to me like you two could really use some peace. What the hell happened?"

"Mercer had a completely different future in mind for his daughter than we did," Sean told the other detective.

Donavan nodded. "We got the three men he brought with him," he told Sean. "My guess is that they wanted to live more than their boss did." Donavan looked from Sean to the visibly shaken woman beside him. "You two okay?" he asked, concerned.

"Well, there're no bullet holes," Sean answered, glancing first at January, then down at himself. "And with Mercer no longer presiding over his drug empire, I'd say that the rest of the situation is looking pretty good—at least for now." He knew that nothing remained permanent in the cartel world. He slipped his arm around January's shoulders. "I'm going to take

January home. Tell your lieutenant I'll be there in the morning to file all the reports he needs."

Donavan nodded, a small smile curving his mouth. "That'll definitely make his day. But as for Mercer's drug empire, killing him is like cutting off the head of a hydra. No matter how hard you try to prevent it, another head is bound to pop up, and then it starts all over again."

"Yeah, I know," Sean agreed with a sigh. "But with any luck, there'll be some breathing space in between heads."

"We can only hope," Donavan said as he went to join the rest of his team to canvas the aftermath of the crime scene.

Sean looked back at January. "Are you ready to go home?"

It was a rhetorical question. He was taking her home whether she was ready or not. She looked drained and exhausted.

"Your home or mine?" she asked.

"You pick," he told her. This wasn't the time to pressure her in any way. She needed to feel like she had some sort of control over her life, however minor.

"Could we go to yours?" January asked. "I don't think I'm up to facing Maya yet. When I see her, I'm going to have to tell her that her daddy's dead." Her eyes filled with tears. "I need some time to figure out how to do that."

Before going to the safe house, they had left Maya back at January's town house. Both of her sisters and her cousin Carly were taking turns looking after the little girl. Because Maya seemed to have taken to all three of them, January felt she didn't have to worry about leaving the little girl with them, although she hadn't reckoned on being gone for so long.

And now, even though she wanted to go rushing back to see Maya—had it really been almost three days?—January knew she couldn't go, not until she had had a chance to get her thoughts organized so she could explain to Maya what had happened. She needed to use the calmest, most neutral manner she could to sign to the girl and explain why she wasn't going to be going back to her father.

"Maybe we can break it to her later," Sean suggested. "For now, until all this is ironed out, maybe one of us should think about adopting her." He looked at January, trying to read her expression. "Does that sound like it might be a possibility?"

"Yes, it is," she agreed, then said, "Although there is another possibility."

Sean's eyes met hers and he knew what she was suggesting—or at least he thought he did.

"We could adopt her together," Sean said.

Although that thought had been what she was entertaining, the moment she heard the words out loud, January knew that was what she wanted to do. Adopt Maya together with Sean.

But there was one problem with that standing in their way.

"They won't allow two single people to adopt her," she pointed out.

She was surprised to see Sean shaking his head. "Not a problem," he told her.

She wasn't going to question him about that. Or push his statement to its logical conclusion. She didn't want to be disappointed in case she was wrong.

For now, she was just going to take solace in the fact that they were both alive and that a horrible, horrible man no longer posed a threat to any of them. Most importantly, not to Maya.

Eventually, January fervently hoped, Maya would come to realize that, as well, and see that her life was actually so much better off without a narcissistic man in it. A man who made his living selling poison to anyone who could come up with the money to buy it, even if it meant that they would be committing their own horrible crimes in order to get it.

That thought, however, was far too wearying to contemplate right now. All she wanted to do, January thought, was to sink into Sean's arms and find comfort there.

He didn't even have to mean anything by it, she thought. All he had to do was just *be*. The rest of it, if there ever was going to be a rest of it, could take care of itself tomorrow.

SEAN DROVE UP to January's town house. Parking his vehicle directly in front, he got out and rounded the hood to get to the passenger side. He opened her door and put his hand out to her, silently indicating that she should take it.

When she did, he closed his fingers over hers, helping her out of her seat.

"Let's go inside," he told January. "You need your rest. You went through a lot today."

The smile she gave him was one that looked exceptionally weary. "So did you."

"Yes, but there's just one difference. It's my job. I deliberately signed on for it. You didn't." And then he smiled as he recalled, "Instead, you barged your way into it."

"You know why. I wanted the stage that we set to be believable," she told him quietly. "If I wasn't there, since Mercer knew I had custody of Maya, it wouldn't be believable. Besides," she said with a smile playing on her lips, "Not everyone can play 'pretend' effectively with a doll."

Sean blew out a breath. "I know, and I'm not about to argue with you over that," Sean told her. "The end result is that Maya is no longer in any sort of danger from her father or *because* of her father. And she has you to thank for that."

Still holding her hand, Sean slowly guided January to her front door. He waited for her to hand him the key to her town house. When she did, Sean put the key into the lock, disarmed the security system and opened the front door.

Once he ushered January inside, Sean rearmed the security system, going through the motions in order to make her feel safe.

And once he was finished, then and only then did

the detective who had fallen so deeply in love with her take January back into his arms and proceed to make her feel personally safe while holding her against him.

Chapter Twenty-Two

The tall, dark-haired, willowy young woman had fire in her light brown eyes as she came storming into the police station a little more than thirty-six hours after Mercer's demise had become the news media's lead story.

"Is it true?" were the woman's opening words to the desk sergeant.

Sergeant Wallace Harrison had been selected for his present position because nothing flustered him. He looked now at the Latin whirlwind who had planted herself squarely in front of his desk. "Well, ma'am, you're going to have to be a little more specific than that," Harrison told her in a warm Southern drawl that had been known to disarm the most indignant of people.

Ruby Duarte took a deep breath, doing her best to sound at least a little calmer. The dark-haired cashier with aspirations of becoming a nurse and who was presently enrolled in online courses toward that end attempted to appeal to the robust looking sergeant's best instincts. "The news bulletin on TV saying that Elias Mercer was killed yesterday while breaking into a safe house," she said as she tried to start from the beginning.

This was above the sergeant's pay grade to discuss. "Why don't I have you talk to one of the detectives involved in that case?" Harrison suggested.

Ruby was not about to be put off. "I don't want to talk to a detective," she cried. "I want to find out if my daughter was there."

"Your daughter?" the desk sergeant repeated, doing his best trying to follow her.

Despite her young age—she was twenty-four—Ruby Duarte was ordinarily a very quiet, reserved person. Mercer and his henchmen had used brute force to keep her from seeing Maya for years now. Not to be put off, she had come up with another plan. She had been secretly putting money aside and attempting to better herself. Her plan was to one day be able to steal her daughter away from the cartel drug lord.

"One day" had come sooner than Ruby had anticipated. She was eager to make it a reality before something else wound up separating her from her little girl. She was not going to put up with anything else keeping them apart.

"Yes!" Ruby declared, desperate to finally be reunited with Maya. "Someone told me that she was brought to this police station. Her name is Maya." Maybe a description would shake up the desk sergeant's memory. "She's five years old and she's hearing impaired. I need to see her," Ruby cried. "Please."

A light went off in his head and the desk sergeant nodded. The pieces were all beginning to come together. Harrison knew who she was talking about. "You wait right here," he told the frantic young mother, getting on the phone. He put in a call to the Narcotics Division.

"Yeah, hi," he said to the detective who answered. "This is Sergeant Harrison at the front desk. Is Detective Stafford still up there?" He was given an affirmative answer. "Great. Would you ask him to come down to my desk? There's someone here claiming to be that little girl's mother. Right."

Hanging up, Harrison looked at the distraught young woman in front of him. "Detective Stafford said he would be right down. You can wait over there if you like." He pointed to several chairs that were lined up next to one another by the far wall.

"If it's all the same to you, I'll wait right here," Ruby told the sergeant, afraid she might miss connecting with the detective if she was anywhere else in the police station. There was a great deal of activity going on in the area.

BECAUSE SHE WANTED to be sure that all her *t*'s were crossed and her *i*'s dotted so that nothing would get in the way of her being able to adopt Maya, January had come with Sean to the police station. She gave her statement about what had taken place at the safe house and then signed all the necessary documents. She wanted no oversights or holdups getting in her way when the time came.

The adoption was beginning to look more and more like a real possibility. She and Sean had been up half the night, discussing the matter. They had come to the mutual agreement that the best thing for the little girl would be if they got married so that the adoption could go off without a problem.

January knew that, in Sean's case, getting married was just a means to a desired end—being able to adopt Maya. But she wasn't going to dwell on that.

"So, in essence, this is going to be a marriage of convenience," January had teased Sean in order to hide her insecurity.

"Trust me, convenience has absolutely nothing to do with you." The detective had laughed just before he took her into his arms.

Sean had merely intended to continue holding January until she fell asleep. But, inevitably, they wound up making love.

January had woken up this morning with a whole new frame of mind, ready to take on the world and make everything in it right.

They had gone together to see Maya. January then went through the draining task of telling the little girl that her father was gone, and he wasn't going to be coming back.

It took a long time for Maya to calm down and stop crying. But like the little trouper she had blossomed into, by the time they left her with Carly, Maya had started to come around.

AFTER JANUARY GAVE her statement at the police station, she slowly regained her normal hopeful attitude. The adoption, no matter how it came about, was going to be a good thing for all of them, she thought—and then the desk sergeant had called, telling Sean that Maya's mother was down there, asking for her.

"Is the desk sergeant sure this woman is Maya's mother?" January asked, fearing the worst. "Because you know how these groupies have a tendency to come out of the woodwork, wanting to elbow their way into the limelight with some sort of made-up story."

And then, worried, January fell silent. If this woman really *was* Maya's mother, then the idea of adopting the little girl was beginning to seem like less of an option.

"We'll go down and talk to her to find out one way or another if she's on the level," Sean told her.

Sensing that January desperately needed support, Sean took her hand and squeezed it as they headed to the elevator.

"But if she *is* Maya's mother, how could she have put up with being separated from her child?" January asked angrily. There was no way she would have gone along with that if Maya had been hers.

"Maybe she had no choice," Sean suggested. "You saw what Mercer was like. That guy was pretty damn intimidating. He could have threatened Maya's mother—or both of them. And he had the backup thugs to do it."

January shot Sean a disgruntled look. "I hate it when you're being rational."

"I'll work on it," he promised, killing the smile that rose to his lips.

The moment they stepped off the elevator, January

immediately spotted Ruby in front of the sergeant's desk. There was no wondering if she was the girl's mother.

January groaned. "Oh lord, she looks like a grown version of Maya."

Sean was looking at the woman, as well. "You see it, too," he noted. "I thought maybe it was just me."

Having heard the elevator's bell announce its arrival, Ruby looked over in that direction. Seeing the police detective coming toward her, she lost no time in striding over to him. She wound up meeting him and the woman accompanying him halfway.

"Is she here?" Ruby asked anxiously. Desperately wanting an answer and beside herself with worry, she had no time for formalities. "Is my baby here? She's not hurt, is she?"

"No, she's not hurt," Sean assured her. "But she's not here, either."

Ruby grew progressively more distressed. "Then where is she?" she demanded, looking from the detective to the woman with him.

It was January who spoke up. Considering the situation, her voice was deliberately calm, belying her own inner turmoil as she reassured Maya's mother. "She's with my two sisters and my cousin, a pediatric nurse— and she's very safe."

Ruby looked bewildered. Was this another detective? "Who are you?"

"I'm Maya's social worker," January explained, then introduced herself. "January Colton. And you are?"

Ruby drew herself up, knowing that her appearance probably left something to be desired. But she had come rushing over in her cashier's uniform the moment she heard the breaking news.

"My name is Ruby Duarte. Maya Duarte is my daughter." The last words came out in an almost stifled sob.

"Duarte, not Mercer?" Sean asked. Given the situation, that probably meant the cartel chieftain hadn't married the woman. He needed to delve deeper into the background story, Sean thought.

"Elias didn't want me to have any claim to our daughter, but given his line of work, he wanted to keep his options open just in case having a daughter wound up being a threat to his business dealings somewhere down the line." There were tears shimmering in the woman's brown eyes as she told him.

January read between the lines. There was no mistaking the animosity that existed between Ruby and her daughter's late father.

Ruby suddenly took January's hand. January sensed that Maya's mother thought the close contact would keep her from lying. She saw desperation in Ruby's tear-filled eyes.

"Where is Maya?" she asked again. "Can you take me to her?"

"How long has it been since you've seen her?" Sean asked.

"Officially, not since she was a baby and Elias took her away from me," Ruby answered.

The way she had phrased her reply begged another question. "And unofficially?" January asked.

"I have a picture of Maya that was taken five months

ago. I have a friend who managed to find out where Maya was going to be one day. He covertly snapped this photograph for me." Ruby took out her phone and showed them the picture. She smiled ruefully as she told them, "I keep it next to me on my nightstand."

Looking at it with January, Sean nodded as he handed the phone back to Ruby. "I just need to substantiate a few things and then we can take you to see your daughter," he told the woman.

Ruby pressed her lips together as she nodded. January saw Maya's mother fighting back tears again. Tears that matched the ones she felt in her soul, January thought as she contemplated losing the child she had never really had.

THE NEXT HOUR, right after Ruby Duarte's story had been verified, was probably the hardest hour January had ever had to go through.

When she, Sean and Ruby finally arrived at the town house where her sisters and cousin were waiting with Maya, January could feel her heart breaking into little pieces. If this wound up going as well as she thought it would, January knew she was going to be saying goodbye to a little girl she had taken into her heart in an incredibly short amount of time.

Who would have ever thought that a bond between her and the frightened little girl could have formed so quickly? January couldn't help marveling. She had come to care for a great many children in her line of work, but never to this extent.

But there was no denying that, right from the beginning, she had wanted nothing but the best for Maya. And the best was uniting the little girl with her mother.

A mother who obviously loved Maya a great deal.

When she and Sean walked in, Maya greeted them both with unabashed delight, hugging first one, then the other and then beginning the process all over again.

"Boy, she certainly did seem to miss you two," Simone observed.

"The entire time you were gone, she was totally antsy," Tatum told them. "Like she was afraid you wouldn't be coming back."

All three women in the room looked at the stranger who had come in with January and Sean.

"January, who's this?" Simone asked, taking the lead and looking at Ruby.

"This is Maya's mother," January answered, her voice completely devoid of any emotion for the moment.

The pain of letting go was almost too much to bear, but for Maya's sake, January knew she had to do it. This wasn't about her or what she wanted, this was about Maya and what was best for the little girl.

Maya was watching January as if she somehow sensed that this person who had come in with her and Sean was someone special. Turning, Maya signed the question to January.

As she started to reply, she was surprised to see Ruby taking over. Signing to Maya, Ruby introduced herself to her daughter.

Maya looked by turns stunned, then hesitant and finally, a very shy smile came to her lips. She obviously had no memory of her mother, but she appeared very willing to finally have a real mother in her life.

"You know how to sign," January heard herself saying to Ruby. For some reason, she hadn't thought that Ruby would know how.

"The moment I discovered that my baby couldn't hear, I started learning how to communicate with her. Even when Elias took her from me and threatened me with dire consequences if I ever tried to reconnect with her, I just continued learning, hoping that she and I would someday be together again. I never gave up hope," Ruby said with feeling, signing the sentiment as she said it. "Never."

January took a deep breath. "Well, looks like you were right," she said. Ignoring how she felt inside, January forced herself to put on a positive face for Maya's sake.

Doing her best to rally, she told Maya's mother, "I bought some things for her. Let me go and pack them for you."

January was trying her best to leave the room with some shred of dignity before she broke down altogether and cried.

"That would be very nice of you," Ruby replied gratefully. And then, pausing, she looked from January to Sean. "Could I talk to the two of you for a minute before we leave?"

"Of course," Sean agreed. He gestured over to the side, but not before asking January's relatives for a favor. "You won't mind staying with Maya a little longer, right?"

"You take as long as you like," Simone said encouragingly, speaking for all three of them. She waved the detective and her sister off.

"What did you want to say to us?" January asked Maya's mother the moment they had all stepped aside.

Ruby appeared a little uneasy as she began to speak. "I couldn't help noticing that Maya seems to have formed a real bond with both of you. She clearly trusts you and I can see that she's very fond of both you and the detective."

January exchanged looks with Sean. "Yes," she agreed. "Your daughter's a very bright, sweet little girl."

Sean handed Maya's mother his business card. "If you need anything at all, I can be reached at this number day or night."

Ruby looked at the card before pocketing it. "Well, as it happens," she told them, "I think I am going to have to impose on you."

January was instantly alert. Was this going to be good or bad? "Oh?"

"Since you both seem to have formed a bond with my daughter, I was wondering if you would mind very much helping me with what is going to be the difficult transition of becoming Maya's mother again. I know I have no right to ask after everything you have already done, but I thought, since it's obvious that she likes you both so much, it would be easier for her to have you—"

"Say no more," January cried. "I'd love to help you and Maya reconnect."

"*We* would love to help you and Maya reconnect,"

Sean corrected, giving January a look that told her he intended to be in on this, as well.

Ruby looked completely relieved. "I can't thank you both enough for going out of your way like this and helping out," Ruby told them with overwhelming sincerity.

"No need to thank us. Just seeing Maya smile like that," January said, gesturing toward the little girl, "is more than enough for me."

"For us," Sean corrected her.

January nodded as she smiled. She was finally starting to relax.

This could turn out well, after all, she thought as she echoed Sean's words. "For us."

Chapter Twenty-Three

It was several days later before a routine began to form and fall into place. Things finally settled down.

Much to Ruby Duarte's relief and joy, with January and Sean's help, she was able to step back into Maya's life. With what turned out to be a minimum of effort, the woman reclaimed her rightful place as the little girl's mother.

"I will always, always be grateful to both of you," Ruby told January and Sean. "I want you to feel free to come by any time. You'll always be welcome here."

"Just don't forget to invite us to your graduation ceremony," January told Maya's mother, referring to the nursing degree that Ruby was earning.

"Count on it," Ruby promised, standing beside her daughter in the brand-new apartment January had helped her find for herself and Maya.

"So," Sean commented as they drove away, "looks like everything is going well for Maya and her mom. Why don't we go out and celebrate?"

"You mean, like, on a date?" January asked. With all the time they had spent together protecting Maya and then making plans for her future, they had never actually been out on a date.

"Exactly like on a date. How about we have dinner at your sister's restaurant? I hear the food's great," he said with a grin.

"Sure," January replied, but there was no enthusiasm in her voice.

As they drove there, Sean found that he was doing most of the talking. If January responded at all, it was in one-or two-word answers.

Arriving at the restaurant, Sean parked his sedan, but remained seated, observing his companion. This didn't bode well for his plans for the evening, he thought.

"You're awfully quiet tonight," he noted. "Something wrong?"

January was just going to shrug off his concern, but then thought better of it. She wasn't in the habit of lying and she wasn't about to start now. Besides, she had discovered that Sean had a way of seeing through her, so there was no use in even pretending everything was all right.

She knew this would probably sound foolish since, technically, she had just seen the girl, but January still told him what was eating away at her.

"I miss Maya," January confessed. There was this painful, gaping hole in her heart. She knew exactly how Ruby must have felt when Kid had taken her daughter from her.

Sean surprised her with his response. He didn't make a comment about her overreacting. Instead, he told her, "So do I." Stunned, she stared at the police detective. "But you have to admit," he went on, "that Maya's better off with her mother."

January sighed. "Yes, I know," she reluctantly agreed, then tried to rally by focusing on another aspect of this little drama. "Well, at least this turned out well for you."

She had lost him. "How do you mean?" Sean asked.

"Well, with her mother coming forward to claim Maya," January explained, "you've got to admit that certainly lets you off the hook." Belatedly, she forced herself to smile at him, as if this outcome at least benefited Sean.

"Off the hook?" he repeated, amazed that January would even think of putting it that way. "Did it ever occur to you that I didn't want to be off the hook? If anything," Sean went on, "I wanted to be *on* the hook." Didn't she understand that? he couldn't help wondering.

Her eyebrows drew together. Sean was lying to her. He was trying to be kind, but he was lying, she concluded. "No, you didn't. With the exception of my dad and my uncle, no man I've ever met *wants* to be on the hook. Men prefer to be free, to come and go as they damn well please," January insisted, and Sean wasn't going to convince her otherwise.

"And this is coming from where?" the detective asked. "From your vast relationship experience?"

"All right," she conceded. So this wasn't firsthand experience on her part, but that didn't make her conclusion any less valid. "It's coming from observing people as a social worker. It comes from having woman after woman pour out their hearts to me because they believed the fabricated lies of some guy who promised to be there and love them forever, only to disappear the moment it had the air of becoming serious—or she became pregnant."

Sean nodded. Just as he'd thought. If tonight was going to turn out the way he hoped, he had to convince her that she was laboring under a misapprehension.

"If you ask me, you've been dealing with a deck that's only been stacked one way." He paused for a minute, looking at her. And then he made up his mind.

He was going to push ahead. His heart gave him no choice.

"This wasn't the way I wanted to do this," he told her. "But maybe I should."

It was her turn not to understand. "Maybe you should what?"

He could feel his heart beginning to accelerate as he continued. "I was going to ask you if you would consider making our living arrangement permanent."

His question didn't clear up anything for her. It just made things even more obscure. "You want to move in with me on a permanent basis?" she asked, attempting to make some kind of sense out of what Sean was telling her.

"No, I want you to marry me on a permanent basis." Watching her face, he asked, "What do you say?"

She was surprised when she actually found her tongue. "I—"

And that was when two members of her family suddenly descended on them.

"Hey, Jan, Sean," Carly cried, looking obviously delighted. "Tatum said you were having dinner here." January's cousin made herself at home, taking a seat.

"So, how have you been?" Simone asked, sitting on the other side of her cousin. If she and Carly realized they were interrupting something, they certainly weren't acting as if they were aware of it. "We were going to grab a bite to eat here ourselves, and then Tatum told us that you two were already here." She beamed at her sister and her police detective. "So here we are," she announced—as if that was actually necessary.

January dearly loved her entire family, but she couldn't help thinking that her sister and her cousin couldn't have come at a worse possible time. Sean had asked her a question—*the* question—and was obviously waiting for an answer.

January looked at the police detective apologetically. This was normal behavior as far as her family was concerned, with members from both sides thinking nothing of popping up out of the blue without any warning and just commingling. But she knew this wasn't something he was used to taking in stride. She regarded Sean ruefully.

"Before I answer your question," January said to him, "how do you feel about being part of a crazy family like this? Because this—" she circled the general area that included her sister and her cousin with her hand "—isn't unusual. This is actually part of the norm."

January watched his face intently for some indication that the man was debating heading for the hills for his own self-preservation.

"How do *I* feel about being part of it?" Sean echoed.

January nodded. "That's the question."

Sean's couldn't have smiled any wider if he had tried. "I feel great about it," he told her with unabashed enthusiasm.

Simone exchanged looks with her sister and then stared at the detective. "What are you two talking about? *What* about our crazy family?" Simone asked.

Sean had just given her his answer, so she was just about to give him hers—and it was a positive one.

"Well, if you must know," January began, "Sean and I have just decided—"

Sean's cell phone went off just then, interrupting what January had been about to share. "Hold that thought," he requested, looking down at his cell phone's screen. "I've got to take this call. It's from my lieutenant."

Maybe it had to do with something more about the dead cartel chieftain, he thought.

Rising from the table, Sean stepped away to give Walters his full attention. He knew that if he remained sitting where he was, he wouldn't be able to concentrate on what his lieutenant had to say. Not under the present circumstances.

The moment Sean walked away from the table, Simone looked at her sister. "So, give," she ordered. "Did he just ask you to marry him?"

Carly was only half a beat behind Simone. "More importantly, did you say yes?"

Oh no, she wasn't about to do this on her own. In her mind, she and Sean were already a couple. "You heard Sean. He wants to be here before anything's said," January told the other two women.

Simone pretended to ignore her sister and turned toward their cousin. "Look at that face," she said, nodding toward January. "She's grinning from ear to ear. She said yes," the oldest Colton sister said confidently. Then she glanced at January. "You did say yes, didn't you?"

January shook her head. "I told you, Simone, it's not exclusively my story to tell."

"C'mon, Jan, don't be that way. We've been through so many things together. You can't just pick now to shut us out," Carly complained.

Simone looked up to see the man she assumed was going to be her future brother-in-law heading back to their table.

"Ah, speak of the devil," she said, winking at Sean as he drew close. "We were just trying to get your partner in crime to spill the beans and tell us what's going on."

In light of the expression she saw on the detective's face, Simone dropped her teasing tone. "Sean?" she asked seriously. "Is something wrong?"

He looked at the three women seated at the table,

wondering how he was going to break what had to be the worst possible news they would ever hear.

For that matter, how was he going to find the words to tell January?

Something had frozen within him the second he had heard the news himself, and now he had to be the one to say those crushing words out loud to January and her sister and cousin.

And once the words were out, Sean knew he couldn't unsay them, couldn't find a way to take back the pain they would create.

But whether or not he could take them back didn't change the fact that it had happened.

And they needed to know.

"Sean," January said in a very still voice. "What is it? You're scaring me. Who was that just now on the phone?"

He was just making this worse, Sean thought. His not saying anything just deepened the tension, the horror of the situation that had just come to pass.

"That was my lieutenant," Sean told her. Each word he uttered felt as if it weighed a ton as it came out of his mouth.

"And?" Carly pressed, growing as uneasy as her cousins.

"For heaven sakes, Sean, it can't be *that* bad," Simone insisted. "Just what did this lieutenant of yours say?"

In the course of his career, he had been the bearer of this kind of awful news a number of times. It was something he had never gotten used to. But in all that time, the news had never been a personal matter.

It was today.

"I was just informed of a double homicide," he heard himself telling the women.

"A double homicide," Carly repeated, as if repeating the words would make her able to absorb the news better. And understand it.

"Who were the victims?" Simone asked, her voice suddenly stony, removed.

He felt January reach for his hand, wrapping her fingers around it in an attempt to brace herself.

Sean squeezed her hand before uttering the words no one wanted to hear. He would have been willing to give up his own life to spare her and her family this anguish and grief.

"Ernest and Alfred Colton. Your father and uncle," he added numbly before saying, "They were gunned down tonight as they left their office."

He was aware of January trying to muffle the anguished sob that rose to her lips.

She failed.

Taking her into his arms, Sean made her and the other two women a promise right then and there. "I'm not going to rest until I find out who did this to your father and uncle—and why."

And he would love January forever and help in the darkest times. Times like this one, where the world seemed to be falling apart for the Colton family.

No one said a word. They all too busy dealing with

the overwhelming, gut-wrenching pain and grief generated by this sudden crime that had come out of nowhere.

One question invaded and dominated all of their minds: Why?

* * * * *

COMING SOON!

We really hope you enjoyed reading this book. If you're looking for more romance, be sure to head to the shops when new books are available on

Thursday 7th January

To see which titles are coming soon, please visit

millsandboon.co.uk/nextmonth

MILLS & BOON

LET'S TALK
Romance

For exclusive extracts, competitions
and special offers, find us online:

facebook.com/millsandboon

@MillsandBoon

@MillsandBoonUK

Get in touch on 01413 063232

For all the latest titles coming soon, visit
millsandboon.co.uk/nextmonth

WANT EVEN MORE
ROMANCE?
SUBSCRIBE AND SAVE TODAY!

'Mills & Boon books, the perfect way to escape for an hour or so.'

MISS W. DYER

'Excellent service, promptly delivered and very good subscription choices.'

MISS A. PEARSON

'You get fantastic special offers and the chance to get books before they hit the shops.'

MRS V. HALL

Visit millsandboon.co.uk/Subscribe and save on brand new books.

MILLS & BOON
A ROMANCE FOR EVERY READER

- **FREE** delivery direct to your door

- **EXCLUSIVE** offers every month

- **SAVE** up to 25% on pre-paid subscriptions

SUBSCRIBE AND SAVE

millsandboon.co.uk/Subscribe

MILLS & BOON

THE HEART OF ROMANCE

A ROMANCE FOR EVERY KIND OF READER

MODERN

Prepare to be swept off your feet by sophisticated, sexy and seductive heroes, in some of the world's most glamourous and romantic locations, where power and passion collide.
8 stories per month.

HISTORICAL

Escape with historical heroes from time gone by. Whether your passion is for wicked Regency Rakes, muscled Vikings or rugged Highlanders, awaken the romance of the past.
6 stories per month.

MEDICAL

Set your pulse racing with dedicated, delectable doctors in the high-pressure world of medicine, where emotions run high and passion, comfort and love are the best medicine.
6 stories per month.

True Love

Celebrate true love with tender stories of heartfelt romance, from the rush of falling in love to the joy a new baby can bring, and a focus on the emotional heart of a relationship.
8 stories per month.

Desire

Indulge in secrets and scandal, intense drama and plenty of sizzling hot action with powerful and passionate heroes who have it all: wealth, status, good looks…everything but the right woman.
6 stories per month.

HEROES

Experience all the excitement of a gripping thriller, with an intense romance at its heart. Resourceful, true-to-life women and strong, fearless men face danger and desire - a killer combination!
8 stories per month.

DARE

Sensual love stories featuring smart, sassy heroines you'd want as a best friend, and compelling intense heroes who are worthy of them.
4 stories per month.

To see which titles are coming soon, please visit

millsandboon.co.uk/nextmonth

JOIN US ON SOCIAL MEDIA!

Stay up to date with our latest releases, author news and gossip, special offers and discounts, and all the behind-the-scenes action from Mills & Boon...

 millsandboon

 millsandboonuk

 millsandboon

It might just be true love...

GET YOUR ROMANCE FIX!

MILLS & BOON
— *blog* —

Get the latest romance news, exclusive author
interviews, story extracts and much more!

blog.millsandboon.co.uk

MILLS & BOON

HISTORICAL

Awaken the romance of the past

Escape with historical heroes from time gone by. Whether your passion is for wicked Regency Rakes, muscled Viking warriors or rugged Highlanders, indulge your fantasies and awaken the romance of the past.

Six Historical stories published every month, find them all at

millsandboon.co.uk/ Historical

MILLS & BOON

MODERN

Power and Passion

Prepare to be swept off your feet by
sophisticated, sexy and seductive heroes, in
some of the world's most glamourous and
romantic locations, where power and
passion collide.

ght Modern stories published every month, find them all at:

millsandboon.co.uk/Modern

MILLS & BOON
DARE

Sexy. Passionate. Bold.

Sensual love stories featuring smart, sassy
heroines you'd want as a best friend, and
compelling intense heroes who are worthy
of them.

Four DARE stories published every month, find them all at
millsandboon.co.uk/DARE

MILLS & BOON
True Love
Romance from the Heart

Celebrate true love with tender stories of
heartfelt romance, from the rush of falling
in love to the joy a new baby can bring,
and a focus on the emotional
heart of a relationship.

ight True Love stories published every month, find them all at:

millsandboon.co.uk/TrueLove

MILLS & BOON
MEDICAL
Pulse-Racing Passion

Set your pulse racing with dedicated, delectable doctors in the high-pressure world of medicine, where emotions run high and passion, comfort and love are the best medicine.

Eight Medical stories published every month, find them all a

millsandboon.co.uk